H. G. WELLS

The Sleeper Awakes

Edited with an Introduction by PATRICK PARRINDER
Notes by ANDY SAWYER

PENGUIN CLASSICS

PENGUIN BOOKS

Published by the Penguin Group
Penguin Books Ltd, 80 Strand, London WC2R ORL, England
Penguin Books (USA) Inc., 375 Hudson Street, New York, New York 10014, USA
Penguin Group (Canada), 10 Alcorn Avenue, Toronto, Ontario, Canada M4V 3B2
(a division of Pearson Penguin Canada Inc.)
Penguin Ireland, 25 St Stephen's Green, Dublin 2, Ireland
(a division of Penguin Books Ltd)
Penguin Group (Australia), 250 Camberwell Road,
Camberwell, Victoria 3124, Australia (a division of Pearson Australia Group Pty Ltd)
Penguin Books India Pvt Ltd, 11 Community Centre,
Panchsheel Park, New Delhi – 110 017, India
Penguin Group (NZ), cnr Airborne and Rosedale Roads, Albany,
Auckland 1310, New Zealand (a division of Pearson New Zealand Ltd)
Penguin Books (South Africa) (Pty) Ltd, 24 Sturdee Avenue,
Rosebank 2196, South Africa

Penguin Books Ltd, Registered Offices: 80 Strand, London WC2R ORL, England

www.penguin.com

First published as *When the Sleeper Wakes* 1899
Revised edition published as *The Sleeper Awakes* 1910
This edition first published in Penguin Classics 2005

1

Text copyright © the Literary Executors of the Estate of H. G. Wells
Introduction, Biographical Note, Further Reading, Note on the Text
copyright © Patrick Parrinder, 2005
Notes and Note on Places in the Text copyright © Andy Sawyer, 2005
All rights reserved

The moral right of the editors has been asserted

Set in 10.25/12.25 pt PostScript Adobe Sabon
Typeset by Rowland Phototypesetting Ltd, Bury St Edmunds, Suffolk
Printed in England by Clays Ltd, St Ives plc

PENGUIN CLASSICS

THE SLEEPER AWAKES

H. G. WELLS, the third son of a small shopkeeper, was born in Bromley in 1866. After two years' apprenticeship in a draper's shop, he became a pupil-teacher at Midhurst Grammar School and won a scholarship to study under T. H. Huxley at the Normal School of Science, South Kensington. He taught biology before becoming a professional writer and journalist. He wrote more than a hundred books, including novels, essays, histories and programmes for world regeneration.

Wells, who rose from obscurity to world fame, had an emotionally and intellectually turbulent life. His prophetic imagination was first displayed in pioneering works of science fiction such as *The Time Machine* (1895), *The Island of Doctor Moreau* (1896), *The Invisible Man* (1897) and *The War of the Worlds* (1898). Later he became an apostle of socialism, science and progress, whose anticipations of a future world state include *The Shape of Things to Come* (1933). His controversial views on sexual equality and women's rights were expressed in the novels *Ann Veronica* (1909) and *The New Machiavelli* (1911). He was, in Bertrand Russell's words, 'an important liberator of thought and action'.

Wells drew on his own early struggles in many of his best novels, including *Love and Mr Lewisham* (1900), *Kipps* (1905), *Tono-Bungay* (1909) and *The History of Mr Polly* (1910). His educational works, some written in collaboration, include *The Outline of History* (1920) and *The Science of Life* (1930). His *Experiment in Autobiography* (2 vols., 1934) reviews his world. He died in London in 1946.

PATRICK PARRINDER took his MA and Ph.D. at Cambridge University, where he held a Fellowship at King's College and published his first two books on Wells, *H. G. Wells* (1970) and *H. G. Wells: The Critical Heritage* (1972). He has been Chairman of the H. G. Wells Society and editor of *The Wellsian*, and has also written on James Joyce, science fiction, literary criticism and the history of the English novel. His book *Shadows of the Future* (1995) brings together his interests in Wells, science fiction and

literary prophecy. Since 1986 he has been Professor of English at the University of Reading.

ANDY SAWYER is the librarian of the Science Fiction Foundation Collection at the University of Liverpool Library, and Course Director of the MA in Science Fiction Studies offered by the School of English. He also teaches a science fiction module for undergraduates. He has published widely on science fiction and related literatures, and has co-edited a collection of essays, *Speaking Science Fiction* (2000). He is also Reviews Editor of *Foundation: the International Review of Science Fiction* and Associate Editor of the forthcoming *Encyclopedia of Themes in Science Fiction and Fantasy*.

CONTENTS

Biographical Note

Herbert George Wells was born on 21 September 1866 at Bromley, Kent, a small market town soon to be swallowed up by the suburban growth of outer London. His father, formerly a professional gardener and a county cricketer renowned for his fast bowling, owned a small business in Bromley High Street selling china goods and cricket bats. The house was grandly known as Atlas House, but the centre of family life was a cramped basement kitchen underneath the shop. Soon Joseph Wells's cricketing days were cut short by a broken leg, and the family fortunes looked bleak.

Young 'Bertie' Wells had already shown great academic promise, but when he was thirteen his family broke up and he was forced to earn his own living. His father was bankrupt, and his mother left home to become resident housekeeper at Uppark, the great Sussex country house where she had worked as a lady's maid before her marriage. Wells was taken out of school to follow his two elder brothers into the drapery trade. After serving briefly as a pupil-teacher and a pharmacist's assistant, in 1881 he was apprenticed to a department store in Southsea, working a thirteen-hour day and sleeping in a dormitory with his fellow-apprentices. This was the unhappiest period of his life, though he would later revisit it in comic romances such as *Kipps* (1905) and *The History of Mr Polly* (1910). Kipps and Polly both manage to escape from their servitude as drapers, and in 1883, helped by his long-suffering mother, Wells cancelled his indentures and obtained a post as teaching assistant at Midhurst Grammar School near Uppark. His intellectual development, long held back, now progressed astonishingly. He passed a series of examinations in science subjects and, in September 1884, entered the Normal School of Science, South Kensington (later to become part of Imperial College of Science and Technology) on a government scholarship.

Wells was a born teacher, as many of his books would show, and at first he was an enthusiastic student. He had the good fortune to be taught biology and zoology by one of the most influential scientific thinkers of the Victorian age, Darwin's friend and supporter T. H. Huxley. Wells never forgot Huxley's teaching, but the other professors were more humdrum, and his interest in their courses rapidly waned. He scraped through second-year physics, but failed his third-year geology exam and left South Kensington in 1887 without taking a degree. He was thrilled by the theoretical framework and imaginative horizons of natural science, but impatient of practical detail and the grinding, routine tasks of laboratory work. He cut his classes and spent his time reading literature and history, satisfying the curiosity he had earlier felt while exploring the long-neglected library at Uppark. He started a college magazine, the *Science Schools Journal*, and argued for socialism in student debates.

In the summer of 1887 Wells became science master at a small private school in North Wales, but a few weeks later he was knocked down and injured by one of his pupils on the football field. Sickly and undernourished as a result of three years of student poverty, he suffered severe kidney and lung damage. After months of convalescence at Uppark he was able to return to science teaching at Henley House School, Kilburn. In 1890 he passed his University of London B.Sc. (Hons.) with a first class in zoology and obtained a post as a biology tutor for the University Correspondence College. In 1891 he married his cousin Isabel Wells, but they had little in common and soon Wells fell in love with one of his students, Amy Catherine Robbins (usually known as 'Jane'). They started living together in 1893, and married two years later when his divorce came through.

During his years as a biology tutor Wells slowly began making his way as a writer and journalist. He wrote for the

Educational Times, edited the *University Correspondent*, and in 1891 published a philosophical essay, 'The Rediscovery of the Unique', in the prestigious *Fortnightly Review*. His first book was a *Textbook of Biology* (1893). But no sooner was it published than his health again collapsed, forcing him to give up teaching and rely entirely on his literary earnings. His future seemed highly precarious, yet soon he was in regular demand as a writer of short stories and humorous essays for the burgeoning newspapers and magazines of the period. He became a fiction reviewer and, for a short period in 1895, a theatre critic.

Ever since his student days Wells had worked intermittently on a story about time-travelling and the possible future of the human race. An early version was published in the *Science Schools Journal* as 'The Chronic Argonauts', but now, after numerous redrafts and much encouragement from the poet and editor W. E. Henley, it finally took shape as *The Time Machine* (1895). Its success was instantaneous, and while it was running as a magazine serial Wells was already being spoken of as a 'man of genius'. He was celebrated as the inventor of the 'scientific romance', a combination of adventure novel and philosophical tale in which the hero becomes involved in a life-and-death struggle resulting from some unforeseen scientific development. There was now a ready market for his fiction, and *The Island of Doctor Moreau* (1896), *The Invisible Man* (1897), *The War of the Worlds* (1898), *When the Sleeper Wakes* (1899; later revised as *The Sleeper Awakes*, 1910), *The First Men in the Moon* (1901) and several other volumes followed quickly from his pen.

By the turn of the twentieth century Wells was established as a popular author in England and America, and his books were rapidly being translated into French, German, Spanish, Russian and other European languages. Already his fame had begun to eclipse that of his predecessor in scientific romance, the French author Jules Verne, who had dominated the field since the 1860s. But Wells, an increasingly self-conscious artist, had larger ambitions than to go down in history as a boys' adventure novelist like Jules Verne. *Love and Mr Lewisham* (1900) was his first attempt at realistic fiction, comic in spirit and manifestly reflecting his own experiences as a student and teacher. By the end of the Edwardian decade, when he wrote his 'Condition of England' novels *Tono-Bungay* (1909) and *The New Machi-avelli* (1911), Wells had become one of the leading novelists of his day, the friend and rival of such literary figures as Arnold Bennett, Joseph Conrad, Ford Madox Ford and Henry James.

But Wells was never a devotee of art for art's sake; he was a prophetic writer with a social and political message. His first major non-fictional work was *Anticipations* (1902), a book of futurological essays setting out the possible effects of scientific and technological progress in the twentieth century. *Anticipations* brought him into contact with the Fabian Society and launched his career as a political journalist and an influential voice of the British left. During his Fabian period Wells wrote *A Modern Utopia* (1905), but failed in his attempt to challenge the bureaucratic, reformist outlook of the Society's leaders such as Bernard Shaw (a lifelong friend and rival) and Beatrice Webb. Wells's Edwardian scientific romances such as *The Food of the Gods* (1904) and *The War in the Air* (1908), though full of humorous touches, are propagandist in intent. In other 'future war' stories of this period he predicted the tank and the atomic bomb.

Success as an author brought about great changes in his personal life. Ill-health had forced him to leave London for the Kent coast in 1898, but in the long run the only legacy of his footballing injury was the diabetes that affected him in old age. He commissioned a house, Spade House, overlooking the English Channel at Sandgate, from the architect C. F. A. Voysey, and here his and Jane's two sons were born – George Philip or 'Gip', who became a zoology professor and collabo-rated with his father and Julian Huxley on the biology encyclo-pedia *The Science of Life* (1930), and Frank, who worked in the film industry. Wells gave generous support to his parents and to his eldest brother, who was a fellow-fugitive from the drapery trade. Increasingly, however, he looked for emotional fulfilment outside the family, and his sexual affairs became notorious. He had a daughter in 1909 with Amber Reeves, a leading young Fabian economist, and in 1914 the novelist and critic Rebecca West gave birth to his son Anthony West, whose troubled childhood would later be reflected in his own novel *Heritage* (1955) and in his biography of his father.

As Wells's personal life became the gossip of literary London, his roles as imaginative writer and political journalist or prophet came increasingly into conflict. *Ann Veronica* (1909) was an example of topical, controversial fiction, dramatizing and commenting on such issues as women's rights, sexual equality and contemporary morals. It was the first of Wells's 'discussion novels' in which his personal relationships were often very thinly disguised. His later fiction takes a great variety of forms, but it all belongs to the broad category of the novel of ideas. At one extreme is the realistic reporting of *Mr Britling Sees It Through* (1916) – still valuable and unique as a portrayal of the English 'home front' in the First World War – while at the other extreme are brief fables such as *The Undying Fire* (1919) and *The Croquet Player* (1936), political allegories about world events each cast in the form of a prophetic dialogue.

Wells was by no means an experimental novelist like his younger contemporaries James Joyce and Virginia Woolf, but he was often technically innovative, and in some of his books the boundaries between fiction and non-fiction begin to break down. Sometimes he would take a classic from an earlier, pre-modern epoch as his literary model: *A Modern Utopia* (1905), for example, refers back to Sir Thomas More's *Utopia* and Plato's *Republic*. His bestselling historical works *The Outline of History* (1920) and *A Short History of the World* (1922) break with historical conventions by looking forward to the next stage in history. These works were written in order to draw the lessons of the First World War and to ensure that, if possible, its carnage would never be repeated; Wells saw history as a 'race between education and catastrophe'. The same concerns led to his future-history novel *The Shape of Things to Come* (1933), later rewritten for the cinema as *Things to Come*, an epic science-fiction film produced in 1936 by Alexander Korda. Both novel and film contain dire warnings about the inevitable outbreak and disastrous consequences of the Second World War.

By the 1920s, Wells was not only a famous author but a public figure whose name was rarely out of the newspapers. He briefly worked for the Ministry of Propaganda in 1918, producing a memorandum on war aims which anticipated the setting-up of the League of Nations. In 1922 and 1923 he stood for Parliament as a Labour candidate. He sought to influence world leaders, including two US Presidents, Theodore Roosevelt and Franklin D. Roosevelt. His meeting with Lenin in the Kremlin in 1920 and his interview in 1934 with Lenin's successor Josef Stalin were publicized all over the world. His high-pitched, piping voice was often heard on BBC radio. In 1933 he was elected president of International PEN, the writers' organization campaigning for intellectual freedom. In the same year his books were publicly burnt by the Nazis in Berlin, and he was banned from visiting Fascist Italy. His ideas strongly influenced the Pan-European Union, the pressure group advocating European unity between the wars.

But Wells became convinced that nothing less than global unity was needed if humanity was not to destroy itself. In *The Open Conspiracy* (1928) and other books he outlined his theories of world citizenship and world government. As the Second World War drew nearer he felt that his mission had been a failure and his warnings had gone unheeded. His last great campaign, for which he tried to obtain international support, was for human rights. The proposal set out in his Penguin Special *The Rights of Man* (1940) helped to bring about the United Nations declaration of 1948. He spent the war years at his house in Hanover Terrace, Regent's Park, and was awarded a D.Litt. by London University in 1943. His last book, *Mind at the End of Its Tether* (1945), was a despairing, pessimistic work, even bleaker in its prospects for mankind than *The Time Machine* fifty years earlier. He died at Hanover Terrace on 13 August 1946. He was restless and tireless to the end, a prophet eternally dissatisfied with himself and with humanity. 'Some day', he had written in a whimsical 'Auto-Obituary' three years earlier, 'I shall write a book, a *real* book.' He had published over fifty works of fiction and, in total, some 150 books and pamphlets.

                                                    Patrick Parrinder

Introduction

(New readers are advised that this Introduction makes the details of the plot explicit.)

The Sleeper Awakes begins on the rocky coastline of North Cornwall, a region usually associated with the legends of King Arthur and the writings of Thomas Hardy rather than with H. G. Wells. There is a meeting on the coast path between two strangers: Isbister the watercolourist and Graham, an insomniac who is apparently on the point of throwing himself over the cliff-edge. Isbister persuades Graham to accompany him to the village of Boscastle, pausing on the way to look down into the abyss of Blackapit – clearly a name of ill omen, although it can be found on any good map of the area. Later that afternoon, Graham falls into the cataleptic trance from which he will not awake for 203 years. His nervous collapse at the seaside forms a brief prelude to what is surely Wells's most disturbing novel of the future, a chilling vision of an industrial slave-state anticipating Aldous Huxley's *Brave New World* and George Orwell's *Nineteen Eighty-Four*. As Orwell wrote forty years after its first publication, 'Everyone who has ever read *The Sleeper Awakes* remembers it.'[1]

What we remember most, perhaps, is the frenzied pace and colossal size of the Wellsian super-city, an image that was to leave its impression on countless science-fiction writers and illustrators. Graham's first view of London in the year 2100, when he goes on to the balcony in chapter 5, is awesome and overwhelming. The soaring heights and plunging depths of the metropolitan cityscape have the sublimity of a great natural spectacle, such as the Cornish cliffs among which Graham fell asleep; and Wells frequently uses the words 'cliff' and 'cliff-like' to evoke the buildings with their towering façades. But the streets are roofed over with glass, and few people ever go outside the city walls. Everything in this future world seems man-made, but on a scale that dwarfs the crowds thronging in the streets. And the streets themselves are in perpetual motion, like a giant system of conveyor belts running at different speeds – the 'moving ways'. As Graham looks out from his balcony the noise is incessant, the feeling of claustrophobia almost inescapable. The mechanized city of the future has imprisoned, not liberated, the human spirit.

Wells's novel, much revised in the form in which it is printed here, was first published in 1899 under the title *When the Sleeper Wakes*. It was a very different kind of fiction from the speculative scientific romances beginning with *The Time Machine* (1895) with which he had made his name. *The Time Machine* pursues a fantastic, if apparently scientific, hypothesis into the far future; *The Sleeper Awakes* uses direct extrapolation from the present into the near future. Here is how Wells summed up the difference in his *Experiment in Autobiography* (1934):

> The future depicted in the *Time Machine* was a mere fantasy based on the idea of the human species developing about divergent lines, but the future in [*The Sleeper Awakes*] was essentially an exaggeration of contemporary tendencies: higher buildings, bigger towns, wickeder capitalists and labour more downtrodden than ever and more desperate. Everything was bigger, quicker and more crowded; there was more and more flying and the wildest financial speculation. It was our contemporary world in a state of highly inflamed distension.[2]

The sharp contrast between *The Sleeper Awakes* and his earlier romances almost certainly explains why, far from inventing a time machine or other technological device to take Graham into the future, Wells falls back on a hoary literary convention – that of suspended animation – deriving from traditional folktales and Washington Irving's story of Rip van Winkle.

The Sleeper Awakes as an Anti-utopia

The situation of a man waking up after 200 years or more provides the storyline of many late nineteenth-century utopian romances, including W. H. Hudson's *A Crystal Age* (1887), Edward Bellamy's *Looking Backward 2000–1887* (1888) and William Morris's *News from Nowhere* (1890). But Graham is both more and less than the conventional literary visitor to a more perfect or more advanced society. Thanks to the accumulation of his investments he is the nominal Owner and Master of the World in 2100, a focus of immense public curiosity and an object of popular worship. But the society that he 'owns' is an inferno of discontent and savage oppression, and its rulers are deeply alarmed by his unexpected awakening.

Graham, we soon learn, has not woken up by chance, but in response to a near-lethal injection administered on the orders of Ostrog, the leader of popular opposition to the ruling White Council. His body has been put on public exhibition while he slept, but now that he is awake no one wants to answer his questions. Until he is rescued by Ostrog's forces and introduced to Asano, his Japanese guide, he meets with none of the customary hospitality shown to a utopian visitor. Later, when he is allowed to meet people and taken on conducted tours of the city, the aim seems to be to distract him and keep him out of the way of the new rulers. For the most part he is bewildered, not enlightened, by his experiences, and the reader shares his bewilderment. Wells's prose is full of sentences beginning 'He looked', 'He saw', 'He perceived' and the like; it is third-person narration as close as is possible to first-person narration. This means that *The Sleeper Awakes* is not an anti-utopia in the satirical mode like *Brave New World* or Wells's own 'A Story of the Days to Come' (1899), not to mention the Swiftian final chapters of his *The First Men in the Moon* (1901). There are a few moments of grotesque humour in the book, such as the description of the Babble Machines, but these are for light relief only. *The Sleeper Awakes* is a sensational adventure story in which Graham himself is neither seen from outside nor held at an ironic distance.

If not a satire, however, Wells's novel is clearly a warning. 'England, awake!' is both a line from William Blake's epic poem 'Jerusalem' and the title of a patriotic song, and one of the meanings of the revised title *The Sleeper Awakes* is that the sleeper's eyes are opened. To this extent Graham, a former political radical who is, however, not a 'far-sighted man' (chapter 2), may be seen as representing England. His misery on the Cornish coast and his pale, drawn, joyless face seem to suggest the figure of Cassandra, the Trojan prophetess set apart from her contemporaries by the curse of foreknowledge; but the nineteenth-century Graham is an activist busily engaged in promoting social change, though without any idea of where it will lead. Is his sleeplessness, perhaps, a sign of unconscious knowledge? If so, what is the future catastrophe to which Wells believes that England ought to be alerted?

The short answer, which the novelist gave in his 1921 preface, is the 'nightmare of Capitalism triumphant'. The novel reflects the specific conditions of capitalism as perceived by Wells and his contemporaries at the end of the nineteenth century. Its principal features are American rather than English, just as the novel's skyscrapers were taking shape in *fin-de-siècle* Chicago and New York rather than in London. The 'gilded age' that followed the American Civil War saw not only the amassing of vast fortunes but the building of great industrial and financial corporations such as US Steel, Standard Oil and J. P. Morgan and Company. These corporations, known as the 'trusts', were presided over by 'robber barons' such as Morgan, J. D. Rockefeller and Andrew Carnegie. The widespread outrage at their activities led to the Sherman Anti-Trust Act, passed by Congress in 1890 with the aim of preserving free competition and curbing the growth of monopolies. But opposition to the trusts had little success until Theodore Roosevelt's presidency, which began two years after *When the Sleeper Wakes* was published. In Wells's novel, these attempts to set limits to monopoly capitalism have manifestly failed. Graham's huge estate has been swollen by a legacy from Isbister the watercolourist who, we learn, has moved to America after turning every cliff-face in England into advertising space. But Graham's Trustees are faced with seething discontent and growing resistance from the forces of militant trade unionism. In the original text of *When the Sleeper Wakes*, Graham was owner of only half the world, and the economy was controlled by private monopolies such as the Food Trust, the Pill Company, the Labour Company and so on. In the revised *Sleeper Awakes* of 1910, Wells changed the terms 'Trust' and 'Company' to 'Department', implying that they are no longer distinct corporations but parts of a vast holding company which rules the whole world without any competition. This system, in which political and economic power are one and the same, is what economists would call state capitalism; it resembles the command economies of the twentieth-century Soviet bloc rather than the market economies of the United States and its allies.

Wells revised his novel in 1910 because, as he said, he had skimped the writing of *When the Sleeper Wakes* through illness. He very slightly reshaped the plot and made a large number of stylistic improvements, but he also took the opportunity of updating the text, particularly the aviation chapters, where, for example, the obsolete term 'aeropile' was replaced by 'monoplane' throughout.[3] What he could not do, of course, was to tear up his novel and start again from scratch, even though the social, technological and geopolitical developments of the Edwardian decade had made a number of his forecasts look obsolete. In *Anticipations* (1902) he had already acknowledged that the vision of huge, bloated cities surrounded by an abandoned countryside was out of date, since the suburban sprawl and ribbon development made possible by the motor car were likely to determine future development. Similarly, the choice of London as the capital of a unified world state with Paris, not Berlin or New York, as its most significant rival reminds us that *When the Sleeper Wakes* was written immediately before the outbreak of the Boer War (1899–1902), when the military and economic power of the British Empire was at its height. The principal symbol of the world state in the novel is the giant white statue in the Hall of the Atlas, a statue possibly alluding to Kipling's justification of European imperialism as the 'White Man's burden'. In Wells's account of the overthrow of the

White Council and the rise of Ostrog – the disaffected member of the ruling elite who stages a revolt in Graham's name – the rest of the world is barely present. It is, however, Ostrog's use of black colonial troops from Senegal and South Africa to put down risings in Paris and London that sets the stage for the final confrontation between Ostrog and Graham.

The Song of the Revolt

As the awakened Sleeper in a nightmare near-future society, Graham from time to time wonders if he is still dreaming. The novel's affiliations, however, are less with the traditional dream-vision than with the phantasmagoric urban landscapes of the *Arabian Nights*. As he becomes accustomed to his position as Owner of the World, Graham takes on the role of the Caliph of Baghdad, Haroun al-Raschid, while Ostrog becomes his chief minister or 'Grand Vizier' (Chapter 17). In chapters 20 and 21 Graham, encouraged by Ostrog's niece Helen Wotton, imitates the legendary Caliph wandering around the streets of his city incognito and at night. It is during this nocturnal expedition, which involves a symbolic descent from the Dome of St Paul's to the city's underside, that Graham sees the full extent of the people's degradation and enslavement. These chapters, in particular, must have inspired Orwell's depiction of the proles of *Nineteen Eighty-Four*. But where Orwell's working classes are mindless and apathetic, Wells's are defiant and on the edge of revolt, as in the following brief episode:

> Looking over the parapet, Graham saw that beneath was a wharf under yet more tremendous archings than any he had seen. Three barges, smothered in floury dust, were being unloaded of their cargoes of powdered felspar by a multitude of coughing men, each guiding a little truck; the dust filled the place with a choking mist, and turned the electric glare yellow. The vague shadows of these workers gesticulated about their feet, and rushed to and fro against a long stretch of whitewashed wall. Every now and then one would stop to cough.
>
> A shadowy, huge mass of masonry rising out of the inky water,

brought to Graham's mind the thought of the multitude of ways and galleries and lifts that rose floor above floor overhead between him and the sky. The men worked in silence under the supervision of two of the Labour Police; their feet made a hollow thunder on the planks along which they went to and fro. And as he looked at this scene, some hidden voice in the darkness began to sing.

'Stop that!' shouted one of the policemen, but the order was disobeyed, and first one and then all the white-stained men who were working there had taken up the beating refrain, singing it defiantly – the Song of the Revolt. (Chapter 21)

Here we are among the foundations of the city's massive, top-heavy architecture. The 'choking mist', the men's coughing and the dim, poisonous glare of the electric lights convey the idea of a subterranean dungeon, yet the wharf is only at sea level, or what would have been ground level in the old London. The reverberation of the men's footsteps, as well as the thickness of arches and walls, suggests the sheer weight of masonry piled above them. The passage vividly evokes the plight of the poor, the slaves of the Labour Department, who are condemned to work and sleep in the city's deepest caverns. It is they, not the bombastic statue in the Hall of the Atlas, who really support what Karl Marx called the economic 'base' and cultural 'super-structure' of capitalist society. (The fact that the felspar the men are unloading is used in the manufacture of decorative tilework for luxury apartments is an added irony.) Give or take some of the details, we might be reading an excerpt from a social-realist novel about late nineteenth-century London. The workers, 'vague shadows' brought to life by their diseased coughing and by their rebellious singing, are stock figures in a kind of Agitprop art; there is little subtlety in the future world of *The Sleeper Awakes*. The novel's political message, however, is distinctly ambiguous, since the danger against which Wells is warning is not simply that of class exploitation under a rampant, hypertrophied capitalist system. The popular democracy represented by the Song of the Revolt and the novel's mass meetings, marches, demonstrations and street fighting is heroic, but also shortsighted and – so far – counter-productive. The people have toppled the leadership of the White Council, but they are manifestly no better off under Ostrog's dictatorship.

Ostrog and Wells's Political Philosophy

'Who will win – Ostrog or the People?' Wells asked in a conclusion, later deleted, to the 1910 preface to *The Sleeper Awakes*.[4] What, we might wonder, lies behind the name Ostrog? The word is a Russian root with various possible meanings – there is a St Ostrog and a town called Ostrog in the Ukraine, as well as the Ostrogoths who helped to destroy the Roman Empire – but it is surely significant that Ostrog in *The Sleeper Awakes* has a brother named Lincoln, presumably after Abraham Lincoln, the great champion of nineteenth-century American democracy. By 1899 it seems likely that Wells already knew something of Moisei Ostrogorsky (1854–1919), the Russian political theorist whose study of British and American politics, *Democracy and the Organization of Political Parties*, was first offered to Macmillan in 1895 and eventually published by them in 1902.[5] Wells's first published reference to Ostrogorsky came in *Mankind in the Making* (1903), and in *The Work, Wealth and Happiness of Mankind* thirty years later he recalled discussing Ostrogorsky's 'fruitful studies of modern democracy' with their mutual friend Graham Wallas.[6] Ostrogorsky was a true democrat, an advocate of single-issue pressure groups and a critic of the electoral chicanery and corruption endemic to party-machine politics. The name Ostrog suggests that Ostrogorsky may be destined to take his place beside Lincoln in the pantheon of democratic heroes; but, if so, the names seem deliberately intended to mislead the populace, since none of the rulers of twenty-second-century London has any respect for democratic ideals. Ostrog is also known as the 'Boss', the word used in the United States for a wealthy and powerful political fixer whose task is to deliver the vote for his party.[7]

In the world of *The Sleeper Awakes*, the two-party system has disappeared and the growth of plutocracy has gone unchecked. The result has been two centuries of social stagnation.

The ruling classes, paraded in front of us at the cocktail party in chapter 15, are frivolous, complacent and self-regarding. The White Council capitulates almost without a struggle, since its leaders evidently have no stomach for fighting. We are told that no shots have been fired in anger for a century and a half, which suggests that the whole social order, not just Graham, has been sleeping. Wells, however, implies that neither Ostrog's easy victory nor his apparent overthrow are the end of the story. Stagnation, as his protagonist had argued in *The Time Machine*, brings about a 'slow movement of degeneration', while war and necessity are powerful stimulants to political organization and technological progress.[8] The battle between Ostrog (or what he represents) and the people is certainly not over, but Wells's own sympathies in this battle are harder to pin down than we might expect. And, however much we may wish to cheer on Graham and his followers, the issue on which Wells's hero finally takes his stand – the use of black soldiers against the white working class – has unmistakable racist overtones.

Graham owes his position as the people's champion not to an informed democratic choice but to the irrational, semi-religious cult of the Sleeper that has spread among the oppressed workers. They look to him less as their tribune than as their saviour. In chapter 19, 'Ostrog's Point of View', the 'Boss' shows his contempt for Graham's outdated democratic and humanitarian ideals. (Even the Song of the Revolt, he alleges, is a propaganda device that has been deliberately planted in the minds of the workers.) At the time when *The Sleeper Awakes* was written, the working classes had only recently been given the vote, women were still excluded from politics, and 'Western democracy' had yet to become the ideological rallying-point of the capitalist world. Criticism of democracy, as a system inherently liable to be corrupted by gerrymandering, political rabble-rousing, mass hysteria and the power of the press, was widespread. Wells in his futurological treatise *Anticipations* wrote of parliamentary democracy as an organism with a 'life-history' – as, in other words, a political ideal that must in time grow old and die. In *The Sleeper Awakes* the democratic ideals of Wells's time have been superseded by a universal tyranny, yet in other contexts, such as his future-history novel *The Shape of Things to Come* (1933), Wells drew a positive message from the passing of democracy.

One of the late nineteenth century's objections to democracy was that it forced politicians to kowtow to the racism, jingoism and xenophobia of the popular masses – or, at least, of those with the power to inflame the masses. This, perhaps, is why Wells shows Graham opposing Ostrog's cynical geopolitics with an appeal to racial prejudice and national pride. The narrative unmistakably invokes racist stereotypes, since Ostrog's reason for using black troops is, apparently, that they are more feared, better disciplined and less likely to mutiny and join the revolt than the white Labour Police. Graham and his followers, for their part, think of the African soldiers as particularly savage and brutal invaders. Such racial stereotyping in fiction was quite commonplace at the height of European imperialism when Wells was writing, though he himself later emerged as an outspoken critic of racism and nationalism. His vision was one of global unification – of the construction of a world state in place of individual nation-states – and it is significant that *The Sleeper Awakes* portrays a debased and corrupted world state, while Ostrog is a dictator with a global vision of a sterile and self-serving kind. Much of human history, Wells would later argue, consisted of failed and self-deluded attempts to construct the universal empire that modern communications had made both necessary and possible.

But Ostrog, as Wells conceded in his 1921 preface, is not entirely successful as a fictional creation. Supposedly a strong man and a master strategist, his actions and words are those of a glib politician who bungles his opportunities inexcusably. A less arrogant, more honest and more charismatic leader might well have retained Graham's support. Ostrog is in no sense a formidable intellectual exponent of tyranny such as Huxley's World Controller, Mustapha Mond, in *Brave New World* or Orwell's chief torturer O'Brien in *Nineteen Eighty-Four*. We have only to set him beside such a figure as Dostoyevsky's Grand Inquisitor in *The Brothers Karamazov* to see the comparative weakness of *The Sleeper Awakes* as a novel of ideas.

Graham as a Romance Hero

But, of course, *The Sleeper Awakes* is not just a novel of ideas but an exciting adventure story – a deliberate work of popular fiction – and Graham's decision to join the revolt owes as much to the beautiful and courageous Helen Wotton as it does to political principle and moral duty. It was the scenes between Graham and Helen that gave Wells his most agonized second thoughts when he revised the story, and he did his best to remove any hints of sexual desire between his hero and heroine. An element of sentimental romance based on the erotic attraction between a girl of the future and a man of the nineteenth century was central to the plot of all three utopian romances – Hudson's *A Crystal Age*, Bellamy's *Looking Backward* and Morris's *News from Nowhere* – mentioned earlier. We might expect that such anachronic love-affairs would come to nothing, but in *Looking Backward* the hero succeeds in staying in the future and marrying his utopian beloved. Wells evidently recognized the absurdity of this. The last meeting between Graham and Helen at the end of chapter 24 gave him considerable trouble, and was several times revised. In the 1899 version they part without a kiss or any physical contact, but in obvious emotional distress; in the 1910 revision they share an awkward embrace; and in the final version (printed here) Wells explains that 'The bare thought of personal love was swept aside by the tremendous necessities of [Graham's] position' (chapter 24).[9] Helen, as this sentence rather brutally reminds us, is always seen from Graham's perspective. A member of the elite who turns against her own class, her history and motivation are obscure, and the effect of the revisions is to make her recede from view rather than emerge as a fully realized character. She is, however, the necessary catalyst who transforms Graham, the awakened Sleeper and bewildered visitor, into a genuine hero and champion of his people.

The Sleeper Awakes predicts numerous technological inventions, including television, video and the harnessing of wind-power to generate electricity, but the most sensational prediction for Wells and his first readers was undoubtedly that of powered flight. The novel was written some five years before the Wright brothers got off the ground, when it was still uncertain whether heavier-than-air rather than lighter-than-air craft represented the future of aviation. There had been popular descriptions of aerial warfare before Wells, such as George Griffith's *The Angel of the Revolution* (1893), but they generally showed battles between airships rather than aeroplanes. Wells guessed rightly on this crucial point, even if the technological level of his aviation chapters seems rather quaint. Through learning to fly, Graham finds the possibility of freeing himself from the grim and overarching city, and when the time comes his skill in the air apparently saves the day for his followers. Not only was Wells one of the first novelists to portray the heroism of the fighter pilot, but he anticipates aerial dogfights and some of the tactics used to break up German bomber formations in the 1940 Battle of Britain. (It is true that Graham has to bring down the enemy planes by the perilous method of ramming rather than by machine-gun or cannon fire.) Graham's exhilaration as he learns to control his aircraft and, later, flies into battle is most movingly conveyed, and in this respect *The Sleeper Awakes* anticipates W. B. Yeats's famous poem 'An Irish Airman Foresees His Death' written nearly two decades later. Unlike the Irish nationalist airman in Yeats's poem, Graham has been urged to fight by public duty and by 'cheering crowds', but both men feel a 'lonely impulse of delight':

> I balanced all, brought all to mind,
> The years to come seemed waste of breath,
> A waste of breath the years behind
> In balance with this life, this death.[10]

It is the thrill of aeronautical mastery, quite as much as the possibility of saving humanity from a nightmare of capitalist oppression, that makes Graham's long sleep worthwhile. When we first saw him near Boscastle he had come from the direction of Newquay and must, therefore, have passed Tintagel, the legendary home of Arthur, Britain's 'once and future king'.

Graham, as the predestined Owner of the World, is also a kind of future king. His final incarnation as an airborne knight-errant fighting off the dark hordes may be seen as a new version of the Arthurian Last Battle that gripped the imagination of so many of Wells's Victorian predecessors. Graham, unlike the hero of *Looking Backward*, could never have settled down happily in a twenty-second-century society so fundamentally different in most respects from the society he has known. It is better for the awakened Sleeper to dismiss Helen from his mind and go down fighting than to live out his years, in the words that Tennyson attributed to King Arthur, 'Among new men, strange faces, other minds'.[11]

P. P.

NOTES

1.   George Orwell, review of a reprinted edition of *The Sleeper Awakes* (12 July 1940) in Orwell, *Complete Works*, ed. Peter Davison, 20 vols. (London: Secker, 1998), xii, p. 211. Orwell also discussed *The Sleeper Awakes* in *The Road to Wigan Pier* and in his 1946 obituary of Wells.

2.   H. G. Wells, *Experiment in Autobiography: Discoveries and Conclusions of a Very Ordinary Brain (Since 1866)*, 2 vols. (London: Gollancz and Cresset Press, 1966), ii, p. 645.

3.   For a summary of Wells's other textual revisions see the Note on the Text.

4.   H. G. Wells, *The Sleeper Awakes* (London: Nelson, [1910]), p. ii.

5.   See Gaetano Quagliariello, *Politics Without Parties: Moisei Ostrogorsky and the Debate on Political Parties on the Eve of the Twentieth Century* (Aldershot: Ashgate, 1996), esp. pp. 26–8, 100–101.

6.   H. G. Wells, *Mankind in the Making* (London: Chapman & Hall, 1903), p. 267n; *The Work, Wealth and Happiness of Mankind* (London: Heinemann, 1932), p. 24.

7.   H. G. Wells explains this sense of the word 'Boss' in *Anticipations of the Reaction of Mechanical and Scientific Progress upon Human Life and Thought* (London: Chapman & Hall, 1902), pp. 155–6n.

8. H. G. Wells, *The Time Machine: An Invention* (London: Heinemann, 1895), p. 84.

9. For the 1910 version of this scene, see the Note on the Text.

10. W. B. Yeats, *Collected Poems* (London: Macmillan, 1950), p. 152.

11. Tennyson, *Poems and Plays* (London: Oxford University Press, 1965), p. 67.

Further Reading

The most vivid and memorable account of Wells's life and times is his own *Experiment in Autobiography* (2 vols., London: Gollancz and Cresset Press, 1934). It has been reprinted several times. A 'postscript' containing the previously suppressed narrative of his sexual liaisons was published as *H. G. Wells in Love*, edited by his son G. P. Wells (London: Faber & Faber, 1984). His more recent biographers draw on this material, as well as on the large body of letters and personal papers archived at the University of Illinois and elsewhere. The fullest and most scholarly biographies are *The Time Traveller* by Norman and Jeanne Mackenzie (2nd edn, London: Hogarth Press, 1987) and *H. G. Wells: Desperately Mortal* by David C. Smith (New Haven and London: Yale University Press, 1986). Smith has also edited a generous selection of Wells's *Correspondence* (4 vols., London: Pickering & Chatto, 1998). Another highly readable, if controversial and idiosyncratic, biography is *H. G. Wells: Aspects of a Life* (London: Hutchinson, 1984) by Wells's son Anthony West. Michael Foot's *H. G.: The History of Mr Wells* (London and New York: Doubleday, 1995) is enlivened by its author's personal knowledge of Wells and his circle.

Two illuminating general interpretations of Wells and his writings are Michael Draper's *H. G. Wells* (Basingstoke: Macmillan, 1987) and Brian Murray's *H. G. Wells* (New York: Continuum, 1990). Both are introductory in scope, but Draper's approach is critical and philosophical, while Murray packs a remarkable amount of biographical and historical detail into a short space. John Hammond's *An H. G. Wells Companion* (London and Basingstoke: Macmillan, 1979) and

H. G. Wells (Harlow and London: Longman, 2001) combine criticism with useful contextual material. *H. G. Wells: The Critical Heritage*, edited by Patrick Parrinder (London: Routledge, 1972), is a collection of reviews and essays of Wells published during his lifetime. A number of specialized critical and scholarly studies of Wells concentrate on his scientific romances. These include Bernard Bergonzi's pioneering study of *The Early H. G. Wells* (Manchester: Manchester University Press, 1961); John Huntington, *The Logic of Fantasy: H. G. Wells and Science Fiction* (New York: Columbia University Press, 1982); and Patrick Parrinder, *Shadows of the Future: H. G. Wells, Science Fiction and Prophecy* (Liverpool: Liverpool University Press, 1995). Peter Kemp's *H. G. Wells and the Culminating Ape* (London and Basingstoke: Macmillan, 1982) offers a lively and, at times, lurid tracing of Wells's 'biological themes and imaginative obsessions', while Roslynn D. Haynes's *H. G. Wells: Discoverer of the Future* (London and Basingstoke: Macmillan, 1980) surveys his use of scientific ideas. W. Warren Wagar, *H. G. Wells and the World State* (New Haven: Yale University Press, 1961) and John S. Partington, *Building Cosmopolis* (Aldershot: Ashgate, 2003) are studies of his political thought and his schemes for world government. John S. Partington has also edited *The Wellsian* (The Netherlands: Equilibris, 2003), a selection of essays from the H. G. Wells Society's annual critical journal of the same name. The American branch of the Wells Society maintains a highly informative website at http://hgwellsusa.50megs.com

P. P.

Note on the Text

Apart from *The Time Machine*, *The Sleeper Awakes* has the most complex textual history of any of Wells's science fiction. Its original conception may possibly have come from an early unpublished draft of *The Time Machine* set in the relatively near future. Wells began writing the novel in May 1897 while staying at Budleigh Salterton in Devon, though it is not known whether he visited Boscastle. On 22 January 1898, struggling with revisions, he told George Gissing that 'I'm midway between a noble performance and a noble disaster' (*George Gissing and H. G. Wells*, ed. Royal A. Gettmann, London: Hart-Davis, 1961, p. 79). The novel, titled *When the Sleeper Wakes*, was finished six weeks later, immediately before Wells and his wife left London for their first visit to Italy. In November, after months of illness, he completed a few further revisions. *When the Sleeper Wakes* ran as an illustrated serial in London in the *Graphic* (January–May 1899), and in New York in *Harper's Weekly* (7 January–5 May). First book publication was by Harper in London and New York in May.

Nine years later, Wells wrote to an agent suggesting a 'big popular serial' that 'might be a sort of caricature of myself as a prophetic journalist . . . full of a dream of seeing the world five hundred years ahead', but all that came of this was the revised version of *When the Sleeper Wakes*, now titled *The Sleeper Awakes*, published by Nelson in London in 1910 with a specially written preface (Norman and Jeanne Mackenzie, *The Time Traveller: The Life of H. G. Wells*, London: Weidenfeld, 1973, pp. 234–5). This version was not published in the United States until 2000. *When the Sleeper Wakes*, however, was frequently reprinted, not only in the United States but in England, where Macmillan purchased the copyright from Harper in 1903. There were Macmillan reprints in 1914 and 1922. *The Sleeper Awakes* appeared in a double-column 'pulp' edition (Newnes' Sixpenny Novels) in 1915, and in 1921 Wells undertook a further revision of the text and wrote a new preface. The new text first appeared under the Collins imprint, although – very confusingly – Collins later produced cheap paperback reprints of *When the Sleeper Wakes*, titled *The Sleeper Awakes* on the front cover and incorporating the new introduction (A. H. Watkins, *Catalogue of the H. G. Wells Collection in the Bromley Public Libraries*, Bromley: London Borough of Bromley Public Libraries, 1974, pp. 53, 68). The 1921 text of *The Sleeper Awakes* was reprinted, very slightly corrected, as Volume II of the Atlantic Edition of the Works of H. G. Wells (London: T. Fisher Unwin, and New York: Scribner's, 1924), and this seems to have been the only American publication of the revised novel during Wells's lifetime.

The Atlantic Edition was intended to provide definitive texts of all Wells's works, and it is this version which is reprinted here, subject to the modifications set out below. Wells's preface to the Atlantic text, also reprinted, is an extended and slightly revised version of his 1910 preface. The Atlantic texts were copy-edited and printed in the United States and were frequently based on earlier US editions, but in the case of *The Sleeper Awakes* the Atlantic version represents the culmination of the British line of texts.

In the present edition, punctuation and spelling have been modernized, and hyphens have been removed from some twenty words, e.g. 'blood-shot', 'to-day', 'wind-screen'. Other compound words have been joined together or separated according to modern British practice, e.g. 'Newquay' (in Cornwall) for 'New Quay', 'anyone' for 'any one', 'businessman' for 'business man', 'fingernails' for 'finger nails', 'pleasure-seekers' for 'pleasure seekers', 'self-pity' for 'self pity' and 'warlords' for 'war lords'; but 'dining halls for 'dining-halls' and 'reading rooms' for 'reading-rooms'. Hyphens have been added where necessary to compounds used adjectivally ('eight-mile', 'nineteenth-century'). The capitalization in 'Negro' has been standardized, 'enquiry' has been substituted for 'inquiry' where this is authorized by the earlier British line of texts, and the spelling of 'waggons' and 'connexions' have been modernized. In four instances, commas have been restored or added for ease of reading. The other substantive emendations are listed below.

Housestyling of punctuation and spelling has also been implemented to make the text more accessible to the reader: single quotation marks (for doubles) with doubles inside singles as needed; end punctuation placed outside end quotation marks when appropriate; spaced N-dashes (for the heavier, longer M-dash) and M-dashes (for the double-length 2M-dash); 'iz' spellings (e.g. recognize, not recognise), and acknowledgements and judgement, not acknowledgments and judgment; no full stop after personal titles (Dr, Mr, Mrs) or chapter titles, which may not follow the capitalization of the copy-text.

SOURCES OF SUBSTANTIVE EMENDATIONS

(C = Collins, N = Nelson)

Page:line	Reading adopted	Atlantic reading rejected
87:7	way off in (C)	way in
117:5	farthest (C)	furthest
207:26	upwards (N)	upward
229:34	upwards (N)	upward

SELECTED VARIANT READINGS

(i) In the 1910 revision, when he changed the novel's title from *When the Sleeper Wakes* to *The Sleeper Awakes*, Wells made some 150 separate emendations, ranging from alterations of single words and the correction of obvious printer's errors to the deletion of whole sections. A large number of the changes were stylistic, eliminating redundancy and verbal repetitions in conformity with Wells's customary method of revising his published texts. Other changes are too drastic to represent here, notably the deletion of some eight descriptive pages from the end of chapter 14, and of four pages, including a long dialogue between Graham and Helen, from chapter 24 (chapter 23 of *When the Sleeper Wakes*). The final paragraphs of this chapter were also rewritten in 1910 and again in 1921 (see below). For a critical appraisal of these changes, and also of Wells's revisions between the serial and the first printed version of *When the Sleeper Wakes*, see Gareth Davies-Morris's 'Afterword' to the Bison Books edition of *The Sleeper Awakes* (Lincoln, NE and London: University of Nebraska Press, 2000).

Some of Wells's smaller-scale revisions in 1910 are also of considerable interest. He replaced the word 'aeropile' by 'monoplane' everywhere, and renamed the Food Trust, Pill Company and Labour Company as the Food Department, Pill Department and Labour Department respectively. Graham became owner of the world, no longer merely of half the world. A brief selection of other variants is given below.

Page:line	The Sleeper Awakes (1924)	When the Sleeper Wakes
21:7	'Do you mean – he was stiff and hard?'	'It was a cataleptic rigour at first, wasn't it?'
23:24	'Rather,' said Isbister.	'It is,' said Isbister. 'As a matter of fact, it's a case for a public trustee, if only we had such a functionary.'
129:8	men.	men. Save London, there were only four other cities in Britain – Edinburgh, Portsmouth, Manchester and Shrewsbury.

Page:line	The Sleeper Awakes (1924)	When the Sleeper Wakes
137:12	wear	are shareholders in the Medical Faculty Company, and wear
212 (chapter title)	Graham Speaks his Word	While the Aeroplanes Were Coming
231:36–7 up	treachery. [The vision	treachery. He was beaten but London was saved. London was saved! [The thought

(ii) Wells revised *The Sleeper Awakes* again very thoroughly in 1921, making over 100 detailed changes to the text, nearly all for stylistic reasons. In further revising the text for the Atlantic edition, he changed 'van' to 'vane' everywhere but made only eight other small changes. His 1921 preface was not reprinted in the Atlantic edition. In other reprints of this preface during Wells's lifetime, the word 'fantasias' (line 4) sometimes appears as 'fantasies', possibly a misprint. The preface to Volume II of the Atlantic Edition, in which *The Sleeper Awakes* appears, is a revised version of Wells's 1910 preface. In particular, Wells added two new paragraphs at the end, deleting the final two sentences of the earlier version. A selection of textual variants from the novel itself is given below.

Page:line	The Sleeper Awakes (1924)	The Sleeper Awakes (1910)
16:10	chair.	chair, seemed almost to fall into it.
22:17	end.'	end.' ['And these Martians.'
49:29	bunch	thick crowd
53:17–18	immense legal significance – legal rather than practical –	very considerable significance

Page:line	The Sleeper Awakes (1924)	The Sleeper Awakes (1910)
76:30	platform	platform and given some drink,
97:10–11	a dream of his arm being pierced	something
116:22	things to be done	duties
132:3	Manchurian	Chinese
144:29–30	He did at least drive them from	After a while they did at least abandon
157:10	faded.	faded. Her slender beauty came compellingly between him and certain immediate temptations of ignoble passion. But he did not see her again until three full days were past.
158.13	'I	He felt a regal impulse to assist her. 'I
190.5	a ladder	a ladder – the first ladder he had seen since his awakening –
191.15	a silent, watchful	an excited, undignified
217	[Footnote added]	
221.33–8	There was no . . . he said.	They were both clear that he must go. There was no step back from these towering heroisms. Her eyes brimmed with tears. She came towards him with a curious movement of her hands, as though she felt her way and could not see; she seized his hand and kissed it.

Page:line	The Sleeper Awakes (1924)	The Sleeper Awakes (1910)
		'To wake,' she cried, 'for this!'
		He held her clumsily for a moment, and kissed the hair of her bowed head, and then thrust her away, and turned towards the man in yellow.
		He could not speak. The gesture of his arm said 'Onward.'
232.6–9	[Although he . . . and stays.	It *must* be a dream! Yet surely he would meet her. She at least was real. He would wake and meet her.
		Although he could not look at it, he was suddenly aware that the earth was very near.

Page:line	The Sleeper Awakes (1924)	The Sleeper Awakes (1921)
15:1	go	return
54:30	an inheritance	a vast inheritance
54:35	was	series of magnificent impressions was

There is no previous edition of *The Sleeper Awakes* with a critical textual apparatus. I am indebted to the textual notes provided by John Lawton and Leon Stover for their recent editions of *When the Sleeper Wakes*, as well as to the Bison Books edition of *The Sleeper Awakes*. Details of the chronology of Wells's composition of *When the Sleeper Wakes* and its serialization are taken from J. R. Hammond, *An H. G. Wells*

Chronology (Basingstoke: Macmillan, 1999), and from David C. Smith's unpublished annotated Wells bibliography. The surviving manuscripts of *When the Sleeper Wakes* and the corrected galley proofs of the Atlantic Edition of *The Sleeper Awakes* are in the H. G. Wells Collection at the Rare Book and Special Collections Library, University of Illinois at Urbana-Champaign.

P. P.

THE SLEEPER AWAKES

PREFACE TO THE ATLANTIC EDITION

When the Sleeper Wakes, whose title I have altered to *The Sleeper Awakes*, was first published as a book in 1899 after a serial appearance in the *Graphic* and one or two American and colonial periodicals. It was one of the most ambitious and least satisfactory of my earlier books, and in 1911 I took the opportunity afforded by its reprinting to make a number of excisions and alterations.[1] Like most of my earlier work, it was written under considerable pressure; there are marks of haste not only in the writing of the latter part, but in the very construction of the story. Except for certain streaks of a slovenliness which seems to be an almost unavoidable defect in me, there is little to be ashamed of in the writing of the opening portion; but it will be fairly manifest to the critic that instead of being put aside and thought over through a leisurely interlude, the ill-conceived latter part was pushed to its end. I was at that time overworked, and badly in need of a holiday. In addition to various necessary journalistic tasks, I had in hand another book, *Love and Mr Lewisham*, which had taken a very much stronger hold upon my affections than this present story. My circumstances demanded that one or other should be finished before I took any rest, and so I wound up the Sleeper sufficiently to make it a marketable work, hoping to be able to revise it before the book printers at any rate got hold of it. But fortune was against me. I came back to England from Italy only to fall dangerously ill, and I still remember the impotent rage and strain of my attempt to put some sort of finish to my story of Mr Lewisham, with my temperature at a hundred and two. I couldn't endure the thought of leaving that book a fragment.

I did afterwards contrive to save it from the consequences of that febrile spurt – *Love and Mr Lewisham* is indeed one of my most carefully balanced books – but the Sleeper escaped me.

It is more than a score of years now since the Sleeper was written, and that young man of thirty-one is already too remote for me to attempt any very drastic reconstruction of his work. I have played now merely the part of an editorial elder brother: cut out relentlessly a number of long tiresome passages that showed all too plainly the fagged, toiling brain, the heavy sluggish *driven* pen, and straightened out certain indecisions at the end. Except for that, I have done no more than hack here and there at clumsy phrases and repetitions. The worst thing in the earlier version, and the thing that rankled most in my mind, was the treatment of the relations of Helen Wotton and Graham. Haste in art is almost always vulgarization, and I slipped into the obvious vulgarity of making what the newspaper syndicates call a 'love interest' out of Helen. There was even a clumsy intimation that instead of going up in the flying-machine to fight, Graham might have given in to Ostrog, and married Helen. I have now removed the suggestion of these uncanny connubialities. Not the slightest intimation of any sexual interest could in truth have arisen between these two. They loved, but as a girl and her heroic grandfather might love. I have found it possible, without any very serious disarrangement, to clear all that objectionable stuff out of the story, and so a little ease my conscience on the score of this ungainly lapse. I have also, with a few strokes of the pen, eliminated certain dishonest and regrettable suggestions that the People beat Ostrog. My Graham dies, as all his kind must die, with no certainty of either victory or defeat.

The air fighting reads queerly nowadays, but when it is remembered – and there will be a footnote at the proper place to remind the reader of the fact – that it was imagined ten years before there was any flying and fifteen years before there was fighting in the air, then its oddity will be understandable. The idea that special landing and starting stages would be necessary was very prevalent then; the story turns on it. Most of the early experimental machines, Maxim's for example, got up speed on a rail before they jumped into the air. There is a great exaggeration of instability and of the technical difficulty of flying. The final nosedive was in the original version, but the spin and one or two other realistic touches have been put in. Even the automobiles described in this story, let the reader remember, are intelligent anticipations. When this book was written there was a speed limit for mechanically propelled vehicles in England of four miles an hour.

I will not discuss the thesis of the story at any length here because the reader will find that done in *Anticipations*,[2] a later volume in this series. It will be clear that the chief assumptions upon which the scene is framed amount to a prolongation of the lines of tendency that were most conspicuous in the last decade of the nineteenth century. The analysis of these tendencies and their possible persistence, is very slight. The story was written ten years before any flying machine got off the ground, but the flying is, I submit, fairly well imagined, and it is interesting in the light of recent events to find that the idea of black troops being brought from Africa to subjugate Europeans occurred to me as a suitable device to bring about my climax. Ostrog my mature mind finds an impossible figure. The thesis is that he is a man of enormous knowledge and capacity. But he bungles his situations incredibly.

[1924]

PREFACE [1921]

This book, *The Sleeper Awakes*, was written in that remote and comparatively happy year, 1898. It is the first of a series of books which I have written at intervals since that time: *The World Set Free* is the latest; they are all 'fantasias of possibility'; each one takes some great creative tendency, or group of tendencies, and develops its possible consequences in the future. *The War in the Air* did that for example with aviation, and is perhaps, as a forecast, the most successful of them all. The present volume takes up certain ideas already very much discussed in the concluding years of the last century, the idea of the growth of the towns and the depopulation of the countryside and the degradation of labour through the higher organization of industrial production. 'Suppose these forces to go on', that is the fundamental hypothesis of the story.

The 'Sleeper' is of course the average man, who owns everything – did he but choose to take hold of his possessions – and who neglects everything. He wakes up to find himself the puppet of a conspiracy of highly intellectual men in a world which is a practical realization of Mr Belloc's nightmare of the Servile State.[1] And the book resolves itself into as vigorous an imagination as the writer's quality permitted of this world of base servitude in hypertrophied cities.

Will such a world ever exist?

I will confess I doubt it. At the time when I wrote this story I had a considerable belief in its possibility, but later on, in *Anticipations*, I made a very careful analysis of the causes of town aggregation and showed that a period of town dispersal was already beginning. And the thesis of a gradual systematic enslavement of organized labour, presupposes an intelligence, a power of combination and a *wickedness* in the class of rich financiers and industrial organizers, such as this class certainly does not possess, and probably cannot possess. A body of men who had the character and the largeness of imagination necessary to combine and overcome the natural insubordination of the worker would have a character and largeness of imagination too fine and great for any such plot against humanity. I was young in those days, I was thirty-two, I had met few big businessmen, and I still thought them as wicked, able men. It was only later that I realized that on the contrary they were, for the most part, rather foolish plungers, fortunate and energetic rather than capable, vulgar rather than wicked, and quite incapable of worldwide constructive plans or generous combined action. 'Ostrog', in *The Sleeper Awakes*, gave way to reality when I drew Uncle Ponderevo in *Tono-Bungay*. The great city of this story is no more than a nightmare of Capitalism triumphant, a nightmare that was dreamt nearly a quarter of a century ago. It is a fantastic possibility no longer possible. Much evil may be in store for mankind, but to this immense, grim organization of servitude, our race will never come.

H. G. WELLS

EASTON GLEBE, DUNMOW, 1921

CONTENTS

CHAPTER I

INSOMNIA

One afternoon at low water Mr Isbister, a young artist lodging at Boscastle, walked from that place to the picturesque cove of Pentargen, desiring to examine the caves there. Halfway down the precipitous path to the Pentargen beach he came suddenly upon a man sitting in an attitude of profound distress beneath a projecting mass of rock. The hands of this man hung limply over his knees, his eyes were red and staring before him, and his face was wet with tears.

He glanced round at Isbister's footfall. Both men were disconcerted, Isbister the more so, and to override the awkwardness of his involuntary pause he remarked, with an air of mature conviction, that the weather was hot for the time of year.

'Very,' answered the stranger shortly, hesitated a second, and added in a colourless tone, 'I can't sleep.'

Isbister stopped abruptly. 'No?' was all he said, but his bearing conveyed his helpful impulse.

'It may sound incredible,' said the stranger, turning weary eyes to Isbister's face and emphasizing his words with a languid hand, 'but I have had no sleep – no sleep at all for six nights.'

'Had advice?'

'Yes. Bad advice for the most part. Drugs. My nervous system. . . . They are all very well for the run of people. It's hard to explain. I dare not take . . . sufficiently powerful drugs.'

'That makes it difficult,' said Isbister.

He stood helplessly in the narrow path, perplexed what to do. Clearly the man wanted to talk. An idea natural enough under the circumstances, prompted him to keep the conversation going. 'I've never suffered from sleeplessness myself,' he said in a tone of commonplace gossip, 'but in those cases I have known, people have usually found something—'

'I dare make no experiments.'

He spoke wearily. He gave a gesture of rejection, and for a space both men were silent.

'Exercise?' suggested Isbister diffidently, with a glance from his interlocutor's face of wretchedness to the touring costume he wore.

'That is what I have tried. Unwisely perhaps. I have followed the coast, day after day – from Newquay. It has only added muscular fatigue to the mental. The cause of this unrest was overwork – trouble. There was something—'

He stopped as if from sheer fatigue. He rubbed his forehead with a lean hand. He resumed speech like one who talks to himself.

'I am a lone wolf, a solitary man, wandering through a world in which I have no part. I am wifeless – childless – who is it speaks of the childless as the dead twigs on the tree of life? I am wifeless, childless – I could find no duty to do. No desire even in my heart. One thing at last I set myself to do.

'I said, I *will* do this; and to do it, to overcome the inertia of this dull body, I resorted to drugs. Great God, I've had enough of drugs! I don't know if *you* feel the heavy inconvenience of the body, its exasperating demand of time from the mind – time – life! Live! We only live in patches. We have to eat, and then come the dull digestive complacencies – or irritations. We have to take the air or else our thoughts grow sluggish, stupid, run into gulfs and blind alleys. A thousand distractions arise from within and without, and then come drowsiness and sleep. Men seem to live for sleep. How little of a man's day is his own – even at the best! And then come those false friends, those Thug helpers, the alkaloids that stifle natural fatigue and kill rest – black coffee, cocaine—'

'I see,' said Isbister.

'I did my work,' said the sleepless man with a querulous intonation.

'And this is the price?'

'Yes.'

For a little while the two remained without speaking.

'You cannot imagine the craving for rest that I feel – a hunger and thirst. For six long days, since my work was done, my mind has been a whirlpool, swift, unprogressive and incessant, a torrent of thoughts leading nowhere, spinning round swift and steady—'

He paused. 'Towards the gulf.'

'You must sleep,' said Isbister decisively, and with an air of a remedy discovered. 'Certainly you must sleep.'

'My mind is perfectly lucid. It was never clearer. But I know I am drawing towards the vortex. Presently—'

'Yes?'

'You have seen things go down an eddy? Out of the light of the day, out of this sweet world of sanity – down—'

'But,' expostulated Isbister.

The man threw out a hand towards him, and his eyes were wild, and his voice suddenly high. 'I shall kill myself. If in no other way – at the foot of yonder dark precipice there, where the waves are green, and the white surge lifts and falls, and that little thread of water trembles down. There at any rate is . . . sleep.'

'That's unreasonable,' said Isbister, startled at the man's hysterical gust of emotion. 'Drugs are better than that.'

'There at any rate is sleep,' repeated the stranger, not heeding him.

Isbister looked at him. 'It's not a cert, you know,' he remarked. 'There's a cliff like that at Lulworth Cove – as high, anyhow – and a little girl fell from top to bottom. And lives today – sound and well.'

'But those rocks there?'

'One might lie on them rather dismally through a cold night, broken bones grating as one shivered, chill water splashing over you. Eh?'

Their eyes met. 'Sorry to upset your ideals,' said Isbister with a sense of devil-may-careish brilliance. 'But a suicide over that cliff (or any cliff for the matter of that), really, as an artist –' He laughed. 'It's so damned amateurish.'

'But the other thing,' said the sleepless man irritably, 'the other thing. No man can keep sane if night after night—'

'Have you been walking along this coast alone?'

'Yes.'

'Silly sort of thing to do. If you'll excuse my saying so. Alone! As you say; body fag[1] is no cure for brain fag. Who told you to? No wonder; walking! And the sun on your head, heat, fag, solitude, all the day long, and then, I suppose, you go to bed and try very hard – eh?'

Isbister stopped short and looked at the sufferer doubtfully.

'Look at these rocks!' cried the seated man with a sudden force of gesture. 'Look at that sea that has shone and quivered there for ever! See the white spume rush into darkness under that great cliff. And this blue vault, with the blinding sun pouring from the dome of it. It is your world. You accept it, you rejoice in it. It warms and supports and delights you. And for me —'

He turned his head and showed a ghastly face, bloodshot pallid eyes and bloodless lips. He spoke almost in a whisper. 'It is the garment of my misery. The whole world . . . is the garment of my misery.'

Isbister looked at all the wild beauty of the sunlit cliffs about them and back to that face of despair. For a moment he was silent.

He started, and made a gesture of impatient rejection. 'You get a night's sleep,' he said, 'and you won't see much misery out here. Take my word for it.'

He was quite sure now that this was a providential encounter. Only half an hour ago he had been feeling horribly bored. Here was employment the bare thought of which was righteous self-applause. He took possession forthwith. The first need of this exhausted being was companionship. He flung himself down on the steeply sloping turf beside the motionless seated figure, and threw out a skirmishing line of gossip.

His hearer lapsed into apathy; he stared dismally seaward, and spoke only in answer to Isbister's direct questions – and not to all of those. But he made no objection to this benevolent intrusion upon his despair.

He seemed even grateful, and when presently Isbister, feeling that his unsupported talk was losing vigour, suggested that they should reascend the steep and go towards Boscastle, alleging the view into Blackapit, he submitted quietly. Halfway up he began talking to himself, and abruptly turned a ghastly face on his helper. 'What can be happening?' he asked with a gaunt illustrative hand. 'What can be happening? Spin, spin, spin, spin. It goes round and round, round and round for evermore.'

He stood with his hand circling.

'It's all right, old chap,' said Isbister with the air of an old friend. 'Don't worry yourself. Trust to me.'

The man dropped his hand. They went over the brow and to the headland beyond Penally, with the sleepless man gesticulating ever and again, and speaking fragmentary things concerning his whirling brain. At the headland they stood by the seat that looks into the dark mysteries of Blackapit, and then he sat down. Isbister had resumed his talk whenever the path had widened sufficiently for them to walk abreast. He was enlarging upon the complex difficulty of making Boscastle Harbour in bad weather, when suddenly and quite irrelevantly his companion interrupted him again.

'My head is not like what it was,' he said. 'It's not like what it was. There is a sort of oppression, a weight. No – not drowsiness, would God it were! It is like a shadow, a deep shadow falling suddenly and swiftly across something busy. Spin, spin into the darkness. The tumult of thought, the confusion, the eddy and eddy. I can't express it. I can hardly keep my mind on it – steadily enough to tell you.'

He stopped feebly.

'Don't trouble, old chap,' said Isbister. 'I think I can understand. At any rate, it don't matter very much just at present about telling me, you know.'

The sleepless man thrust his knuckles into his eyes and rubbed them. Isbister talked while this rubbing continued, and then he had a fresh idea. 'Come down to my room,' he said, 'and try a pipe. I can show you some sketches of this Blackapit. If you'd care?'

The other rose obediently and followed him down the steep.

Several times Isbister heard him stumble as they came down, and his movements were slow and hesitating. 'Come in with me,' said Isbister, 'and try some cigarettes and the blessed gift of alcohol. If you take alcohol?'

The stranger hesitated at the garden gate. He seemed no longer aware of his actions. 'I don't drink,' he said slowly, coming up the garden path, and after a moment's interval repeated absently, 'No – I don't drink. It goes round. Spin, it goes – spin —'

He stumbled at the doorstep and entered the room with the bearing of one who sees nothing.

Then he sat down heavily in the easy chair. He leant forward with his brows on his hands and became motionless. Presently there was a faint sound in his throat.

Isbister moved about the room with the nervousness of an inexperienced host, making little remarks that scarcely required answering. He crossed the room to his portfolio, placed it on the table and noticed the mantel clock.

'I don't know if you'd care to have supper with me,' he said with an unlighted cigarette in his hand, his mind troubled with ideas of a furtive administration of chloral.[2] 'Only cold mutton, you know, but passing sweet. Welsh. And a tart, I believe.' He repeated this after momentary silence.

The seated man made no answer. Isbister stopped, match in hand, regarding him.

The stillness lengthened. The match went out, the cigarette was put down unlit. The man was certainly very still. Isbister took up the portfolio, opened it, put it down, hesitated. 'Per-haps,' he whispered doubtfully. Presently he glanced at the door and back to the figure. Then he stole on tiptoe out of the room, glancing at his companion after each elaborate pace.

He closed the door noiselessly. The house door was standing open, and he went out beyond the porch, and stood where the monkshood[3] rose at the corner of the garden bed. From this point he could see the stranger through the open window, still and dim, sitting head on hand. He had not moved.

A number of children going along the road stopped and regarded the artist curiously. A boatman exchanged civilities with him. He felt that possibly his circumspect attitude and position looked peculiar and unaccountable. Smoking, perhaps, might seem more natural. He drew pipe and pouch from his pocket, filled the pipe slowly.

'I wonder,' ... he said, with a scarcely perceptible loss of complacency. 'At any rate one must give him a chance.' He struck a match in the virile way, and proceeded to light his pipe.

He heard his landlady behind him, coming with his lamp lit from the kitchen. He turned, gesticulating with his pipe, and stopped her at the door of his sitting room. He had some difficulty in explaining the situation in whispers, for she did not know he had a visitor. She retreated again with the lamp, still a little mystified to judge from her manner, and he resumed his hovering at the corner of the porch, flushed and less at his ease.

Long after he had smoked out his pipe, and when the bats were abroad, curiosity dominated his complex hesitations, and he stole back into his darkling[4] sitting room. He paused in the doorway. The stranger was still in the same attitude, dark against the window. Save for the singing of some sailors aboard one of the little slate-carrying ships in the harbour the evening was very still. Outside, the spikes of monkshood and delphinium[5] stood erect and motionless against the shadow of the hillside. Something flashed into Isbister's mind; he started, and leaning over the table, listened. An unpleasant suspicion grew stronger; became conviction. Astonishment seized him and became – dread!

No sound of breathing came from the seated figure!

He crept slowly and noiselessly round the table, pausing twice to listen. At last he could lay his hand on the back of the armchair. He bent down until the two heads were ear to ear.

Then he bent still lower to look up at his visitor's face. He started violently and uttered an exclamation. The eyes were void spaces of white.

He looked again and saw that they were open and with the pupils rolled under the lids. He was afraid. He took the man by the shoulder and shook him. 'Are you asleep?' he said, with his voice jumping, and again, 'Are you asleep?'

A conviction took possession of his mind that this man was dead. He became active and noisy, strode across the room, blundering against the table as he did so, and rang the bell.

'Please bring a light at once,' he said in the passage. 'There is something wrong with my friend.'

He returned to the motionless seated figure, grasped the shoulder, shook it, shouted. The room was flooded with yellow glare as his landlady entered with the light. His face was white as he turned blinking towards her. 'I must fetch a doctor,' he said. 'It is either death or a fit. Is there a doctor in the village? Where is a doctor to be found?'

CHAPTER 2
THE TRANCE

The state of cataleptic rigour into which this man had fallen, lasted for an unprecedented length of time, and then he passed slowly to the flaccid state, to a lax attitude suggestive of profound repose. Then it was his eyes could be closed.

He was removed from the hotel to the Boscastle surgery, and from the surgery, after some weeks, to London. But he still resisted every attempt at reanimation. After a time, for reasons that will appear later, these attempts were discontinued. For a great space he lay in that strange condition, inert and still – neither dead nor living but, as it were, suspended, hanging midway between nothingness and existence. His was a darkness unbroken by a ray of thought or sensation, a dreamless inanition, a vast space of peace. The tumult of his mind had swelled and risen to an abrupt climax of silence. Where was the man? Where is any man when insensibility takes hold of him?

'It seems only yesterday,' said Isbister. 'I remember it all as though it happened yesterday – clearer, perhaps, than if it had happened yesterday.'

It was the Isbister of the last chapter, but he was no longer a young man. The hair that had been brown and a trifle in excess of the fashionable length, was iron grey and clipped close, and the face that had been pink and white was buff and ruddy. He had a pointed beard shot with grey. He talked to an elderly man who wore a summer suit of drill[1] (the summer of that year was unusually hot). This was Warming, a London solicitor and next of kin to Graham, the man who had fallen into the trance. And the two men stood side by side in a room in a house in London regarding his recumbent figure.

was a yellow figure lying lax upon a water-bed and clad in a flowing shirt, a figure with a shrunken face and a stubby beard, lean limbs and lank nails, and about it was a case of thin glass. This glass seemed to mark off the sleeper from the reality of life about him, he was a thing apart, a strange, isolated abnormality. The two men stood close to the glass, peering in.

'The thing gave me a shock,' said Isbister. 'I feel a queer sort of surprise even now when I think of his white eyes. They were white, you know, rolled up. Coming here again brings it all back to me.'

'Have you never seen him since that time?' asked Warming.

'Often wanted to come,' said Isbister; 'but business nowadays is too serious a thing for much holiday keeping. I've been in America most of the time.'

'If I remember rightly,' said Warming, 'you were an artist?'

'Was. And then I became a married man. I saw it was all up with black and white, very soon – at least for a mediocrity, and I jumped on to process. Those posters on the Cliffs at Dover are by my people.'

'Good posters,' admitted the solicitor, 'though I was sorry to see them there.'

'Last as long as the cliffs, if necessary,' exclaimed Isbister with satisfaction. 'The world changes. When he fell asleep, twenty years ago, I was down at Boscastle with a box of water-colours and a noble, old-fashioned ambition. I didn't expect that some day my pigments would glorify the whole blessed coast of England, from Land's End round again to the Lizard. Luck comes to a man very often when he's not looking.'

Warming seemed to doubt the quality of the luck. 'I just missed seeing you, if I recollect aright.'

'You came back by the trap[2] that took me to Camelford railway station. It was close on the Jubilee, Victoria's Jubilee,[3] because I remember the seats and flags in Westminster, and the row with the cabman at Chelsea.'

'The Diamond Jubilee, it was,' said Warming; 'the second one.'

'Ah, yes! At the proper Jubilee – the Fifty Year affair – I was down at Wookey – a boy. I missed all that. . . . What a fuss we

had with him! My landlady wouldn't take him in, wouldn't let
him stay – he looked so queer when he was rigid. We had to
carry him in a chair up to the hotel. And the Boscastle doctor
– it wasn't the present chap, but the GP[4] before him – was at
him until nearly two, with me and the landlord holding lights
and so forth.'

'Do you mean – he was stiff and hard?'

'Stiff! – wherever you bent him he stuck. You might have
stood him on his head and he'd have stopped. I never saw such
stiffness. Of course this' – he indicated the prostrate figure by
a movement of his head – 'is quite different. And the little
doctor – what was his name?'

'Smithers?'

'Smithers it was – was quite wrong in trying to fetch him
round too soon, according to all accounts. The things he did!
Even now it makes me feel all – ugh! Mustard, snuff, pricking.
And one of those beastly little things, not dynamos—'

'Coils.'

'Yes. You could see his muscles throb and jump, and he
twisted about. There were just two flaring yellow candles, and
all the shadows were shivering, and the little doctor nervous
and putting on side, and *him* – stark and squirming in the most
unnatural ways. Well, it made me dream.'

Pause.

'It's a strange state,' said Warming.

'It's a sort of complete absence,' said Isbister. 'Here's the
body, empty. Not dead a bit, and yet not alive. It's like a seat
vacant and marked "engaged". No feeling, no digestion, no
beating of the heart – not a flutter. *That* doesn't make me feel
as if there was a man present. In a sense it's more dead than
death, for these doctors tell me that even the hair has stopped
growing. Now with the proper dead, the hair will go on
growing—'

'I know,' said Warming, with a flash of pain in his expression.

They peered through the glass again. Graham was indeed in
a strange state, in the flaccid phase of a trance, but a trance
unprecedented in medical history. Trances had lasted for as
much as a year before – but at the end of that time it had ever

been a waking or a death; sometimes first one and then the other. Isbister noted the marks the physicians had made in injecting nourishment, for that had been resorted to to postpone collapse; he pointed them out to Warming, who had been trying not to see them.

'And while he has been lying here,' said Isbister, with the zest of a life freely spent, 'I have changed my plans in life; married, raised a family, my eldest lad – I hadn't begun to think of sons then – is an American citizen and looking forward to leaving Harvard. There's a touch of grey in my hair. And this man, not a day older nor wiser (practically) than I was in my downy days. It's curious to think of.'

Warming turned. 'And I have grown old too. I played cricket with him when I was still only a boy. And he looks a young man still. Yellow perhaps. But that *is* a young man nevertheless.'

'And there's been the War,'[5] said Isbister.

'From beginning to end.'

'I've understood,' said Isbister after a pause, 'that he had some moderate property of his own?'

'That is so,' said Warming. He coughed primly. 'As it happens – I have charge of it.'

'Ah!' Isbister thought, hesitated and spoke: 'No doubt – his keep here is not expensive – no doubt it will have improved – accumulated?'

'It has. He will wake up very much better off – if he wakes – than when he slept.'

'As a businessman,' said Isbister, 'that thought has naturally been in my mind. I have indeed sometimes thought that, speaking commercially of course, this sleep may be a very good thing for him. That he knows what he is about, so to speak, in being insensible so long. If he had lived straight on—'

'I doubt if he would have premeditated as much,' said Warming. 'He was not a far-sighted man. In fact—'

'Yes?'

'We differed on that point. I stood to him somewhat in the relation of a guardian. You have probably seen enough of affairs to recognize that occasionally a certain friction – But even if that was the case, there is a doubt whether he will ever awake. This sleep exhausts slowly, but it exhausts. Apparently he is sliding slowly, very slowly and tediously, down a long slope, if you can understand me?'

'It will be a pity to lose his surprise. There's been a lot of change these twenty years. It's Rip Van Winkle[6] come real.'

'There has been a lot of change certainly,' said Warming. 'And, among other changes, I have changed. I am an old man.'

Isbister hesitated, and then feigned a belated surprise. 'I shouldn't have thought it.'

'I was forty-three when his bankers – you remember you wired to his bankers – sent on to me.'

'I got their address from the cheque book in his pocket,' said Isbister.

'Well, the addition is not difficult,' said Warming.

There was another pause, and then Isbister gave way to an unavoidable curiosity. 'He may go on for years yet,' he said, and had a moment of hesitation. 'We have to consider that. His affairs, you know, may fall some day into the hands of – someone else, you know.'

'That, if you will believe me, Mr Isbister, is one of the problems most constantly before my mind. We happen to be – as a matter of fact, there are no very trustworthy connections of ours. It is a grotesque and unprecedented position.'

'Rather,' said Isbister.

'It seems to me it's a case of some public body, some practically undying guardian. If he really is going on living – as the doctors, some of them, think. As a matter of fact, I have gone to one or two public men about it. But so far nothing has been done.'

'It wouldn't be a bad idea to hand him over to some public body – the British Museum Trustees, or the Royal College of Physicians. Sounds a bit odd, of course, but the whole situation is odd.'

'The difficulty is to induce them to take him.'

'Red tape, I suppose?'

'Partly.'

Pause. 'It's a curious business, certainly,' said Isbister. 'And compound interest[7] has a way of mounting up.'

'It has,' said Warming. 'And now the gold supplies are running short there is a tendency towards . . . appreciation.'

'I've felt that,' said Isbister with a grimace. 'But it makes it better for *him*.'

'*If* he awakes.'

'If he awakes,' echoed Isbister. 'Do you notice the pinched-in look of his nose, and the way in which his eyelids sink?'

Warming looked and thought for a space. 'I doubt if he will awake,' he said at last.

'I never properly understood,' said Isbister, 'what it was brought this on. He told me something about overstudy. I've often been curious.'

'He was a man of considerable gifts, but spasmodic, emotional. He had grave domestic troubles, divorced his wife in fact, and it was as a relief from that, I think, that he took up politics of the rabid sort. He was a fanatical Radical – a Socialist – or typical Liberal, as they used to call themselves, of the advanced school. Energetic – flighty – undisciplined. Overwork upon a controversy did this for him. I remember the pamphlet he wrote – a curious production. Wild, whirling stuff. There were one or two prophecies. Some of them are already exploded, some of them are established facts. But for the most part to read such a thesis is to realize how full the world is of unanticipated things. He will have much to learn, much to unlearn, when he awakes. If ever an awakening comes.'

'I'd give anything to be there,' said Isbister, 'just to hear what he would say to it all.'

'So would I,' said Warming. 'Aye! so would I,' with an old man's sudden turn to self-pity. 'But I shall never see him awake.'

He stood looking thoughtfully at the waxen figure. 'He will never awake,' he said at last. He sighed. 'He will never awake again.'

CHAPTER 3
THE AWAKENING

But Warming was wrong in that. An awakening came.

What a wonderfully complex thing! this simple seeming unity – the self! Who can trace its reintegration as morning after morning we awaken, the flux and confluence of its countless factors interweaving, rebuilding, the dim first stirrings of the soul, the growth and synthesis of the unconscious to the subconscious, the subconscious to dawning consciousness, until at last we recognize ourselves again. And as it happens to most of us after the night's sleep, so it was with Graham at the end of his vast slumber. A dim mist of sensation taking shape, a cloudy dreariness, and he found himself vaguely somewhere, recumbent, faint, but alive.

The pilgrimage towards a personal being seemed to traverse vast gulfs, to occupy epochs. Gigantic dreams that were terrible realities at the time, left vague perplexing memories, strange creatures, strange scenery, as if from another planet. There was a distinct impression, too, of a momentous conversation, of a name – he could not tell what name – that was subsequently to recur, of some queer long-forgotten sensation of vein and muscle, of a feeling of vast hopeless effort, the effort of a man near drowning in darkness. Then came a panorama of dazzling unstable confluent scenes. . . .

Graham became aware that his eyes were open and regarding some unfamiliar thing.

It was something white, the edge of something, a frame of wood. He moved his head slightly, following the contour of this shape. It went up beyond the top of his eyes. He tried to think where he might be. Did it matter, seeing he was so wretched? The colour of his thoughts was a dark depression. He felt the featureless misery of one who wakes towards the hour of dawn. He had an uncertain sense of whispers and footsteps hastily receding.

The movement of his head involved a perception of extreme physical weakness. He supposed he was in bed in the hotel at the place in the valley – but he could not recall that white edge. He must have slept. He remembered now that he had wanted to sleep. He recalled the cliff and waterfall again, and then recollected something about talking to a passer-by. . . .

How long had he slept? What was that sound of pattering feet? And that rise and fall, like the murmur of breakers on pebbles? He put out a languid hand to reach his watch from the chair whereon it was his habit to place it, and touched some smooth hard surface like glass. This was so unexpected that it startled him extremely. Quite suddenly he rolled over, stared for a moment, and struggled into a sitting position. The effort was unexpectedly difficult, and it left him giddy and weak – and amazed.

He rubbed his eyes. The riddle of his surroundings was confusing but his mind was quite clear – evidently his sleep had benefited him. He was not in a bed at all as he understood the word, but lying naked on a very soft and yielding mattress, in a trough of dark glass. The mattress was partly transparent, a fact he observed with a sense of insecurity, and below it was a mirror reflecting him greyly. About his arm – and he saw with a shock that his skin was strangely dry and yellow – was bound a curious apparatus of rubber, bound so cunningly that it seemed to pass into his skin above and below. And this bed was placed in a case of greenish-coloured glass (as it seemed to him), a bar in the white framework of which had first arrested his attention. In the corner of the case was a stand of glittering and delicately made apparatus, for the most part quite strange appliances, though a maximum and minimum thermometer[1] was recognizable.

The slightly greenish tint of the glass-like substance which surrounded him on every hand obscured what lay behind, but he perceived it was a vast apartment of splendid appearance, and with a very large and simple white archway facing him. Close to the walls of the cage were articles of furniture, a table covered with a silvery cloth, silvery like the side of a fish, a couple of graceful chairs, and on the table a number of dishes with substances piled on them, a bottle and two glasses. He realized that he was intensely hungry.

He could see no one, and after a period of hesitation scrambled off the translucent mattress and tried to stand on the clean white floor of his little apartment. He had miscalculated his strength, however, and staggered and put his hand against the glass-like pane before him to steady himself. For a moment it resisted his hand, bending outward like a distended bladder, then it broke with a slight report and vanished – a pricked bubble. He reeled out into the general space of the hall, greatly astonished. He caught at the table to save himself, knocking one of the glasses to the floor – it rang but did not break – and sat down in one of the armchairs.

When he had a little recovered he filled the remaining glass from the bottle and drank – a colourless liquid it was, but not water, with a pleasing faint aroma and taste and a quality of immediate support and stimulus. He put down the vessel and looked about him.

The apartment lost none of its size and magnificence now that the greenish transparency that had intervened was removed. The archway he saw led to a flight of steps, going downward without the intermediation of a door, to a spacious transverse passage. This passage ran between polished pillars of some white-veined substance of deep ultramarine, and along it came the sound of human movements, and voices and a deep undeviating droning note. He sat, now fully awake, listening alertly, forgetting the viands in his attention.

Then with a shock he remembered that he was naked, and casting about him for covering, saw a long black robe thrown on one of the chairs beside him. This he wrapped about him and sat down again, trembling.

His mind was still a surging perplexity. Clearly he had slept, and had been removed in his sleep. But where? And who were those people, the distant crowd beyond the deep blue pillars?

Boscastle? He poured out and partially drank another glass of the colourless fluid.

What was this place? – this place that to his senses seemed subtly quivering like a thing alive? He looked about him at the clean and beautiful form of the apartment, unstained by ornament, and saw that the roof was broken in one place by a circular shaft full of light, and as he looked a steady, sweeping shadow[2] blotted it out and passed, and came again and passed. 'Beat, beat,' that sweeping shadow had a note of its own in the subdued tumult that filled the air.

He would have called out, but only a little sound came into his throat. Then he stood up and, with the uncertain steps of a drunkard, made his way towards the archway. He staggered down the steps, tripped on the corner of the black cloak he had wrapped about himself, and saved himself by catching at one of the blue pillars.

The passage ran down a cool vista of blue and purple and ended remotely in a railed space like a balcony brightly lit and projecting into a space of haze, a space like the interior of some gigantic building. Beyond and remote were vast and vague architectural forms. The tumult of voices rose now loud and clear, and on the balcony and with their backs to him, gesticulating and apparently in animated conversation, were three figures, richly dressed in loose and easy garments of bright soft colourings. The noise of a great multitude of people poured up over the balcony, and once it seemed the top of a banner passed, and once some brightly coloured object, a pale blue cap or garment thrown up into the air perhaps, flashed athwart the space and fell. The shouts sounded like English, there was a reiteration of 'wake!' He heard some indistinct shrill cry, and abruptly these three men began laughing.

'Ha, ha, ha!' laughed one – a red-haired man in a short purple robe. 'When the Sleeper wakes – *When*!'

He turned his eyes full of merriment along the passage. His face changed, the whole man changed, became rigid. The other two turned swiftly at his exclamation and stood motionless. Their faces assumed an expression of consternation, an expression that deepened into awe.

Suddenly Graham's knees bent beneath him, his arm against the pillar collapsed limply, he staggered forward and fell upon his face.

CHAPTER 4
THE SOUND OF A TUMULT

Graham's last impression before he fainted was of the ringing of bells. He learnt afterwards that he was insensible, hanging between life and death, for the better part of an hour. When he recovered his senses he was back on his translucent couch, and there was a stirring warmth at heart and throat. The dark apparatus, he perceived, had been removed from his arm, which was bandaged. The white framework was still about him, but the greenish transparent substance that had filled it was altogether gone. A man in a deep violet robe, one of those who had been on the balcony, was looking keenly into his face.

Remote but insistent was a clamour of bells and confused sounds, that suggested to his mind the picture of a great number of people shouting together. Something seemed to fall across this tumult, a door suddenly closed.

Graham moved his head. 'What does this all mean?' he said slowly. 'Where am I?'

He saw the red-haired man who had been first to discover him. A voice seemed to be asking what he had said, and was abruptly stilled.

The man in violet answered in a soft voice, speaking English with a slightly foreign accent, or so at least it seemed to the Sleeper's ears. 'You are quite safe. You were brought hither from where you fell asleep. It is quite safe. You have been here some time – sleeping. In a trance.'

He said something further that Graham could not hear, and a little phial was handed across to him. Graham felt a cooling spray, a fragrant mist played over his forehead for a moment, and his sense of refreshment increased. He closed his eyes in satisfaction.

'Better?' asked the man in violet, as Graham's eyes reopened. He was a pleasant-faced man of thirty perhaps, with a pointed flaxen beard and a clasp of gold at the neck of his violet robe.

'Yes,' said Graham.

'You have been asleep some time. In a cataleptic trance. You have heard? Catalepsy? It may seem strange to you at first, but I can assure you everything is well.'

Graham did not answer, but these words served their reassuring purpose. His eyes went from face to face of the three people about him. They were regarding him strangely. He knew he ought to be somewhere in Cornwall, but he could not square these things with that impression.

A matter that had been in his mind during his last waking moments at Boscastle recurred, a thing resolved upon and somehow neglected. He cleared his throat.

'Have you wired my cousin?' he asked. 'E. Warming, 27, Chancery Lane?'

They were all assiduous to hear. But he had to repeat it. 'What an odd *blurr* in his accent!' whispered the red-haired man. 'Wire, sir?' said the young man with the flaxen beard, evidently puzzled.

'He means send an electric telegram,' volunteered the third, a pleasant-faced youth of nineteen or twenty. The flaxen-bearded man gave a cry of comprehension. 'How stupid of me! You may be sure everything shall be done, sir,' he said to Graham. 'I am afraid it would be difficult to – *wire* to your cousin. He is not in London now. But don't trouble about arrangements yet; you have been asleep a very long time and the important thing is to get over that, sir.' (Graham concluded the word was sir, but this man pronounced it '*Sire*'.)

'Oh!' said Graham, and became quiet.

It was all very puzzling, but apparently these people in unfamiliar dress knew what they were about. Yet they were odd and the room was odd. It seemed he was in some newly established place. He had a sudden flash of suspicion! Surely

this wasn't some hall of public exhibition! If it was he would
give Warming a piece of his mind. But it scarcely had that
character. And in a place of public exhibition he would not
have discovered himself naked.

Then suddenly, he realized what had happened. There was
no perceptible interval of suspicion, no dawn to his knowledge.
Abruptly he knew that his trance had lasted for a vast interval;
as if by some process of thought-reading he interpreted the awe
in the faces that peered into his. He looked at them strangely,
full of intense emotion. It seemed they read his eyes. He framed
his lips to speak and could not. A queer impulse to hide his
knowledge came into his mind almost at the moment of his
discovery. He looked at his bare feet, regarding them silently.
His impulse to speak passed. He was trembling exceedingly.

They gave him some pink fluid with a greenish fluorescence
and a meaty taste, and the assurance of returning strength grew.

'That – that makes me feel better,' he said hoarsely, and there
were murmurs of respectful approval. He knew now quite
clearly. He made to speak again, and again he could not.

He pressed his throat and tried a third time. 'How long?' he
asked in a level voice. 'How long have I been asleep?'

'Some considerable time,' said the flaxen-bearded man,
glancing quickly at the others.

'How long?'

'A very long time.'

'Yes – yes,' said Graham, suddenly testy. 'But I want – Is it –
it is – some years? Many years? There was something – I forget
what. I feel – confused. But you –' He sobbed. 'You need not
fence with me. How long—?'

He stopped, breathing irregularly. He squeezed his eyes with
his knuckles and sat waiting for an answer.

They spoke in undertones.

'Five or six?' he asked faintly. 'More?'

'Very much more than that.'

'More!'

'More.'

He looked at them and it seemed as though imps were twitching the muscles of his face. He looked his question.

'Many years,' said the man with the red beard.

Graham struggled into a sitting position. He wiped a rheumy tear from his face with a lean hand. 'Many years!' he repeated. He shut his eyes tight, opened them, and sat looking about him from one unfamiliar thing to another.

'How many years?' he asked.

'You must be prepared to be surprised.'

'Well?'

'More than a gross of years.'[1]

He was irritated at the strange word. 'More than a *what*?'

Two of them spoke together. Some quick remarks that were made about 'decimal' he did not catch.

'How long did you say?' asked Graham. 'How long? Don't look like that. Tell me.'

Among the remarks in an undertone, his ear caught six words: 'More than a couple of centuries.'

'*What*?' he cried, turning on the youth who he thought had spoken. 'Who says –? What was that? A couple of *centuries*!'

'Yes,' said the man with the red beard. 'Two hundred years.'

Graham repeated the words. He had been prepared to hear of a vast repose, and yet these concrete centuries defeated him.

'Two hundred years,' he said again, with the figure of a great gulf opening very slowly in his mind; and then, 'Oh, but—!'

They said nothing.

'You – did you say—?'

'Two hundred years. Two centuries of years,' said the man with the red beard.

There was a pause. Graham looked at their faces and saw that what he had heard was indeed true.

'But it can't be,' he said querulously. 'I am dreaming. Trances – trances don't last. That is not right – this is a joke you have played upon me! Tell me – some days ago, perhaps, I was walking along the coast of Cornwall—?'

His voice failed him.

The man with the flaxen beard hesitated. 'I'm not very strong in history, sir,' he said weakly, and glanced at the others.

'That was it, sir,' said the youngster. 'Boscastle, in the old Duchy of Cornwall[2] – it's in the south-west country beyond the dairy meadows. There is a house there still. I have been there.'

'Boscastle!' Graham turned his eyes to the youngster. 'That was it – Boscastle. Little Boscastle. I fell asleep – somewhere there. I don't exactly remember. I don't exactly remember.'

He pressed his brows and whispered, 'More than *two hundred years*!'

He began to speak quickly with a twitching face, but his heart was cold within him. 'But if it *is* two hundred years, every soul I know, every human being that ever I saw or spoke to before I went to sleep, must be dead.'

They did not answer him.

'The Queen and the Royal Family, her Ministers, Church and State. High and low, rich and poor, one with another ... Is there England still? ...

'That's a comfort! Is there London? ...

'This *is* London, eh? And you are my assistant-custodian; assistant-custodian. And these –? Eh? Assistant-custodians too!'

He sat with a gaunt stare on his face. 'But why am I here? No! Don't talk. Be quiet. Let me —'

He sat silent, rubbed his eyes, and, uncovering them, found another little glass of pinkish fluid held towards him. He took the dose. Directly he had taken it he began to weep naturally and refreshingly.

Presently he looked at their faces, suddenly laughed through his tears, a little foolishly. 'But – two – hun – dred – years!' he said. He grimaced hysterically and covered his face again.

After a space he grew calm. He sat up, his hands hanging over his knees in almost precisely the same attitude in which Isbister had found him on the cliff at Pentargen. His attention was attracted by a thick domineering voice, the footsteps of an advancing personage. 'What are you doing? Why was I not warned? Surely you could tell? Someone will suffer for this. The man must be kept quiet. Are the doorways closed? All the doorways? He must be kept perfectly quiet. He must not be told. Has he been told anything?'

The man with the fair beard made some inaudible remark, and Graham looking over his shoulder saw approaching a short, fat and thickset beardless man, with aquiline nose and heavy neck and chin. Very thick black and slightly sloping eyebrows that almost met over his nose and overhung deep grey eyes, gave his face an oddly formidable expression. He scowled momentarily at Graham and then his regard returned to the man with the flaxen beard. 'These others,' he said in a voice of extreme irritation. 'You had better go.'

'Go?' said the red-bearded man.

'Certainly – go now. But see the doorways are closed as you go.'

The two men addressed turned obediently, after one reluctant glance at Graham, and instead of going through the archway as he expected, walked straight to the dead wall of the apartment opposite the archway. A long strip of this apparently solid wall rolled up with a snap,[3] hung over the two retreating men and fell again, and immediately Graham was alone with the newcomer and the purple-robed man with the flaxen beard.

For a space the thickset man took not the slightest notice of Graham, but proceeded to interrogate the other – obviously his subordinate – upon the treatment of their charge. He spoke clearly, but in phrases only partially intelligible to Graham. The awakening seemed not only a matter of surprise but of consternation and annoyance to him. He was evidently profoundly excited.

'You must not confuse his mind by telling him things,' he repeated again and again. 'You must not confuse his mind.'

His questions answered, he turned quickly and eyed the awakened sleeper with an ambiguous expression.

'Feel queer?' he asked.

'Very.'

'The world, what you see of it, seems strange to you?'

'I suppose I have to live in it, strange as it seems.'

'I suppose so, now.'

'In the first place, hadn't I better have some clothes?'

'They –' said the thickset man and stopped, and the flaxen-bearded man met his eye and went away. 'You will very speedily have clothes,' said the thickset man.

'Is it true indeed, that I have been asleep two hundred – ?' asked Graham.

'They have told you that, have they? Two hundred and three, as a matter of fact.'

Graham accepted the indisputable now with raised eyebrows and depressed mouth. He sat silent for a moment, and then asked a question, 'Is there a mill or dynamo near here?' He did not wait for an answer. 'Things have changed tremendously, I suppose?' he said.

'What is that shouting?' he asked abruptly.

'Nothing,' said the thickset man impatiently. 'It's people. You'll understand better later – perhaps. As you say, things have changed.' He spoke shortly, his brows were knit, and he glanced about him like a man trying to decide in an emergency. 'We must get you clothes and so forth, at any rate. Better wait here until they can be procured. No one will come near you. You want shaving.'

Graham rubbed his chin.

The man with the flaxen beard came back towards them, turned suddenly, listened for a moment, lifted his eyebrows at the older man, and hurried off through the archway towards the balcony. The tumult of shouting grew louder, and the thickset man turned and listened also. He cursed suddenly under his breath, and turned his eyes upon Graham with an unfriendly expression. It was a surge of many voices, rising and falling, shouting and screaming, and once came a sound like blows and sharp cries, and then a snapping like the crackling of dry sticks. Graham strained his ears to draw some single thread of sound from the woven tumult.

Then he perceived, repeated again and again, a certain formula. For a time he doubted his ears. But surely these were the words: 'Show us the Sleeper! Show us the Sleeper!'

The thickset man rushed suddenly to the archway.

'Wild!' he cried. 'How do they know? Do they know? Or is it guessing?'

There was perhaps an answer.

'I can't come,' said the thickset man; 'I have *him* to see to. But shout from the balcony.'

There was an inaudible reply.

'Say he is not awake. Anything! I leave it to you.'

He came hurrying back to Graham. 'You must have clothes at once,' he said. 'You cannot stop here – and it will be impossible to—'

He rushed away, Graham calling unanswered questions after him. In a moment he was back.

'I can't tell you what is happening. It is too complex to explain. In a moment you shall have your clothes made. Yes – in a moment. And then I can take you away from here. You will find out our troubles soon enough.'

'But those voices. They were shouting—?'

'Something about the Sleeper – that's you. They have some twisted idea. I don't know what it is. I know nothing.'

A shrill bell jetted acutely across the indistinct mingling of remote noises, and this brusque person sprang to a little group of appliances in the corner of the room. He listened for a moment, regarding a ball of crystal, nodded, and said a few words; then he walked to the wall through which the two men had vanished. It rolled up again like a curtain, and he stood waiting.

Graham lifted his arm and was astonished to find what strength the restoratives had given him. He thrust one leg over the side of the couch and then the other. His head no longer swam. He could scarcely credit his rapid recovery. He sat feeling his limbs.

The man with the flaxen beard re-entered from the archway, and as he did so the cage of a lift came sliding down in front of the thickset man, and a lean, grey-bearded man, carrying a roll and wearing a tightly fitting costume of dark green, appeared therein.

'This is the tailor,' said the thickset man with an introductory gesture. 'It will never do for you to wear that black. I cannot understand how it got here. But I shall. I shall. You will be as rapid as possible?' he said to the tailor.

The man in green bowed, and, advancing, seated himself by Graham on the bed. His manner was calm, but his eyes were full of curiosity. 'You will find the fashions altered, Sire,' he said. He glanced from under his brows at the thickset man.

He opened the roller with a quick movement, and a confusion

of brilliant fabrics poured out over his knees. 'You lived, Sire, in a period essentially cylindrical – the Victorian. With a tendency to the hemisphere in hats. Circular curves always. Now –' He flicked out a little appliance the size and appearance of a keyless watch, whirled the knob, and behold – a little figure in white appeared kinetoscope[4] fashion on the dial, walking and turning. The tailor caught up a pattern of bluish white satin. 'That is my conception of your immediate treatment,' he said.

The thickset man came and stood by the shoulder of Graham. 'We have very little time,' he said.

'Trust me,' said the tailor. 'My machine follows. What do you think of this?'

'What is that?' asked the man from the nineteenth century.

'In your days they showed you a fashion-plate,' said the tailor, 'but this is our modern development. See here.' The little figure repeated its evolutions, but in a different costume. 'Or this,' and with a click another small figure in a more voluminous type of robe marched on to the dial. The tailor was very quick in his movements, and glanced twice towards the lift as he did these things.

It rumbled again, and a crop-haired anaemic[5] lad with features of the Chinese type, clad in coarse pale blue canvas, appeared together with a complicated machine, which he pushed noiselessly on little castors into the room. Incontinently the little kinetoscope was dropped, Graham was invited to stand in front of the machine and the tailor muttered some instructions to the crop-haired lad, who answered in guttural tones and with words Graham did not recognize. The boy then went to conduct an incomprehensible monologue in the corner, and the tailor pulled out a number of slotted arms terminating in little discs, pulling them out until the discs were flat against the body of Graham, one at each shoulder blade, one at the elbows, one at the neck and so forth, so that at last there were, perhaps, two score of them upon his body and limbs. At the same time, some other person entered the room by the lift, behind Graham. The tailor set moving a mechanism that initiated a faint-sounding rhythmic movement of parts in the machine, and in another moment he was knocking up the levers and Graham was released. The tailor replaced his cloak of black, and the man with the flaxen beard proffered him a little glass of some refreshing fluid. Graham saw over the rim of the glass a pale-faced young man regarding him with a singular fixity.

The thickset man had been pacing the room fretfully, and now turned and went through the archway towards the balcony, from which the noise of a distant crowd still came in gusts and cadences. The crop-headed lad handed the tailor a roll of the bluish satin and the two began fixing this in the mechanism in a manner reminiscent of a roll of paper in a nineteenth-century printing machine. Then they ran the entire thing on its easy, noiseless bearings across the room to a remote corner where a twisted cable looped rather gracefully from the wall. They made some connection and the machine became energetic and swift.

'What is that doing?' asked Graham, pointing with the empty glass to the busy figures and trying to ignore the scrutiny of the newcomer. 'Is that – some sort of force[6] – laid on?'

'Yes,' said the man with the flaxen beard.

'Who is *that*?' He indicated the archway behind him.

The man in purple stroked his little beard, hesitated, and answered in an undertone, 'He is Howard, your chief guardian. You see, Sire – it's a little difficult to explain. The Council appoints a guardian and assistants. This hall has under certain restrictions been public. In order that people might satisfy themselves. We have barred the doorways for the first time. But I think – if you don't mind, I will leave him to explain.'

'Odd!' said Graham. 'Guardian? Council?' Then turning his back on the newcomer, he asked in an undertone, 'Why is this man *glaring* at me? Is he a mesmerist?'[7]

'Mesmerist! He is a capillotomist.'[8]

'Capillotomist!'

'Yes – one of the chief. His yearly fee is sixdoz lions.'[9]

It sounded sheer nonsense. Graham snatched at the last phrase with an unsteady mind. 'Sixdoz lions?' he said.

'Didn't you have lions? I suppose not. You had the old pounds? They are our monetary units.'

'But what was that you said – sixdoz?'

'Yes. Six dozen, Sire. Of course things, even these little things, have altered. You lived in the days of the decimal system, the Arab system – tens, and little hundreds and thousands. We have eleven numerals now. We have single figures for both ten and eleven, two figures for a dozen, and a dozen dozen makes a gross, a great hundred, you know, a dozen gross a dozand, and a dozand dozand a myriad. Very simple?'

'I suppose so,' said Graham. 'But about this cap – what was it?'

The man with the flaxen beard glanced over his shoulder.

'Here are your clothes!' he said. Graham turned round sharply and saw the tailor standing at his elbow smiling, and holding some palpably new garments over his arm. The crop-headed boy, by means of one finger, was impelling the complicated machine towards the lift by which he had arrived. Graham stared at the completed suit. 'You don't mean to say—!'

'Just made,' said the tailor. He dropped the garments at the feet of Graham, walked to the bed on which Graham had so recently been lying, flung out the translucent mattress, and turned up the looking-glass. As he did so a furious bell summoned the thickset man to the corner. The man with the flaxen beard rushed across to him and then hurried out by the archway.

The tailor was assisting Graham into a dark purple combination garment, stockings, vest and pants in one, as the thickset man came back from the corner to meet the man with the flaxen beard returning from the balcony. They began speaking quickly in an undertone, their bearing had an unmistakable quality of anxiety. Over the purple under-garment came a complex garment of bluish white, and Graham was clothed in the fashion once more and saw himself, sallow-faced, unshaven and shaggy still, but at least naked no longer, and in some indefinable unprecedented way graceful.

'I must shave,' he said regarding himself in the glass.

'In a moment,' said Howard.

The persistent stare ceased. The young man closed his eyes, reopened them, and with a lean hand extended, advanced on

Graham. Then he stopped, with his hand slowly gesticulating, and looked about him.

'A seat,' said Howard impatiently, and in a moment the flaxen-bearded man had a chair behind Graham. 'Sit down, please,' said Howard.

Graham hesitated, and in the other hand of the wild-eyed man he saw the glint of steel.

'Don't you understand, Sire?' cried the flaxen-bearded man with hurried politeness. 'He is going to cut your hair.'

'Oh!' cried Graham enlightened. 'But you called him—'

'A capillotomist – precisely! He is one of the finest artists in the world.'

Graham sat down abruptly. The flaxen-bearded man disappeared. The capillotomist came forward, examined Graham's ears and surveyed him, felt the back of his head, and would have sat down again to regard him but for Howard's audible impatience. Forthwith with rapid movements and a succession of deftly handled implements he shaved Graham's chin, clipped his moustache, and cut and arranged his hair. All this he did without a word, with something of the rapt air of a poet inspired. And as soon as he had finished Graham was handed a pair of shoes.

Suddenly a loud voice shouted – it seemed from a piece of machinery in the corner – 'At once – at once. The people know all over the city. Work is being stopped. Work is being stopped. Wait for nothing, but come.'

This shout appeared to perturb Howard exceedingly. By his gestures it seemed to Graham that he hesitated between two directions. Abruptly he went towards the corner where the apparatus stood about the little crystal ball. As he did so the undertone of tumultuous shouting from the archway that had continued during all these occurrences rose to a mighty sound, roared as if it were sweeping past, and fell again as if receding swiftly. It drew Graham after it with an irresistible attraction. He glanced at the thickset man, and then obeyed his impulse. In two strides he was down the steps and in the passage, and in a score he was out upon the balcony upon which the three men had been standing.

CHAPTER 5
THE MOVING WAYS[1]

He went to the railings of the balcony and stared upward. An exclamation of surprise at his appearance, and the movements of a number of people came from the great area below.

His first impression was of overwhelming architecture. The place into which he looked was an aisle of Titanic[2] buildings, curving spaciously in either direction. Overhead mighty cantilevers sprang together across the huge width of the place, and a tracery of translucent[3] material shut out the sky. Gigantic globes of cool white light shamed the pale sunbeams that filtered down through the girders and wires. Here and there a gossamer suspension bridge dotted with foot passengers flung across the chasm and the air was webbed with slender cables. A cliff of edifice hung above him, he perceived as he glanced upward, and the opposite façade was grey and dim and broken by great archings, circular perforations, balconies, buttresses, turret projections, myriads of vast windows and an intricate scheme of architectural relief. Athwart these ran inscriptions horizontally and obliquely in an unfamiliar lettering. Here and there close to the roof cables of a peculiar stoutness were fastened, and drooped in a steep curve to circular openings on the opposite side of the space, and even as Graham noted these a remote and tiny figure of a man clad in pale blue arrested his attention. This little figure was far overhead across the space beside the higher fastening of one of these festoons, hanging forward from a little ledge of masonry and handling some well-nigh invisible strings dependent from the line. Then suddenly, with a swoop that sent Graham's heart into his mouth, this man had rushed down the curve and vanished through a round opening on the hither side of the way. Graham had been looking up as he came out upon the balcony, and the things he saw above and opposed to him had at first seized his attention to the exclusion of anything else. Then suddenly he discovered the roadway! It was not a roadway at all, as Graham understood such things, for in the nineteenth century the only roads and streets were beaten tracks of motionless earth, jostling rivulets of vehicles between narrow footways. But this roadway was three hundred feet across, and it moved; it moved, all save the middle, the lowest part. For a moment the motion dazzled his mind. Then he understood.

Under the balcony this extraordinary roadway ran swiftly to Graham's right, an endless flow rushing along as fast as a nineteenth-century express train, an endless platform of narrow transverse overlapping slats with little interspaces that permitted it to follow the curvatures of the street. Upon it were seats, and here and there little kiosks, but they swept by too swiftly for him to see what might be therein. From this nearest and swiftest platform a series of others descended to the centre of the space. Each moved to the right, each perceptibly slower than the one above it, but the difference in pace was small enough to permit anyone to step from any platform to the one adjacent, and so walk uninterruptedly from the swiftest to the motionless middle way. Beyond this middle way was another series of endless platforms rushing with varying pace to Graham's left. And seated in crowds upon the two widest and swiftest platforms, or stepping from one to another down the steps, or swarming over the central space, was an innumerable and wonderfully diversified multitude of people.

'You must not stop here,' shouted Howard suddenly at his side. 'You must come away at once.'

Graham made no answer. He heard without hearing. The platforms ran with a roar and the people were shouting. He saw women and girls with flowing hair, beautifully robed, with bands crossing between the breasts. These first came out of the confusion. Then he perceived that the dominant note in that kaleidoscope of costume was the pale blue that the tailor's boy had worn. He became aware of cries of 'The Sleeper. What has happened to the Sleeper?' and it seemed as though the rushing platforms before him were suddenly spattered with the pale

buff of human faces, and then still more thickly. He saw
pointing fingers. The motionless central area of this huge arcade
just opposite to the balcony was densely crowded with blue-clad
people. Some sort of struggle had sprung into life. People
seemed to be pushed up the running platforms on either side,
and carried away against their will. They would spring off so
soon as they were beyond the thick of the confusion, and run
back towards the conflict.

'It is the Sleeper. Verily it is the Sleeper,' shouted voices. 'That
is never the Sleeper,' shouted others. More and more faces were
turned to him. At the intervals along this central area Graham
noted openings, pits, apparently the heads of staircases going
down with people ascending out of them and descending into
them. The struggle centred about the one of these nearest to
him. People were running down the moving platforms to this,
leaping dexterously from platform to platform. The clustering
people on the higher platforms seemed to divide their interest
between this point and the balcony. A number of sturdy little
figures clad in a uniform of bright red, and working methodi-
cally together, were employed in preventing access to this
descending staircase. About them a crowd was rapidly accumu-
lating. Their brilliant colour contrasted vividly with the whitish-
blue of their antagonists, for the struggle was indisputable.

He saw these things with Howard shouting in his ear and
shaking his arm. And then suddenly Howard was gone and he
stood alone.

The cries of 'The Sleeper!' grew in volume, and the people
on the nearer platform were standing up. The nearer platform
he perceived was empty to the right of him, and far across
the space the platform running in the opposite direction was
coming crowded and passing away bare. With incredible swiftness a vast crowd had gathered in the central space before
his eyes; a dense swaying mass of people, and the shouts grew
from a fitful crying to a voluminous incessant clamour: 'The
Sleeper! The Sleeper!' and yells and cheers, a waving of garments and cries of 'Stop the ways!' They were also crying
another name strange to Graham. It sounded like 'Ostrog'.[4] The
slower platforms were soon thick with active people, running

against the movement so as to keep themselves opposite to him.

'Stop the ways,' they cried. Agile figures ran up from the centre to the swift road nearest to him, were borne rapidly past him, shouting strange, unintelligible things, and ran back obliquely to the central way. One thing he distinguished: 'It is indeed the Sleeper. It is indeed the Sleeper,' they testified.

For a space Graham stood motionless. Then he became vividly aware that all this concerned him. He was pleased at his wonderful popularity, he bowed, and, seeking a gesture of longer range, waved his arm. He was astonished at the uproar this provoked. The tumult about the descending stairway rose to furious violence. He was aware of crowded balconies, of men sliding along ropes, of men in trapeze-like seats hurling athwart the space. He heard voices behind him, a number of people descending the steps through the archway; he suddenly perceived that his guardian Howard was back again and gripping his arm painfully, and shouting inaudibly in his ear.

He turned, and Howard's face was white. 'Come back,' he heard. 'They will stop the ways. The whole city will be in confusion.'

There appeared a number of men hurrying along the passage of blue pillars behind Howard, the red-haired man, the man with the flaxen beard, a tall man in vivid vermilion, a crowd of others in red carrying staves, and all these people had anxious eager faces.

'Get him away,' cried Howard.

'But why?' said Graham. 'I don't see —'

'You must come away!' said the man in red in a resolute voice. His face and eyes were resolute too. Graham's glances went from face to face, and he was suddenly aware of that most disagreeable flavour in life, compulsion. Someone gripped his arm. . . .

He was being dragged away. It seemed as though the tumult suddenly became two, as if half the shouts that had come in from this wonderful roadway had sprung into the passages of the great building behind him. Marvelling and confused, feeling an impotent desire to resist, Graham was half led, half thrust, along the passage of blue pillars, and suddenly he found himself alone with Howard in a lift and moving swiftly upward.

CHAPTER 6
THE HALL OF THE ATLAS

From the moment when the tailor had bowed his farewell to the moment when Graham found himself in the lift, was altogether barely five minutes. As yet the haze of his vast interval of sleep hung about him, as yet the initial strangeness of his being alive at all in this remote age touched everything with wonder, with a sense of the irrational, with something of the quality of a realistic dream. He was still detached, an astonished spectator, still but half involved in life. What he had seen, and especially the last crowded tumult, framed in the setting of the balcony, had a spectacular turn like a thing witnessed from the box of a theatre. 'I don't understand,' he said. 'What was the trouble? My mind is in a whirl. Why were they shouting? What is the danger?'

'We have our troubles,' said Howard. His eyes avoided Graham's enquiry. 'This is a time of unrest. And, in fact, your appearance, your waking just now, has a sort of connection —'

He spoke jerkily, like a man not quite sure of his breathing. He stopped abruptly.

'I don't understand,' said Graham.

'It will be clearer later,' said Howard.

He glanced uneasily upward, as though he found the progress of the lift slow.

'I shall understand better, no doubt, when I have seen my way about a little,' said Graham puzzled. 'It will be – it is bound to be perplexing. At present it is all so strange. Anything seems possible. Anything. In the details even. Your counting, I understand, is different.'

The lift stopped, and they stepped out into a narrow but

very long passage between high walls, along which ran an extraordinary number of tubes and big cables.

'What a huge place this is!' said Graham. 'Is it all one building? What place is it?'

'This is one of the city ways for various public services. Light and so forth.'

'Was it a social trouble – that – in the great roadway place? How are you governed? Have you still a police?'

'Several,' said Howard.

'Several?'

'About fourteen.'

'I don't understand.'

'Very probably not. Our social order will probably seem very complex to you. To tell you the truth, I don't understand it myself very clearly. Nobody does. You will, perhaps – by and by. We have to go to the Council.'

Graham's attention was divided between the urgent necessity of his enquiries and the people in the passages and halls they were traversing. For a moment his mind would be concentrated upon Howard and the halting answers he made, and then he would lose the thread in response to some vivid unexpected impression. Along the passages, in the halls, half the people seemed to be men in the red uniform. The pale blue canvas that had been so abundant in the aisle of moving ways did not appear. Invariably these men looked at him, and saluted him and Howard as they passed.

He had a clear vision of entering a long corridor, and there were a number of girls sitting on low seats, as though in a class. He saw no teacher, but only a novel apparatus from which he fancied a voice proceeded. The girls regarded him and his conductor, he thought, with curiosity and astonishment. But he was hurried on before he could form a clear idea of the gathering. He judged they knew Howard and not himself, and that they wondered who he might be. This Howard, it seemed, was a person of importance. But then he was merely Graham's guardian. That was odd.

There came a passage in twilight, and into this passage a footway hung so that he could see the feet and ankles of people going to and fro thereon, but no more of them. Then vague impressions of galleries and of casual astonished passers-by turning round to stare after the two of them with their red-clad guard.

The stimulus of the restoratives he had taken was only temporary. He was speedily fatigued by this excessive haste. He asked Howard to slacken his speed. Presently he was in a lift that had a window upon the great street space, but this was glazed and did not open, and they were too high for him to see the moving platforms below. But he saw people going to and fro along cables and along strange, frail-looking bridges.

Thence they passed across the street and at a vast height above it. They crossed by means of a narrow bridge closed in with glass, so clear that it made him giddy even to remember it. The floor of it also was of glass. From his memory of the cliffs between Newquay and Boscastle, so remote in time, and so recent in his experience, it seemed to him that they must be nearly four hundred feet above the moving ways. He stopped, looked down between his legs upon the swarming blue and red multitudes, minute and foreshortened, struggling and gesticulating still towards the little balcony far below, a little toy balcony, it seemed, where he had so recently been standing. A thin haze and the glare of the mighty globes of light obscured everything. A man seated in a little openwork cradle shot by from some point still higher than the little narrow bridge, rushing down a cable as swiftly almost as if he were falling. Graham stopped involuntarily to watch this strange passenger vanish below, and then his eyes went back to the tumultuous struggle.

Along one of the faster ways rushed a bunch of red spots. This broke up into individuals as it approached the balcony, and went pouring down the slower ways towards the dense struggling crowd on the central area. These men in red appeared to be armed with sticks or truncheons; they seemed to be striking and thrusting. A great shouting, cries of wrath, screaming, burst out and came up to Graham, faint and thin. 'Go on,' cried Howard, laying hands on him.

Another man rushed down a cable. Graham suddenly glanced up to see whence he came, and beheld through the glassy roof and the network of cables and girders, dim rhythmically passing forms like the vans of windmills, and between them glimpses of a remote and pallid sky. Then Howard had thrust him forward across the bridge, and he was in a little narrow passage decorated with geometrical patterns.

'I want to see more of that,' cried Graham, resisting.

'No, no,' cried Howard, still gripping his arm. 'This way. You must go this way.' And the men in red following them seemed ready to enforce his orders.

Some Negroes in a curious wasp-like uniform of black and yellow appeared down the passage, and one hastened to throw up a sliding shutter that had seemed a door to Graham, and led the way through it. Graham found himself in a gallery overhanging the end of a great chamber. The attendant in black and yellow crossed this, thrust up a second shutter and stood waiting.

This place had the appearance of an ante-room. He saw a number of people in the central space, and at the opposite end a large and imposing doorway at the top of a flight of steps, heavily curtained but giving a glimpse of some still larger hall beyond. He perceived white men in red and other Negroes in black and yellow standing stiffly about those portals.

As they crossed the gallery he heard a whisper from below, 'The Sleeper,' and was aware of a turning of heads, a hum of observation. They entered another little passage in the wall of this antechamber, and then he found himself on an iron-railed gallery of metal that passed round the side of the great hall he had already seen through the curtains. He entered the place at the corner, so that he received the fullest impression of its huge proportions. The black in the wasp uniform stood aside like a well-trained servant, and closed the valve behind him.

Compared with any of the places Graham had seen thus far, this second hall appeared to be decorated with extreme richness. On a pedestal at the remoter end, and more brilliantly lit than any other object, was a gigantic white figure of Atlas,[1] strong and strenuous, the globe upon his bowed shoulders. It was the first thing to strike his attention, it was so vast, so patiently and painfully real, so white and simple. Save for this figure and for a dais in the centre, the wide floor of the place was a shining vacancy. The dais was remote in the greatness of the area; it would have looked a mere slab of metal had it not been for the group of seven men who stood about a table on it, and gave an inkling of its proportions. They were all dressed in white robes, they seemed to have arisen that moment from their seats, and they were regarding Graham steadfastly. At the end of the table he perceived the glitter of some mechanical appliances.

Howard led him along the end gallery until they were opposite this mighty labouring figure. Then he stopped. The two men in red who had followed them into the gallery came and stood on either hand of Graham.

'You must remain here,' murmured Howard, 'for a few moments,' and, without waiting for a reply, hurried away along the gallery.

'But, *why* –?' began Graham.

He moved as if to follow Howard, and found his path obstructed by one of the men in red. 'You have to wait here, Sire,' said the man in red.

'*Why*?'

'Orders, Sire.'

'Whose orders?'

'Our orders, Sire.'

Graham looked his exasperation.

'What place is this?' he said presently. 'Who are those men?'

'They are the lords of the Council, Sire.'

'What Council?'

'*The* Council.'

'Oh!' said Graham, and after an equally ineffectual attempt at the other man, went to the railing and stared at the distant men in white, who stood watching him and whispering together.

The Council? He perceived there were now eight, though how the newcomer had arrived he had not observed. They made no gestures of greeting; they stood regarding him as in the nineteenth century a group of men might have stood in the street regarding a distant balloon that had suddenly floated into view. What council could it be that gathered there, that little body of men beneath the significant white Atlas, secluded from every eavesdropper in this impressive spaciousness? And why should he be brought to them, and be looked at strangely and spoken of inaudibly? Howard appeared beneath, walking quickly across the polished floor towards them. As he drew near he bowed and performed certain peculiar movements, apparently of a ceremonious nature. Then he ascended the steps of the dais, and stood by the apparatus at the end of the table.

Graham watched that visible inaudible conversation. Occasionally one of the white-robed men would glance towards him. He strained his ears in vain. The gesticulation of two of the speakers became animated. He glanced from them to the passive faces of his attendants. . . . When he looked again Howard was extending his hands and moving his head like a man who protests. He was interrupted, it seemed, by one of the white-robed men rapping the table.

The conversation lasted an interminable time to Graham's sense. His eyes rose to the still giant at whose feet the Council sat. Thence they wandered to the walls of the hall. It was decorated in long painted panels of a quasi-Japanese type, many of them very beautiful. These panels were grouped in a great and elaborate framing of dark metal, which passed into the metallic caryatidae[2] of the galleries and the great structural lines of the interior. The facile grace of these panels enhanced the mighty white effort that laboured in the centre of the scheme. Graham's eyes came back to the Council, and Howard was descending the steps. As he drew nearer his features could be distinguished, and Graham saw that he was flushed and blowing out his cheeks. His countenance was still disturbed when presently he reappeared along the gallery.

'This way,' he said concisely, and they went on in silence to a little door that opened at their approach. The two men in red stopped on either side of this door. Howard and Graham passed in, and Graham, glancing back, saw the white-robed Council still standing in a close group and looking at him. Then the door closed behind him with a heavy thud, and for the first time since his awakening he was in silence. The floor, even, was noiseless to his feet.

Howard opened another door, and they were in the first of two contiguous chambers furnished in white and green. 'What Council was that?' began Graham. 'What were they discussing? What have they to do with me?' Howard closed the door carefully, heaved a huge sigh, and said something in an undertone. He walked slantingways across the room and turned, blowing out his cheeks again. 'Ugh!' he grunted, a man relieved.

Graham stood regarding him.

'You must understand,' began Howard abruptly, avoiding Graham's eyes, 'that our social order is very complex. A half explanation, a bare unqualified statement would give you false impressions. As a matter of fact – it is a case of compound interest partly – your small fortune, and the fortune of your cousin Warming which was left to you – and certain other beginnings – have become very considerable. And in other ways that will be hard for you to understand, you are become a person of significance – of immense legal significance – legal rather than practical – involved in the world's affairs.'

He stopped.

'Yes?' said Graham.

'We have grave social troubles.'

'Yes?'

'Things have come to such a pass that, in fact, it is advisable to seclude you here.'

'Keep me prisoner!' exclaimed Graham.

'Well – to ask you to keep in seclusion.'

Graham turned on him. 'This is strange!' he said.

'No harm will be done you.'

'No harm!'

'But you must be kept here—'

'While I learn my position, I presume.'

'Precisely.'

'Very well then. Begin. Why *harm*?'

'Not now.'

'Why not?'

'It is too long a story, Sire.'

'All the more reason I should begin at once. You say I am a

person of importance. What was that shouting I heard? Why is a great multitude shouting and excited because my trance is over, and who are the men in white in that huge council chamber?'

'All in good time, Sire,' said Howard. 'But not crudely, not crudely. This is one of those flimsy times when no man has a settled mind. Your awakening – no one expected your awakening. The Council is consulting.'

'What council?'

'The Council you saw.'

Graham made a petulant movement. 'This is not right,' he said. 'I should be told what is happening.'

'You must wait. Really you must wait.'

Graham sat down abruptly. 'I suppose since I have waited so long to resume life,' he said, 'that I must wait a little longer.'

'That is better,' said Howard. 'Yes, that is much better. And I must leave you alone. For a space. While I attend the discussion in the Council. . . . I am sorry.'

He went towards the noiseless door, hesitated and vanished.

Graham walked to the door, tried it, found it securely fastened in some way he never came to understand, turned about, paced the room restlessly, made the circuit of the room, and sat down. He remained sitting for some time with folded arms and knitted brow, biting his fingernails and trying to piece together the kaleidoscopic impressions of this first hour of awakened life; the vast mechanical spaces, the endless series of chambers and passages, the great struggle that roared and splashed through these strange ways, the little group of remote unsympathetic men beneath the colossal Atlas, Howard's mysterious behaviour. There was an inkling of some great inheritance already in his mind – an inheritance perhaps misapplied – of some unprecedented importance and opportunity. What had he to do? And this room's secluded silence was eloquent of imprisonment!

It came into Graham's mind with irresistible conviction that this was all a dream. He tried to shut his eyes and succeeded, but that time-honoured device led to no awakening.

Presently he began to touch and examine all the unfamiliar appointments of the two small rooms in which he found himself.

In a long oval panel of mirror he saw himself and stopped astonished. He was clad in a graceful costume of purple and bluish white, with a little greyshot beard trimmed to a point, and his hair, its blackness streaked now with bands of grey, arranged over his forehead in an unfamiliar but pleasing manner. He seemed a man of five-and-forty perhaps. For a moment he did not perceive this was himself.

A flash of laughter came with the recognition. 'To call on old Warming like this!' he exclaimed, 'and make him take me out to lunch!'

Then he thought of meeting first one and then another of the few familiar acquaintances of his early manhood, and in the midst of his amusement realized that every soul with whom he might jest had died many score of years ago. The thought smote him abruptly and keenly; he stopped short, the expression of his face changed to a white consternation.

The tumultuous memory of the moving platforms and the huge façade of that wonderful street reasserted itself. The shouting multitudes came back, clear and vivid, and those remote, inaudible, unfriendly councillors in white. He felt himself a little figure, very small and ineffectual, pitifully conspicuous. And all about him, the world was – *strange*.

CHAPTER 7
IN THE SILENT ROOMS

Presently Graham resumed his examination of his apartments. Curiosity kept him moving in spite of his fatigue. The inner room, he perceived, was high and its ceiling dome-shaped, with an oblong aperture in the centre opening into a funnel in which a wheel of broad vanes seemed to be rotating, apparently driving the air up the shaft. The faint humming note of its easy motion was the only clear sound in that quiet place. As these vanes sprang up one after the other, Graham could get transient glimpses of the sky. He was surprised to see a star.

This drew his attention to the fact that the bright lighting of these rooms was due to a multitude of very faint glow lamps set about the cornices. There were no windows. And he began to recall that along all the vast chambers and passages he had traversed with Howard he had observed no windows at all. Had there been windows? There were windows on the street indeed, but were they for light? Or was the whole city lit day and night for evermore, so that there was no night there?

And another thing dawned upon him. There was no fireplace in either room. Was the season summer, and were these merely summer apartments, or was the whole city uniformly heated or cooled? He became interested in these questions, began examining the smooth texture of the walls, the simply constructed bed, the ingenious arrangements by which the labour of bedroom service was practically abolished. And over everything was a curious absence of deliberate ornament, a bare grace of form and colour, that he found very pleasing to the eye. There were several comfortable chairs, a light table on silent runners carrying several bottles of fluids and glasses, and two plates bearing a clear substance like jelly. Then he noticed there were no books, no newspapers, no writing materials. 'The world has changed indeed,' he thought.

He observed one entire side of the outer room was set with rows of peculiar double cylinders inscribed with green lettering on white that harmonized with the decorative scheme of the room, and in the centre of this side projected a little apparatus about a yard square and having a white smooth face to the room. A chair faced this. He had a transitory idea that these cylinders might be books, or a modern substitute for books, but at first it did not seem so.

The lettering on the cylinders puzzled him. It seemed like Russian. Then he noticed a suggestion of mutilated English about certain of the words.

'Ɵi Man huwdbi Kiŋ,'

forced itself on him as 'The Man who would be King'.[1] 'Phonetic spelling,' he said. He remembered reading a story with that title, then he recalled the story vividly, one of the best stories in the world. But this thing before him was not a book as he understood it. He puzzled out the titles of two adjacent cylinders. 'The Heart of Darkness' he had never heard of before nor 'The Madonna of the Future'[2] – no doubt if they were indeed stories, they were by post-Victorian authors.

He puzzled over this peculiar cylinder for some time and replaced it. Then he turned to the square apparatus and examined that. He opened a sort of lid and found one of the double cylinders within, and on the upper edge a little stud like the stud of an electric bell. He pressed this and a rapid clicking began and ceased. He became aware of voices and music, and noticed a play of colour on the smooth front face. He suddenly realized what this might be, and stepped back to regard it.

On the flat surface was now a little picture, very vividly coloured, and in this picture were figures that moved. Not only did they move, but they were conversing in clear small voices. It was exactly like reality viewed through an inverted opera-glass and heard through a long tube. His interest was seized at once by the situation, which presented a man pacing up and down and vociferating angry things to a pretty but petulant woman. Both were in the picturesque costume that seemed so strange to Graham. 'I have worked,' said the man, 'but what have you been doing?'

'Ah!' said Graham. He forgot everything else, and sat down in the chair. Within five minutes he heard himself named, heard 'when the Sleeper wakes', used jestingly as a proverb for remote postponement, and passed himself by, a thing remote and incredible. But in a little while he knew those two people like intimate friends.

At last the miniature drama came to an end, and the square face of the apparatus was blank again.

It was a strange world into which he had been permitted to look, unscrupulous, pleasure-seeking, energetic, subtle, a world too of dire economic struggle; there were allusions he did not understand, incidents that conveyed strange suggestions of altered moral ideals, flashes of dubious enlightenment. The blue canvas that bulked so largely in his first impression of the city ways appeared again and again as the costume of the common people. He had no doubt the story was contemporary, and its intense realism was undeniable. And the end had been a tragedy that oppressed him. He sat staring at the blankness.

He started and rubbed his eyes. He had been so absorbed in the latter-day substitute for a novel, that he awoke to the little green and white room with more than a touch of the surprise of his first awakening.

He stood up, and abruptly he was back in his own wonderland. The clearness of the kinetoscope drama passed, and the struggle in the vast place of streets, the ambiguous Council, the swift phases of his waking hour, came back. These people had spoken of the Council with suggestions of a vague universality of power. And they had spoken of the Sleeper; it had not really struck him vividly at the time that he was the Sleeper. He had to recall precisely what they had said. . . .

He walked into the bedroom and peered up through the quick intervals of the revolving fan. As the fan swept round, a dim turmoil like the noise of machinery came in rhythmic eddies. All else

was silence. Though the perpetual day still irradiated his apartments, he perceived the intermittent strip of sky was now deep
blue – black almost, with a dust of little stars. . . .

He resumed his examination of the rooms. He could find no
way of opening the padded door, no bell nor other means of
calling for attendance. His feeling of wonder was in abeyance;
but he was curious, anxious for information. He wanted to
know exactly how he stood to these new things. He tried to
compose himself to wait until someone came to him. Presently
he became restless and eager for information, for distraction,
for fresh sensations.

He went back to the apparatus in the other room, and had
soon puzzled out the method of replacing the cylinders by
others. As he did so, it came into his mind that it must be these
little appliances had fixed the language so that it was still clear
and understandable after two hundred years. The haphazard
cylinders he substituted displayed a musical fantasia. At first it
was beautiful, and then it was sensuous. He presently recognized what appeared to him to be an altered version of the
story of Tannhauser.[3] The music was unfamiliar. But the ren-
dering was realistic, and with a contemporary unfamiliarity.
Tannhauser did not go to a Venusberg, but to a Pleasure City.
What was a Pleasure City? A dream, surely, the fancy of a
fantastic, voluptuous writer.

He became interested, curious. The story developed with a
flavour of strangely twisted sentimentality. Suddenly he did not
like it. He liked it less as it proceeded.

He had a revulsion of feeling. These were no pictures, no
idealizations, but photographed realities.[4] He wanted no more
of the twenty-second century Venusberg. He forgot the part
played by the model in nineteenth-century art, and gave way to
an archaic indignation. He rose, angry and half ashamed at
himself for witnessing this thing even in solitude. He pulled
forward the apparatus, and with some violence sought for a
means of stopping its action. Something snapped. A violet spark
stung and convulsed his arm and the thing was still. When he
attempted next day to replace these Tannhauser cylinders by
another pair, he found the apparatus broken. . . .

He struck out a path oblique to the room and paced to and fro, struggling with intolerable vast impressions. The things he had derived from the cylinders and the things he had seen, conflicted, confused him. It seemed to him beyond measure incredible that in his thirty years of life he had never tried to shape a picture of these coming times. 'We were making the future,' he said, 'and hardly any of us troubled to think what future we were making. And here it is!

'What have they got to, what has been done? How do I come into the midst of it all?' The vastness of street and house he was prepared for, the multitudes of people. But conflicts in the city ways! And the systematized sensuality of a class of rich men!

He thought of Bellamy,[5] the hero of whose Socialistic Utopia had so oddly anticipated this actual experience. But here was no Utopia, no Socialistic state. He had already seen enough to realize that the ancient antithesis of luxury, waste and sensuality on the one hand and abject poverty on the other, still prevailed. He knew enough of the essential factors of life to understand that correlation. And not only were the buildings of the city gigantic and the crowds in the street gigantic, but the voices he had heard in the ways, the uneasiness of Howard, the very atmosphere spoke of gigantic discontent. What country was he in? Still England it seemed, and yet strangely 'un-English'. His mind glanced at the rest of the world, and saw only an enigmatical veil.

He prowled about his apartment, examining everything as a caged animal might do. He was very tired, with that feverish exhaustion that does not admit of rest. He listened for long spaces under the ventilator to catch some distant echo of the tumults he felt must be proceeding in the city.

He began to talk to himself. 'Two hundred and three years!' he said to himself over and over again, laughing stupidly. 'Then I am two hundred and thirty-three years old! The oldest inhabitant. Surely they haven't reversed the tendency of our time and gone back to the rule of the oldest. My claims are indisputable. Mumble, mumble. I remember the Bulgarian atrocities[6] as though it was yesterday. 'Tis a great age! Ha ha!' He was surprised at first to hear himself laughing, and then laughed again deliberately and louder. Then he realized that he was behaving foolishly. 'Steady,' he said. 'Steady!'

His pacing became more regular. 'This new world,' he said. 'I don't understand it. *Why?* ... But it is all *why*!'

'I suppose they can fly[7] and do all sorts of things. Let me try and remember just how it began.'

He was surprised at first to find how vague the memories of his first thirty years had become. He remembered fragments, for the most part trivial moments, things of no great importance that he had observed. His boyhood seemed the most accessible at first, he recalled school books and certain lessons in mensuration. Then he revived the more salient features of his life, memories of the wife long since dead, her magic influence now gone beyond corruption, of his rivals and friends and betrayers, of the decision of this issue and that, and then of his last years of misery, of fluctuating resolves, and at last of his strenuous studies. In a little while he perceived he had it all again; dim perhaps, like metal long laid aside, but in no way defective or injured, capable of re-polishing. And the hue of it was a deepening misery. Was it worth re-polishing? By a miracle he had been lifted out of a life that had become intolerable. ...

He reverted to his present condition. He wrestled with the facts in vain. It became an inextricable tangle. He saw the sky through the ventilator pink with dawn. An old persuasion came out of the dark recesses of his memory. 'I must sleep,' he said. It appeared as a delightful relief from this mental distress and from the growing pain and heaviness of his limbs. He went to the strange little bed, lay down and was presently asleep. ...

He was destined to become very familiar indeed with these apartments before he left them, for he remained imprisoned for three days. During that time no one, except Howard, entered the rooms. The marvel of his fate mingled with and in some way minimized the marvel of his survival. He had awakened to mankind it seemed only to be snatched away into this unaccountable solitude. Howard came regularly with sustaining and nutritive fluids, and light and pleasant foods, quite strange to Graham. He always closed the door carefully as he entered. On matters of detail he was increasingly obliging, but the bearing of Graham on the great issues that were evidently being contested so closely beyond the sound-proof walls that enclosed him, he would not elucidate. He evaded, as politely as possible, every question on the position of affairs in the outer world.

And in those three days Graham's incessant thoughts went far and wide. All that he had seen, all this elaborate contrivance to prevent him seeing, worked together in his mind. Almost every possible interpretation of his position he debated – even, as it chanced, the right interpretation. Things that presently happened to him, became at least credible by virtue of this seclusion. When at length the moment of his release arrived, it found him prepared. . . .

Howard's bearing went far to deepen Graham's impression of his own strange importance; the door between its opening and closing seemed to admit with him a breath of momentous happening. His enquiries became more definite and searching. Howard retreated through protests and difficulties. The awakening was unforeseen, he repeated; it happened to have fallen in with the trend of a social convulsion. 'To explain it I must tell you the history of a gross and a half of years,' protested Howard.

'The thing is this,' said Graham. 'You are afraid of something I shall do. In some way I am arbitrator – I might be arbitrator.'

'It is not that. But you have – I may tell you this much – the automatic increase of your property puts great possibilities of interference in your hands. And in certain other ways you have influence, with your eighteenth-century notions.'

'Nineteenth-century,' corrected Graham.

'With your old-world notions, anyhow, ignorant as you are of every feature of our State.'

'Am I a fool?'

'Certainly not.'

'Do I seem to be the sort of man who would act rashly?'

'You were never expected to act at all. No one counted on your awakening. No one dreamt you would ever awake. The Council had surrounded you with antiseptic conditions. As a matter of fact, we thought that you were dead – a mere arrest of decay. And – but it is too complex. We dare not suddenly – while you are still half awake.'

'It won't do,' said Graham. 'Suppose it is as you say – why am I not being crammed night and day with facts and warnings and all the wisdom of the time to fit me for my responsibilities? Am I any wiser now than two days ago, if it is two days, when I awoke?'

Howard pulled his lip.

'I am beginning to feel – every hour I feel more clearly – a system of concealment of which you are the face. Is this Council, or committee, or whatever they are, cooking the accounts of my estate? Is that it?'

'That note of suspicion –' said Howard.

'Ugh!' said Graham. 'Now, mark my words, it will be ill for those who have put me here. It will be ill. I am alive. Make no doubt of it, I am alive. Every day my pulse is stronger and my mind clearer and more vigorous. No more quiescence. I am a man come back to life. And I want to *live* —'

'*Live!*'

Howard's face lit with an idea. He came towards Graham and spoke in an easy confidential tone.

'The Council secludes you here for your good. You are restless. Naturally – an energetic man! You find it dull here. But we are anxious that everything you may desire – every desire – every sort of desire ... There may be something. Is there any sort of company?'

He paused meaningly.

'Yes,' said Graham thoughtfully. 'There is.'

'Ah! *Now*! We have treated you neglectfully.'

'The crowds in yonder streets of yours.'

'That,' said Howard, 'I am afraid – But—'

Graham began pacing the room. Howard stood near the door watching him. The implication of Howard's suggestion was only half evident to Graham. Company? Suppose he were to accept the proposal, demand some sort of *company*? Would there be any possibilities of gathering from the conversation of this additional person some vague inkling of the struggle that had broken out so vividly at his waking moment? He meditated again, and the suggestion took colour. He turned on Howard abruptly.

'What do you mean by company?'

Howard raised his eyes and shrugged his shoulders. 'Human beings,' he said, with a curious smile on his heavy face.

'Our social ideas,' he said, 'have a certain increased liberality, perhaps, in comparison with your times. If a man wishes to relieve such a tedium as this – by feminine society, for instance. We think it no scandal. We have cleared our minds of formulae. There is in our city a class, a necessary class, no longer despised – discreet—'

Graham stopped dead.

'It would pass the time,' said Howard. 'It is a thing I should perhaps have thought of before, but as a matter of fact so much is happening—'

He indicated the exterior world.

Graham hesitated. For a moment the figure of a possible woman dominated his mind with an intense attraction. Then he flashed into anger.

'*No!*' he shouted.

He began striding rapidly up and down the room. 'Everything you say, everything you do, convinces me – of some great issue in which I am concerned. I do not want to pass the time, as you call it. Yes, I know. Desire and indulgence are life in a sense – and death! Extinction! In my life before I slept I had worked out that pitiful question. I will not begin again. There is a city, a multitude – And meanwhile I am here like a rabbit in a bag.'

His rage surged high. He choked for a moment and began to wave his clenched fists. He gave way to an anger fit, he swore archaic curses. His gestures had the quality of physical threats.

'I do not know who your party may be. I am in the dark, and you keep me in the dark. But I know this, that I am secluded here for no good purpose. For no good purpose. I warn you, I warn you of the consequences. Once I come at my power—'

He realized that to threaten thus might be a danger to himself. He stopped. Howard stood regarding him with a curious expression.

'I take it this is a message to the Council,' said Howard.

Graham had a momentary impulse to leap upon the man, fell or stun him. It must have shown upon his face; at any rate

Howard's movement was quick. In a second the noiseless door had closed and the man from the nineteenth century was alone.

For a moment he stood rigid, with clenched hands half raised. Then he flung them down. 'What a fool I have been!' he said, and gave way to his anger, stamping about the room and shouting curses. . . . For a long time he kept himself in a sort of frenzy, raging at his position, at his own folly, at the knaves who had imprisoned him. He did this because he did not want to look calmly at his position. He clung to his anger – because he was afraid of fear.

Presently he was reasoning with himself. This imprisonment was unaccountable, but no doubt the legal forms – new legal forms – of the time permitted it. It must of course be legal. These people were two hundred years further on in the march of civilization than the Victorian generation. It was not likely they would be less – humane. Yet they had cleared their minds of formulae! Was humanity a formula as well as chastity?

His imagination set to work to suggest things that might be done to him. The attempts of his reason to dispose of these suggestions, though for the most part logically valid, were quite unavailing. 'Why should anything be done to me?

'If the worst comes to the worst,' he found himself saying at last, 'I can give up what they want. But what do they want? And why don't they ask me for it instead of cooping me up?'

He returned to his former preoccupation with the Council's possible intentions. He began to reconsider the details of Howard's behaviour, sinister glances, inexplicable hesitations. Then for a time his mind circled about the idea of escaping from these rooms; but whither could he escape into this vast, crowded world? He would be worse off than a Saxon yeoman suddenly dropped into nineteenth-century London. And besides, how could anyone escape from these rooms?

'How can it benefit anyone if harm should happen to me?'

He thought of the tumult, the great social trouble of which he was so unaccountably the axis. A text, irrelevant enough and yet curiously insistent, came floating up out of the darkness of his memory. This also a Council had said:[8]

'It is expedient for us that one man should die for the people.'

CHAPTER 8
THE ROOF SPACES

As the fans in the circular aperture of the inner room rotated and permitted glimpses of the night, dim sounds drifted in thereby. And Graham, standing underneath, was startled by the sound of a voice.

He peered up and saw in the intervals of the rotation, dark and dim, the face and shoulders of a man regarding him. Then a dark hand was extended, the swift vane struck it, swung round and beat on with a little brownish patch on the edge of its thin blade, and something began to fall therefrom upon the floor, dripping silently.

Graham looked down, and there were spots of blood at his feet. He looked up again in a strange excitement. The figure had gone.

He remained motionless – his every sense intent upon the flickering patch of darkness. He became aware of some faint, remote, dark specks floating lightly through the outer air. They came down towards him, fitfully, eddyingly, and passed aside out of the uprush from the fan. A gleam of light flickered, the specks flashed white, and then the darkness came again. Warmed and lit as he was, he perceived that it was snowing within a few feet of him.

Graham walked across the room and came back to the ventilator again. He saw the head of a man pass near. There was a sound of whispering. Then a smart blow on some metallic substance, effort, voices, and the vanes stopped. A gust of snowflakes whirled into the room, and vanished before they touched the floor. 'Don't be afraid,' said a voice.

Graham stood under the van. 'Who are you?' he whispered.

For a moment there was nothing but a swaying of the fan, and then the head of a man was thrust cautiously into the opening. His face appeared nearly inverted to Graham; his dark hair was wet with dissolving flakes of snow upon it. His arm went up into the darkness holding something unseen. He had a youthful face and bright eyes, and the veins of his forehead were swollen. He seemed to be exerting himself to maintain his position.

For several seconds neither he nor Graham spoke.

'You were the Sleeper?' said the stranger at last.

'Yes,' said Graham. 'What do you want with me?'

'I come from Ostrog, Sire.'

'Ostrog?'

The man in the ventilator twisted his head round so that his profile was towards Graham. He appeared to be listening. Suddenly there was a hasty exclamation, and the intruder sprang back just in time to escape the sweep of the released fan. And when Graham peered up there was nothing visible but the slowly falling snow.

It was perhaps a quarter of an hour before anything returned to the ventilator. But at last came the same metallic interference again; the fans stopped and the face reappeared. Graham had remained all this time in the same place, alert and tremulously excited.

'Who are you? What do you want?' he said.

'We want to speak to you, Sire,' said the intruder. 'We want – I can't hold the thing. We have been trying to find a way to you – these three days.'

'Is it rescue?' whispered Graham. 'Escape?'

'Yes, Sire. If you will.'

'You are my party – the party of the Sleeper?'

'Yes, Sire.'

'What am I to do?' said Graham.

There was a struggle. The stranger's arm appeared, and his hand was bleeding. His knees came into view over the edge of the funnel. 'Stand away from me,' he said, and he dropped rather heavily on his hands and one shoulder at Graham's feet. The released ventilator whirled noisily. The stranger rolled over, sprang up nimbly and stood panting, hand to a bruised shoulder, and with his bright eyes on Graham.

'You are indeed the Sleeper,' he said. 'I saw you asleep. When it was the law that anyone might see you.'

'I am the man who was in a trance,' said Graham. 'They have imprisoned me here. I have been here since I awoke – at least three days.'

The intruder seemed about to speak, heard something, glanced swiftly at the door, and suddenly left Graham and ran towards it, shouting quick incoherent words. A bright wedge of steel flashed in his hand, and he began tap, tap, a quick succession of blows upon the hinges. 'Mind!' cried a voice. 'Oh!' The voice came from above.

Graham glanced up, saw the soles of two feet, ducked, was struck on the shoulder by one of them, and a heavy weight bore him to the ground. He fell on his knees and forward, and the weight went over his head. He knelt up and saw a second man from above seated before him.

'I did not see you, Sire,' panted the man. He rose and assisted Graham to rise. 'Are you hurt, Sire?' he panted. A succession of heavy blows on the ventilator began, something fell close to Graham's face, and a shivering edge of white metal danced, fell over, and lay flat upon the floor.

'What is this?' cried Graham, confused and looking at the ventilator. 'Who are you? What are you going to do? Remember, I understand nothing.'

'Stand back,' said the stranger, and drew him from under the ventilator as another fragment of metal fell heavily.

'We want you to come, Sire,' panted the newcomer, and Graham glancing at his face again, saw a new cut had changed from white to red on his forehead, and a couple of little trickles of blood were starting therefrom. 'Your people call for you.'

'Come where? My people?'

'To the hall above the markets. Your life is in danger here. We have spies. We learnt but just in time. The Council has decided – this very day – either to drug or kill you. And everything is ready. The people are drilled, the wind-vane police,[1] the engineers, and half the way-gearers[2] are with us. We have the halls crowded – shouting. The whole city shouts against the Council. We have arms.' He wiped the blood with his hand. 'Your life here is not worth—'

'But why arms?'

'The people have risen to protect you, Sire. What?'

He turned quickly as the man who had first come down made a hissing with his teeth. Graham saw the latter start back, gesticulate to them to conceal themselves, and move as if to hide behind the opening door.

As he did so Howard appeared, a little tray in one hand and his heavy face downcast. He started, looked up, the door slammed behind him, the tray tilted sideways, and the steel wedge struck him behind the ear. He went down like a felled tree, and lay as he fell athwart the floor of the outer room. The man who had struck him bent hastily, studied his face for a moment, rose, and returned to his work at the door.

'Your poison!' said a voice in Graham's ear.

Then abruptly they were in darkness. The innumerable cornice lights had been extinguished. Graham saw the aperture of the ventilator with ghostly snow whirling above it and dark figures moving hastily. Three knelt on the van. Some dim thing – a ladder – was being lowered through the opening, and a hand appeared holding a fitful yellow light.

He had a moment of hesitation. But the manner of these men, their swift alacrity, their words, marched so completely with his own fears of the Council, with his idea and hope of a rescue, that it lasted not a moment. And his people awaited him!

'I do not understand,' he said. 'I trust. Tell me what to do.'

The man with the cut brow gripped Graham's arm. 'Clamber up the ladder,' he whispered. 'Quick. They will have heard—'

Graham felt for the ladder with extended hands, put his foot on the lower rung and, turning his head, saw over the shoulder of the nearest man, in the yellow flicker of the light, the first-comer astride over Howard and still working at the door. Graham turned to the ladder again, and was thrust by his conductor and helped up by those above, and then he was standing on something hard and cold and slippery outside the ventilating funnel.

He shivered. He was aware of a great difference in the

temperature. Half a dozen men stood about him, and light flakes of snow touched hands and face and melted. For a moment it was dark, then for a flash a ghastly violet white, and then everything was dark again.

He saw he had come out upon the roof of the vast city structure[3] which had replaced the miscellaneous houses, streets and open spaces of Victorian London. The place upon which he stood was level, with huge serpentine cables lying athwart it in every direction. The circular wheels of a number of windmills loomed indistinct and gigantic through the darkness and snow-fall, and roared with a varying loudness as the fitful wind rose and fell. Some way off an intermittent white light smote up from below, touched the snow eddies with a transient glitter, and made an evanescent spectre in the night; and here and there, low down, some vaguely outlined wind-driven mechanism flickered with livid sparks.

All this he appreciated in a fragmentary manner as his rescuers stood about him. Someone threw a thick soft cloak of fur-like texture about him, and fastened it by buckled straps at waist and shoulders. Things were said briefly, decisively. Someone thrust him forward.

Before his mind was yet clear a dark shape gripped his arm. 'This way,' said this shape, urging him along, and pointed Graham across the flat roof in the direction of a dim semicircular haze of light. Graham obeyed.

'Mind!' said a voice, as Graham stumbled against a cable. 'Between them and not across them,' said the voice. And, 'We must hurry.'

'Where are the people?' said Graham. 'The people you said awaited me?'

The stranger did not answer. He left Graham's arm as the path grew narrower, and led the way with rapid strides. Graham followed blindly. In a minute he found himself running. 'Are the others coming?' he panted, but received no reply. His companion glanced back and ran on. They came to a sort of pathway of open metalwork, transverse to the direction they had come, and they turned aside to follow this. Graham looked back, but the snowstorm had hidden the others.

'Come on!' said his guide. Running now, they drew near a little windmill spinning high in the air. 'Stoop,' said Graham's guide, and they avoided an endless band running roaring up to the shaft of the vane. 'This way!' and they were ankle deep in a gutter full of drifted thawing snow, between two low walls of metal that presently rose waist high. 'I will go first,' said the guide. Graham drew his cloak about him and followed. Then suddenly came a narrow abyss across which the gutter leapt to the snowy darkness of the further side. Graham peeped over the side once and the gulf was black. For a moment he regretted his flight. He dared not look again, and his brain spun as he waded through the half liquid snow.

Then out of the gutter they clambered and hurried across a wide flat space damp with thawing snow, and for half its extent dimly translucent to lights that went to and fro underneath. He hesitated at this unstable looking substance, but his guide ran on unheeding, and so they came to and clambered up slippery steps to the rim of a great dome of glass. Round this they went. Far below a number of people seemed to be dancing, and music filtered through the dome. . . . Graham fancied he heard a shouting through the snowstorm, and his guide hurried him on with a new spurt of haste. They clambered panting to a space of huge windmills, one so vast that only the lower edge of its vanes came rushing into sight and rushed up again and was lost in the night and the snow. They hurried for a time through the colossal metallic tracery of its supports, and came at last above a place of moving platforms like the place into which Graham had looked from the balcony. They crawled across the sloping transparency that covered this street of plat-forms, crawling on hands and knees because of the slipperiness of the snowfall.

For the most part the glass was bedewed, and Graham saw only hazy suggestions of the forms below, but near the pitch of the transparent roof the glass was clear, and he found himself looking sheerly down upon it all. For a while, in spite of the urgency of his guide, he gave way to vertigo and lay spread-eagled on the glass, sick and paralysed. Far below, mere stirring specks and dots, went the people of the unsleeping city in their perpetual daylight, and the moving platforms ran on their incessant journey. Messengers and men on unknown businesses shot along the drooping cables and the frail bridges were crowded with men. It was like peering into a gigantic glass hive, and it lay vertically below him with only a tough glass of unknown thickness to save him from a fall. The street showed warm and lit, and Graham was wet now to the skin with thawing snow, and his feet were numbed with cold. For a space he could not move. 'Come on!' cried his guide, with terror in his voice. 'Come on!'

Graham reached the pitch of the roof by an effort.

Over the ridge, following his guide's example, he turned about and slid backward down the opposite slope very swiftly, amid a little avalanche of snow. While he was sliding he thought of what would happen if some broken gap should come in his way. At the edge he stumbled to his feet ankle deep in slush, thanking heaven for an opaque footing again. His guide was already clambering up a metal screen to a level expanse.

Through the spare snowflakes above this loomed another line of vast windmills, and then suddenly the amorphous tumult of the rotating wheels was pierced with a deafening sound. It was a mechanical shrilling of extraordinary intensity that seemed to come simultaneously from every point of the compass.

'They have missed us already!' cried Graham's guide in an accent of terror, and suddenly, with a blinding flash, the night became day.

Above the driving snow, from the summits of the wind-wheels, appeared vast masts carrying globes of livid light. They receded in illimitable vistas in every direction. As far as his eye could penetrate the snowfall they glared.

'Get on this,' cried Graham's conductor, and thrust him forward to a long grating of snowless metal that ran like a band between two slightly sloping expanses of snow. It felt warm to Graham's benumbed feet, and a faint eddy of steam rose from it.

'Come on!' shouted his guide ten yards off, and, without waiting, ran swiftly through the incandescent glare towards the iron supports of the next range of wind-wheels. Graham, recovering from his astonishment, followed as fast, convinced of his imminent capture. . . .

In a score of seconds they were within a tracery of glare and black shadows shot with moving bars beneath the monstrous wheels. Graham's conductor ran on for some time, and suddenly darted sideways and vanished into a black shadow in the corner of the foot of a huge support. In another moment Graham was beside him.

They cowered panting and stared out.

The scene upon which Graham looked was very wild and strange. The snow had now almost ceased; only a belated flake passed now and again across the picture. But the broad stretch of level before them was a ghastly white, broken only by gigantic masses and moving shapes and lengthy strips of impenetrable darkness, vast ungainly Titans of shadow. All about them huge metallic structures, iron girders, inhumanly vast as it seemed to him, interlaced, and the edges of wind-wheels, scarcely moving in the lull, passed in great shining curves more and more steeply up into a luminous haze. Wherever the snow-spangled light struck down, beams and girders, and incessant bands running with a halting, indomitable resolution, passed upward and downward into the black. And with all that mighty activity, with an omnipresent sense of motive and design, this snowclad desolation of mechanism seemed void of all human presence save themselves, seemed as trackless and deserted and unfrequented by men as some inaccessible Alpine snowfield.

'They will be chasing us,' cried the leader. 'We are scarcely halfway there yet. Cold as it is we must hide here for a space – at least until it snows more thickly again.'

His teeth chattered in his head.

'Where are the markets?' asked Graham staring out. 'Where are all the people?'

The other made no answer.

'*Look*!' whispered Graham, crouched close, and became very still.

The snow had suddenly become thick again, and sliding with the whirling eddies out of the black pit of the sky came something, vague and large and very swift. It came down in a steep curve and swept round, wide wings extended and a trail of white condensing steam behind it, rose with an easy swiftness and went gliding up the air, swept horizontally forward in a wide curve, and vanished again in the steaming specks of snow. And through the ribs of its body Graham saw two little men, very minute and active, searching the snowy areas about him, as it seemed to him, with field-glasses. For a second they were clear, then hazy through a thick whirl of snow, then small and distant, and in a minute they were gone.

'*Now*!' cried his companion. 'Come!'

He pulled Graham's sleeve, and incontinently the two were running headlong down the arcade of ironwork beneath the wind-wheels. Graham, running blindly, collided with his leader, who had turned back on him suddenly. He found himself within a dozen yards of a black chasm. It extended as far as he could see right and left. It seemed to cut off their progress in either direction.

'Do as I do,' whispered his guide. He lay down and crawled to the edge, thrust his head over and twisted until one leg hung. He seemed to feel for something with his foot, found it, and went sliding over the edge into the gulf. His head reappeared. 'It is a ledge,' he whispered. 'In the dark all the way along. Do as I did.'

Graham hesitated, went down upon all fours, crawled to the edge, and peered into a velvety blackness. For a sickly moment he had courage neither to go on nor retreat, then he sat and hung his leg down, felt his guide's hands pulling at him, had a horrible sensation of sliding over the edge into the unfathomable, splashed, and felt himself in a slushy gutter, impenetrably dark.

'This way,' whispered the voice, and he began crawling along the gutter through the trickling thaw, pressing himself against the wall. They continued along it for some minutes. He seemed to pass through a hundred stages of misery, to pass minute after minute through a hundred degrees of cold, damp and exhaustion. In a little while he ceased to feel his hands and feet.

The gutter sloped downwards. He observed that they were now many feet below the edge of the buildings. Rows of spectral white shapes like the ghosts of blind-drawn windows rose above them. They came to the end of a cable fastened above one of these white windows, dimly visible and dropping into impenetrable shadows. Suddenly his hand came against his guide's. '*Still*!' whispered the latter very softly.

He looked up with a start and saw the huge wings of the flying machine[4] gliding slowly and noiselessly overhead athwart the broad band of snow-flecked grey-blue sky. In a moment it was hidden again.

'Keep still; they were just turning.'

For a while both were motionless, then Graham's companion stood up, and reaching towards the fastenings of the cable fumbled with some indistinct tackle.

'What is that?' asked Graham.

The only answer was a faint cry. The man crouched motionless. Graham peered and saw his face dimly. He was staring down the long ribbon of sky, and Graham, following his eyes, saw the flying machine small and faint and remote. Then he saw that the wings spread on either side, that it headed towards them, that every moment it grew larger. It was following the edge of the chasm towards them.

The man's movements became convulsive. He thrust two cross bars into Graham's hand. Graham could not see them, he ascertained their form by feeling. They were slung by thin cords to the cable. On the cord were hand grips of some soft elastic substance. 'Put the cross between your legs,' whispered the guide hysterically, 'and grip the holdfasts. Grip tightly, grip!'

Graham did as he was told.

'Jump,' said the voice. 'In heaven's name, jump!'

For one momentous second Graham could not speak. He was glad afterwards that darkness hid his face. He said nothing. He began to tremble violently. He looked sideways at the swift shadow that swallowed up the sky as it rushed upon him.

'Jump! Jump – in God's name! Or they will have us,' cried Graham's guide, and in the violence of his passion thrust him forward.

Graham tottered convulsively, gave a sobbing cry, a cry in spite of himself, and then, as the flying machine swept over them, fell forward into the pit of that darkness, seated on the cross wood and holding the ropes with the clutch of death. Something cracked, something rapped smartly against a wall. He heard the pulley of the cradle hum on its rope. He heard the aeronauts shout. He felt a pair of knees digging into his back. . . . He was sweeping headlong through the air, falling through the air. All his strength was in his hands. He would have screamed but he had no breath.

He shot into a blinding light that made him grip the tighter. He recognized the great passage with the running ways, the hanging lights and interlacing girders. They rushed upward and by him. He had a momentary impression of a great round mouth yawning to swallow him up.

He was in the dark again, falling, falling, gripping with aching hands, and behold! a clap of sound, a burst of light, and he was in a brightly lit hall with a roaring multitude of people beneath his feet. The people! His people! A proscenium,[5] a stage rushed up towards him, and his cable swept down to a circular aperture to the right of this. He felt he was travelling slower, and suddenly very much slower. He distinguished shouts of 'Saved! The Master. He is safe!' The stage rushed up towards him with rapidly diminishing swiftness. Then—

He heard the man clinging behind him shout as if suddenly terrified, and this shout was echoed by a shout from below. He felt that he was no longer gliding along the cable but falling with it. There was a tumult of yells, screams and cries. He felt something soft against his extended hand, and the impact of a broken fall quivering through his arm. . . .

He wanted to be still and the people were lifting him. He believed afterwards he was carried to the platform, but he was never sure. He did not notice what became of his guide. When his mind was clear again he was on his feet; eager hands were assisting him to stand. He was in a big alcove, occupying the position that in his previous experience had been devoted to the lower boxes. If this was indeed a theatre.

A mighty tumult was in his ears, a thunderous roar, the shouting of a countless multitude. 'It is the Sleeper! The Sleeper is with us!'

'The Sleeper is with us! The Master – the Owner! The Master is with us. He is safe.'

Graham had a surging vision of a great hall crowded with people. He saw no individuals, he was conscious of a froth of pink faces, of waving arms and garments, he felt the occult influence of a vast crowd pouring over him, buoying him up. There were balconies, galleries, great archways giving remoter perspectives, and everywhere people, a vast arena of people, densely packed and cheering. Across the nearer space lay the collapsed cable like a huge snake. It had been cut by the men of the flying machine at its upper end, and had crumpled down into the hall. Men seemed to be hauling this out of the way. But the whole effect was vague, the very buildings throbbed and leapt with the roar of the voices.

He stood unsteadily and looked at those about him. Someone supported him by one arm. 'Let me go into a little room,' he said, weeping; 'a little room,' and could say no more. A man in black stepped forward, took his disengaged arm. He was aware of officious men opening a door before him. Someone guided him to a seat. He staggered. He sat down heavily and covered his face with his hands; he was trembling violently, his nervous control was at an end. He was relieved of his cloak, he could not remember how; his purple hose he saw were black with wet. People were running about him, things were happening, but for some time he gave no heed to them.

He had escaped. A myriad cries told him that. He was safe. These were the people who were on his side. For a space he sobbed for breath, and then he sat still with his face covered. The air was full of the shouting of innumerable men.

CHAPTER 9
THE PEOPLE MARCH

He became aware of someone urging a glass of clear fluid upon his attention, looked up and discovered this was a dark young man in a yellow garment. He took the dose forthwith, and in a moment he was glowing. A tall man in a black robe stood by his shoulder, and pointed to the half-open door into the hall. This man was shouting close to his ear, and yet what was said was indistinct because of the tremendous uproar from the great theatre. Behind the man was a girl in a silvery grey robe, whom Graham, even in this confusion, perceived to be beautiful. Her dark eyes, full of wonder and curiosity, were fixed on him, her lips trembled apart. A partially opened door gave a glimpse of the crowded hall, and admitted a vast uneven tumult, a hammering, clapping and shouting that died away and began again and rose to a thunderous pitch, and so continued intermittently all the time that Graham remained in the little room. He watched the lips of the man in black and gathered that he was making some explanation.

He stared stupidly for some moments at these things and then stood up abruptly; he grasped the arm of this shouting person.

'Tell me!' he cried. 'Who am I? Who am I?'

The others came nearer to hear his words. 'Who am I?' His eyes searched their faces.

'They have told him nothing!' cried the girl.

'Tell me, tell me!' cried Graham.

'You are the Master of the Earth. You are owner of the world.'

He did not believe he heard aright. He resisted the persuasion. He pretended not to understand, not to hear. He lifted his voice again. 'I have been awake three days – a prisoner three days. I judge there is some struggle between a number of people in this city – it is London?'

'Yes,' said the younger man.

'And those who meet in the great hall with the white Atlas? How does it concern me? In some way it has to do with me. *Why*, I don't know. Drugs? It seems to me that while I have slept the world has gone mad. I have gone mad. . . . Who are those Councillors under the Atlas? Why should they try to drug me?'

'To keep you insensible,' said the man in yellow. 'To prevent your interference.'

'But *why*?'

'Because *you* are the Atlas, Sire,' said the man in yellow. 'The world is on your shoulders. They rule it in your name.'

The sounds from the hall had died into a silence threaded by one monotonous voice. Now suddenly, trampling on these last words, came a deafening tumult, a roaring and thundering, cheer crowded on cheer, voices hoarse and shrill, beating, overlapping, and while it lasted the people in the little room could not hear each other shout.

Graham stood, his intelligence clinging helplessly to the thing he had just heard. 'The Council,' he repeated blankly, and then snatched at a name that had struck him. 'But who is Ostrog?' he said.

'He is the organizer – the organizer of the revolt. Our Leader – in your name.'

'In my name? – And you? Why is he not here?'

'He – has deputed us. I am his brother – his half-brother, Lincoln.[1] He wants you to show yourself to those people and then come on to him. That is why he was sent. He is at the wind-vane offices directing. The people are marching.'

'In your name,' shouted the younger man. 'They have ruled, crushed, tyrannized. At last even—'

'In my name! My name! Master?'

The younger man suddenly became audible in a pause of the outer thunder, indignant and vociferous, a high penetrating voice under his red aquiline nose and bushy moustache. 'No one expected you to wake. No one expected you to wake. They were cunning. Damned tyrants! But they were taken by surprise. They did not know whether to drug you, hypnotize you, kill you.'

Again the hall dominated everything.

'Ostrog is at the wind-vane offices ready – Even now there is a rumour of fighting beginning.'

The man who had called himself Lincoln came close to him. 'Ostrog has it planned. Trust him. We have our organizations ready. We shall seize the flying stages – Even now he may be doing that. Then—'

'This public theatre,' bawled the man in yellow, 'is only a contingent. We have five myriads of drilled men—'

'We have arms,' cried Lincoln. 'We have plans. A leader. Their police have gone from the streets and are massed in the –' (inaudible). 'It is now or never. The Council is rocking – They cannot trust even their drilled men—'

'Hear the people calling to you!'

Graham's mind was like a night of moon and swift clouds, now dark and hopeless, now clear and ghastly. He was Master of the Earth, he was a man sodden with thawing snow. Of all his fluctuating impressions the dominant ones presented an antagonism; on the one hand was the White Council, powerful, disciplined, few, the White Council from which he had just escaped; and on the other, monstrous crowds, packed masses of indistinguishable people clamouring his name, hailing him Master. The other side had imprisoned him, debated his death. These shouting thousands beyond the little doorway had rescued him. But why these things should be so he could not understand.

The door opened, Lincoln's voice was swept away and drowned, and a rush of people followed on the heels of the tumult. These intruders came towards him and Lincoln gesticulating. The voices without explained their soundless lips. 'Show us the Sleeper, show us the Sleeper!' was the burden of the uproar. Men were bawling for 'Order! Silence!'

Graham glanced towards the open doorway, and saw a tall, oblong picture of the hall beyond, a waving, incessant confusion of crowded, shouting faces, men and women together, waving pale blue garments, extended hands. Many were standing; one man in rags of dark brown, a gaunt figure, stood on the seat and waved a black cloth. He met the wonder and expectation of the girl's eyes. What did these people expect from him? He was dimly aware that the tumult outside had changed its character, was in some way beating, marching. His own mind, too, changed. For a space he did not recognize the influence that was transforming him. But a moment that was near to panic passed. He tried to make audible inquiries in vain.

Lincoln was shouting in his ear, but Graham was deafened to that. All the others save the woman gesticulated towards the hall. He perceived what had happened to the uproar. The whole mass of people was chanting together. It was not simply a song, the voices were gathered together and upborne by a torrent of instrumental music, music like the music of an organ, a woven texture of sounds, full of trumpets, full of flaunting banners, full of the march and pageantry of opening war. And the feet of the people were beating time – tramp, tramp.

He was urged towards the door. He obeyed mechanically. The strength of that chant took hold of him, stirred him, emboldened him. The hall opened to him, a vast welter of fluttering colour swaying to the music.

'Wave your arm to them,' said Lincoln. 'Wave your arm to them.'

'This,' said a voice on the other side, 'he must have this.' Arms were about his neck detaining him in the doorway, and a black mantle hung from his shoulders. He threw his arm free of this and followed Lincoln. He perceived the girl in grey close to him, her face lit, her gesture onward. For the instant she became to him, flushed and eager as she was, an embodiment of the song. He emerged in the alcove again. Incontinently the mounting waves of the song broke upon his appearing, and flashed up into a foam of shouting. Guided by Lincoln's hand he marched obliquely across the centre of the stage facing the people.

The hall was a vast and intricate space – galleries, balconies, broad spaces of amphitheatral steps, and great archways. Far away, high up, seemed the mouth of a huge passage full of struggling humanity. The whole multitude was swaying in congested masses. Individual figures sprang out of the tumult, impressed him momentarily, and lost definition again. Close to the platform swayed a beautiful fair woman carried by three men, her hair across her face and brandishing a green staff. Next this group an old careworn man in blue canvas maintained his place in the crush with difficulty, and behind shouted a hairless face, a great cavity of toothless mouth. A voice called that enigmatical word 'Ostrog'. All his impressions were vague save the massive emotion of that trampling song. The multitude were beating time with their feet – marking time, tramp, tramp, tramp, tramp. The green weapons waved, flashed and slanted. Then he saw those nearest to him on a level space before the stage were marching in front of him, passing towards a great archway, shouting 'To the Council!' Tramp, tramp, tramp, tramp. He raised his arm, and the roaring was redoubled. He remembered he had to shout 'March!' His mouth shaped inaudible heroic words. He waved his arm again and pointed to the archway, shouting 'Onward!' They were no longer marking time, they were marching; tramp, tramp, tramp, tramp. In that host were bearded men, old men, youths, fluttering robed bare-armed women, girls. Men and women of the new age! Rich robes, grey rags fluttered together in the whirl of their movement amidst the dominant blue.[2] A monstrous black banner jerked its way to the right. He perceived a blue-clad Negro, a shrivelled woman in yellow, then a group of tall fair-haired, white-faced, blue-clad men pushed theatrically past him. He noted two Chinamen. A tall, sallow, dark-haired, shining-eyed youth, white clad from top to toe, clambered up towards the platform shouting loyally, and sprang down again and receded, looking backward. Heads, shoulders, hands clutching weapons, all were swinging with those marching cadences.

Faces came out of the confusion to him as he stood there, eyes met his and passed and vanished. Men gesticulated to him, shouted inaudible personal things. Most of the faces were flushed, but many were ghastly white. And disease was there, and many a hand that waved to him was gaunt and lean. Men

and women of the new age! Strange and incredible meeting! As
the broad stream passed before him to the right, tributary
gangways from the remote uplands of the hall thrust downward
in an incessant replacement of people; tramp, tramp, tramp,
tramp. The unison of the song was enriched and complicated
by the massive echoes of arches and passages. Men and women
mingled in the ranks; tramp, tramp, tramp, tramp. The whole
world seemed marching. Tramp, tramp, tramp, tramp; his brain
was tramping. The garments waved onward, the faces poured
by more abundantly.

Tramp, tramp, tramp, tramp; at Lincoln's pressure he turned
towards the archway, walking unconsciously in that rhythm,
scarcely noticing his movement for the melody and stir of it.
The multitude, the gesture and song, all moved in that direction,
the flow of people smote downward until the upturned faces
were below the level of his feet. He was aware of a path before
him, of a suite about him, of guards and dignities and Lincoln
on his right hand. Attendants intervened, and ever and again
blotted out the sight of the multitude to the left. Before him
went the backs of the guards in black – three and three and
three. He was marched along a little railed way, and crossed
above the archway with the torrent dipping to flow beneath
and shouting up to him. He did not know whither he went;
he did not want to know. He glanced back across a flaming
spaciousness of hall. Tramp, tramp, tramp, tramp.

CHAPTER 10

THE BATTLE OF THE DARKNESS

He was no longer in the hall. He was marching along a gallery overhanging one of the great streets of the moving platforms that traversed the city. Before him and behind him tramped his guards. The whole concave of the moving ways below was a congested mass of people marching, tramping to the left, shouting, waving hands and arms, pouring along a huge vista, shouting as they came into view, shouting as they passed, shouting as they receded, until the globes of electric light[1] receding in perspective dropped down it seemed and hid the swarming bare heads. Tramp, tramp, tramp, tramp.

The song roared up to Graham now, no longer upborne by music but coarse and noisy, and the beating of the marching feet, tramp, tramp, tramp, tramp, interwove with a thunderous irregularity of footsteps from the undisciplined rabble that poured along the higher ways.

Abruptly he noted a contrast. The buildings on the opposite side of the way seemed deserted, the cables and bridges that laced across the aisle were empty and shadowy. It came into Graham's mind that these also should have swarmed with people.

He felt a curious emotion – throbbing – very fast! He stopped again. The guards before him marched on; those about him stopped as he did. He saw anxiety and fear in their faces. The throbbing had something to do with the lights. He too looked up.

At first it seemed to him a thing that affected the lights simply, an isolated phenomenon having no bearing on the things below. Each huge globe of blinding whiteness was as it were clutched, compressed in a systole that was followed by a transitory diastole, and again a systole like a tightening grip, darkness, light, darkness, in rapid alternation.

Graham became aware that this strange behaviour of the lights had to do with the people below. The appearance of the houses and ways, the appearance of the packed masses changed, became a confusion of vivid lights and leaping shadows. He saw a multitude of shadows had sprung into aggressive existence, seemed rushing up, broadening, widening, growing with steady swiftness – to leap suddenly back and return reinforced. The song and the tramping had ceased. The unanimous march, he discovered, was arrested, there were eddies, a flow sideways, shouts of 'The lights!' Voices were crying together one thing. 'The lights! The lights!' He looked down. In this dancing death of the lights the area of the street had suddenly become a monstrous struggle. The huge white globes became purple-white, purple with a reddish glow, flickered, flickered faster and faster, fluttered between light and extinction, ceased to flicker and became mere fading specks of glowing red in a vast obscurity. In ten seconds the extinction was accomplished, and there was only this roaring darkness, a black monstrosity that had suddenly swallowed up those glittering myriads of men.

He felt invisible forms about him; his arms were gripped. Something rapped sharply against his shin. A voice bawled in his ear, 'It is all right – all right.'

Graham shook off the paralysis of his first astonishment. He struck his forehead against Lincoln's and bawled, 'What is this darkness?'

'The Council has cut the currents that light the city. We must wait – stop. The people will go on. They will—'

His voice was drowned. There was an immense shouting, 'Save the Sleeper. Take care of the Sleeper.' A guard stumbled against Graham and hurt his hand by an inadvertent blow of his weapon. A wild tumult tossed and whirled about him, growing, as it seemed, louder, denser, more furious each moment. Fragments of recognizable sounds drove towards him, were whirled away from him as his mind reached out to grasp them. Men seemed to be shouting conflicting orders, others answered. There was suddenly a succession of piercing screams close beneath them.

A voice bawled in his ear, 'The red police,' and receded forthwith beyond his questions.

A crackling sound grew to distinctness, and therewith a leaping of faint flashes along the edge of the further ways. By their light Graham saw the heads and bodies of a number of men, armed with weapons like those of his guards, leap into an instant's dim visibility. The whole area began to crackle, to flash with little instantaneous streaks of light, and abruptly the darkness rolled back like a curtain.

A glare of light dazzled his eyes, a vast seething expanse of struggling men confused his mind. A shout, a burst of cheering, came across the ways. He looked up to see the source of the light. A man hung far overhead from the upper part of a cable, holding by a rope the blinding star that had driven the darkness back.

Graham's eyes fell to the ways again. A wedge of red a little way along the vista caught his eye. He saw it was a dense mass of red-clad men jammed on the higher further way, their backs against the pitiless cliff of building, and surrounded by a great crowd of antagonists. They were fighting. Weapons flashed and rose and fell, heads vanished at the edge of the contest, and other heads replaced them, the little flashes from the green weapons became little jets of smoky grey while the light lasted.

Abruptly the flare was extinguished and the ways were an inky darkness once more, a tumultuous mystery.

He felt something thrusting against him. He was being pushed along the gallery. Someone was shouting – it might be at him. He was too confused to hear. He was thrust against the wall, and a number of people blundered past him. It seemed to him that his guards were struggling with one another.

Suddenly the cable-hung star-holder appeared again, and the whole scene was white and dazzling. The band of red-coats seemed broader and nearer; its apex was halfway down the ways towards the central aisle. And raising his eyes Graham saw that a number of these men had also appeared now in the darkened lower galleries of the opposite building, and were

firing over the heads of their fellows below at the boiling confusion of people on the lower ways. The meaning of these things
dawned upon him. The march of the people had come upon
an ambush at the very outset. Thrown into confusion by the
extinction of the lights they were now being attacked by the
red police. Then he became aware that he was standing alone,
that his guards and Lincoln were some way off in the direction
along which he had come before the darkness fell. He saw they
were gesticulating to him wildly, running back towards him. A
great shouting came from across the ways. Then it seemed as
though the whole face of the darkened building opposite was
lined and speckled with red-clad men. And they were pointing
over to him and shouting. 'The Sleeper! Save the Sleeper!'
shouted a multitude of throats.

Something struck the wall above his head. He looked up at
the impact and saw a star-shaped splash of silvery metal. He
saw Lincoln near him. Felt his arm gripped. Then, pat, pat; he
had been missed twice.

For a moment he did not understand this. The street was
hidden, everything was hidden, as he looked. The second flare
had burned out.

Lincoln had gripped Graham by the arm, was lugging him
along the gallery. 'Before the next light!' he cried. His haste was
contagious. Graham's instinct of self-preservation overcame the
paralysis of his incredulous astonishment. He became for a
time the blind creature of the fear of death. He ran, stumbling
because of the uncertainty of the darkness, blundered into his
guards as they turned to run with him. Haste was his one desire,
to escape this perilous gallery upon which he was exposed. A
third glare came close on its predecessors. With it came a great
shouting across the ways, an answering tumult from the ways.
The red-coats below, he saw, had now almost gained the central
passage. Their countless faces turned towards him, and they
shouted. The white façade opposite was densely stippled with
red. All these wonderful things concerned him, turned upon
him as a pivot. These were the guards of the Council attempting
to recapture him.

Lucky it was for him that these shots were the first fired in anger for a hundred and fifty years. He heard bullets whacking over his head, felt a splash of molten metal sting his ear, and perceived without looking that the whole opposite façade, an unmasked ambuscade of red police, was crowded and bawling and firing at him.

Down went one of his guards before him, and Graham, unable to stop, leapt the writhing body.

In another second he had plunged unhurt into a black passage, and incontinently someone, coming it may be in a transverse direction, blundered violently into him. He was hurling down a staircase in absolute darkness. He reeled, and was struck again, and came against a wall with his hands. He was crushed by a weight of struggling bodies, whirled round, and thrust to the right. A vast pressure pinned him. He could not breathe, his ribs seemed cracking. He felt a momentary relaxation, and then the whole mass of people moving together, bore him back towards the great theatre from which he had so recently come. There were moments when his feet did not touch the ground. Then he was staggering and shoving. He heard shouts of 'They are coming!' and a muffled cry close to him. His foot blundered against something soft, he heard a hoarse scream under foot. He heard shouts of 'The Sleeper!' but he was too confused to speak. He heard the green weapons crackling. For a space he lost his individual will, became an atom in a panic, blind, unthinking, mechanical. He thrust and pressed back and writhed in the pressure, kicked presently against a step, and found himself ascending a slope. And abruptly the faces all about him leapt out of the black, visible, ghastly-white and astonished, terrified, perspiring, in a livid glare. One face, a young man's, was very near to him, not twenty inches away. At the time it was but a passing incident of no emotional value, but afterwards it came back to him in his dreams. For this young man, wedged upright in the crowd for a time, had been shot and was already dead.

A fourth white star must have been lit by the man on the cable. Its light came glaring in through vast windows and arches and showed Graham that he was now one of a dense mass of flying black figures pressed back across the lower area of the great theatre. This time the picture was livid and fragmentary, slashed and barred with black shadows. He saw that quite near to him the red guards were fighting their way through the people. He could not tell whether they saw him. He looked for Lincoln and his guards. He saw Lincoln near the stage of the theatre surrounded by a crowd of black-badged revolutionaries, lifted up and staring to and fro as if seeking him. Graham perceived that he himself was near the opposite edge of the crowd, that behind him, separated by a barrier, sloped the now vacant seats of the theatre. A sudden idea came to him, and he began fighting his way towards the barrier. As he reached it the glare came to an end.

In a moment he had thrown off the great cloak that not only impeded his movements, but made him conspicuous, and had slipped it from his shoulders. He heard someone trip in its folds. In another he was scaling the barrier and had dropped into the blackness on the further side. Then feeling his way he came to the lower end of an ascending gangway. In the darkness the sound of firing ceased and the roar of feet and voices lulled. Then suddenly he came to an unexpected step and tripped and fell. As he did so pools and islands amidst the darkness about him leapt to vivid light again, the uproar surged louder and the glare of the fifth white star shone through the vast fenestrations[2] of the theatre walls.

He rolled over among some seats, heard a shouting and the whirring rattle of weapons, struggled up and was knocked back again, perceived that a number of black-badged men were all about him firing at the reds below, leaping from seat to seat, crouching among the seats to reload. Instinctively he crouched amidst the seats, as stray shots ripped the pneumatic[3] cushions and cut bright slashes on their soft metal frames. Instinctively he marked the direction of the gangways, the most plausible way of escape for him so soon as the veil of darkness fell again.

A young man in faded blue garments came vaulting over the seats. 'Hullo!' he said, with his flying feet within six inches of the crouching Sleeper's face.

He stared without any sign of recognition, turned to fire, fired, and shouting, 'To hell with the Council!' was about to fire again. Then it seemed to Graham that the half of this man's neck had vanished. A drop of moisture fell on Graham's cheek. The green weapon stopped half raised. For a moment the man stood still with his face suddenly expressionless, then he began to slant forward. His knees bent. Man and darkness fell together. At the sound of his fall Graham rose up and ran for his life until a step down to the gangway tripped him. He scrambled to his feet, turned up the gangway and ran on.

When the sixth star glared he was already close to the yawning throat of a passage. He ran on the swifter for the light, entered the passage and turned a corner into absolute night again. He was knocked sideways, rolled over, and recovered his feet. He found himself one of a crowd of invisible fugitives pressing in one direction. His one thought now was their thought also; to escape out of this fighting. He thrust and struck, staggered, ran, was wedged tightly, lost ground and then was clear again.

For some minutes he was running through the darkness along a winding passage, and then he crossed some wide and open space, passed down a long incline, and came at last down a flight of steps to a level place. Many people were shouting, 'They are coming! The guards are coming. They are firing. Get out of the fighting. The guards are firing. It will be safe in Seventh Way. Along here to Seventh Way!' There were women and children in the crowd as well as men.

The crowd converged on an archway, passed through a short throat and emerged on a wider space again, lit dimly. The black figures about him spread out and ran up what seemed in the twilight to be a gigantic series of steps. He followed. The people dispersed to the right and left. . . . He perceived that he was no longer in a crowd. He stopped near the highest step. Before him, on that level, were groups of seats and a little kiosk. He went up to this and, stopping in the shadow of its eaves, looked about him panting.

Everything was vague and grey, but he recognized that these great steps were a series of platforms of the 'ways', now motionless again. The platform slanted up on either side, and the tall buildings rose beyond, vast dim ghosts, their inscriptions and advertisements indistinctly seen, and up through the girders and cables was a faint interrupted ribbon of pallid sky. A number of people hurried by. From their shouts and voices, it seemed they were hurrying to join the fighting. Other less noisy figures flitted timidly among the shadows.

From very far away down the street he could hear the sound of a struggle. But it was evident to him that this was not the street into which the theatre opened. That former fight, it seemed, had suddenly dropped out of sound and hearing. And they were fighting for him!

For a space he was like a man who pauses in the reading of a vivid book, and suddenly doubts what he has been taking unquestionably. At that time he had little mind for details; the whole effect was a huge astonishment. Oddly enough, while the flight from the Council prison, the great crowd in the hall, and the attack of the red police upon the swarming people were clearly present in his mind, it cost him an effort to piece in his awakening and to revive the meditative interval of the Silent Rooms. At first his memory leapt these things and took him back to the cascade at Pentargen quivering in the wind, and all the sombre splendours of the sunlit Cornish coast. The contrast touched everything with unreality. And then the gap filled, and he began to comprehend his position.

It was no longer absolutely a riddle, as it had been in the Silent Rooms. At least he had the strange, bare outline now. He was in some way the owner of the world, and great political parties were fighting to possess him. On the one hand was the Council with its red police, set resolutely, it seemed, on the usurpation of his property and perhaps his murder; on the other, the revolution that had liberated him, with this unseen 'Ostrog' as its leader. And the whole of this gigantic city was convulsed by their struggle. Frantic development of his world! 'I do not understand,' he cried. 'I do not understand!'

He had slipped out between the contending parties into this liberty of the twilight. What would happen next? What was happening? He figured the red-clad men as busily hunting him, driving the black-badged revolutionists before them.

At any rate chance had given him a breathing space. He could lurk unchallenged by the passers-by, and watch the course of things. His eye followed up the intricate dim immensity of the twilight buildings, and it came to him as a thing infinitely wonderful that above there the sun was rising, and the world was lit and glowing with the old familiar light of day. In a little while he had recovered his breath. His clothing had already dried upon him from the snow.

He wandered for miles along these twilight ways, speaking to no one, accosted by no one – a dark figure among dark figures – the coveted man out of the past, the inestimable unintentional owner of the world. Wherever there were lights or dense crowds or exceptional excitement, he was afraid of recognition, and watched and turned back or went up and down by the middle stairways into some transverse system of ways at a lower or higher level. And though he came on no more fighting, the whole city stirred with battle. Once he had to run to avoid a marching multitude of men that swept the street. Everyone abroad seemed involved. For the most part they were men, and they carried what he judged were weapons. It seemed as though the struggle was concentrated mainly in the quarter of the city from which he came. Ever and again a distant roaring, the remote suggestion of that conflict, reached his ears. Then his caution and his curiosity struggled together. But his caution prevailed, and he continued wandering away from the fighting – so far as he could judge. He went unmolested, unsuspected through the dark. After a time he ceased to hear even a remote echo of the battle, fewer and fewer people passed him, until at last the streets became deserted. The frontages of the buildings grew plain and harsh; he seemed to have come to a district of vacant warehouses. Solitude crept upon him – his pace slackened.

He became aware of a growing fatigue. At times he would turn aside and sit down on one of the numerous benches of the upper ways. But a feverish restlessness, the knowledge of his vital implication in this struggle, would not let him rest in any place for long. Was the struggle on his behalf alone?

And then in a desolate place came the shock of an earthquake – a roaring and thundering – a mighty wind of cold air pouring through the city, the smash of glass, the slip and thud of falling masonry – a series of gigantic concussions. A mass of glass and ironwork fell from the remote roofs into the middle gallery not a hundred yards away from him, and in the distance were shouts and running. He, too, was startled to an aimless activity, and ran first one way and then as aimlessly back.

A man came running towards him. His self-control returned. 'What have they blown up?' asked the man breathlessly. 'That was an explosion,' and before Graham could speak he had hurried on.

The great buildings rose dimly, veiled by a perplexing twilight albeit the rivulet of sky above was now bright with day. He noted many strange features, understanding none at the time; he even spelt out many of the inscriptions in Phonetic lettering. But what profits it to decipher a confusion of odd-looking letters resolving itself, after painful strain of eye and mind, into 'Here is Eadhamite',[4] or, 'Labour Bureau – Little Side'?[5] Grotesque thought, that all these cliff-like houses were his!

The perversity of his experience came to him vividly. In actual fact he had made such a leap in time[6] as romancers have imagined again and again. And that fact realized, he had been prepared. His mind had, as it were, seated itself for a spectacle. And no spectacle unfolded itself, but a great vague danger, unsympathetic shadows and veils of darkness. Somewhere through the labyrinthine obscurity his death sought him. Would he, after all, be killed before he saw? It might be that even at the next corner his destruction ambushed. A great desire to see, a great longing to know, arose in him.

He became fearful of corners. It seemed to him that there was safety in concealment. Where could he hide to be inconspicuous when the lights returned? At last he sat down upon a seat in a recess on one of the higher ways, conceiving he was alone there.

He squeezed his knuckles into his weary eyes. Suppose when he looked again he found the dark trough of parallel ways and that intolerable altitude of edifice gone. Suppose he were to discover the whole story of these last few days, the awakening, the shouting multitudes, the darkness and the fighting, a phantasmagoria, a new and more vivid sort of dream. It must be a dream; it was so inconsecutive, so reasonless. Why were the people fighting for him? Why should this saner world regard him as Owner and Master?

So he thought, sitting blinded; and then he looked again, half hoping in spite of his ears to see some familiar aspect of the life of the nineteenth century, to see, perhaps, the little harbour of Boscastle about him, the cliffs of Pentargen, or the bedroom of his home. But fact takes no heed of human hopes. A squad of men with a black banner tramped athwart the nearer shadows, intent on conflict, and beyond rose that giddy wall of frontage, vast and dark, with the dim incomprehensible lettering showing faintly on its face.

'It is no dream,' he said, 'no dream.' And he bowed his face upon his hands.

CHAPTER II
THE OLD MAN WHO KNEW EVERYTHING

He was startled by a cough close at hand.

He turned sharply, and peering, saw a small, hunched-up figure sitting a couple of yards off in the shadow of the enclosure.

'Have ye any news?' asked the high-pitched wheezy voice of a very old man.

Graham hesitated. 'None,' he said.

'I stay here till the lights come again,' said the old man. 'These blue scoundrels are everywhere – everywhere.'

Graham's answer was inarticulate assent. He tried to see the old man but the darkness hid his face. He wanted very much to respond, to talk, but he did not know how to begin.

'Dark and damnable,' said the old man suddenly. 'Dark and damnable. Turned out of my room among all these dangers.'

'That's hard,' ventured Graham. 'That's hard on you.'

'Darkness. An old man lost in the darkness. And all the world gone mad. War and fighting. The police beaten and rogues abroad. Why don't they bring some Negroes to protect us? . . . No more dark passages for me. I fell over a dead man.

'You're safer with company,' said the old man, 'if it's company of the right sort,' and peered frankly. He rose suddenly and came towards Graham.

Apparently the scrutiny was satisfactory. The old man sat down as if relieved to be no longer alone. 'Eh!' he said, 'but this is a terrible time! War and fighting, and the dead lying there – men, strong men, dying in the dark. Sons! I have three sons. God knows where they are tonight.'

The voice ceased. Then repeated quavering: 'God knows where they are tonight.'

Graham stood revolving a question that should not betray his ignorance. Again the old man's voice ended the pause.

'This Ostrog will win,' he said. 'He will win. And what the world will be like under him no one can tell. My sons are under the wind-vanes, all three. One of my daughters-in-law was his mistress for a while. His mistress! We're not common people. Though they've sent me to wander tonight and take my chance. . . . I knew what was going on. Before most people. But this darkness! And to fall over a dead body suddenly in the dark!'

His wheezy breathing could be heard.

'Ostrog!' said Graham.

'The greatest Boss[1] the world has ever seen,' said the voice.

Graham ransacked his mind. 'The Council has few friends among the people,' he hazarded.

'Few friends. And poor ones at that. They've had their time. Eh! They should have kept to the clever ones. But twice they held election. And Ostrog – And now it has burst out and nothing can stay it, nothing can stay it. Twice they rejected Ostrog – Ostrog the Boss. I heard of his rages at the time – he was terrible. Heaven save them! For nothing on earth can now he has raised the Labour Companies upon them. No one else would have dared. All the blue canvas armed and marching! He will go through with it. He will go through.'

He was silent for a little while. 'This Sleeper,' he said, and stopped.

'Yes,' said Graham. 'Well?'

The senile voice sank to a confidential whisper, the dim, pale face came close. 'The real Sleeper —'

'Yes,' said Graham.

'Died years ago.'

'What?' said Graham, sharply.

'Years ago. Died. Years ago.'

'You don't say so!' said Graham.

'I do. I do say so. He died. This Sleeper who's woke up – they changed in the night. A poor, drugged insensible creature. But I mustn't tell all I know. I mustn't tell all I know.'

For a little while he muttered inaudibly. His secret was too

much for him. 'I don't know the ones that put him to sleep –
that was before my time – but I know the man who injected the
stimulants and woke him again. It was ten to one – wake or
kill. Wake or kill. Ostrog's way.'

Graham was so astonished that he had to interrupt, to make
the old man repeat his words, to re-question vaguely, before he
was sure of the meaning and folly of what he heard. And his
awakening had not been natural! Was that an old man's senile
superstition, too, or had it any truth in it? Feeling in the dark
corners of his memory, he presently came on a dream of his
arm being pierced that might conceivably be an impression of
some such stimulating effect. It dawned upon him that he had
happened upon a lucky encounter, that at last he might learn
something of the new age. The old man wheezed a while and
spat, and then the piping, reminiscent voice resumed:

'First they rejected him. I've followed it all.'

'Rejected whom?' said Graham. 'The Sleeper?'

'Sleeper? *No*. Ostrog. He was terrible – terrible! And he was
promised then, promised certainly the next time. Fools they
were – not to be more afraid of him. Now all the city's his
millstone, and such as we, dust ground upon it. Dust ground
upon it. Until he set to work – the workers cut each other's
throats, and murdered a Chinaman or a Labour policeman
now and then, and left the rest of us in peace. Dead bodies!
Robbing! Darkness! Such a thing hasn't been this gross of
years. Eh! – but 'tis ill on small folks when the great fall out!
It's ill.'

'Did you say – there had not been – what? – for a gross of
years?'

'Eh?' said the old man.

The old man grumbled at his way of clipping his words, and
made him repeat this. 'Fighting and slaying, and weapons in
hand, and fools bawling freedom and the like,' said the old
man. 'Not in all my life has there been that. These are like the
old days – for sure – when the Paris people broke out[2] – three
gross of years ago. That's what I mean hasn't been. But it's the
world's way. It had to come back. I know. I know. This five
years Ostrog has been working, and there has been trouble and

trouble, and hunger and threats and high talk and arms. Blue canvas and murmurs. No one safe. Everything sliding and slipping. And now here we are! Revolt and fighting, and the Council come to its end.'

'You are rather well-informed on these things,' said Graham.

'I know what I hear. It isn't all Babble Machine[3] with me.'

'No,' said Graham, wondering what Babble Machine might be. 'And you are certain this Ostrog – you are certain Ostrog organized this rebellion and arranged for the waking of the Sleeper? Just to assert himself – because he was not elected to the Council?'

'Everyone knows that, I should think,' said the old man. 'Except – just fools. He meant to be master somehow. In the Council or not. Everyone who knows anything knows that. And here we are with dead bodies lying in the dark! Why, where have you been if you haven't heard all about the trouble between Ostrog and the Verneys?[4] And what do you think the troubles are about? The Sleeper? Eh? You think the Sleeper's real and woke of his own accord – eh?'

'I'm a dull man, older than I look, and forgetful,' said Graham. 'Lots of things that have happened – especially of late years – If I was the Sleeper, to tell you the truth, I couldn't know less about them.'

'Eh!' said the voice. 'Old, are you? You don't sound so very old! But it's not everyone keeps his memory to my time of life – truly. But these notorious things! But you're not so old as me – not nearly so old as me. Well! I ought not to judge other men by myself, perhaps. I'm young – for so old a man. Maybe you're old for so young.'

'That's it,' said Graham. 'And I've a queer history. I know very little. History! Practically I know no history. The Sleeper and Julius Caesar[5] are all the same to me. It's interesting to hear you talk of these things.'

'I know a few things,' said the old man. 'I know a thing or two. But – Hark!'

The two men became silent, listening. There was a heavy thud, a concussion that made their seat shiver. The passers-by stopped, shouted to one another. The old man was full of questions; he shouted to a man who passed near. Graham, emboldened by his example, got up and accosted others. None knew what had happened.

He returned to the seat and found the old man muttering vague interrogations in an undertone. For a while they said nothing to one another.

The sense of this gigantic struggle, so near and yet so remote, oppressed Graham's imagination. Was this old man right, was the report of the people right, and were the revolutionaries winning? Or were they all in error, and were the red guards driving all before them? At any time the flood of warfare might pour into this silent quarter of the city and seize upon him again. It behoved him to learn all he could while there was time. He turned suddenly to the old man with a question and left it unsaid. But his motion moved the old man to speech again.

'Eh! but how things work together!' said the old man. 'This Sleeper that all the fools put their trust in! I've the whole history of it – I was always a good one for histories. When I was a boy – I'm that old – I used to read printed books. You'd hardly think it. Likely you've seen none – they rot and dust so – and the Sanitary Company[6] burns them to make ashlarite.[7] But they were convenient in their dirty way. One learnt a lot. These new-fangled Babble Machines – they don't seem new-fangled to you, eh? – they're easy to hear, easy to forget. But I've traced all the Sleeper business from the first.'

'You will scarcely believe it,' said Graham slowly, 'I'm so ignorant – I've been so preoccupied in my own little affairs, my circumstances have been so odd – I know nothing of this Sleeper's history. Who was he?'

'Eh!' said the old man. 'I know, I know. He was a poor nobody, and set on a playful woman, poor soul! And he fell into a trance. There's the old things they had, those brown things – silver photographs[8] – still showing him as he lay, a gross and a half years ago – a gross and a half of years.'

'Set on a playful woman, poor soul,' said Graham softly to himself, and then aloud, 'Yes – well, go on.'

'You must know he had a cousin named Warming, a solitary

man without children, who made a big fortune speculating in roads – the first Eadhamite roads. But surely you've heard? No? Why, – he bought all the patent rights and made a big company. In those days there were grosses of grosses of separate businesses and business companies. Grosses of grosses! His roads killed the railroads – the old things – in two dozen years; he bought up and Eadhamited the tracks. And because he didn't want to break up his great property or let in shareholders, he left it all to the Sleeper, and put it under a Board of Trustees that he had picked and trained. He knew then the Sleeper wouldn't wake, that he would go on sleeping, sleeping till he died. He knew that quite well! And plump! a man in the United States, who had lost two sons in a boat accident, followed that up with another great bequest. His trustees found themselves with a dozen myriads of lions'-worth or more of property at the very beginning.'

'What was his name?'

'Graham.'

'No – I mean – that American's.'

'Isbister.'

'Isbister!' cried Graham. 'Why, I don't even know the name.'

'Of course not,' said the old man. 'Of course not. People don't learn much in the schools nowadays. But I know all about him. He was a rich American who went from England, and he left the Sleeper even more than Warming. How he made it? That I don't know. Something about pictures by machinery. But he made it and left it, and so the Council had its start. It was just a council of trustees at first.'

'And how did it grow?'

'Eh! – but you're not up to things. Money attracts money – and twelve brains are better than one. They played it cleverly. They worked politics with money, and kept on adding to the money by working currency and tariffs. They grew – they grew. And for years the twelve trustees hid the growing of the Sleeper's estate under double names and company titles and all that. The Council spread by title deed, mortgage, share; every political party, every newspaper they bought. If you listen to the old stories you will see the Council growing and growing.

Billions and billions of lions at last – the Sleeper's estate. And all growing out of a whim – out of this Warming's will, and an accident to Isbister's sons.

'Men are strange,' said the old man. 'The strange thing to me is how the Council worked together so long. As many as twelve. But they worked in cliques from the first. And they've slipped back. In my young days speaking of the Council was like an ignorant man speaking of God. We didn't think they could do wrong. We didn't know of their women and all that! Or else I've got wiser.

'Men are strange,' said the old man. 'Here are you, young and ignorant, and me – sevendy years old, and I might reasonably be forgetting – explaining it all to you short and clear.

'Sevendy,' he said, 'sevendy, and I hear and see – hear better than I see. And reason clearly, and keep myself up to all the happenings of things. Sevendy!

'Life is strange. I was twaindy before Ostrog was a baby. I remember him long before he'd pushed his way to the head of the Wind Vanes Control.[9] I've seen many changes. Eh! I've worn the blue.[10] And at last I've come to see this crush and darkness and tumult and dead men carried by in heaps on the ways. And all his doing! All his doing!'

His voice died away in scarcely articulate praises of Ostrog.

Graham thought. 'Let me see,' he said, 'if I have it right.'

He extended a hand and ticked off points upon his fingers. 'The Sleeper has been asleep —'

'Changed,' said the old man.

'Perhaps. And meanwhile the Sleeper's property grew in the hands of Twelve Trustees, until it swallowed up nearly all the great ownership of the world. The Twelve Trustees – by virtue of this property have become masters of the world. Because they are the paying power – just as the old English Parliament used to be —'

'Eh!' said the old man. 'That's so – that's a good comparison. You're not so —'

'And now this Ostrog – has suddenly revolutionized the world by waking the Sleeper – whom no one but the super- stitious, common people had ever dreamt would wake again –

raising the Sleeper to claim his property from the Council, after all these years.'

The old man endorsed this statement with a cough.

'It's strange,' he said, 'to meet a man who learns these things for the first time tonight.'

'Aye,' said Graham, 'it's strange.'

'Have you been in a Pleasure City?'[11] said the old man. 'All my life I've longed –' He laughed. 'Even now,' he said, 'I could enjoy a little fun. Enjoy seeing things, anyhow.' He mumbled a sentence Graham did not understand.

'The Sleeper – when did he awake?' said Graham suddenly.

'Three days ago.'

'Where is he?'

'Ostrog has him. He escaped from the Council not four hours ago. My dear sir, where were you at the time? He was in the hall of the markets – where the fighting has been. All the city was screaming about it. All the Babble Machines. Everywhere it was shouted. Even the fools who speak for the Council were admitting it. Everyone was rushing off to see him – everyone was getting arms. Were you drunk or asleep? And even then! But you're joking! Surely you're pretending. It was to stop the shouting of the Babble Machines and prevent the people gathering that they turned off the electricity – and put this damned darkness upon us. Do you mean to say—?'

'I had heard the Sleeper was rescued,' said Graham. 'But – to come back a minute. Are you sure Ostrog has him?'

'He won't let him go,' said the old man.

'And the Sleeper. Are you sure he is not genuine? I have never heard—'

'So all the fools think. So they think. As if there wasn't a thousand things that were never heard. I know Ostrog too well for that. Did I tell you? In a way I'm a sort of relation of Ostrog's. A sort of relation. Through my daughter-in-law.'

'I suppose—'

'Well?'

'I suppose there's no chance of this Sleeper asserting himself. I suppose he's certain to be a puppet – in Ostrog's hands or the Council's, as soon as the struggle is over.'

'In Ostrog's hands – certainly. Why shouldn't he be a puppet? Look at his position. Everything done for him, every pleasure possible. Why should he want to assert himself?'

'What are these Pleasure Cities?' said Graham, abruptly.

The old man made him repeat the question. When at last he was assured of Graham's words, he nudged him violently. 'That's *too* much,' said he. 'You're poking fun at an old man. I've been suspecting you know more than you pretend.'

'Perhaps I do,' said Graham. 'But no! why should I go on acting? No, I do not know what a Pleasure City is.'

The old man laughed in an intimate way.

'What is more, I do not know how to read your letters, I do not know what money you use, I do not know what foreign countries there are. I do not know where I am. I cannot count. I do not know where to get food, nor drink, nor shelter.'

'Come, come,' said the old man, 'if you had a glass of drink now, would you put it in your ear or your eye?'

'I want you to tell me all these things.'

'He, he! Well, gentlemen who dress in silk must have their fun.' A withered hand caressed Graham's arm for a moment. 'Silk. Well, well! But, all the same, I wish I was the man who was put up as the Sleeper. He'll have a fine time of it. All the pomp and pleasure. He's a queer-looking face. When they used to let anyone go to see him, I've got tickets and been. The image of the real one, as the photographs show him, this substitute used to be. Yellow. But he'll get fed up. It's a queer world. Think of the luck of it. The luck of it. I expect he'll be sent to Capri.[12] It's the best fun for a greener.'[13]

His cough overtook him again. Then he began mumbling enviously of pleasures and strange delights. 'The luck of it, the luck of it! All my life I've been in London, hoping to get my chance.'

'But you don't know that the Sleeper died,' said Graham, suddenly.

The old man made him repeat his words.

'Men don't live beyond ten dozen. It's not in the order of things,' said the old man. 'I'm not a fool. Fools may believe it, but not me.'

Graham became angry with the old man's assurance. 'Whether you are a fool or not,' he said, 'it happens you are wrong about the Sleeper.'

'Eh?'

'You are wrong about the Sleeper. I haven't told you before, but I will tell you now. You are wrong about the Sleeper.'

'How do you know? I thought you didn't know anything – not even about Pleasure Cities.'

Graham paused.

'You don't know,' said the old man. 'How are you to know? It's very few men —'

'I *am* the Sleeper.'

He had to repeat it.

There was a brief pause. 'There's a silly thing to say, sir, if you'll excuse me. It might get you into trouble in a time like this,' said the old man.

Graham, slightly dashed, repeated his assertion.

'I was saying I was the Sleeper. That years and years ago I did indeed fall asleep in a little stone-built village, in the days when there were hedgerows and villages and inns, and all the countryside cut up into little pieces, little fields. Have you never heard of those days? And it is I – I who speak to you – who awakened again these four days since.'

'Four days since! – the Sleeper! But they've *got* the Sleeper. They have him and they won't let him go. Nonsense! You've been talking sensibly enough up to now. I can see it as though I was there. There will be Lincoln like a keeper just behind him; they won't let him go about alone. Trust them. You're a queer fellow. One of these fun pokers. I see now why you have been clipping your words so oddly, but —'

He stopped abruptly, and Graham could see his gesture.

'As if Ostrog would let the Sleeper run about alone! No, you're telling that to the wrong man altogether. Eh! as if I should believe. What's your game? And besides, we've been talking of the Sleeper.'

Graham stood up. 'Listen,' he said. 'I am the Sleeper.'

'You're an odd man,' said the old man, 'to sit here in the dark, talking clipped, and telling a lie of that sort. But —'

Graham's exasperation fell to laughter. 'It is preposterous,' he cried. 'Preposterous. The dream must end. It gets wilder and wilder. Here am I – in this damned twilight – I never knew a dream in twilight before – an anachronism by two hundred years and trying to persuade an old fool that I am myself, and meanwhile – Ugh!'

He moved in gusty irritation and went striding. In a moment the old man was pursuing him. 'Eh! but don't go!' cried the old man. 'I'm an old fool, I know. Don't go. Don't leave me in all this darkness.'

Graham hesitated, stopped. Suddenly the folly of telling his secret flashed into his mind.

'I didn't mean to offend you – disbelieving you,' said the old man coming near. 'It's no manner of harm. Call yourself the Sleeper if it pleases you. 'Tis a foolish trick—'

Graham hesitated, turned abruptly and went on his way.

For a time he heard the old man's hobbling pursuit and his wheezy cries receding. But at last the darkness swallowed him, and Graham saw him no more.

CHAPTER 12
OSTROG

Graham could now take a clearer view of his position. For a long time yet he wandered, but after the talk of the old man his discovery of this Ostrog was clear in his mind as the final inevitable decision. One thing was evident, those who were at the headquarters of the revolt had succeeded very admirably in suppressing the fact of his disappearance. But every moment he expected to hear the report of his death or of his recapture by the Council.

Presently a man stopped before him. 'Have you heard?' he said.

'No!' said Graham, starting.

'Near a dozand,' said the man, 'a dozand men!' and hurried on.

A number of men and a girl passed in the darkness, gesticulating and shouting: 'Capitulated! Given up!' 'A dozand of men.' 'Two dozand of men.' 'Ostrog, Hurrah! Ostrog, Hurrah!' These cries receded, became indistinct.

Other shouting men followed. For a time his attention was absorbed in the fragments of speech he heard. He had a doubt whether all were speaking English. Scraps floated to him, scraps like pigeon English,[1] like 'nigger' dialect, blurred and mangled distortions. He dared accost no one with questions. The impression the people gave him jarred altogether with his preconceptions of the struggle and confirmed the old man's faith in Ostrog. It was only slowly he could bring himself to believe that all these people were rejoicing at the defeat of the Council, that the Council which had pursued him with such power and vigour was after all the weaker of the two sides in conflict. And if that was so, how did it affect him? Several times he hesitated on the verge of fundamental questions. Once he turned and walked for a long way after a little man of rotund inviting outline, but he was unable to master confidence to address him.

It was only slowly that it came to him that he might ask for the 'wind-vane offices' whatever the 'wind-vane offices' might be. His first inquiry simply resulted in a direction to go on towards Westminster. His second led to the discovery of a short cut in which he was speedily lost. He was told to leave the ways to which he had hitherto confined himself – knowing no other means of transit – and to plunge down one of the middle staircases into the blackness of a cross-way. Thereupon came some trivial adventures; chief of these an ambiguous encounter with a gruff-voiced invisible creature speaking in a strange dialect that seemed at first a strange tongue, a thick flow of speech with the drifting corpses of English words therein, the dialect of the latter-day vile. Then another voice drew near, a girl's voice singing, 'tralala tralala'. She spoke to Graham, her English touched with something of the same quality. She professed to have lost her sister, she blundered needlessly into him he thought, caught hold of him and laughed. But a word of vague remonstrance sent her into the unseen again.

The sounds about him increased. Stumbling people passed him, speaking excitedly. 'They have surrendered!' 'The Council! Surely not the Council!' 'They are saying so in the Ways.' The passage seemed wider. Suddenly the wall fell away. He was in a great space and people were stirring remotely. He inquired his way of an indistinct figure. 'Strike straight across,' said a woman's voice. He left his guiding wall, and in a moment had stumbled against a little table on which were utensils of glass. Graham's eyes, now attuned to darkness, made out a long vista with tables on either side. He went down this. At one or two of the tables he heard a clang of glass and a sound of eating. There were people then cool enough to dine, or daring enough to steal a meal in spite of social convulsion and darkness. Far off and high up he presently saw a pallid light of a semicircular shape. As he approached this, a black edge came up and hid it. He stumbled at steps and found himself in a gallery. He heard a sobbing, and found two scared little girls crouched by a railing. These children became silent at the near sound of feet. He tried to console them, but they were very still until he left them. Then as he receded he could hear them sobbing again.

Presently he found himself at the foot of a staircase and near a wide opening. He saw a dim twilight above this and ascended out of the blackness into a street of moving Ways again. Along this a disorderly swarm of people marched shouting. They were singing snatches of the song of the revolt, most of them out of tune. Here and there torches flared, creating brief hysterical shadows. He asked his way and was twice puzzled by that same thick dialect. His third attempt won an answer he could understand. He was two miles from the wind-vane offices in Westminster, but the way was easy to follow.

When at last he did approach the district of the wind-vane offices it seemed to him, from the cheering processions that came marching along the Ways, from the tumult of rejoicing, and finally from the restoration of the lighting of the city, that the overthrow of the Council must already be accomplished. And still no news of his absence came to his ears.

The re-illumination of the city came with startling abruptness. Suddenly he stood blinking, all about him men halted dazzled, and the world was incandescent. The light found him already upon the outskirts of the excited crowds that choked the Ways near the wind-vane offices, and the sense of visibility and exposure that came with it turned his colourless intention of joining Ostrog to a keen anxiety.

He was jostled, obstructed and endangered by men hoarse and weary with cheering his name, some of them bandaged and bloody in his cause. The frontage of the wind-vane offices was illuminated by some moving picture, but what it was he could not see, because in spite of his strenuous attempts the density of the crowd prevented his approaching it. From the fragments of speech he caught, he judged it conveyed news of the fighting about the Council House. Ignorance and indecision made him slow and ineffective in his movements. For a time he could not conceive how he was to get within the unbroken façade of this place. He made his way into the midst of this mass of people,

until he realized that the descending staircase of the central
Way led to the interior of the buildings. This gave him a goal,
but the crowding in the central path was so dense that it was
long before he could reach it. And even then he encountered
intricate obstruction, and had an hour of vivid argument first
in this guard-room and then in that before he could get a note
taken to the one man of all men who was most eager to see
him. His story was laughed to scorn at one place, and wiser for
that, when at last he reached a second stairway he professed
simply to have news of extraordinary importance for Ostrog.
What it was he would not say. They sent his note reluctantly.
He waited in a little room at the foot of the lift shaft, and thither
at last came Lincoln, eager, apologetic, astonished. He stopped
in the doorway scrutinizing Graham, then rushed forward
effusively.

'Yes,' he cried. 'It is you. And you are not dead!'

'My brother is waiting,' explained Lincoln. 'He is alone in
the wind-vane offices. We feared you had been killed in the
theatre. He doubted – and things are very urgent still in spite
of what we are telling them *there* – or he would have come
to you.'

They ascended a lift, passed along a narrow passage, crossed
a great hall, empty save for two hurrying messengers, and
entered a comparatively little room, whose only furniture was
a long settee and a large oval disc[2] of cloudy, shifting grey,
hung by cables from the wall. There Lincoln left Graham for a
space, and he remained alone without understanding the smoky
shapes that drove slowly across this disc.

His attention was arrested by a sound that began abruptly.
It was cheering, the frantic cheering of a vast but very remote
crowd, a roaring exultation. This ended as sharply as it had
begun, like a sound heard between the opening and shutting of
a door. In the outer room was a noise of hurrying steps and a
melodious clinking as if a loose chain was running over the
teeth of a wheel.

Then he heard the voice of a woman, the rustle of unseen
garments. 'It is Ostrog!' he heard her say. A little bell rang
fitfully, and then everything was still again.

Presently came voices, footsteps and movement without. The footsteps of some one person detached itself from the other sounds, and drew near, firm, evenly measured steps. The curtain lifted slowly. A tall, white-haired man, clad in garments of cream-coloured silk, appeared, regarding Graham from under his raised arm.

For a moment the white form remained holding the curtain, then dropped it and stood before it. Graham's first impression was of a very broad forehead, very pale blue eyes deep sunken under white brows, an aquiline nose, and a heavily lined resolute mouth. The folds of flesh over the eyes, the drooping of the corners of the mouth contradicted the upright bearing, and said the man was old. Graham rose to his feet instinctively, and for a moment the two men stood in silence, regarding each other.

'You are Ostrog?' said Graham.

'I am Ostrog.'

'The Boss?'

'So I am called.'

Graham felt the inconvenience of the silence. 'I have to thank you chiefly, I understand, for my safety,' he said presently.

'We were afraid you were killed,' said Ostrog. 'Or sent to sleep again – for ever. We have been doing everything to keep our secret – the secret of your disappearance. Where have you been? How did you get here?'

Graham told him briefly.

Ostrog listened in silence.

He smiled faintly. 'Do you know what I was doing when they came to tell me you had come?'

'How can I guess?'

'Preparing your double.'

'My double?'

'A man as like you as we could find. We were going to hypnotize him, to save him the difficulty of acting. It was imperative. The whole of this revolt depends on the idea that you are awake, alive, and with us. Even now a great multitude of people has gathered in the theatre clamouring to see you. They do not trust. . . . You know, of course – something of your position?'

'Very little,' said Graham.

'It is like this.' Ostrog walked a pace or two into the room and turned. 'You are absolute owner,' he said, 'of the world. You are King of the Earth. Your powers are limited in many intricate ways, but you are the figurehead, the popular symbol of government. This White Council, the Council of Trustees as it is called—'

'I have heard the vague outline of these things.'

'I wondered.'

'I came upon a garrulous old man.'

'I see . . . Our masses – the word comes from your days – you know, of course, that we still have masses – regard you as our actual ruler. Just as a great number of people in your days regarded the Crown as the ruler. They are discontented – the masses all over the earth – with the rule of your Trustees. For the most part it is the old discontent, the old quarrel of the common man with his commonness – the misery of work and discipline and unfitness. But your Trustees have ruled ill. In certain matters, in the administration of the Labour Companies, for example, they have been unwise. They have given endless opportunities. Already we of the popular party were agitating for reforms – when your waking came. Came! If it had been contrived it could not have come more opportunely.' He smiled. 'The public mind, making no allowance for your years of quiescence, had already hit on the thought of waking you and appealing to you, and – Flash!'

He indicated the outbreak by a gesture, and Graham moved his head to show that he understood.

'The Council muddled – quarrelled. They always do. They could not decide what to do with you. You know how they imprisoned you?'

'I see. I see. And now – we win?'

'We win. Indeed we win. Tonight, in five swift hours. Suddenly we struck everywhere. The wind-vane people, the Labour Company and its millions, burst the bonds. We got the pull of the aeroplanes.'[3]

'Yes,' said Graham.

'That was, of course, essential. Or they could have got away.

All the city rose, every third man almost was in it! All the blue, all the public services, save only just a few aeronauts and about half the red police. You were rescued, and their own police of the Ways – not half of them could be massed at the Council House – have been broken up, disarmed or killed. All London is ours – now. Only the Council House remains.

'Half of those who remain to them of the red police were lost in that foolish attempt to recapture you. They lost their heads when they lost you. They flung all they had at the theatre. We cut them off from the Council House there. Truly tonight has been a night of victory. Everywhere your star has blazed. A day ago – the White Council ruled as it has ruled for a gross of years, for a century and a half of years, and then, with only a little whispering, a covert arming here and there, suddenly – So!'

'I am very ignorant,' said Graham. 'I suppose – I do not clearly understand the conditions of this fighting. If you could explain. Where is the Council? Where is the fight?'

Ostrog stepped across the room, something clicked, and suddenly, save for an oval glow, they were in darkness. For a moment Graham was puzzled.

Then he saw that the cloudy grey disc had taken depth and colour, had assumed the appearance of an oval window looking out upon a strange unfamiliar scene.

At the first glance he was unable to guess what this scene might be. It was a daylight scene, the daylight of a wintry day, grey and clear. Across the picture, and halfway as it seemed between him and the remoter view, a stout cable of twisted white wire stretched vertically. Then he perceived that the rows of great wind-wheels he saw, the wide intervals, the occasional gulfs of darkness, were akin to those through which he had fled from the Council House. He distinguished an orderly file of red figures marching across an open space between files of men in black, and realized before Ostrog spoke that he was looking down on the upper surface of latter-day London. The overnight snows had gone. He judged that this mirror was some modern replacement of the camera obscura, but that matter was not explained to him. He saw that though the file of red figures was trotting from left to right, yet they were passing out of the picture to the left. He wondered momentarily, and then saw that the picture was passing silently, panorama fashion, across the oval.

'In a moment you will see the fighting,' said Ostrog at his elbow. 'Those fellows in red you notice are prisoners. This is the roof space of London – all the houses are practically continuous now. The streets and public squares are covered in. The gaps and chasms of your time have disappeared.'

Something out of focus obliterated half the picture. Its form suggested a man. There was a gleam of metal, a flash, something that swept across the oval, as the eyelid of a bird sweeps across its eye, and the picture was clear again. And now Graham beheld men running down among the wind-wheels, pointing weapons from which jetted out little smoky flashes. They swarmed thicker and thicker to the right, gesticulating – it might be they were shouting, but of that the picture told nothing. They and the wind-wheels passed slowly and steadily across the field of the mirror.

'Now,' said Ostrog, 'comes the Council House,' and a black edge crept into view and gathered Graham's attention. Soon it was no longer an edge but a cavity, a huge blackened space amidst the clustering edifices, and from it thin spires of smoke rose into the pallid winter sky. Gaunt ruinous masses of the building, mighty truncated piers and girders, rose dismally out of this cavernous darkness. And over these vestiges of some splendid place, countless minute men were clambering, leaping, swarming.

'This is the Council House,' said Ostrog. 'Their last stronghold. And the fools wasted enough ammunition to hold out for a month in blowing up the buildings all about them – to stop our attack. You heard the smash? It shattered half the brittle glass in the city.'

And while he spoke, Graham saw that beyond this area of ruins, overhanging it and rising to a great height, was a ragged mass of white building. This mass had been isolated by the ruthless destruction of its surroundings. Black gaps marked the passages the disaster had torn apart; big halls had been slashed open and the decoration of their interiors showed dismally in the wintry dawn, and down the jagged walls hung festoons of divided cables and twisted ends of lines and metallic rods. And amidst all the vast details moved little red specks, the red-clothed defenders of the Council. Every now and then faint flashes illuminated the bleak shadows. At the first sight it seemed to Graham that an attack upon this isolated white building was in progress, but then he perceived that the party of the revolt was not advancing but, sheltered amidst the colossal wreckage that encircled this last ragged stronghold of the red-garbed men, was keeping up a fitful firing.

And not ten hours ago he had stood beneath the ventilating fans in a little chamber within that remote building wondering what was happening in the world!

Looking more attentively as this warlike episode moved silently across the centre of the mirror, Graham saw that the white building was surrounded on every side by ruins, and Ostrog proceeded to describe in concise phrases how its defenders had sought by such destruction to isolate themselves from a storm. He spoke of the loss of men that huge downfall had entailed in an indifferent tone. He indicated an improvised mortuary among the wreckage, showed ambulances swarming like cheese-mites along a ruinous groove that had once been a street of moving ways. He was more interested in pointing out the parts of the Council House, the distribution of the besiegers. In a little while the civil contest that had convulsed London was no longer a mystery to Graham. It was no tumultuous revolt had occurred that night, no equal warfare, but a splendidly organized *coup d'état*. Ostrog's grasp of details was astonishing; he seemed to know the business of even the smallest knot of black and red specks that crawled amidst these places.

He stretched a huge black arm across the luminous picture, and showed the room whence Graham had escaped, and across the chasm of ruins the course of his flight. Graham recognized the gulf across which the gutter ran, and the wind-wheels where he had crouched from the flying machine. The rest of his path had succumbed to the explosion. He looked again at the Council House, and it was already half hidden, and on the right a hillside with a cluster of domes and pinnacles, hazy, dim and distant, was gliding into view.

'And the Council is really overthrown?' he said.

'Overthrown,' said Ostrog.

'And I – Is it indeed true that I—?'

'You are Master of the World.'

'But that white flag—'

'That is the flag of the Council – the flag of the Rule of the World. It will fall. The fight is over. Their attack on the theatre was their last frantic struggle. They have only a thousand men or so, and some of these men will be disloyal. They have little ammunition. And we are reviving the ancient arts. We are casting guns.'

'But – help. Is this city the world?'

'Practically this is all they have left to them of their empire. Abroad the cities have either revolted with us or wait the issue. Your awakening has perplexed them, paralysed them.'

'But haven't the Council flying machines? Why is there no fighting with them?'

'They had. But the greater part of the aeronauts were in the revolt with us. They wouldn't take the risk of fighting on our side, but they would not stir against us. We *had* to get a pull with the aeronauts. Quite half were with us, and the others knew it. Directly they knew you had got away, those looking for you dropped. We killed the man who shot at you – an hour ago. And we occupied the flying stages at the outset in every city we could, and so stopped and captured the greater aeroplanes, and as for the little flying machines that turned out – for some did – we kept up too straight and steady a fire for them to get near the Council House. If they dropped they couldn't rise again, because there's no clear space about there for them to get up. Several we have smashed, several others have dropped and surrendered, the rest have gone off to the Continent to find a friendly city if they can before their fuel runs out. Most of these men were only too glad to be taken prisoner and kept out of harm's way. Upsetting in a flying machine isn't a very attractive prospect. There's no chance for the Council that way. Its days are done.'

He laughed and turned to the oval reflection again to show Graham what he meant by flying stages. Even the four nearer ones were remote and obscured by a thin morning haze. But Graham could perceive they were very vast structures, judged even by the standard of the things about them.

And then as these dim shapes passed to the left there came again the sight of the expanse across which the disarmed men in red had been marching. And then the black ruins, and then again the beleaguered white fastness of the Council. It appeared no longer a ghostly pile, but glowing amber in the sunlight, for a cloud shadow had passed. About it the pigmy struggle still hung in suspense, but now the red defenders were no longer firing.

So, in a dusky stillness, the man from the nineteenth century saw the closing scene of the great revolt, the forcible establishment of his rule. With a quality of startling discovery it came to him that this was his world, and not that other he had left behind; that this was no spectacle to culminate and cease; that in this world lay whatever life was still before him, lay all his duties and dangers and responsibilities. He turned with fresh questions. Ostrog began to answer them, and then broke off abruptly. 'But these things I must explain more fully later. At present there are – things to be done. The people are coming by the moving ways towards this ward from every part of the city – the markets and theatres are densely crowded. You are just in time for them. They are clamouring to see you. And abroad they want to see you. Paris, New York, Chicago, Denver, Capri – thousands of cities are up and in a tumult, undecided, and clamouring to see you. They have clamoured that you should be awakened for years, and now it is done they will scarcely believe—'

'But surely – I can't go . . .'

Ostrog answered from the other side of the room, and the picture on the oval disc paled and vanished as the light jerked back again. 'There are kinetotelephotographs,'[4] he said. 'As you bow to the people here – all over the world myriads of myriads of people, packed and still in darkened halls, will see you also. In black and white, of course – not like this. And you will hear their shouts reinforcing the shouting in the hall.

'And there is an optical contrivance we have,' said Ostrog, 'used by some of the posturers and women dancers. It may be novel to you. You stand in a very bright light, and they see not you but a magnified image of you thrown on a screen – so that even the farthest man in the remotest gallery can, if he chooses, count your eyelashes.'

Graham clutched desperately at one of the questions in his mind. 'What is the population of London?' he said.

'Eight and twaindy myriads.'

'Eight and what?'

'More than thirty-three millions.'

These figures went beyond Graham's imagination.

'You will be expected to say something,' said Ostrog. 'Not what you used to call a Speech, but what our people call a Word – just one sentence, six or seven words. Something formal. If I might suggest – "I have awakened and my heart is with you." That is the sort of thing they want.'

'What was that?' asked Graham.

'"I am awakened and my heart is with you." And bow – bow royally. But first we must get you black robes – for black is your colour. Do you mind? And then they will disperse to their homes.'

Graham hesitated. 'I am in your hands,' he said.

Ostrog was clearly of that opinion. He thought for a moment, turned to the curtain and called brief directions to some unseen attendants. Almost immediately a black robe, the very fellow of the black robe Graham had worn in the theatre, was brought. And as he threw it about his shoulders there came from the room without the shrilling of a high-pitched bell. Ostrog turned in interrogation to the attendant, then suddenly seemed to change his mind, pulled the curtain aside and disappeared.

Graham stood with the deferential attendant listening to Ostrog's retreating steps. There was a sound of quick question and answer and of men running. The curtain was snatched back and Ostrog reappeared, his massive face glowing with excitement. He crossed the room in a stride, clicked the room into darkness, gripped Graham's arm and pointed to the mirror.

'Even as we turned away,' he said.

Graham saw his index finger, black and colossal, above the mirrored Council House. He did not understand immediately. And then he perceived that the flagstaff that had carried the white banner was bare.

'Do you mean – ?' he began.

'The Council has surrendered. Its rule is at an end for evermore.

'Look!' and Ostrog pointed to a coil of black that crept in little jerks up the vacant flagstaff, unfolding as it rose.

The oval picture paled as Lincoln pulled the curtain aside and entered.

'They are clamorous,' he said.

Ostrog kept his grip of Graham's arm.

'We have raised the people,' he said. 'We have given them arms. For today at least their wishes must be law.'

Lincoln held the curtain open for Graham and Ostrog to pass through. . . .

On his way to the markets Graham had a transitory glance of a long narrow white-walled room in which men in the universal blue canvas were carrying covered things like biers, and about which men in medical purple hurried to and fro. From this room came groans and wailing. He had an impression of an empty bloodstained couch, of men on other couches, bandaged and bloodstained. It was just a glimpse from a railed footway and then a buttress hid the place and they were going on towards the markets. . . .

The roar of the multitude was near now: it leapt to thunder. And, arresting his attention, a fluttering of black banners, the waving of blue canvas and brown rags, and the swarming vastness of the theatre near the public markets came into view down a long passage. The picture opened out. He perceived they were entering the great theatre of his first appearance, the great theatre he had last seen as a chequer-work of glare and blackness in his flight from the red police. This time he entered it along a gallery at a level high above the stage. The place was now brilliantly lit again. His eyes sought the gangway up which he had fled, but he could not tell it from among its dozens of fellows; nor could he see anything of the smashed seats, deflated cushions, and such like traces of the fight because of the density of the people. Except the stage the whole place was closely packed. Looking down the effect was a vast area of stippled pink, each dot a still upturned face regarding him. At his appearance with Ostrog the cheering died away, the singing died away, a common interest stilled and unified the disorder. It seemed as though every individual of those myriads was watching him.

CHAPTER 13
THE END OF THE OLD ORDER

So far as Graham was able to judge, it was near midday when the white banner of the Council fell. But some hours had to elapse before it was possible to effect the formal capitulation, and so after he had spoken his 'Word' he retired to his new apartments in the wind-vane offices. The continuous excitement of the last twelve hours had left him inordinately fatigued, even his curiosity was exhausted; for a space he sat inert and passive with open eyes, and for a space he slept. He was roused by two medical attendants, come prepared with stimulants to sustain him through the next occasion. After he had taken their drugs and bathed by their advice in cold water, he felt a rapid return of interest and energy, and was presently able and willing to accompany Ostrog through several miles (as it seemed) of passages, lifts, and slides to the closing scene of the White Council's rule.

The way ran deviously through a maze of buildings. They came at last to a passage that curved about, and showed broadening before him an oblong opening, clouds hot with sunset, and the ragged skyline of the ruinous Council House. A tumult of shouts came drifting up to him. In another moment they had come out high up on the brow of the cliff of torn buildings that overhung the wreckage. The vast area opened to Graham's eyes, none the less strange and wonderful for the remote view he had had of it in the oval mirror.

This rudely amphitheatral space seemed now the better part of a mile to its outer edge. It was gold-lit on the left hand, catching the sunlight, and below and to the right clear and cold in the shadow. Above the shadowy grey Council House that

stood in the midst of it, the great black banner of the surrender
still hung in sluggish folds against the blazing sunset. Severed
rooms, halls and passages gaped strangely, broken masses of
metal projected dismally from the complex wreckage, vast
masses of twisted cable dropped like tangled seaweed, and
from its base came a tumult of innumerable voices, violent
concussions and the sound of trumpets. All about this great
white pile was a ring of desolation; the smashed and blackened
masses, the gaunt foundations and ruinous lumber of the fabric
that had been destroyed by the Council's orders, skeletons of
girders, Titanic masses of wall, forests of stout pillars. Amongst
the sombre wreckage beneath, running water flashed and glis-
tened, and far away across the space, out of the midst of a
vague vast mass of buildings, there thrust the twisted end of a
water-main, two hundred feet in the air, thunderously spouting
a shining cascade. And everywhere great multitudes of people.

Wherever there was space and foothold, people swarmed,
little people, small and minutely clear except where the sunset
touched them to indistinguishable gold. They clambered up
the tottering walls, they clung in wreaths and groups about the
high-standing pillars. They swarmed along the edges of the circle
of ruins. The air was full of their shouting, and they were pressing
and swaying towards the central space.

The upper storeys of the Council House seemed deserted, not
a human being was visible. Only the drooping banner of the
surrender hung heavily against the light. The dead were within
the Council House, or hidden by the swarming people, or
carried away. Graham could see only a few neglected bodies in
gaps and corners of the ruins, and amidst the flowing water.

'Will you let them see you, Sire?' said Ostrog. 'They are very
anxious to see you.'

Graham hesitated, and then walked forward to where the
broken verge of wall dropped sheer. He stood looking down, a
lonely, tall, black figure against the sky.

Very slowly the swarming ruins became aware of him. And
as they did so little bands of black-uniformed men appeared
remotely, thrusting through the crowds towards the Council

House. He saw little black heads become pink, looking at him, saw by that means a wave of recognition sweep across the space. It occurred to him that he should accord them some recognition. He held up his arm, then pointed to the Council House and dropped his hand. The voices below became unanimous, gathered volume, came up to him as multitudinous wavelets of cheering.

The western sky was a pallid bluish green and Jupiter shone high in the south, before the capitulation was accomplished. Above was a slow insensible change, the advance of night serene and beautiful; below was hurry, excitement, conflicting orders, pauses, spasmodic developments of organization, a vast ascending clamour and confusion. Before the Council came out, toiling perspiring men, directed by a conflict of shouts, carried forth hundreds of those who had perished in the hand-to-hand conflict within those long passages and chambers. . . .

Guards in black lined the way that the Council would come and as far as the eye could reach into the hazy blue twilight of the ruins, and swarming now at every possible point in the captured Council House and along the shattered cliff of its circumadjacent[1] buildings, were innumerable people, and their voices, even when they were not cheering, were as the soughing of the sea upon a pebble beach. Ostrog had chosen a huge commanding pile of crushed and overthrown masonry, and on this a stage of timbers and metal girders was being hastily constructed. Its essential parts were complete, but humming and clangorous machinery still glared fitfully in the shadows beneath this temporary edifice.

The stage had a small higher portion on which Graham stood with Ostrog and Lincoln close beside him, a little in advance of a group of minor officers. A broader lower stage surrounded this quarter-deck, and on this were the black-uniformed guards of the revolt armed with the little green weapons whose very names Graham still did not know. Those standing about him perceived that his eyes wandered perpetually from the swarming people in the twilight ruins about him to the darkling mass of the White Council House, whence the Trustees would presently come, and to the gaunt cliffs of ruin that encircled him, and so back to the people. The voices of the crowd swelled to a deafening tumult.

He saw the Councillors first afar off in the glare of one of the temporary lights that marked their path, a little group of white figures in a black archway. In the Council House they had been in darkness. He watched them approaching, drawing nearer past first this blazing electric star and then that; the minatory roar of the crowd over whom their power had lasted for a hundred and fifty years marched along beside them. As they drew still nearer their faces came out weary, white and anxious. He saw them blinking up through the glare about him and Ostrog. He contrasted their strange cold looks in the Hall of Atlas. . . . Presently he could recognize several of them; the man who had rapped the table at Howard, a burly man with a red beard, and one delicate-featured, short, dark man with a peculiarly long skull. He noted that two were whispering together and looking behind him at Ostrog. Next there came a tall, dark and handsome man, walking downcast. Abruptly he glanced up, his eyes touched Graham for a moment, and passed beyond him to Ostrog. The way that had been made for them was so contrived that they had to march past and curve about before they came to the sloping path of planks that ascended to the stage where their surrender was to be made.

'The Master, the Master! God and the Master,' shouted the people. 'To hell with the Council!' Graham looked at their multitudes, receding beyond counting into a shouting haze, and then at Ostrog beside him, white and steadfast and still. His eye went again to the group of White Councillors. And then he looked up at the familiar quiet stars overhead. The marvellous element in his fate was suddenly vivid. Could that be his indeed, that little life in his memory two hundred years gone by – and this as well?

CHAPTER 14
FROM THE CROW'S NEST[1]

And so after strange delays and through an avenue of doubt and battle, this man from the nineteenth century came at last to his position at the head of that complex world.

At first when he rose from the long deep sleep that followed his rescue and the surrender of the Council, he did not recognize his surroundings. By an effort he gained a clue in his mind, and all that had happened came back to him, with a quality of insincerity like a story heard, like something read out of a book. And even before his memories were clear, the exultation of his escape, the wonder of his prominence were back in his mind. He was owner of the world; Master of the Earth. This new great age was in the completest sense his. He no longer hoped to discover his experiences a dream; he became anxious now to convince himself that they were real.

An obsequious valet assisted him to dress under the direction of a dignified chief attendant, a little man whose face proclaimed him Japanese, albeit he spoke English like an Englishman. From the latter he learnt something of the state of affairs. Already the revolution was an accepted fact; already business was being resumed throughout the city. Abroad the downfall of the Council had been received for the most part with delight. Nowhere was the Council popular, and the thousand cities of Western America, after two hundred years still jealous of New York, London, and the East, had risen almost unanimously two days before at the news of Graham's imprisonment. Paris was fighting within itself. The rest of the world hung in suspense.

While he was breaking his fast, the sound of a telephone bell[2] jetted from a corner, and his chief attendant called his attention

to the voice of Ostrog making polite inquiries. Graham interrupted his refreshment to reply. Very shortly Lincoln arrived,
and Graham at once expressed a strong desire to talk to people
and to be shown more of the new life that was opening before
him. Lincoln informed him that in three hours' time a representative gathering of officials and their wives would be held in
the state apartments of the wind-vane Chief. Graham's desire
to traverse the ways of the city was, however, at present impossible, because of the enormous excitement of the people. It was,
however, quite possible for him to take a bird's-eye view of the
city from the crow's nest of the wind-vane keeper. To this
accordingly Graham was conducted by his attendant. Lincoln,
with a graceful compliment to the attendant, apologized for
not accompanying them, on account of the present pressure of
administrative work.

Higher even than the most gigantic wind-wheels hung this
crow's nest, a clear thousand feet above the roofs, a little disc-
shaped speck on a spear of metallic filigree, cable stayed. To its
summit Graham was drawn in a little wire-hung cradle. Halfway down the frail-seeming stem was a light gallery about
which hung a cluster of tubes – minute they looked from above
– rotating slowly on the ring of its outer rail. These were the
specula,[3] *en rapport* with the wind-vane keeper's mirrors, in
one of which Ostrog had shown him the coming of his rule.
His Japanese attendant ascended before him and they spent
nearly an hour asking and answering questions.

It was a day full of the promise and quality of spring. The
touch of the wind warmed. The sky was an intense blue and
the vast expanse of London shone dazzling under the morning
sun. The air was clear of smoke and haze, sweet as the air of a
mountain glen.

Save for the irregular oval of ruins about the House of the
Council and the black flag of the surrender that fluttered there,
the mighty city seen from above showed few signs of the swift
revolution that had, to his imagination, in one night and one
day changed the destinies of the world. A multitude of people
still swarmed over these ruins, and the huge openwork stagings
in the distance from which started in times of peace the service

of aeroplanes to the various great cities of Europe and America, were also black with the victors. Across a narrow way of planking raised on trestles that crossed the ruins a crowd of workmen were busy restoring the connection between the cables and wires of the Council House and the rest of the city, preparatory to the transfer thither of Ostrog's headquarters from the wind-vane buildings.

For the rest the luminous expanse was undisturbed. So vast was its serenity in comparison with the areas of disturbance, that presently Graham, looking beyond them, could almost forget the thousands of men lying out of sight in the artificial glare within the quasi-subterranean labyrinth, dead or dying of their overnight wounds, forget the improvised wards with the hosts of surgeons, nurses, and bearers feverishly busy, forget, indeed, all the wonder, consternation and novelty under the electric lights. Down there in the hidden ways of the anthill he knew that the revolution triumphed, that black everywhere carried the day, black favours, black banners, black festoons across the streets. And out here under the fresh sunlight, beyond the crater of the fight, as if nothing had happened to the earth, the forest of wind-vanes that had grown from one or two while the Council had ruled, roared peacefully upon their incessant duty.

Far away, spiked, jagged and indented by the wind-vanes, the Surrey Hills rose blue and faint; to the north and nearer, the sharp contours of Highgate and Muswell Hill[4] were similarly jagged. And all over the countryside, he knew, on every crest and hill where once the hedges had interlaced, and cottages, churches, inns and farmhouses had nestled among their trees, wind-wheels similar to those he saw and bearing like them vast advertisements, gaunt and distinctive symbols of the new age, cast their whirling shadows and stored incessantly the energy that flowed away incessantly through all the arteries of the city. And underneath these wandered the countless flocks and herds of the British Food Trust,[5] his property, with their lonely guards and keepers.

Not a familiar outline anywhere broke the cluster of gigantic shapes below. St Paul's he knew survived, and many of the old

buildings in Westminster, embedded out of sight, arched over
and covered in among the giant growths of this great age. The
Thames, too, made no fall and gleam of silver to break the
wilderness of the city; the thirsty water mains drank up every
drop of its waters before they reached the walls. Its bed and
estuary, scoured and sunken, was now a canal of sea water,
and a race of grimy bargemen brought the heavy materials
of trade from the Pool[6] thereby beneath the very feet of the
workers. Faint and dim in the eastward between earth and sky
hung the clustering masts of the colossal shipping in the Pool.
For all the heavy traffic, for which there was no need of haste,
came in gigantic sailing ships from the ends of the earth, and
the heavy goods for which there was urgency in mechanical
ships of a smaller swifter sort.

And to the south over the hills came vast aqueducts with
sea water for the sewers, and in three separate directions ran
pallid lines – the roads, stippled with moving grey specks. On
the first occasion that offered he was determined to go out and
see these roads. That would come after the flying ship he was
presently to try. His attendant officer described them as a pair
of gently curving surfaces a hundred yards wide, each one for
the traffic going in one direction, and made of a substance
called Eadhamite – an artificial substance, so far as he could
gather, resembling toughened glass. Along this shot a strange
traffic of narrow rubber-shod vehicles, great single wheels,[7]
two- and four-wheeled vehicles, sweeping along at velocities
of from one to six miles a minute. Railroads had vanished; a
few embankments remained as rust-crowned trenches here and
there. Some few formed the cores of Eadhamite ways.

Among the first things to strike his attention had been the
great fleets of advertisement balloons and kites that receded in
irregular vistas northward and southward along the lines of the
aeroplane journeys. No great aeroplanes were to be seen. Their
passages had ceased, and only one little-seeming monoplane[8]
circled high in the blue distance above the Surrey Hills, an
unimpressive soaring speck.

A thing Graham had already learnt, and which he found very
hard to imagine, was that nearly all the towns in the country

and almost all the villages had disappeared. Here and there only, he understood, a gigantic hotel-like edifice stood amid square miles of some single cultivation and preserved the name of a town – as Bournemouth, Wareham or Swanage. Yet the officer had speedily convinced him how inevitable such a change had been. The old order had dotted the country with farm-houses, and every two or three miles was the ruling landlord's estate, and the place of the inn and cobbler, the grocer's shop and church – the village. Every eight miles or so was the country town, where lawyer, corn merchant, wool-stapler, saddler, veterinary surgeon, doctor, draper, milliner and so forth lived. Every eight miles – simply because that eight-mile marketing journey, four there and back, was as much as was comfortable for the farmer. But directly the railways came into play, and after them the light railways, and all the swift new motor cars that had replaced wagons and horses, and so soon as the high roads began to be made of wood and rubber and Eadhamite and all sorts of elastic durable substances – the necessity of having such frequent market towns disappeared. And the big towns grew. They drew the worker with the gravitational force of seemingly endless work, the employer with their suggestion of an infinite ocean of labour.

And as the standard of comfort rose, as the complexity of the mechanism of living increased, life in the country had become more and more costly, or narrow and impossible. The disappearance of vicar and squire, the extinction of the general practitioner by the city specialist, had robbed the village of its last touch of culture. After telephone, kinematograph and phonograph[9] had replaced newspaper, book, schoolmaster and letter, to live outside the range of the electric cables was to live an isolated savage. In the country were neither means of being clothed nor fed (according to the refined conceptions of the time), no efficient doctors for an emergency, no company and no pursuits.

Moreover, mechanical appliances in agriculture made one engineer the equivalent of thirty labourers. So, inverting the condition of the city clerk in the days when London was scarce inhabitable because of the coaly foulness of its air, the labourers now came to the city and its life and delights at night to leave it again in the morning. The city had swallowed up humanity; man had entered upon a new stage in his development. First had come the nomad, the hunter, then had followed the agriculturist of the agricultural state, whose towns and cities and ports were but the headquarters and markets of the countryside. And now, logical consequence of an epoch of invention, was this huge new aggregation of men.

Such things as these, simple statements of fact though they were to contemporary men, strained Graham's imagination to picture. And when he glanced 'over beyond there' at the strange things that existed on the Continent, it failed him altogether.

He had a vision of city beyond city; cities on great plains, cities beside great rivers, vast cities along the sea margin, cities girdled by snowy mountains. Over a great part of the earth the English tongue was spoken; taken together with its Spanish-American and Hindoo[10] and Negro and 'Pidgin' dialects, it was the everyday language of two-thirds of humanity. On the Continent, save as remote and curious survivals, three other languages alone held sway – German, which reached to Antioch and Genoa and jostled Spanish-English at Cadiz,[11] a Gallicized Russian which met the Indian English in Persia and Kurdistan[12] and the 'Pidgin' English in Pekin,[13] and French still clear and brilliant, the language of lucidity, which shared the Mediterranean with the Indian English and German and reached through a Negro dialect to the Congo.[14]

And everywhere now through the city-set earth, save in the administered 'black belt' territories of the tropics, the same cosmopolitan social organization prevailed, and everywhere from Pole to Equator his property and his responsibilities extended. The whole world was civilized; the whole world dwelt in cities; the whole world was his property. . . .

Out of the dim south-west, glittering and strange, voluptuous, and in some way terrible, shone those Pleasure Cities of which the kinematograph-phonograph and the old man in the street had spoken. Strange places reminiscent of the legendary Sybaris,[15] cities of art and beauty, mercenary art and mercenary beauty, sterile wonderful cities of motion and music, whither repaired all who profited by the fierce, inglorious, economic struggle that went on in the glaring labyrinth below.

Fierce he knew it was. How fierce he could judge from the fact that these latter-day people referred back to the England of the nineteenth century as the figure of an idyllic easy-going life. He turned his eyes to the scene immediately before him again, trying to conceive the big factories of that intricate maze. . . .

CHAPTER 15

PROMINENT PEOPLE

The state apartments of the wind-vane keeper would have astonished Graham had he entered them fresh from his nineteenth-century life, but already he was growing accustomed to the scale of the new time. He came out through one of the now familiar sliding panels upon a plateau of landing at the head of a flight of very broad and gentle steps, with men and women far more brilliantly dressed than any he had hitherto seen, ascending and descending. From this position he looked down a vista of subtle and varied ornament in lustreless white and mauve and purple, spanned by bridges that seemed wrought of porcelain and filigree,[1] and terminating far off in a cloudy mystery of perforated screens.

Glancing upward, he saw tier above tier of ascending galleries with faces looking down upon him. The air was full of the babble of innumerable voices and of a music that descended from above, a gay and exhilarating music whose source he did not discover.

The central aisle was thick with people, but by no means uncomfortably crowded; altogether that assembly must have numbered many thousands. They were brilliantly, even fantastically dressed, the men as fancifully as the women, for the sobering influence of the Puritan conception of dignity upon masculine dress had long since passed away. The hair of the men, too, though it was rarely worn long, was commonly curled in a manner that suggested the barber, and baldness had vanished from the earth. Frizzy straight-cut masses that would have charmed Rossetti[2] abounded, and one gentleman, who was pointed out to Graham under the mysterious title of an 'amorist', wore his hair in two becoming plaits à la Marguerite.[3] The pigtail[4] was in evidence; it would seem that citizens of Manchurian extraction were no longer ashamed of their race. There was little uniformity of fashion apparent in the forms of clothing worn. The more shapely men displayed their symmetry in trunk hose, and here were puffs and slashes, and there a cloak and there a robe. The fashions of the days of Leo the Tenth[5] were perhaps the prevailing influence, but the aesthetic conceptions of the Far East were also patent. Masculine embonpoint,[6] which in Victorian times would have been subjected to the buttoned perils, the ruthless exaggeration of tight-legged, tight-armed evening dress, now formed but the basis of a wealth of dignity and drooping folds. Graceful slenderness abounded also. To Graham, a typically stiff man from a typically stiff period, not only did these men seem altogether too graceful in person, but altogether too expressive in their vividly expressive faces. They gesticulated, they expressed surprise, interest, amusement, above all they expressed the emotions excited in their minds by the ladies about them with astonishing frankness. Even at the first glance it was evident that women were in a great majority.

The ladies in the company of these gentlemen displayed in dress, bearing and manner alike, less emphasis and more intricacy. Some affected a classical simplicity of robing and subtlety of fold, after the fashion of the First French Empire,[7] and flashed conquering arms and shoulders as Graham passed. Others had closely fitting dresses without seam or belt at the waist, sometimes with long folds falling from the shoulders. The delightful confidences of evening dress had not been diminished by the passage of two centuries.

Everyone's movements seemed graceful. Graham remarked to Lincoln that he saw men as Raphael's cartoons[8] walking, and Lincoln told him that the attainment of an appropriate set of gestures was part of every rich person's education. The Master's entry was greeted with a sort of tittering applause, but these people showed their distinguished manners by not crowding upon him nor annoying him by any persistent scrutiny, as he descended the steps towards the floor of the aisle.

He had already learnt from Lincoln that these were the leaders of existing London society; almost every person there that night was either a powerful official or the immediate connection of a powerful official. Many had returned from the European Pleasure Cities expressly to welcome him. The aeronautic authorities, whose defection had played a part in the overthrow of the Council only second to Graham's, were very prominent, and so, too, was the Wind-Vane Control. Amongst others there were several of the more prominent officers of the Food Department; the controller of the European Piggeries had a particularly melancholy and interesting countenance and a daintily cynical manner. A bishop in full canonicals passed athwart Graham's vision, conversing with a gentleman dressed exactly like the traditional Chaucer,[9] including even the laurel wreath.

'Who is that?' he asked almost involuntarily.

'The Bishop of London,' said Lincoln.

'No – the other, I mean.'

'Poet Laureate.'

'You still—?'

'He doesn't make poetry, of course. He's a cousin of Wotton – one of the Councillors. But he's one of the Red Rose[10] Royalists – a delightful club – and they keep up the tradition of these things.'

'Asano[11] told me there was a King.'

'The King doesn't belong. They had to expel him. It's the Stuart blood,[12] I suppose; but really—'

'Too much?'

'Far too much.'

Graham did not quite follow all this, but it seemed part of the general inversion of the new age. He bowed condescendingly to his first introduction. It was evident that subtle distinctions of class prevailed even in this assembly, that only to a small proportion of the guests, to an inner group, did Lincoln consider it appropriate to introduce him. This first introduction was the Master Aeronaut, a man whose sun-tanned face contrasted oddly with the delicate complexions about him. Just at present his critical defection from the Council made him a very important person indeed.

His manner contrasted favourably, according to Graham's ideas, with the general bearing. He offered a few commonplace remarks, assurances of loyalty and frank enquiries about the Master's health. His manner was breezy, his accent lacked the easy staccato of latter-day English. He made it admirably clear to Graham that he was a bluff 'aerial dog'[13] – he used that phrase – that there was no nonsense about him, that he was a thoroughly manly fellow and old-fashioned at that, that he didn't profess to know much, and that what he did not know was not worth knowing. He made a curt bow, ostentatiously free from obsequiousness, and passed.

'I am glad to see that type endures,' said Graham.

'Phonographs and kinematographs,' said Lincoln, a little spitefully. 'He has studied from the life.' Graham glanced at the burly form again. It was oddly reminiscent.

'As a matter of fact we bought him,' said Lincoln. 'Partly. And partly he was afraid of Ostrog. Everything rested with him.'

He turned sharply to introduce the Surveyor-General of the Public Schools.[14] This person was a willowy figure in a blue-grey academic gown, he beamed down upon Graham through *pince-nez*[15] of a Victorian pattern, and illustrated his remarks by gestures of a beautifully manicured hand. Graham was immediately interested in this gentleman's functions, and asked him a number of singularly direct questions. The Surveyor-General seemed quietly amused at the Master's fundamental bluntness. He was a little vague as to the monopoly of education his Company possessed; it was done by contract with the syndicate that ran the numerous London Municipalities, but he waxed enthusiastic over educational progress since the Victorian times. 'We have conquered Cram,'[16] he said, 'completely conquered Cram – there is not an examination left in the world. Aren't you glad?'

'How do you get the work done?' asked Graham.

'We make it attractive – as attractive as possible. And if it does not attract then – we let it go. We cover an immense field.'

He proceeded to details, and they had a lengthy conversation. Graham learnt that University Extension[17] still existed in a modified form. 'There is a certain type of girl, for example,' said the Surveyor-General, dilating with a sense of his usefulness, 'with a perfect passion for severe studies – when they are not too difficult, you know. We cater for them by the thousand. At this moment,' he said with a Napoleonic touch, 'nearly five hundred phonographs are lecturing in different parts of London on the influence exercised by Plato and Swift on the love affairs of Shelley, Hazlitt and Burns.[18] And afterwards they write essays on the lectures, and their names in order of merit are put in conspicuous places. You see how your little germ has grown? The illiterate middle-class of your days has quite passed away.'

'About the public elementary schools,' said Graham. 'Do you control them?'

The Surveyor-General did, 'entirely'. Now Graham in his later democratic days had taken a keen interest in these, and his questioning quickened. Certain casual phrases that had fallen from the old man with whom he had talked in the darkness recurred to him. The Surveyor-General in effect endorsed the old man's words. 'We try and make the elementary schools pleasant for the little children. They will have to work so soon. Just a few simple principles – obedience – industry.'

'You teach them very little?'

'Why should we? It only leads to trouble and discontent. We amuse them. Even as it is – there are troubles – agitations. Where the labourers get the ideas, one cannot tell. They tell one another. There are socialistic dreams – anarchy even! Agitators *will* get to work among them. I take it – I have always taken it – that my foremost duty is to fight against popular discontent. Why should people be made unhappy?'

'I wonder,' said Graham thoughtfully. 'But there are a great many things I want to know.'

Lincoln, who had stood watching Graham's face throughout the conversation, intervened. 'There are others,' he said in an undertone.

The Surveyor-General of Schools gesticulated himself away. 'Perhaps,' said Lincoln, intercepting a casual glance, 'you would like to know some of these ladies?'

The daughter of the Manager of the Piggeries was a particularly charming little person with red hair and animated blue eyes. Lincoln left him a while to converse with her, and she displayed herself as quite an enthusiast for the 'dear old days', as she called them, that had seen the beginning of his trance. As she talked she smiled, and her eyes smiled in a manner that demanded reciprocity.

'I have tried,' she said, 'countless times – to imagine those old romantic days. And to you – they are memories. How strange and crowded the world must seem to you! I have seen photographs and pictures of the past, the little isolated houses built of bricks made out of burnt mud and all black with soot from your fires, the railway bridges, the simple advertisements, the solemn savage Puritanical men in strange black coats and those tall hats of theirs, iron railway trains on iron bridges overhead, horses and cattle, and even dogs running half wild about the streets. And suddenly, you have come into this!'

'Into this,' said Graham.

'Out of your life – out of all that was familiar.'

'The old life was not a happy one,' said Graham. 'I do not regret that.'

She looked at him quickly. There was a brief pause. She sighed encouragingly. 'No?'

'No,' said Graham. 'It was a little life – and unmeaning. But this – We thought the world complex and crowded and civilized enough. Yet I see – although in this world I am barely four days old – looking back on my own time, that it was a queer, barbaric time – the mere beginning of this new order. The mere beginning of this new order. You will find it hard to understand how little I know.'

'You may ask me what you like,' she said, smiling at him.

'Then tell me who these people are. I'm still very much in the dark about them. It's puzzling. Are there any Generals?'

'Men in hats and feathers?'

'Of course not. No. I suppose they are the men who control the great public businesses. Who is that distinguished-looking man?'

'That? He's a most important officer. That is Morden. He is managing director of the Antibilious Pill Department.[19] I have heard that his workers sometimes turn out a myriad myriad pills a day in the twenty-four hours. Fancy a myriad myriad!'

'A myriad myriad. No wonder he looks proud,' said Graham. 'Pills! What a wonderful time it is! That man in purple?'

'He is not quite one of the inner circle, you know. But we like him. He is really clever and very amusing. He is one of the heads of the Medical Faculty of our London University. All medical men, you know, wear that purple. But of course people who are paid by fees for *doing* something –' She smiled away the social pretensions of all such people.

'Are any of your great artists or authors here?'

'No authors. They are mostly such queer people – and so preoccupied about themselves. And they quarrel so dreadfully! They will fight, some of them, for precedence on staircases! Dreadful, isn't it? But I think Wraysbury, the fashionable capillotomist, is here. From Capri.'

'Capillotomist,' said Graham. 'Ah! I remember. An artist! Why not?'

'We have to cultivate him,' she said apologetically. 'Our heads are in his hands.' She smiled.

Graham hesitated at the invited compliment, but his glance was expressive. 'Have the arts grown with the rest of civilized things?' he said. 'Who are your great painters?'

She looked at him doubtfully. Then laughed. 'For a moment,' she said, 'I thought you meant –' She laughed again. 'You mean, of course, those good men you used to think so much of because they could cover great spaces of canvas with oil-colours? Great oblongs. And people used to put the things in gilt frames and hang them up in rows in their square rooms. We haven't any. People grew tired of that sort of thing.'

'But what did you think I meant?'

She put a finger significantly on a cheek whose glow was above suspicion, and smiled and looked very arch and pretty and inviting. 'And here,' and she indicated her eyelid.

Graham had an adventurous moment. Then a grotesque memory of a picture he had somewhere seen of Uncle Toby and the Widow[20] flashed across his mind. An archaic shame came upon him. He became acutely aware that he was visible to a great number of interested people. 'I see,' he remarked inadequately. He turned awkwardly away from her fascinating facility. He looked about him to meet a number of eyes that immediately occupied themselves with other things. Possibly he coloured a little. 'Who is that talking with the lady in saffron?' he asked, avoiding her eyes.

The person in question he learnt was one of the great organizers of the American theatres just fresh from a gigantic production in Mexico. His face reminded Graham of a bust of Caligula.[21] Another striking-looking man was the Black Labour Master.[22] The phrase at the time made no deep impression, but afterwards it recurred; – the Black Labour Master? The little lady, in no degree embarrassed, pointed out to him a charming little woman as one of the subsidiary wives of the Anglican Bishop of London. She added encomiums on the episcopal courage – hitherto there had been a rule of clerical monogamy[23] – 'neither a natural nor an expedient condition of things. Why should the natural development of the affections be dwarfed and restricted because a man is a priest?

'And by-the-by,' she added, 'are you an Anglican?' Graham was on the verge of hesitating enquiries about the status of a 'subsidiary wife', apparently an euphemistic phrase, when Lincoln's return broke off this very suggestive and interesting conversation. They crossed the aisle to where a tall man in crimson and two charming persons in Burmese costume (as it seemed to him) awaited him diffidently. From their civilities he passed to other presentations.

In a little while his multitudinous impressions began to organize themselves into a general effect. At first the glitter of the gathering had raised all the democrat in Graham; he had felt hostile and satirical. But it is not in human nature to resist an atmosphere of courteous regard. Soon the music, the light, the play of colours, the shining arms and shoulders about him, the touch of hands, the transient interest of smiling faces, the frothing sound of skilfully modulated voices, the atmosphere of compliment, interest and respect, had woven together into a fabric of indisputable pleasure. Graham for a time forgot his spacious resolutions. He gave way insensibly to the intoxication of the position that was conceded him, his manner became more convincingly regal, his feet walked assuredly, the black robe fell with a bolder fold and pride ennobled his voice. After all, this was a brilliant, interesting world.

He looked up and saw passing across a bridge of porcelain and looking down upon him, a face that was almost immediately hidden, the face of the girl he had seen overnight in the little room beyond the theatre after his escape from the Council. And she was watching him.

For the moment he did not remember where he had seen her, and then came a vague memory of the stirring emotions of their first encounter. But the dancing web of melody about him kept the air of that great marching song from his memory.

The lady to whom he talked repeated her remark, and Graham recalled himself to the quasi-regal flirtation upon which he was engaged.

Yet unaccountably a vague restlessness, a feeling that grew to dissatisfaction, came into his mind. He was troubled as if by some half-forgotten duty, by the sense of things important slipping from him amidst this light and brilliance. The attraction that these ladies who crowded about him were beginning to exercise ceased. He no longer gave vague and clumsy responses to the subtly amorous advances that he was now assured were being made to him, and his eyes wandered for another sight of the girl of the first revolt.

Where precisely had he seen her? . . .

Graham was in one of the upper galleries in conversation with a bright-eyed lady on the subject of Eadhamite – the subject was his choice and not hers. He had interrupted her warm assurances of personal devotion with a matter-of-fact inquiry. He found her, as he had already found several other latter-day women that night, less well informed than charming. Suddenly, struggling against the eddying drift of nearer melody, the song of the Revolt, the great song he had heard in the Hall, hoarse and massive, came beating down to him.

Ah! Now he remembered!

He glanced up startled, and perceived above him an *œil de bœuf*[24] through which this song had come, and beyond, the upper courses of cable, the blue haze, and the pendant fabric of the lights of the public ways. He heard the song break into a tumult of voices and cease. He perceived quite clearly the drone and tumult of the moving platforms and a murmur of many people. He had a vague persuasion that he could not account for, a sort of instinctive feeling that outside in the ways a huge crowd must be watching this place in which their Master amused himself.

Though the song had stopped so abruptly, though the special music of this gathering reasserted itself, the *motif* of the marching song, once it had begun, lingered in his mind.

The bright-eyed lady was still struggling with the mysteries of Eadhamite when he perceived the girl he had seen in the theatre again. She was coming now along the gallery towards him; he saw her first before she saw him. She was dressed in a faintly luminous grey, her dark hair about her brows was like a cloud, and as he saw her the cold light from the circular opening into the ways fell upon her downcast face.

The lady in trouble about the Eadhamite saw the change in his expression, and grasped her opportunity to escape. 'Would you care to know that girl, Sire?' she asked boldly. 'She is Helen Wotton – a niece of Ostrog's. She knows a great many serious things. She is one of the most serious persons alive. I am sure you will like her.'

In another moment Graham was talking to the girl, and the bright-eyed lady had fluttered away.

'I remember you quite well,' said Graham. 'You were in that little room. When all the people were singing and beating time with their feet. Before I walked across the Hall.'

Her momentary embarrassment passed. She looked up at him, and her face was steady. 'It was wonderful,' she said, hesitated, and spoke with a sudden effort. 'All those people would have died for you, Sire. Countless people did die for you that night.'

Her face glowed. She glanced swiftly aside to see that no other heard her words.

Lincoln appeared some way off along the gallery, making his way through the press towards them. She saw him and turned to Graham strangely eager, with a swift change to confidence and intimacy. 'Sire,' she said quickly, 'I cannot tell you now and here. But the common people are very unhappy; they are oppressed – they are misgoverned. Do not forget the people, who faced death – death that you might live.'

'I know nothing –' began Graham.

'I cannot tell you now.'

Lincoln's face appeared close to them. He bowed an apology to the girl.

'You find the new world amusing, Sire?' asked Lincoln with smiling deference, and indicating the space and splendour of the gathering by one comprehensive gesture. 'At any rate, you find it changed.'

'Yes,' said Graham, 'changed. And yet, after all, not so greatly changed.'

'Wait till you are in the air,' said Lincoln. 'The wind has fallen; even now an aeroplane awaits you.'

The girl's attitude awaited dismissal.

Graham glanced at her face, was on the verge of a question, found a warning in her expression, bowed to her and turned to accompany Lincoln.

CHAPTER 16
THE MONOPLANE

The Flying Stages of London were collected together in an irregular crescent on the southern side of the river. They formed three groups of two each and retained the names of ancient suburban hills or villages. They were named in order, Roehampton, Wimbledon Park, Streatham, Norwood, Blackheath and Shooter's Hill. They were uniform structures rising high above the general roof surfaces. Each was about four thousand yards long and a thousand broad, and constructed of the compound of aluminium and iron that had replaced iron in architecture. Their higher tiers formed an openwork of girders through which lifts and staircases ascended. The upper surface was a uniform expanse, with portions – the starting carriers – that could be raised and were then able to run on very slightly inclined rails to the end of the fabric.

Graham went to the flying stages by the public ways. He was accompanied by Asano, his Japanese attendant. Lincoln was called away by Ostrog, who was busy with his administrative concerns. A strong guard of the wind-vane police awaited the Master outside the wind-vane offices, and they cleared a space for him on the upper moving platform. His passage to the flying stages was unexpected, nevertheless a considerable crowd gathered and followed him to his destination. As he went along, he could hear the people shouting his name, and saw numberless men and women and children in blue come swarming up the staircases in the central path, gesticulating and shouting. He could not hear what they shouted. He was struck again by the evident existence of a vulgar dialect among the poor of the city. When at last he descended, his guards were immediately surrounded by a dense excited crowd. Afterwards it occurred to him that some had attempted to reach him with petitions. His guards cleared a passage for him with difficulty.

He found a monoplane in charge of an aeronaut awaiting him on the westward stage. Seen close this mechanism was no longer small. As it lay on its launching carrier upon the wide expanse of the flying stage, its aluminium body skeleton[1] was as big as the hull of a twenty-ton yacht. Its lateral supporting sails, braced and stayed with metal nerves almost like the nerves of a bee's wing and made of some sort of glassy artificial membrane, cast their shadow over many hundreds of square yards. The chairs for the engineer and his passenger hung free to swing by a complex tackle within the protecting ribs of the frame and well abaft the middle. The passenger's chair was protected by a windguard and guarded about with metallic rods carrying air cushions. It could, if desired, be completely closed in, but Graham was anxious for novel experiences and desired that it should be left open. The aeronaut sat behind a glass that sheltered his face. The passenger could secure himself firmly in his seat, and this was almost unavoidable on landing, or he could move along by means of a little rail and rod to a locker at the stem of the machine where his personal luggage, his wraps and restoratives were placed, and which also with the seats, served as a makeweight to the parts of the central engine that projected to the propeller at the stern.

The flying stage about him was empty save for Asano and their suite of attendants. Directed by the aeronaut he placed himself in his seat. Asano stepped through the bars of the hull, and stood below on the stage waving his hand. He seemed to slide along the stage to the right and vanish.

The engine was humming loudly, the propeller spinning, and for a second the stage and the buildings beyond were gliding swiftly and horizontally past Graham's eye; then these things seemed to tilt up abruptly. He gripped the little rods on either side of him instinctively. He felt himself moving upward, heard the air whistle over the top of the windscreen. The propeller screw moved round with powerful rhythmic impulses – one, two, three, pause; one, two, three – which the engineer controlled very delicately. The machine began a quivering vibration that continued throughout the flight, and the roof areas seemed running away to starboard very quickly and growing rapidly smaller. He looked from the face of the engineer through the ribs of the machine. Looking sideways, there was nothing very startling in what he saw – a rapid funicular railway[2] might have given the same sensations. He recognized the Council House and the Highgate Ridge. And then he looked straight down between his feet.

Physical terror possessed him, a passionate sense of insecurity. He held tight. For a second or so he could not lift his eyes. Some hundred feet or more sheer below him was one of the big wind-vanes of south-west London, and beyond it the southernmost flying stage crowded with little black dots. These things seemed to be falling away from him. For a second he had an impulse to pursue the earth. He set his teeth, he lifted his eyes by a muscular effort, and the moment of panic passed.

He remained with his teeth set hard, his eyes staring into the sky. Throb, throb, throb – beat, went the engine; throb, throb, throb – beat. He gripped his bars tightly, glanced at the aeronaut, and saw a smile upon his sun-tanned face. He smiled in return – perhaps a little artificially. 'A little strange at first,' he shouted before he recalled his dignity. But he dared not look down again for some time. He stared over the aeronaut's head to where a rim of vague blue horizon crept up the sky. He could not banish the thought of possible accidents from his mind. Throb, throb, throb – beat; suppose some trivial screw went wrong in that supporting engine! Suppose –! He made a grim effort to dismiss all such suppositions. He did at least drive them from the foreground of his thoughts. And up he went steadily, higher and higher into the clear air.

Once the mental shock of moving unsupported through the air was over, his sensations ceased to be unpleasant, became very speedily pleasurable. He had been warned of air sickness. But he found the pulsating movement of the monoplane as it drove up the faint south-west breeze was very little in excess of the pitching of a boat head on to broad rollers in a moderate gale, and he was constitutionally a good sailor. And the keenness of the more rarefied air into which they ascended produced a sense of lightness and exhilaration. He looked up and saw the blue sky above fretted with cirrus clouds. His eye came cautiously down through the ribs and bars to a shining flight of white birds that hung in the lower sky. Then going lower and less apprehensively, he saw the slender figure of the wind-vane keeper's crow's nest shining golden in the sunlight and growing smaller every moment. As his eye fell with more confidence now, there came a blue line of hills, and then London, already to leeward, an intricate space of roofing. Its near edge came sharp and clear, and banished his last apprehensions in a shock of surprise. For the boundary of London was like a wall, like a cliff, a steep fall of three or four hundred feet, a frontage broken only by terraces here and there, a complex decorative façade.

That gradual passage of town into country through an extensive sponge of suburbs, which was so characteristic a feature of the great cities of the nineteenth century, existed no longer. Nothing remained of it here but a waste of ruins, variegated and dense with thickets of the heterogeneous growths that had once adorned the gardens of the belt, interspersed among levelled brown patches of sown ground, and verdant stretches of winter greens. The latter even spread among the vestiges of houses. But for the most part the reefs and skerries[3] of ruins, the wreckage of suburban villas, stood among their streets and roads, queer islands amidst the levelled expanses of green and brown, abandoned indeed by the inhabitants years since, but too substantial, it seemed, to be cleared out of the way of the wholesale horticultural mechanisms of the time.

The vegetation of this waste undulated and frothed amidst the countless cells of crumbling house walls, and broke along the foot of the city wall in a surf of bramble and holly and ivy and teazle and tall grasses. Here and there gaudy pleasure palaces towered amidst the puny remains of Victorian times, and cable ways slanted to them from the city. That winter day they seemed deserted. Deserted, too, were the artificial gardens among the ruins. The city limits were indeed as sharply defined as in the ancient days when the gates were shut at nightfall and the robber foeman prowled to the very walls. A huge semi-circular throat poured out a vigorous traffic upon the Eadhamite Bath Road.[4] So the first prospect of the world beyond the city flashed on Graham, and dwindled. And when at last he could look vertically downward again, he saw below him the vegetable fields of the Thames valley – innumerable minute oblongs of ruddy brown, intersected by shining threads, the sewage ditches.

His exhilaration increased rapidly, became a sort of intoxication. He found himself drawing deep breaths of air, laughing aloud, desiring to shout. That desire became too strong for him, and he shouted. They curved about towards the south. They drove with a slight list to leeward, and with a slow alternation of movement, first a short, sharp ascent and then a long downward glide that was very swift and pleasing. During these downward glides the propeller was inactive altogether. These ascents gave Graham a glorious sense of successful effort; the descents through the rarefied air were beyond all experience. He wanted never to leave the upper air again.

For a time he was intent upon the landscape that ran swiftly northward beneath him. Its minute, clear detail pleased him exceedingly. He was impressed by the ruin of the houses that had once dotted the country, by the vast treeless expanse of country from which all farms and villages had gone, save for crumbling ruins. He had known the thing was so, but seeing it so was an altogether different matter. He tried to make out familiar places within the hollow basin of the world below, but at first he could distinguish no data now that the Thames valley was left behind. Soon, however, they were driving over a sharp chalk hill that he recognized as the Guildford Hog's Back, because of the familiar outline of the gorge at its eastward end, and because of the ruins of the town that rose steeply on either lip of this gorge. And from that he made out other points, Leith Hill, the sandy wastes of Aldershot, and so forth. Save where the broad Eadhamite Portsmouth Road, thickly dotted with rushing shapes, followed the course of the old railway, the gorge of the Wey was choked with thickets.

The whole expanse of the Downs escarpment, so far as the grey haze permitted him to see, was set with wind-wheels to which the largest of the city was but a younger brother. They stirred with a stately motion before the south-west wind. And here and there were patches dotted with the sheep of the British Food Trust, and here and there a mounted shepherd made a spot of black. Then rushing under the stern of the monoplane came the Wealden Heights, the line of Hindhead, Pitch Hill and Leith Hill, with a second row of wind-wheels that seemed striving to rob the downland whirlers of their share of breeze. The purple heather was speckled with yellow gorse, and on the further side a drove of black oxen stampeded before a couple of mounted men. Swiftly these swept behind, and dwindled and lost colour, and became scarce moving specks that were swallowed up in haze.

And when these had vanished in the distance Graham heard a peewit[5] wailing close at hand. He perceived he was now above the South Downs, and staring over his shoulder saw the battlements of Portsmouth Landing Stage towering over the ridge of Portsdown Hill. In another moment there came into sight a spread of shipping like floating cities, the little white cliffs of the Needles dwarfed and sunlit, and the grey and glittering waters of the narrow sea. They seemed to leap the Solent in a moment, and in a few seconds the Isle of Wight was running past; and then beneath him spread a wider and wider extent of sea, here purple with the shadow of a cloud, here grey, here a burnished mirror, and here a spread of cloudy greenish blue. The Isle of Wight grew smaller and smaller. In a few more minutes a strip of grey haze detached itself from other strips that were clouds, descended out of the sky and became a coastline – sunlit and pleasant – the coast of northern France. It rose, it took colour, became definite and detailed, and the counterpart of the Downland of England was speeding by below.

In a little time, as it seemed, Paris came above the horizon, and hung there for a space, and sank out of sight again as the monoplane circled about to the north. But he perceived the Eiffel Tower[6] still standing, and beside it a huge dome surmounted by a pinpoint Colossus. And he perceived, too, though he did not understand it at the time, a slanting drift of smoke.

The aeronaut said something about 'trouble in the underways', that Graham did not heed. But he marked the minarets and towers and slender masses that streamed skyward above the city wind-vanes, and knew that in the matter of grace at least Paris still kept in front of her larger rival. And even as he looked a pale-blue shape ascended very swiftly from the city like a dead leaf driving up before a gale. It curved round and soared towards them, growing rapidly larger and larger. The aeronaut was saying something. 'What?' said Graham, loth to take his eyes from this. 'London aeroplane, Sire,' bawled the aeronaut, pointing.

They rose and curved about northward as it drew nearer. Nearer it came and nearer, larger and larger. The throb, throb, throb – beat, of the monoplane's flight, that had seemed so potent and so swift, suddenly appeared slow by comparison with this tremendous rush. How great the monster seemed, how swift and steady! It passed quite closely beneath them, driving along silently, a vast spread of wire-netted translucent wings, a thing alive. Graham had a momentary glimpse of the rows and rows of wrapped-up passengers, slung in their little cradles behind windscreens, of a white-clothed engineer crawling against the gale along a ladder way, of spouting engines beating together, of the whirling wind-screw,[7] and of a wide waste of wing. He exulted in the sight. And in an instant the thing had passed.

It rose slightly and their own little wings swayed in the rush of its flight. It fell and grew smaller. Scarcely had they moved, as it seemed, before it was again only a flat blue thing that dwindled in the sky. This was the aeroplane that went to and fro between London and Paris. In fair weather and in peaceful times it came and went four times a day.

They beat across the Channel, slowly as it seemed now to Graham's enlarged ideas, and Beachy Head rose greyly to the left of them.

'Land,' called the aeronaut, his voice small against the whistling of the air over the windscreen.

'Not yet,' bawled Graham, laughing. 'Not land yet. I want to learn more of this machine.'

'I meant –' said the aeronaut.

'I want to learn more of this machine,' repeated Graham.

'I'm coming to you,' he said, and had flung himself free of his chair and taken a step along the guarded rail between them. He stopped for a moment, and his colour changed and his hands tightened. Another step and he was clinging close to the aeronaut. He felt a weight on his shoulder, the pressure of the air. His hat was a whirling speck behind. The wind came in gusts over his windscreen and blew his hair in streamers past his cheek. The aeronaut made some hasty adjustments for the shifting of the centres of gravity and pressure.

'I want to have these things explained,' said Graham. 'What do you do when you move that engine forward?'

The aeronaut hesitated. Then he answered, 'They are complex, Sire.'

'I don't mind,' shouted Graham. 'I don't mind.'

There was a moment's pause. 'Aeronautics is the secret – the privilege—'[8]

'I know. But I'm the Master, and I mean to know.' He laughed, full of this novel realization of power that was his gift from the upper air.

The monoplane curved about, and the keen fresh wind cut across Graham's face and his garment lugged at his body as the stem pointed round to the west. The two men looked into each other's eyes.

'Sire, there are rules—'

'Not where I am concerned,' said Graham. 'You seem to forget.'

The aeronaut scrutinized his face. 'No,' he said. 'I do not forget, Sire. But in all the earth – no man who is not a sworn aeronaut – has ever a chance. They come as passengers—'

'I have heard something of the sort. But I'm not going to argue these points. Do you know why I have slept two hundred years? To fly!'

'Sire,' said the aeronaut, 'the rules – if I break the rules—'

Graham waved the penalties aside.

'Then if you will watch me—'

'No,' said Graham, swaying and gripping tight as the machine lifted its nose again for an ascent. 'That's not my game. I want to do it myself. Do it myself if I smash for it! No! I will. See I am going to clamber by this – to come and share your seat. Steady! I mean to fly of my own accord if I smash at the end of it. I will have something to pay for my sleep. Of all other things – In my past it was my dream to fly. Now – keep your balance.'

'A dozen spies are watching me, Sire!'

Graham's temper was at end. Perhaps he chose it should be. He swore. He swung himself round the intervening mass of levers and the monoplane swayed.

'Am I Master of the Earth?' he said. 'Or is your Society? Now. Take your hands off those levers, and hold my wrists. Yes – so. And now, how do we turn her nose down to the glide?'

'Sire,' said the aeronaut.

'What is it?'

'You will protect me?'

'Lord! Yes! If I have to burn London. Now!'

And with that promise Graham bought his first lesson in aerial navigation. 'It's clearly to your advantage, this journey,' he said with a loud laugh – for the air was like strong wine – 'to teach me quickly and well. Do I pull this? Ah! So! Hullo!'

'Back, Sire! Back!'

'Back – right. One – two – three – good God! Ah! Up she goes! But this is living!'

And now the machine began to dance the strangest figures in the air. Now it would sweep round a spiral of scarcely a hundred yards diameter, now rush up into the air and swoop down again, steeply, swiftly, falling like a hawk, to recover in a rushing loop that swept it high again. In one of these descents it seemed driving straight at the drifting park of balloons in the south-east, and only curved about and cleared them by a sudden recovery of dexterity. The extraordinary swiftness and smoothness of the motion, the extraordinary effect of the rarefied air upon his constitution, threw Graham into a careless fury.

But at last a queer incident came to sober him, to send him flying down once more to the crowded life below with all its dark insoluble riddles. As he swooped, came a tap and something flying past, and a drop like a drop of rain. Then as he went on down he saw something like a white rag whirling down in his wake. 'What was that?' he asked. 'I did not see.'

The aeronaut glanced, and then clutched at the lever to recover, for they were sweeping down. When the monoplane was rising again he drew a deep breath and replied, 'That,' and he indicated the white thing still fluttering down, 'was a swan.'

'I never saw it,' said Graham.

The aeronaut made no answer, and Graham saw little drops upon his forehead.

They drove horizontally while Graham clambered back to the passenger's place out of the lash of the wind. And then came a swift rush down, with the wind-screw whirling to check their fall, and the flying stage growing broad and dark before them. The sun, sinking over the chalk hills in the west, fell with them, and left the sky a blaze of gold.

Soon men could be seen as little specks. He heard a noise coming up to meet him, a noise like the sound of waves upon a pebbly beach, and saw that the roofs about the flying stage were dense with his people rejoicing over his safe return. A black mass was crushed together under the stage, a darkness stippled with innumerable faces, and quivering with the minute oscillation of waved white handkerchiefs and waving hands.

CHAPTER 17
THREE DAYS

Lincoln awaited Graham in an apartment beneath the flying stages. He seemed curious to learn all that had happened, pleased to hear of the extraordinary delight and interest which Graham took in flying. Graham was in a mood of enthusiasm. 'I must learn to fly,' he cried. 'I must master that. I pity all poor souls who have died without this opportunity. The sweet swift air! It is the most wonderful experience in the world.'

'You will find our new times full of wonderful experiences,' said Lincoln. 'I do not know what you will care to do now. We have music that may seem novel.'

'For the present,' said Graham, 'flying holds me. Let me learn more of that. Your aeronaut was saying there is some trades union objection to one's learning.'

'There is, I believe,' said Lincoln. 'But for you – ! If you would like to occupy yourself with that, we can make you a sworn aeronaut tomorrow.'

Graham expressed his wishes vividly and talked of his sensations for a while. 'And as for affairs,' he asked abruptly. 'How are things going on?'

Lincoln waved affairs aside. 'Ostrog will tell you that tomorrow,' he said. 'Everything is settling down. The Revolution accomplishes itself all over the world. Friction is inevitable here and there, of course; but your rule is assured. You may rest secure with things in Ostrog's hands.'

'Would it be possible for me to be made a sworn aeronaut, as you call it, forthwith – before I sleep?' said Graham, pacing. 'Then I could be at it the very first thing tomorrow again.' . . .

'It would be possible,' said Lincoln thoughtfully. 'Quite poss-

ible. Indeed, it shall be done.' He laughed. 'I came prepared to
suggest amusements, but you have found one for yourself. I
will telephone to the aeronautical offices from here and we will
return to your apartments in the Wind-Vane Control. By the
time you have dined the aeronauts will be able to come. You
don't think that after you have dined you might prefer –?' He
paused.

'Yes?' said Graham.

'We had prepared a show of dancers – they have been brought
from the Capri theatre.'

'I hate ballets,' said Graham, shortly. 'Always did. That other
– That's not what I want to see. We had dancers in the old
days. For the matter of that, they had them in ancient Egypt.
But flying—'

'True,' said Lincoln. 'Though our dancers—'

'They can afford to wait,' said Graham; 'they can afford to
wait. I know. I'm not a Latin.[1] There's questions I want to ask
some expert – about your machinery. I'm keen. I want no
distractions.'

'You have the world to choose from,' said Lincoln: 'whatever
you want is yours.'

Asano appeared, and under the escort of a strong guard they
returned through the city streets to Graham's apartments. Far
larger crowds had assembled to witness his return than his
departure had gathered, and the shouts and cheering of these
masses of people sometimes drowned Lincoln's answers to the
endless questions Graham's aerial journey had suggested. At
first Graham had acknowledged the cheering and cries of the
crowd by bows and gestures, but Lincoln warned him that
such a recognition would be considered incorrect behaviour.
Graham, already a little wearied by rhythmic civilities, ignored
his subjects for the remainder of his public progress.

Directly they arrived at his apartments Asano departed in
search of kinematographic renderings of machinery in motion,
and Lincoln despatched Graham's commands for models of
machines and small machines to illustrate the various mechanical advances of the last two centuries. The little group of
appliances for telegraphic communication attracted the Master

so strongly that his delightfully prepared dinner, served by a number of charmingly dexterous girls, waited for a space. The habit of smoking had almost ceased from the face of the earth, but when he expressed a wish for that indulgence, enquiries were made and some excellent cigars were discovered in Florida, and sent to him by pneumatic despatch while the dinner was still in progress. Afterwards came the aeronauts, and a feast of ingenious wonders in the hands of a latter-day engineer. For the time, at any rate, the neat dexterity of counting and numbering machines, building machines, spinning engines, patent doorways, explosive motors, grain and water elevators, slaughterhouse machines and harvesting appliances, was more fascinating to Graham than any bayadère.[2] 'We were savages,' was his refrain, 'we were savages. We were in the stone age – compared with this. . . . And what else have you?'

There came also practical psychologists with some very interesting developments in the art of hypnotism. The names of Milne Bramwell, Fechner, Liebault, William James, Myers and Gurney,[3] he found, bore a value now that would have astonished their contemporaries. Several practical applications of psychology were now in general use; it had largely superseded drugs, antiseptics and anaesthetics in medicine; was employed by almost all who had any need of mental concentration. A real enlargement of human faculty seemed to have been effected in this direction. The feats of 'calculating boys', the wonders, as Graham had been wont to regard them, of mesmerizers, were now within the range of anyone who could afford the services of a skilled hypnotist. Long ago the old examination methods in education had been destroyed by these expedients. Instead of years of study, candidates had substituted a few weeks of trances, and during the trances expert coaches had simply to repeat all the points necessary for adequate answering, adding a suggestion of the post-hypnotic recollection of these points. In process mathematics particularly, this aid had been of singular service; and it was now invariably invoked by such players of chess and games of manual dexterity as were still to be found. In fact all operations conducted under finite rules, of a quasi-mechanical sort that is, were now systematically relieved from the wanderings of imagination and emotion, and brought to an unexampled pitch of accuracy. Little children of the labouring classes, so soon as they were of sufficient age to be hypnotized, were thus converted into beautifully punctual and trustworthy machine-minders, and released forthwith from the long, long thoughts of youth. Aeronautical pupils who gave way to giddiness could be relieved of their imaginary terrors. In every street were hypnotists ready to print permanent memories upon the mind.[4] If anyone desired to remember a name, a series of numbers, a song, or a speech, it could be done by this method; and conversely memories could be effaced, habits removed, and desires eradicated – a sort of psychic surgery was, in fact, in general use. Indignities, humbling experiences, were thus forgotten; widows would obliterate their previous husbands, angry lovers release themselves from their slavery. To graft desires however was still impossible, and the facts of thought transference were yet unsystematized. The psychologists illustrated their expositions with some astounding experiments in mnemonics made through the agency of a troupe of pale-faced children in blue.

Graham, like most of the people of his former time, distrusted the hypnotist, or he might then and there have eased his mind of many painful preoccupations. But in spite of Lincoln's assurances he held to the old theory that to be hypnotized was in some way the surrender of his personality, the abdication of his will. At the banquet of wonderful experiences that was beginning, he wanted very keenly to remain absolutely himself.

The next day, and another day, and yet another day passed in such interests as these. Each morning Graham spent many hours in the glorious entertainment of flying. On the third, he soared across middle France, and within sight of the snow-clad Alps. These vigorous exercises gave him restful sleep; he recovered almost wholly from the spiritless anaemia of his first awakening. And whenever he was not in the air and awake, Lincoln was assiduous in the cause of his amusement; all that was novel and curious in contemporary invention was brought to him, until at last his appetite for novelty was well-nigh glutted. One might fill a dozen inconsecutive volumes with the strange things they exhibited. Each afternoon he held his court for an hour or so. He found his interest in his contemporaries becoming personal and intimate. At first he had been alert chiefly for unfamiliarity and peculiarity; any foppishness in their dress, any discordance with his preconceptions of nobility in their status and manners had jarred upon him, and it was remarkable to him how soon that strangeness and the faint hostility that arose from it, disappeared; how soon he came to appreciate the true perspective of his position, and see the old Victorian days remote and quaint. He was particularly amused by the red-haired daughter of the Manager of the European Piggeries. On the second evening after dinner he made the acquaintance of a latter-day dancing girl, and found her an astonishing artist. And after that, more hypnotic wonders. The third night Lincoln was moved to suggest that the Master should repair to a Pleasure City, but this Graham declined, nor would he accept the services of the hypnotists in his aeronautical experiments. The link of locality held him to London; he found a delight in topographical identifications that he would have missed abroad. 'Here – or a hundred feet below here,' he could say, 'I used to eat my midday cutlets during my London University days.[5] Underneath here was Waterloo[6] and the tiresome hunt for confusing trains. Often have I stood waiting down there, bag in hand, and stared up into the sky above the forest of signals, little thinking I should walk some day a hundred yards in the air. And now in that very sky that was once a grey smoke canopy, I circle in a monoplane.'

Graham was so occupied with these distractions that the vast political movements in progress outside his quarters had but a small share of his attention. Those about him told him little. Daily came Ostrog, the Boss, his Grand Vizier, his mayor of the palace, to report in vague terms the steady establishment of his rule; 'a little trouble' soon to be settled in this city, 'a slight disturbance' in that. The song of the social revolt came to him no more; he never learnt that it had been forbidden in the municipal limits; and all the great emotions of the crow's nest slumbered in his mind.

Presently he found himself, in spite of his interest in the

daughter of the Pig Manager, or it may be by reason of the thoughts her conversation suggested, remembering the girl Helen Wotton who had spoken to him so oddly at the wind-vane keeper's gathering. The impression she had made was a deep one, albeit the incessant surprise of novel circumstances had kept him from brooding upon it for a space. But now her memory was coming to its own. He wondered what she had meant by those broken half-forgotten sentences; the picture of her eyes and the earnest passion of her face became more vivid as his mechanical interests faded.

CHAPTER 18
GRAHAM REMEMBERS

She came upon him at last in a little gallery that ran from the wind-vane offices towards his state apartments. The gallery was long and narrow, with a series of recesses, each with an arched fenestration that looked upon a court of palms. He came upon her suddenly in one of these recesses. She was seated. She turned her head at the sound of his footsteps and started at the sight of him. Every touch of colour vanished from her face. She rose instantly, made a step towards him as if to address him, and hesitated. He stopped and stood still, expectant. Then he perceived that a nervous tumult silenced her; perceived, too, that she must have sought speech with him to be waiting for him in this place.

'I have wanted to see you,' he said. 'A few days ago you wanted to tell me something – you wanted to tell me of the people. What was it you had to tell me?'

She looked at him with troubled eyes.

'You said the people were unhappy?'

For a moment she was silent still.

'It must have seemed strange to you,' she said abruptly.

'It did. And yet—'

'It was an impulse.'

'Well?'

'That is all.'

She looked at him with a face of hesitation. She spoke with an effort. 'You forget,' she said, drawing a deep breath.

'What?'

'The people—'

'Do you mean—?'

'You forget the people.'

He looked interrogative.

'Yes. I know you are surprised. For you do not understand what you are. You do not know the things that are happening.'

'Well?'

'You do not understand.'

'Not clearly, perhaps. But – tell me.'

She turned to him with sudden resolution. 'It is so hard to explain. I have meant to, I have wanted to. And now – I cannot. I am not ready with words. But about you – there is something. It is Wonder. Your sleep – your awakening. These things are miracles. To me at least – and to all the common people. You who lived and suffered and died, you who were a common citizen, wake again, live again, to find yourself Master almost of the earth.'

'Master of the Earth,' he said. 'So they tell me. But try and imagine how little I know of it.'

'Cities – Trusts – the Labour Department—'

'Principalities, powers, dominions[1] – the power and the glory. Yes, I have heard them shout. I know. I am Master. King, if you wish. With Ostrog, the Boss—'

He paused.

She turned upon him and surveyed his face with a curious scrutiny. 'Well?'

He smiled. 'To take the responsibility.'

'That is what we have begun to fear.' For a moment she said no more. 'No,' she said slowly. '*You* will take the responsibility. You will take the responsibility. The people look to you.'

She spoke softly. 'Listen! For at least half the years of your sleep – in every generation – multitudes of people, in every generation greater multitudes of people, have prayed that you might awake – *prayed*.'

Graham moved to speak and did not.

She hesitated, and a faint colour crept back to her cheek. 'Do you know that you have been to myriads – King Arthur, Barbarossa[2] – the King who would come in his own good time and put the world right for them?'

'I suppose the imagination of the people—'

'Have you not heard our proverb, "When the Sleeper wakes"? While you lay insensible and motionless there – thousands came. Thousands. Every first of the month you lay in state with a white robe upon you and the people filed by you. When I was a little girl I saw you like that, with your face white and calm.'

She turned her face from him and looked steadfastly at the painted wall before her. Her voice fell. 'When I was a little girl I used to look at your face . . . it seemed to me fixed and waiting, like the patience of God.

'That is what we thought of you,' she said. 'That is how you seemed to us.'

She turned shining eyes to him, her voice was clear and strong. 'In the city, in the earth, a myriad myriad men and women are waiting to see what you will do, full of strange expectations.'

'Yes?'

'Ostrog – no one – can take that responsibility.'

Graham looked at her in surprise, as her face lit with emotion. She seemed at first to have spoken with an effort, and to have fired herself by speaking.

'Do you think,' she said, 'that you who have lived that little life so far away in the past, you who have fallen into and risen out of this miracle of sleep – do you think that the wonder and reverence and hope of half the world has gathered about you only that you may live another little life? . . . That you may shift the responsibility to any other man?'

'I know how great this kingship of mine is,' he said haltingly. 'I know how great it seems. But is it real? It is incredible – dreamlike. Is it real, or is it only a great delusion?'

'It is real,' she said; 'if you dare.'

'After all, like all kingship, my kingship is Belief. It is an illusion in the minds of men.'

'If you dare!' she said.

'But—'

'Countless men,' she said, 'and while it is in their minds – they will obey.'

'But I know nothing. That is what I had in mind. I know

nothing. And these others – the Councillors, Ostrog. They are wiser, cooler, they know so much, every detail. And, indeed, what are these miseries of which you speak? What am I to know? Do you mean—'

He stopped blankly.

'I am still hardly more than a girl,' she said. 'But to me the world seems full of wretchedness. The world has altered since your day, altered very strangely. I have prayed that I might see you and tell you these things. The world has changed. As if a canker had seized it – and robbed life of – everything worth having.'

She turned a flushed face upon him, moving suddenly. 'Your days were the days of freedom. Yes – I have thought. I have been made to think, for my life – has not been happy. Men are no longer free – no greater, no better than the men of your time. That is not all. This city – is a prison. Every city now is a prison. Mammon[3] grips the key in his hand. Myriads, countless myriads, toil from the cradle to the grave. Is that right? Is that to be – for ever? Yes, far worse than in your time. All about us, beneath us, sorrow and pain. All the shallow delight of such life as you find about you, is separated by just a little from a life of wretchedness beyond any telling. Yes, the poor know it – they know they suffer. These countless multitudes who faced death for you two nights since –! You owe your life to them.'

'Yes,' said Graham, slowly. 'Yes. I owe my life to them.'

'You come,' she said, 'from the days when this new tyranny of the cities was scarcely beginning. It is a tyranny – a tyranny. In your days the feudal warlords had gone, and the new lordship of wealth had still to come. Half the men in the world still lived out upon the free countryside. The cities had still to devour them. I have heard the stories out of the old books – there was nobility! Common men led lives of love and faithfulness then – they did a thousand things. And you – you come from that time.'

'It was not – But never mind. How is it now—?'

'Gain and the Pleasure Cities! Or slavery – unthanked, unhonoured slavery.'

'Slavery!' he said.

'Slavery.'

'You don't mean to say that human beings are chattels.'

'Worse. That is what I want you to know, what I want you to see. I know you do not know. They will keep things from you, they will take you presently to a Pleasure City. But you have noticed men and women and children in pale-blue canvas, with thin yellow faces and dull eyes?'

'Everywhere.'

'Speaking a horrible dialect, coarse and weak.'

'I have heard it.'

'They are the slaves – your slaves. They are the slaves of the Labour Department you own.'

'The Labour Department! In some way – that is familiar. Ah! now I remember. I saw it when I was wandering about the city, after the lights returned, great fronts of buildings coloured pale blue. Do you really mean—?'

'Yes. How can I explain it to you? Of course the blue uniform struck you. Nearly a third of our people wear it – more assume it now every day. This Labour Department has grown imperceptibly.'

'What *is* this Labour Department?' asked Graham.

'In the old times, how did you manage with starving people?'

'There was the workhouse[4] – which the parishes maintained.'

'Workhouse! Yes – there was something. In our history lessons. I remember now. The Labour Department ousted the workhouse. It grew – partly – out of something – you, perhaps, may remember it – an emotional religious organization called the Salvation Army[5] – that became a business company. In the first place it was almost a charity. To save people from workhouse rigours. There had been a great agitation against the workhouse. Now I come to think of it, it was one of the earliest properties your Trustees acquired. They bought the Salvation Army and reconstructed it as this. The idea in the first place was to organize the labour of starving homeless people.'

'Yes.'

'Nowadays there are no workhouses, no refuges and charities, nothing but that Department. Its offices are everywhere. That blue is its colour. And any man, woman or child who comes to be hungry and weary and with neither home nor friend nor resort, must go to the Department in the end – or seek some way of death. The Euthanasy[6] is beyond their means – for the poor there is no easy death. And at any hour in the day or night there is food, shelter and a blue uniform for all comers – that is the first condition of the Department's incorporation – and in return for a day's shelter the Department extracts a day's work, and then returns the visitor's proper clothing and sends him or her out again.'

'Yes?'

'Perhaps that does not seem so terrible to you. In your time men starved in your streets. That was bad. But they died – *men*. These people in blue – The proverb runs: "Blue canvas once and ever." The Department trades in their labour, and it has taken care to assure itself of the supply. People come to it starving and helpless – they eat and sleep for a night and day, they work for a day, and at the end of the day they go out again. If they have worked well they have a penny or so – enough for a theatre or a cheap dancing place, or a kinemato-graph story, or a dinner or a bet. They wander about after that is spent. Begging is prevented by the police of the ways. Besides, no one gives. They come back again the next day or the day after – brought back by the same incapacity that brought them first. At last their proper clothing wears out, or their rags get so shabby that they are ashamed. Then they must work for months to get fresh. If they want fresh. A great number of children are born under the Department's care. The mother owes them a month thereafter – the children they cherish and educate until they are fourteen, and they pay two years' service. You may be sure these children are educated for the blue canvas. And so it is the Department works.'

'And none are destitute in the city?'

'None. They are either in blue canvas or in prison. We have abolished destitution. It is engraved upon the Department's checks.'

'If they will not work?'

'Most people will work at that pitch, and the Department has powers. There are stages of unpleasantness in the work –

stoppage of food – and a man or woman who has refused to work once is known by a thumb-marking system in the Department's offices all over the world. Besides, who can leave the city poor? To go to Paris costs two lions. And for insubordination there are the prisons – dark and miserable – out of sight below. There are prisons now for many things.'

'And a third of the people wear this blue canvas?'

'More than a third. Toilers, living without pride or delight or hope, with the stories of Pleasure Cities ringing in their ears, mocking their shameful lives, their privations and hardships. Too poor even for the Euthanasy, the rich man's refuge from life. Dumb, crippled millions, countless millions, all the world about, ignorant of anything but limitations and unsatisfied desires. They are born, they are thwarted and they die. That is the state to which we have come.'

For a space Graham sat downcast.

'But there has been a revolution,' he said. 'All these things will be changed. Ostrog—'

'That is our hope. That is the hope of the world. But Ostrog will not do it. He is a politician. To him it seems things must be like this. He does not mind. He takes it for granted. All the rich, all the influential, all who are happy, come at last to take these miseries for granted. They use the people in their politics, they live in ease by their degradation. But you – you who come from a happier age – it is to you the people look. To you.'

He looked at her face. Her eyes were bright with unshed tears. He felt a rush of emotion. For a moment he forgot this city, he forgot the race, and all those vague remote voices, in the immediate humanity of her beauty.

'But what am I to do?' he said with his eyes upon her.

'Rule,' she answered, bending towards him and speaking in a low tone. 'Rule the world as it has never been ruled, for the good and happiness of men. For you might rule it – you could rule it.

'The people are stirring. All over the world the people are stirring. It wants but a word – but a word from you – to bring them all together. Even the middle sort of people are restless – unhappy.

'They are not telling you the things that are happening. The people will not go back to their drudgery – they refuse to be disarmed. Ostrog has awakened something greater than he dreamt of – he has awakened hopes.'

His heart was beating fast. He tried to seem judicial, to weigh considerations.

'They only want their leader,' she said.

'And then?'

'You could do what you would; – the world is yours.'

He sat, no longer regarding her. Presently he spoke. 'The old dreams, and the thing I have dreamt, liberty, happiness. Are they dreams? Could one man – *one man* –?' His voice sank and ceased.

'Not one man, but all men – give them only a leader to speak the desire of their hearts.'

He shook his head, and for a time there was silence.

He looked up suddenly, and their eyes met. 'I have not your faith,' he said, 'I have not your youth. I am here with power that mocks me. No – let me speak. I want to do – not right – I have not the strength for that – but something rather right than wrong. It will bring no millennium, but I am resolved now that I will rule. What you have said has awakened me. . . . You are right. Ostrog must know his place. And I will learn –. . . . One thing I promise you. This Labour slavery shall end.'

'And you will rule?'

'Yes. Provided – There is one thing.'

'Yes?'

'That you will help me.'

'*I*! – a girl!'

'Yes. Does it not occur to you I am absolutely alone?'

She started and for an instant her eyes had pity. 'Need you ask whether I will help you?' she said.

'I am very helpless.'

'Father and Master,' she said. 'The world is yours.'

There came a tense silence, and then the beating of a clock striking the hour. Graham rose.

'Even now,' he said, 'Ostrog will be waiting.' He hesitated, facing her. 'When I have asked him certain questions – There is much I do not know. It may be, that I will go to see with my own eyes the things of which you have spoken. And when I return—?'

'I shall know of your going and coming. I will wait for you here again.'

They regarded one another steadfastly, questioningly, and then he turned from her towards the wind-vane office.

CHAPTER 19

OSTROG'S POINT OF VIEW

Graham found Ostrog waiting to give a formal account of his day's stewardship. On previous occasions he had passed over this ceremony as speedily as possible, in order to resume his aerial experiences, but now he began to ask quick short questions. He was very anxious to take up his empire forthwith. Ostrog brought flattering reports of the development of affairs abroad. In Paris and Berlin, Graham perceived that he was saying, there had been trouble, not organized resistance indeed, but insubordinate proceedings. 'After all these years,' said Ostrog, when Graham pressed inquiries; 'the Commune has lifted its head again. That is the real nature of the struggle, to be explicit.' But order had been restored in those cities. Graham, the more deliberately judicial for the stirring emotions he felt, asked if there had been any fighting. 'A little,' said Ostrog. 'In one quarter only. But the Senegalese[1] division of our African agricultural police – the Consolidated African Companies have a very well-drilled police – was ready, and so were the aeroplanes. We expected a little trouble in the continental cities, and in America. But things are very quiet in America. They are satisfied with the overthrow of the Council. For the time.'

'Why should you expect trouble?' asked Graham abruptly.

'There is a lot of discontent – social discontent.'

'The Labour Department?'

'You are learning,' said Ostrog with a touch of surprise. 'Yes. It is chiefly the discontent with the Labour Department. It was that discontent supplied the motive force of this overthrow – that and your awakening.'

'Yes?'

Ostrog smiled. He became explicit. 'We had to stir up their discontent, we had to revive the old ideals of universal happiness – all men equal – all men happy – no luxury that everyone may not share – ideas that have slumbered for two hundred years. You know that? We had to revive these ideals, impossible as they are – in order to overthrow the Council. And now—'

'Well?'

'Our revolution is accomplished, and the Council is overthrown, and people whom we have stirred up – remain surging. There was scarcely enough fighting. . . . We made promises, of course. It is extraordinary how violently and rapidly this vague out-of-date humanitarianism has revived and spread. We who sowed the seed even, have been astonished. In Paris, as I say – we have had to call in a little external help.'

'And here?'

'There is trouble. Multitudes will not go back to work. There is a general strike. Half the factories are empty and the people are swarming in the Ways. They are talking of a Commune. Men in silk and satin have been insulted in the streets. The blue canvas is expecting all sorts of things from you. . . . Of course there is no need for you to trouble. We are setting the Babble Machines to work with counter suggestions in the cause of law and order. We must keep the grip tight; that is all.'

Graham thought. He perceived a way of asserting himself. But he spoke with restraint.

'Even to the pitch of bringing a Negro police,' he said.

'They are useful,' said Ostrog. 'They are fine loyal brutes, with no wash of ideas in their heads – such as our rabble has. The Council should have had them as police of the Ways, and things might have been different. Of course, there is nothing to fear except rioting and wreckage. You can manage your own wings now, and you can soar away to Capri if there is any smoke or fuss. We have the pull of all the great things; the aeronauts are privileged and rich, the closest trades union in the world, and so are the engineers of the wind-vanes. We have the air, and the mastery of the air is the mastery of the earth. No one of any ability is organizing against us. They have no leaders – only the sectional leaders of the secret society we organized before your very opportune awakening. Mere busy-bodies and sentimentalists they are, and bitterly jealous of each other. None of them is man enough for a central figure. The only trouble will be a disorganized upheaval. To be frank – that may happen. But it won't interrupt your aeronautics. The days when the People could make revolutions are past.'

'I suppose they are,' said Graham. 'I suppose they are.' He mused. 'This world of yours has been full of surprises to me. In the old days we dreamt of a wonderful democratic life, of a time when all men would be equal and happy.'

Ostrog looked at him steadfastly. 'The day of democracy is past,' he said. 'Past for ever. That day began with the bowmen of Creçy,[2] it ended when marching infantry, when common men in masses ceased to win the battles of the world, when costly cannon, great ironclads, and strategic railways became the means of power. Today is the day of wealth. Wealth now is power as it never was power before – it commands earth and sea and sky. All power is for those who can handle wealth. On your behalf. . . . You must accept facts, and these are facts. The world for the Crowd! The Crowd as Ruler! Even in your days that creed had been tried and condemned. Today it has only one believer – a multiplex, silly one – the man in the Crowd.'

Graham did not answer immediately. He stood lost in sombre preoccupations.

'No,' said Ostrog. 'The day of the common man is past. On the open countryside one man is as good as another, or nearly as good. The earlier aristocracy had a precarious tenure of strength and audacity. They were tempered – tempered. There were insurrections, duels, riots. The first real aristocracy, the first permanent aristocracy, came in with castles and armour, and vanished before the musket and bow. But this is the second aristocracy. The real one. Those days of gunpowder and democracy were only an eddy in the stream. The common man now is a helpless unit. In these days we have this great machine of the city, and an organization complex beyond his understanding.'

'Yet,' said Graham, 'there is something resists, something you are holding down – something that stirs and presses.'

'You will see,' said Ostrog, with a forced smile that would

brush these difficult questions aside. 'I have not roused the force to destroy myself – trust me.'

'I wonder,' said Graham.

Ostrog stared.

'*Must* the world go this way?' said Graham with his emotions at the speaking point. 'Must it indeed go in this way? Have all our hopes been vain?'

'What do you mean?' said Ostrog. 'Hopes?'

'I come from a democratic age. And I find an aristocratic tyranny!'

'Well, – but you are the chief tyrant.'

Graham shook his head.

'Well,' said Ostrog, 'take the general question. It is the way that change has always travelled. Aristocracy, the prevalence of the best – the suffering and extinction of the unfit, and so to better things.'

'But aristocracy! those people I met—'

'Oh! not *those*!' said Ostrog. 'But for the most part they go to their death. Vice and pleasure! They have no children. That sort of stuff will die out. If the world keeps to one road, that is, if there is no turning back. An easy road to excess, convenient Euthanasia for the pleasure-seekers singed in the flame, that is the way to improve the race!'

'Pleasant extinction,' said Graham. 'Yet –' He thought for an instant. 'There is that other thing – the Crowd, the great mass of poor men. Will that die out? That will not die out. And it suffers, its suffering is a force that even you—'

Ostrog moved impatiently, and when he spoke, he spoke rather less evenly than before.

'Don't trouble about these things,' he said. 'Everything will be settled in a few days now. The Crowd is a huge foolish beast. What if it does not die out? Even if it does not die, it can still be tamed and driven. I have no sympathy with servile men. You heard those people shouting and singing two nights ago. They were *taught* that song. If you had taken any man there in cold blood and asked why he shouted, he could not have told you. They think they are shouting for you, that they are loyal and devoted to you. Just then they were ready to slaughter the

Council. Today – they are already murmuring against those who have overthrown the Council.'

'No, no,' said Graham. 'They shouted because their lives were dreary, without joy or pride, and because in me – in me – they hoped.'

'And what was their hope? What is their hope? What right have they to hope? They work ill and they want the reward of those who work well. The hope of mankind – what is it? That some day the Over-man[3] may come, that some day the inferior, the weak and the bestial may be subdued or eliminated. Subdued if not eliminated. The world is no place for the bad, the stupid, the enervated. Their duty – it's a fine duty too! – is to die. The death of the failure! That is the path by which the beast rose to manhood, by which man goes on to higher things.'

Ostrog took a pace, seemed to think, and turned on Graham. 'I can imagine how this great world state of ours seems to a Victorian Englishman. You regret all the old forms of representative government – their spectres still haunt the world, the voting councils and parliaments and all that eighteenth-century tomfoolery. You feel moved against our Pleasure Cities. I might have thought of that, – had I not been busy. But you will learn better. The people are mad with envy – they would be in sympathy with you. Even in the streets now, they clamour to destroy the Pleasure Cities. But the Pleasure Cities are the excretory organs of the State, attractive places that year after year draw together all that is weak and vicious, all that is lascivious and lazy, all the easy roguery of the world, to a graceful destruction. They go there, they have their time, they die childless, all the pretty silly lascivious women die childless, and mankind is the better. If the people were sane they would not envy the rich their way of death. And you would emancipate the silly brainless workers that we have enslaved, and try to make their lives easy and pleasant again. Just as they have sunk to what they are fit for.' He smiled a smile that irritated Graham oddly. 'You will learn better. I know those ideas; in my boyhood I read your Shelley and dreamt of Liberty. There is no liberty save wisdom and self-control. Liberty is within – not without. It is each man's own affair. Suppose – which is impossible –

that these swarming yelping fools in blue get the upper hand of us, what then? They will only fall to other masters. So long as there are sheep Nature will insist on beasts of prey. It would mean but a few hundred years' delay. The coming of the aristocrat is fatal and assured. The end will be the Over-man – for all the mad protests of humanity. Let them revolt, let them win and kill me and my like. Others will arise – other masters. The end will be the same.'

'I wonder,' said Graham doggedly.

For a moment he stood downcast.

'But I must see these things for myself,' he said, suddenly assuming a tone of confident mastery. 'Only by seeing can I understand. I must learn. That is what I want to tell you, Ostrog. I do not want to be King in a Pleasure City; that is not my pleasure. I have spent enough time with aeronautics – and those other things. I must learn how people live now, how the common life has developed. Then I shall understand these things better. I must learn how common people live – the labour people more especially – how they work, marry, bear children, die —'

'You get that from our realistic novelists,' suggested Ostrog, suddenly preoccupied.

'I want reality,' said Graham.

'There are difficulties,' said Ostrog, and thought. 'On the whole—

'I did not expect—

'I had thought – And yet perhaps – You say you want to go through the Ways of the city and see the common people.'

Suddenly he came to some conclusion. 'You would need to go disguised,' he said. 'The city is intensely excited, and the discovery of your presence among them might create a fearful tumult. Still this wish of yours to go into this city – this idea of yours – Yes, now I think the thing over, it seems to me not altogether – It can be contrived. If you would really find an interest in that! You are, of course, Master. You can go soon if you like. Asano will be able to manage a disguise. He would go with you. After all it is not a bad idea of yours.'

'You will not want to consult me in any matter?' asked Graham suddenly, struck by an odd suspicion.

'Oh, dear, no! No! I think you may trust affairs to me for a time, at any rate,' said Ostrog, smiling. 'Even if we differ—'

Graham glanced at him sharply.

'There is no fighting likely to happen soon?' he asked abruptly.

'Certainly not.'

'I have been thinking about those Negroes. I don't believe the people intend any hostility to me, and after all I am the Master. I do not want any Negroes brought to London. It is an archaic prejudice perhaps, but I have peculiar feelings about Europeans and the subject races. Even about Paris—'

Ostrog stood watching him from under his drooping brows. 'I am not bringing Negroes to London,' he said slowly. 'But if—'

'You are not to bring armed Negroes to London, whatever happens,' said Graham. 'In that matter I am quite decided.'

Ostrog bowed deferentially.

CHAPTER 20
IN THE CITY WAYS

And that night, unknown and unsuspected, Graham, dressed in the costume of an inferior wind-vane official keeping holiday and accompanied by Asano in Labour Department canvas, surveyed the city through which he had wandered when it was veiled in darkness. But now he saw it lit and waking, a whirlpool of life. In spite of the surging and swaying of the forces of revolution, in spite of the unusual discontent, the mutterings of the greater struggle of which the first revolt was but the prelude, the myriad streams of commerce still flowed wide and strong. He knew now something of the dimensions and quality of the new age, but he was not prepared for the infinite surprise of the detailed view, for the torrent of colour and vivid impressions that poured past him.

This was his first real contact with the people of these latter days. He realized that all that had gone before, saving his glimpses of the public theatres and markets, had had its element of seclusion, had been a movement within the comparatively narrow political quarter, that all his previous experiences had revolved immediately about the question of his own position. But here was the city at the busiest hours of night, the people to a large extent returned to their own immediate interests, the resumption of the real informal life, the common habits of the new time.

They emerged at first into a street whose opposite ways were crowded with the blue canvas liveries. This swarm Graham saw was a portion of a procession – it was odd to see a procession parading the city *seated*.[1] They carried banners of coarse black stuff with red letters. 'No disarmament,' said the banners, for the most part in crudely daubed letters and with variant spelling, and 'Why should we disarm?' 'No disarming.' 'No disarming.' Banner after banner went by, a stream of banners flowing past, and at last at the end, the song of the revolt and a noisy band of strange instruments. 'They all ought to be at work,' said Asano. 'They have had no food these two days, or they have stolen it.'

Presently Asano made a detour to avoid the congested crowd that gaped upon the occasional passage of dead bodies from hospital to a mortuary, the gleanings after death's harvest of the first revolt.

That night few people were sleeping, everyone was abroad. A vast excitement, perpetual crowds perpetually changing, surrounded Graham; his mind was confused and darkened by an incessant tumult, by the cries and enigmatical fragments of the social struggle that was as yet only beginning. Everywhere festoons and banners of black and strange decorations, intensified the impression of his popularity. Everywhere he caught snatches of that crude thick dialect that served the illiterate class, the class, that is, beyond the reach of phonograph culture, in their commonplace intercourse. Everywhere this trouble of disarmament was in the air, with a quality of immediate stress of which he had had no inkling during his seclusion in the wind-vane quarter. He perceived that as soon as he returned he must discuss this with Ostrog, this and the greater issues of which it was the expression, in a far more conclusive way than he had so far done. Throughout that night, even in the earlier hours of their wanderings about the city, the spirit of unrest and revolt swamped his attention to the exclusion of countless strange things he might otherwise have observed.

This preoccupation made his impressions fragmentary. Yet amidst so much that was strange and vivid, no subject, however personal and insistent, could exert undivided sway. There were spaces when the revolutionary movement passed clean out of his mind, was drawn aside like a curtain from before some startling new aspect of the time. Helen had swayed his mind to this intense earnestness of inquiry, but there came times when she, even, receded beyond his conscious thoughts. At one moment, for example, he found they were traversing the religious quarter, for the easy transit about the city afforded by the moving ways rendered sporadic churches and chapels no longer necessary – and his attention was arrested by the façade of one of the Christian sects.

They were travelling seated on one of the swift upper ways, the place leapt upon them at a bend and advanced rapidly towards them. It was covered with inscriptions from top to base, in vivid white and blue, save where a coarse and glaring kinematograph transparency presented a realistic New Testament scene, and where a vast festoon of black to show that the popular religion followed the popular politics, hung across the lettering. Graham had already become familiar with the phonotype writing and these inscriptions arrested him, being to his sense for the most part almost incredible blasphemy. Among the less offensive were 'Salvation on the First Floor and turn to the Right.' 'Put your Money on your Maker.' 'The Sharpest Conversion in London, Expert Operators! Look Slippy!' 'What Christ would say to the Sleeper; – Join the Up-to-date Saints!' 'Be a Christian – without hindrance to your present Occupation.' 'All the Brightest Bishops on the Bench tonight and Prices as Usual.' 'Brisk Blessings for Busy Businessmen.'

'But this is appalling!' said Graham, as that deafening scream of mercantile piety towered above them.

'What is appalling?' asked his little officer, apparently seeking vainly for anything unusual in this shrieking enamel.

'This! Surely the essence of religion is reverence.'

'Oh that!' Asano looked at Graham. 'Does it shock you?' he said in the tone of one who makes a discovery. 'I suppose it would, of course. I had forgotten. Nowadays the competition for attention is so keen, and people simply haven't the leisure to attend to their souls, you know, as they used to do.' He smiled. 'In the old days you had quiet Sabbaths and the countryside. Though somewhere I've read of Sunday afternoons that—'

'But that,' said Graham, glancing back at the receding blue and white. 'That is surely not the only—'

'There are hundreds of different ways. But of course if a sect doesn't *tell* it doesn't pay. Worship has moved with the times. There are high-class sects with quieter ways – costly incense and personal attentions and all that. These people are extremely popular and prosperous. They pay several dozen lions for those apartments to the Council – to you, I should say.'

Graham still felt a difficulty with the coinage, and this mention of a dozen lions brought him abruptly to that matter. In a moment the screaming temples and their swarming touts were forgotten in this new interest. A turn of a phrase suggested, and an answer confirmed the idea that gold and silver were both demonetized, that stamped gold which had begun its reign amidst the merchants of Phoenicia[2] was at last dethroned. The change had been graduated but swift, brought about by an extension of the system of cheques that had even in his previous life already practically superseded gold in all the larger business transactions. The common traffic of the city, the common currency indeed of all the world, was conducted by means of the little brown, green and pink council cheques for small amounts, printed with a blank payee. Asano had several with him, and at the first opportunity he supplied the gaps in his set. They were printed not on tearable paper but on a semi-transparent fabric of silken flexibility, interwoven with silk. Across them all sprawled a facsimile[3] of Graham's signature, his first encounter with the curves and turns of that familiar autograph for two hundred and three years.

Some intermediary experiences made no impression sufficiently vivid to prevent the matter of the disarmament claiming his thoughts again; a blurred picture of a Theosophist[4] temple that promised MIRACLES in enormous letters of unsteady fire was least submerged perhaps, but then came the view of the dining hall in Northumberland Avenue.[5] That interested him very greatly.

By the energy and thought of Asano he was able to view this place from a little screened gallery reserved for the attendants of the tables. The building was pervaded by a distant muffled hooting, piping and bawling of which he did not at first understand the import, but which recalled a certain mysterious leathery voice he had heard after the resumption of the lights on the night of his solitary wandering.

He had grown accustomed to vastness and great numbers of people, nevertheless this spectacle held him for a long time. It was as he watched the table service more immediately beneath, and interspersed with many questions and answers concerning details, that the realization of the full significance of the feast of several thousand people came to him.

It was his constant surprise to find that points that one might have expected to strike vividly at the very outset never occurred to him until some trivial detail suddenly shaped as a riddle and pointed to the obvious thing he had overlooked. He discovered only now that this continuity of the city, this exclusion of weather, these vast halls and ways, involved the disappearance of the household; that the typical Victorian 'Home', the little brick cell containing kitchen and scullery,[6] living rooms and bedrooms, had, save for the ruins that diversified the country-side, vanished as surely as the wattle hut.[7] But now he saw what had indeed been manifest from the first, that London, regarded as a living place, was no longer an aggregation of houses but a prodigious hotel, an hotel with a thousand classes of accommo-dation, thousands of dining halls, chapels, theatres, markets and places of assembly, a synthesis of enterprises, of which he chiefly was the owner. People had their sleeping rooms, with, it might be, antechambers, rooms that were always sanitary at least whatever their degree of comfort and privacy, and for the rest they lived much as many people had lived in the new-made giant hotels of the Victorian days, eating, reading, thinking, playing, conversing, all in places of public resort, going to their work in the industrial quarters of the city or doing business in their offices in the trading section.

He perceived at once how necessarily this state of affairs had developed from the Victorian city. The fundamental reason for the modern city had ever been the economy of co-operation. The chief thing to prevent the merging of the separate house-holds in his own generation was simply the still imperfect civili-zation of the people, the strong barbaric pride, passions and prejudices, the jealousies, rivalries and violence of the middle and lower classes, which had necessitated the entire separation of contiguous households. But the change, the taming of the people, had been in rapid progress even then. In his brief thirty years of previous life he had seen an enormous extension of the habit of consuming meals from home, the casually patronized horse-box coffee-house had given place to the open and crowded Aërated Bread Shop[8] for instance, women's clubs had had their beginning, and an immense development of reading rooms, lounges and libraries had witnessed to the growth of social confidence. Those promises had by this time attained to their complete fulfilment. The locked and barred household had passed away.

These people below him belonged, he learnt, to the lower middle class, the class just above the blue labourers, a class so accustomed in the Victorian period to feed with every precaution of privacy that its members, when occasion confronted them with a public meal, would usually hide their embarrassment under horseplay or a markedly militant demeanour. But these gaily, if lightly dressed people below, albeit vivacious, hurried and uncommunicative, were dexterously mannered and certainly quite at their ease with regard to one another.

He noted a slight significant thing; the table, as far as he could see, was and remained delightfully neat, there was nothing to parallel the confusion, the broadcast crumbs, the splashes of viand and condiment,[9] the overturned drink and displaced ornaments, which would have marked the stormy progress of the Victorian meal. The table furniture was very different. There were no ornaments, no flowers, and the table was without a cloth, being made, he learnt, of a solid substance having the texture and appearance of damask. He discerned that this damask substance was patterned with gracefully designed trade advertisements.

In a sort of recess before each diner was a complex apparatus of porcelain and metal. There was one plate of white porcelain, and by means of taps for hot and cold volatile fluids the diner washed this himself between the courses; he also washed his elegant white metal knife and fork and spoon as occasion required.

Soup and the chemical wine[10] that was the common drink were delivered by similar taps, and the remaining covers travelled automatically in tastefully arranged dishes down the table along silver rails. The diner stopped these and helped himself at his discretion. They appeared at a little door at one end of the table, and vanished at the other. That democratic sentiment in decay, that ugly pride of menial souls which renders equals loth to wait on one another, was very strong he found among these people. He was so preoccupied with these details that it was only as he was leaving the place that he remarked the huge advertisement dioramas that marched majestically along the upper walls and proclaimed the most remarkable commodities.

Beyond this place they came into a crowded hall, and he discovered the cause of the noise that had perplexed him. They paused at a turnstile at which a payment was made.

Graham's attention was immediately arrested by a violent, loud hoot, followed by a vast leathery voice. 'The Master is sleeping peacefully,' it vociferated. 'He is in excellent health. He is going to devote the rest of his life to aeronautics. He says women are more beautiful than ever. Galloop! Wow! Our wonderful civilization astonishes him beyond measure. Beyond all measure. Galloop. He puts great trust in Boss Ostrog, absolute confidence in Boss Ostrog. Ostrog is to be his chief minister; is authorized to remove or reinstate public officers – all patronage will be in his hands. All patronage in the hands of Boss Ostrog! The Councillors have been sent back to their own prison above the Council House.'

Graham stopped at the first sentence, and, looking up, beheld a foolish trumpet face from which this was brayed. This was the General Intelligence Machine. For a space it seemed to be gathering breath, and a regular throbbing from its cylindrical body was audible. Then it trumpeted 'Galloop, Galloop,' and broke out again.

'Paris is now pacified. All resistance is over. Galloop! The black police hold every position of importance in the city. They fought with great bravery, singing songs written in praise of their ancestors by the poet Kipling. Once or twice they got out of hand, and tortured and mutilated wounded and captured insurgents, men and women. Moral – don't go rebelling. Haha! Galloop, Galloop! They are lively fellows. Lively brave fellows. Let this be a lesson to the disorderly banderlog[11] of this city. Yah! Banderlog! Filth of the earth! Galloop, Galloop!'

The voice ceased. There was a confused murmur of disapproval among the crowd. 'Damned niggers.' A man began to harangue near them. 'Is this the Master's doing, brothers? Is this the Master's doing?'

'Black police!' said Graham. 'What is that? You don't mean—'

Asano touched his arm and gave him a warning look, and forthwith another of these mechanisms screamed deafeningly and gave tongue in a shrill voice. 'Yahaha, Yahah, Yap! Hear a live paper yelp! Live paper. Yaha! Shocking outrage in Paris. Yahahah! The Parisians exasperated by the black police to the pitch of assassination. Dreadful reprisals. Savage times come again. Blood! Blood! Yaha!' The nearer Babble Machine hooted stupendously, 'Galloop, Galloop,' drowned the end of the sentence, and proceeded in a rather flatter note than before with novel comments on the horrors of disorder. 'Law and order must be maintained,' said the nearer Babble Machine.

'But,' began Graham.

'Don't ask questions here,' said Asano, 'or you will be involved in an argument.'

'Then let us go on,' said Graham, 'for I want to know more of this.'

As he and his companion pushed their way through the excited crowd that swarmed beneath these voices, towards the exit, Graham conceived more clearly the proportion and features of this room. Altogether, great and small, there must have been nearly a thousand of these erections, piping, hooting, bawling, and gabbling in that great space, each with its crowd of excited listeners, the majority of them men dressed in blue canvas. There were all sizes of machines, from the little gossiping mechanisms that chuckled out mechanical sarcasm in odd corners, through a number of grades to such fifty-foot giants as that which had first hooted over Graham.

This place was unusually crowded because of the intense

public interest in the course of affairs in Paris. Evidently the struggle had been much more savage than Ostrog had represented it. All the mechanisms were discoursing upon that topic, and the repetition of the people made the huge hive buzz with such phrases as 'Lynched policemen,' 'Women burnt alive,' 'Fuzzy Wuzzy.'[12] 'But does the Master allow such things?' asked a man near him. 'Is *this* the beginning of the Master's rule?'

Is *this* the beginning of the Master's rule? For a long time after he had left the place, the hooting, whistling and braying of the machines pursued him; 'Galloop, Galloop,' 'Yahahah, Yaha, Yap! Yaha!' Is *this* the beginning of the Master's rule?

Directly they were out upon the ways he began to question Asano closely on the nature of the Parisian struggle. 'This disarmament! What was their trouble? What does it all mean?' Asano seemed chiefly anxious to reassure him that it was 'all right.' 'But these outrages!' 'You cannot have an omelette,' said Asano, 'without breaking eggs. It is only the rough people. Only in one part of the city. All the rest is all right. The Parisian labourers are the wildest in the world, except ours.'

'What! the Londoners?'

'No, the Japanese. They have to be kept in order.'

'But burning women alive!'

'A Commune!' said Asano. 'They would rob you of your property. They would do away with property and give the world over to mob rule. You are Master, the world is yours. But there will be no Commune here. There is no need for black police here.

'And every consideration has been shown. It is their own Negroes – French-speaking Negroes. Senegal regiments, and Niger and Timbuctoo.'[13]

'Regiments?' said Graham, 'I thought there was only one—'

'No,' said Asano, and glanced at him. 'There is more than one.'

Graham felt unpleasantly helpless.

'I did not think,' he began and stopped abruptly. He went off at a tangent to ask for information about these Babble Machines. For the most part, the crowd present had been shabbily or even raggedly dressed, and Graham learnt that so far as the more prosperous classes were concerned, in all the more comfortable private apartments of the city were fixed Babble Machines that would speak directly a lever was pulled. The tenant of the apartment could connect this with the cables of any of the great News Syndicates that he preferred. When he learnt this presently, he demanded the reason of their absence from his own suite of apartments. Asano was embarrassed. 'I never thought,' he said. 'Ostrog must have had them removed.'

Graham stared. 'How was I to know?' he exclaimed.

'Perhaps he thought they would annoy you,' said Asano.

'They must be replaced directly I return,' said Graham after an interval.

He found a difficulty in understanding that this newsroom and the dining hall were not great central places, that such establishments were repeated almost beyond counting all over the city. But ever and again during the night's expedition his ears would pick out from the tumult of the ways the peculiar hooting of the organ of Boss Ostrog, 'Galloop, Galloop!' or the shrill 'Yahaha, Yaha Yap! – Hear a live paper yelp!' of its chief rival.

Repeated, too, everywhere, were such *crèches*[14] as the one he now entered. It was reached by a lift, and by a glass bridge that flung across the dining hall and traversed the ways at a slight upward angle. To enter the first section of the place necessitated the use of his solvent signature under Asano's direction. They were immediately attended to by a man in a violet robe and gold clasp, the insignia of practising medical men. He perceived from this man's manner that his identity was known, and proceeded to ask questions on the strange arrangements of the place without reserve.

On either side of the passage, which was silent and padded, as if to deaden the footfall, were narrow little doors, their size and arrangement suggestive of the cells of a Victorian prison. But the upper portion of each door was of the same greenish transparent stuff that had enclosed him at his awakening, and within, dimly seen, lay in every case a very young baby in a little nest of wadding. Elaborate apparatus watched the atmosphere and rang a bell far away in the central office at the slightest departure from the optimum of temperature and moisture. A system of such *crèches* had almost entirely replaced the hazardous adventures of the old-world nursing. The attendant presently called Graham's attention to the wet nurses,[15] a vista of mechanical figures, with arms, shoulders and breasts of astonishingly realistic modelling, articulation and texture, but mere brass tripods below, and having in the place of features a flat disc bearing advertisements likely to be of interest to mothers.

Of all the strange things that Graham came upon that night, none jarred more upon his habits of thought than this place. The spectacle of the little pink creatures, their feeble limbs swaying uncertainly in vague first movements, left alone, without embrace or endearment, was wholly repugnant to him. The attendant doctor was of a different opinion. His statistical evidence showed beyond dispute that in the Victorian times the most dangerous passage of life was the arms of the mother, that there human mortality had ever been most terrible. On the other hand this *crèche* company, the International Crèche Syndicate, lost not one-half per cent of the million babies or so that formed its peculiar care. But Graham's prejudice was too strong even for those figures.

Along one of the many passages of the place they presently came upon a young couple in the usual blue canvas peering through the transparency and laughing hysterically at the bald head of their first-born. Graham's face must have showed his estimate of them, for their merriment ceased and they looked abashed. But this little incident accentuated his sudden realization of the gulf between his habits of thought and the ways of the new age. He passed on to the crawling rooms and the Kindergarten, perplexed and distressed. He found the endless long playrooms were empty! the latter-day children at least still spent their nights in sleep. As they went through these, the little officer pointed out the nature of the toys, developments of those devised by that inspired sentimentalist Froebel.[16] There were nurses here, but much was done by machines that sang and danced and dandled.

Graham was still not clear upon many points. 'But so many orphans,' he said perplexed, reverting to a first misconception, and learnt again that they were not orphans.

So soon as they had left the *crèche* he began to speak of the horror the babies in their incubating cases had caused him. 'Is motherhood gone?' he said. 'Was it a cant?[17] Surely it was an instinct. This seems so unnatural – abominable almost.'

'Along here we shall come to the dancing place,' said Asano by way of reply. 'It is sure to be crowded. In spite of all the political unrest it will be crowded. The women take no great interest in politics – except a few here and there. You will see the mothers – most young women in London are mothers. In that class it is considered a creditable thing to have one child – a proof of animation. Few middle-class people have more than one. With the Labour Department it is different. As for motherhood! They still take an immense pride in the children. They come here to look at them quite often.'

'Then do you mean that the population of the world—?'

'Is falling? Yes. Except among the people under the Labour Department. In spite of scientific discipline they are reckless—'

The air was suddenly dancing with music, and down a way they approached obliquely, set with gorgeous pillars as it seemed of clear amethyst, flowed a concourse of gay people and a tumult of merry cries and laughter. He saw curled heads, wreathed brows, and a happy intricate flutter of gamboge pass triumphant across the picture.

'You will see,' said Asano with a faint smile. 'The world has changed. In a moment you will see the mothers of the new age. Come this way. We shall see those yonder again very soon.'

They ascended a certain height in a swift lift, and changed to a slower one. As they went on the music grew upon them, until it was near and full and splendid, and, moving with its glorious intricacies they could distinguish the beat of innumerable dancing feet. They made a payment at a turnstile and emerged upon the wide gallery that overlooked the dancing place, and upon the full enchantment of sound and sight.

'Here,' said Asano, 'are the fathers and mothers of the little ones you saw.'

The hall was not so richly decorated as that of the Atlas, but saving that, it was, for its size, the most splendid Graham had seen. The beautiful white-limbed figures that supported the galleries reminded him once more of the restored magnificence of sculpture; they seemed to writhe in engaging attitudes, their faces laughed. The source of the music that filled the place was hidden, and the whole vast shining floor was thick with dancing couples. 'Look at them,' said the little officer, 'see how much they show of motherhood.'

The gallery they stood upon ran along the upper edge of a huge screen that cut the dancing hall on one side from a sort of outer hall that showed through broad arches the incessant onward rush of the city ways. In this outer hall was a great crowd of less brilliantly dressed people, as numerous almost as those who danced within, the great majority wearing the blue uniform of the Labour Department that was now so familiar to Graham. Too poor to pass the turnstiles to the festival, they were yet unable to keep away from the sound of its seductions. Some of them even had cleared spaces, and were dancing also, fluttering their rags in the air. Some shouted as they danced, jests and odd allusions Graham did not understand. Once some-one began whistling the refrain of the revolutionary song, but it seemed as though that beginning was promptly suppressed. The corner was dark and Graham could not see. He turned to the hall again. Above the caryatidae were marble busts of men whom that age esteemed great moral emancipators and pion-eers; for the most part their names were strange to Graham, though he recognized Grant Allen, Le Gallienne,[18] Nietzsche, Shelley and Godwin.[19] Great black festoons and eloquent senti-ments reinforced the huge inscription that partially defaced the upper end of the dancing place, and asserted that 'The Festival of the Awakening' was in progress.

'Myriads are taking holiday or staying from work because of that, quite apart from the labourers who refuse to go back,' said Asano. 'These people are always ready for holidays.'

Graham walked to the parapet and stood leaning over, look-ing down at the dancers. Save for two or three remote whisper-ing couples, who had stolen apart, he and his guide had the gallery to themselves. A warm breath of scent and vitality came up to him. Both men and women below were lightly clad, bare-armed, open-necked, as the universal warmth of the city permitted. The hair of the men was often a mass of effeminate curls, their chins were always shaven, and many of them had flushed or coloured cheeks. Many of the women were very pretty, and all were dressed with elaborate coquetry. As they swept by beneath, he saw ecstatic faces with eyes half closed in pleasure.

'What sort of people are these?' he asked abruptly.

'Workers – prosperous workers. What you would have called the middle class. Independent tradesmen with little separate businesses have vanished long ago, but there are store servers, managers, engineers of a hundred sorts. Tonight is a holiday of course, and every dancing place in the city will be crowded, and every place of worship.'

'But – the women?'

'The same. There's a thousand forms of work for women now. But you had the beginning of the independent working-woman in your days. Most women are independent now. Most of these are married more or less – there are a number of methods of contract – and that gives them more money, and enables them to enjoy themselves.'

'I see,' said Graham, looking at the flushed faces, the flash and swirl of movement, and still thinking of that nightmare of pink helpless limbs. 'And these are – mothers.'

'Most of them.'

'The more I see of these things the more complex I find your problems. This, for instance, is a surprise. That news from Paris was a surprise.'

In a little while he spoke again:

'These are mothers. Presently, I suppose, I shall get into the modern way of seeing things. I have old habits of mind clinging about me – habits based, I suppose, on needs that are over and done with. Of course, in our time, a woman was supposed not only to bear children, but to cherish them, to devote herself to them, to educate them – all the essentials of moral and mental education a child owed its mother. Or went without. Quite a number, I admit, went without. Nowadays, clearly, there is no more need for such care than if they were butterflies. I see that! Only there was an ideal – that figure of a grave, patient woman, silently and serenely mistress of a home, mother and maker of men – to love her was a sort of worship—'

He stopped and repeated, 'A sort of worship.'

'Ideals change,' said the little man, 'as needs change.'

Graham awoke from an instant reverie and Asano repeated his words. Graham's mind returned to the thing at hand.

'Of course I see the perfect reasonableness of this. Restraint, soberness, the matured thought, the unselfish act, they are necessities of the barbarous state, the life of dangers. Dourness is man's tribute to unconquered nature. But man has conquered nature now for all practical purposes – his political affairs are managed by Bosses with a black police – and life is joyous.'

He looked at the dancers again. 'Joyous,' he said.

'There are weary moments,' said the little officer, reflectively.

'They all look young. Down there I should be visibly the oldest man. And in my own time I should have passed as middle-aged.'

'They are young. There are few old people in this class in the work cities.'

'How is that?'

'Old people's lives are not so pleasant as they used to be, unless they are rich to hire lovers and helpers. And we have an institution called Euthanasy.'

'Ah! that Euthanasy!' said Graham. 'The easy death?'

'The easy death. It is the last pleasure. The Euthanasy Company does it well. People will pay the sum – it is a costly thing – long beforehand, go off to some Pleasure City and return impoverished and weary, very weary.'

'There is a lot left for me to understand,' said Graham after a pause. 'Yet I see the logic of it all. Our array of angry virtues and sour restraints was the consequence of danger and insecurity. The Stoic, the Puritan, even in my time, were vanishing types. In the old days man was armed against Pain, now he is eager for Pleasure. There lies the difference. Civilization has driven pain and danger so far off – for well-to-do people. And only well-to-do people matter now. I have been asleep two hundred years.'

For a minute they leant on the balustrading, following the intricate evolution of the dance. Indeed the scene was very beautiful.

'Before God,' said Graham, suddenly, 'I would rather be a wounded sentinel freezing in the snow than one of these painted fools!'

'In the snow,' said Asano, 'one might think differently.'

'I am uncivilized,' said Graham, not heeding him. 'That is the trouble. I am primitive – Palaeolithic. *Their* fountain of rage and fear and anger is sealed and closed, the habits of a lifetime make them cheerful and easy and delightful. You must bear with my nineteenth-century shocks and disgusts. These people, you say, are skilled workers and so forth. And while these dance, men are fighting – men are dying in Paris to keep the world – that they may dance.'

Asano smiled faintly. 'For that matter, men are dying in London,' he said.

There was a moment's silence.

'Where do these sleep?' asked Graham.

'Above and below – an intricate warren.'

'And where do they work? This is – the domestic life.'

'You will see little work tonight. Half the workers are out or under arms. Half these people are keeping holiday. But we will go to the work places if you wish it.'

For a time Graham watched the dancers, then suddenly turned away. 'I want to see the workers. I have seen enough of these,' he said.

Asano led the way along the gallery across the dancing hall. Presently they came to a transverse passage that brought a breath of fresher, colder air.

Asano glanced at this passage as they went past, stopped, went back to it, and turned to Graham with a smile. 'Here, Sire,' he said, 'is something – will be familiar to you at least – and yet – But I will not tell you. Come!'

He led the way along a closed passage that presently became

cold. The reverberation of their feet told that this passage was
a bridge. They came into a circular gallery that was glazed in
from the outer weather, and so reached a circular chamber
which seemed familiar, though Graham could not recall distinctly when he had entered it before. In this was a ladder up
which they went, and came into a high, dark, cold place in
which was another almost vertical ladder. This they ascended,
Graham still perplexed.

But at the top he understood, and recognized the metallic
bars to which he clung. He was in the cage under the ball of
St Paul's. The dome rose but a little way above the general
contour of the city, into the still twilight, and sloped away,
shining greasily under a few distant lights, into a circumambient
ditch of darkness.

Out between the bars he looked upon the wind-clear northern
sky and saw the starry constellations all unchanged. Capella
hung in the west, Vega was rising, and the seven glittering
points of the Great Bear[20] swept overhead in their stately circle
about the Pole.

He saw these stars in a clear gap of sky. To the east and
south the great circular shapes of complaining wind-wheels
blotted out the heavens, so that the glare about the Council
House was hidden. To the south-west hung Orion,[21] showing
like a pallid ghost through a tracery of ironwork and interlacing
shapes above a dazzling coruscation of lights. A bellowing and
siren screaming that came from the flying stages warned the
world that one of the aeroplanes was ready to start. He
remained for a space gazing towards the glaring stage. Then his
eyes went back to the northward constellations.

For a long time he was silent. 'This,' he said at last, smiling
in the shadow, 'seems the strangest thing of all. To stand in the
dome of St Paul's and look once more upon these familiar,
silent stars!'

Thence Graham was taken by Asano along devious ways to
the great gambling and business quarters where the bulk of the
fortunes in the city were lost and made. It impressed him as a
well-nigh interminable series of very high halls, surrounded by
tiers upon tiers of galleries into which opened thousands of

offices, and traversed by a complicated multitude of bridges, footways, aerial motor rails and trapeze and cable leaps. And here more than anywhere the note of vehement vitality, of uncontrollable, hasty activity, rose high. Everywhere was violent advertisement, until his brain swam at the tumult of light and colour. And Babble Machines of a peculiarly rancid tone were abundant and filled the air with strenuous squealing and an idiotic slang. 'Skin your eyes and slide,' 'Gewhoop, Bonanza,' 'Gollipers come and hark!'

The place seemed to him to be dense with people either profoundly agitated or swelling with obscure cunning, yet he learnt that it was comparatively empty, that the great political convulsion of the last few days had reduced transactions to an unprecedented minimum. In one hall were long avenues of roulette tables, each with a silent, watchful crowd about it; in another a yelping Babel of white-faced women and red-necked leathery-lunged men bought and sold the shares of an absolutely fictitious business undertaking which every five minutes paid a dividend of ten per cent and cancelled a certain proportion of its shares by means of a lottery wheel.

These business activities were prosecuted with an energy that readily passed into violence, and Graham approaching a dense crowd found at its centre a couple of prominent merchants in violent controversy with teeth and nails on some delicate point of business etiquette. Something still remained in life to be fought for. Further he had a shock at a vehement announcement in phonetic letters of scarlet flame, each twice the height of a man, that 'WE ASSURE THE PROPRAIET'R.[22] WE ASSURE THE PROPRAIET'R.'

'Who's the proprietor?' he asked.

'You.'

'But what do they assure me?' he asked. 'What do they assure me?'

'Didn't you have assurance?'

Graham thought. 'Insurance?'

'Yes – Insurance. I remember that was the older word. They are insuring your life. Dozands of people are taking out policies, myriads of lions are being put on you. And further on other people are buying annuities. They do that on everybody who is at all prominent. Look there!'

A crowd of people surged and roared, and Graham saw a vast black screen suddenly illuminated in still larger letters of burning purple. 'Anuetes on the Propraiet'r – x 5 pr. G.' The people began to boo and shout at this, a number of hard-breathing, wild-eyed men came running past, clawing with hooked fingers at the air. There was a furious crush about a little doorway.

Asano did a brief, inaccurate calculation. 'Seventeen per cent per annum is their annuity on you. They would not pay so much per cent if they could see you now, Sire. But they do not know. Your own annuities used to be a very safe investment, but now you are sheer gambling, of course. This is probably a desperate bid. I doubt if people will get their money.'

The crowd of would-be annuitants grew so thick about them that for some time they could move neither forward nor backward. Graham noticed what appeared to him to be a high proportion of women among the speculators, and was reminded again of the economic independence of their sex. They seemed remarkably well able to take care of themselves in the crowd, using their elbows with particular skill, as he learnt to his cost. One curly-headed person caught in the pressure for a space, looked steadfastly at him several times, almost as if she recognized him, and then, edging deliberately towards him, touched his hand with her arm in a scarcely accidental manner, and made it plain by a look as ancient as Chaldea[23] that he had found favour in her eyes. And then a lank, grey-bearded man, perspiring copiously in a noble passion of self-help, blind to all earthly things save that glaring bait, thrust between them in a cataclysmal rush towards that alluring 'x 5 pr. G.'

'I want to get out of this,' said Graham to Asano. 'This is not what I came to see. Show me the workers. I want to see the people in blue. These parasitic lunatics—'

He found himself wedged into a struggling mass of people.

CHAPTER 21

THE UNDERSIDE[1]

From the Business Quarter they presently passed by the running ways into a remote quarter of the city, where the bulk of the manufactures was done. On their way the platforms crossed the Thames twice, and passed in a broad viaduct across one of the great roads that entered the city from the north. In both cases his impression was swift and in both very vivid. The river was a broad wrinkled glitter of black sea water, overarched by buildings, and vanishing either way into a blackness starred with receding lights. A string of black barges passed seaward, manned by blue-clad men. The road was a long and very broad and high tunnel, along which big-wheeled machines drove noiselessly and swiftly. Here, too, the distinctive blue of the Labour Department was in abundance. The smoothness of the double tracks, the largeness and the lightness of the big pneumatic wheels in proportion to the vehicular body, struck Graham most vividly. One lank and very high carriage with longitudinal metallic rods hung with the dripping carcasses of many hundred sheep arrested his attention unduly. Abruptly the edge of the archway cut and blotted out the picture.

Presently they left the way and descended by a lift and traversed a passage that sloped downward, and so came to a descending lift again. The appearance of things changed. Even the pretence of architectural ornament disappeared, the lights diminished in number and size, the architecture became more and more massive in proportion to the spaces as the factory quarters were reached. And in the dusty biscuit-making[2] place of the potters, among the felspar[3] mills, in the furnace rooms of the metal workers, among the incandescent lakes of crude

Eadhamite, the blue canvas clothing was on man, woman and child.

Many of these great and dusty galleries were silent avenues of machinery, endless raked-out ashen furnaces testified to the revolutionary dislocation, but wherever there was work it was being done by slow-moving workers in blue canvas. The only people not in blue canvas were the overlookers of the work-places and the orange-clad Labour Police. And fresh from the flushed faces of the dancing halls, the voluntary vigours of the Business Quarter, Graham could note the pinched faces, the feeble muscles, and weary eyes of many of the latter-day workers. Such as he saw at work were noticeably inferior in physique to the few gaily dressed managers and forewomen who were directing their labours. The burly labourers of the old Victorian times had followed the dray horse[4] and all such living force producers, to extinction; the place of his costly muscles was taken by some dexterous machine. The latter-day labourer, male as well as female, was essentially a machine-minder and feeder, a servant and attendant, or an artist under direction.

The women, in comparison with those Graham remembered, were as a class distinctly plain and flat-chested.[5] Two hundred years of emancipation from the moral restraints of Puritanical religion, two hundred years of city life, had done their work in eliminating the strain of feminine beauty and vigour from the blue canvas myriads. To be brilliant physically or mentally, to be in any way attractive or exceptional, had been and was still a certain way of emancipation to the drudge, a line of escape to the Pleasure City and its splendours and delights, and at last to the Euthanasy and peace. To be steadfast against such inducements was scarcely to be expected of meanly nourished souls. In the young cities of Graham's former life, the newly aggregated labouring mass had been a diverse multitude, still stirred by the tradition of personal honour and a high morality; now it was differentiating into an instinct class, with a moral and physical difference of its own – even with a dialect of its own.

They penetrated downward, ever downward, towards the

working places. Presently they passed underneath one of the streets of the moving ways, and saw its platforms running on their rails far overhead, and chinks of white light between the transverse slits. The factories that were not working were sparsely lighted; to Graham they and their shrouded aisles of giant machines seemed plunged in gloom, and even where work was going on the illumination was far less brilliant than upon the public ways.

Beyond the blazing lakes of Eadhamite he came to the warren of the jewellers, and, with some difficulty and by using his signature, obtained admission to these galleries. They were high and dark, and rather cold. In the first a few men were making ornaments of gold filigree, each man at a little bench by himself, and with a little shaded light. The long vista of light patches, with the nimble fingers brightly lit and moving among the gleaming yellow coils, and the intent face like the face of a ghost, in each shadow, had the oddest effect.

The work was beautifully executed but without any strength of modelling or drawing, for the most part intricate grotesques or the ringing of the changes on a geometrical *motif*. These workers wore a peculiar white uniform without pockets or sleeves. They assumed this on coming to work, but at night they were stripped and examined before they left the premises of the Department. In spite of every precaution, the Labour policeman told them in a depressed tone, the Department was not infrequently robbed.

Beyond was a gallery of women busied in cutting and setting slabs of artificial ruby, and next to these were men and women working together upon the slabs of copper net that formed the basis of *cloisonné* tiles.[6] Many of these workers had lips and nostrils a livid white,[7] due to a disease caused by a peculiar purple enamel that chanced to be much in fashion. Asano apologized to Graham for this offensive sight, but excused himself on the score of the convenience of this route. 'This is what I wanted to see,' said Graham; 'this is what I wanted to see,' trying to avoid a start at a particularly striking disfigurement.

'She might have done better with herself than that,' said Asano.

Graham made some indignant comments.

'But, Sire, we simply could not stand that stuff without the purple,' said Asano. 'In your days people could stand such crudities, they were nearer the barbaric by two hundred years.'

They continued along one of the lower galleries of this *cloisonné* factory, and came to a little bridge that spanned a vault. Looking over the parapet, Graham saw that beneath was a wharf under yet more tremendous archings than any he had seen. Three barges, smothered in floury dust, were being unloaded of their cargoes of powdered felspar by a multitude of coughing men, each guiding a little truck; the dust filled the place with a choking mist, and turned the electric glare yellow. The vague shadows of these workers gesticulated about their feet, and rushed to and fro against a long stretch of whitewashed wall. Every now and then one would stop to cough.

A shadowy, huge mass of masonry rising out of the inky water, brought to Graham's mind the thought of the multitude of ways and galleries and lifts that rose floor above floor overhead between him and the sky. The men worked in silence under the supervision of two of the Labour Police; their feet made a hollow thunder on the planks along which they went to and fro. And as he looked at this scene, some hidden voice in the darkness began to sing.

'Stop that!' shouted one of the policemen, but the order was disobeyed, and first one and then all the white-stained men who were working there had taken up the beating refrain, singing it defiantly – the Song of the Revolt. The feet upon the planks thundered now to the rhythm of the song, tramp, tramp, tramp. The policeman who had shouted glanced at his fellow, and Graham saw him shrug his shoulders. He made no further effort to stop the singing.

And so they went through these factories and places of toil, seeing many painful and grim things. That walk left on Graham's mind a maze of memories, fluctuating pictures of swathed halls and crowded vaults seen through clouds of dust, of intricate machines, the racing threads of looms, the heavy beat of stamping machinery, the roar and rattle of belt and armature, of ill-lit subterranean aisles of sleeping places, illimitable vistas of pinpoint lights. Here was the smell of tanning, and here the reek of a brewery, and here unprecedented reeks. Everywhere were pillars and cross archings of such a massiveness as Graham had never before seen, thick Titans of greasy, shining brickwork crushed beneath the vast weight of that complex city world, even as these anaemic millions were crushed by its complexity. And everywhere were pale features, lean limbs, disfigurement and degradation.

Once and again, and again a third time, Graham heard the Song of the Revolt during his long, unpleasant research in these places, and once he saw a confused struggle down a passage and learnt that a number of these serfs had seized their bread before their work was done. Graham was ascending towards the ways again when he saw a number of blue-clad children running down a transverse passage, and presently perceived the reason of their panic in a company of the Labour Police armed with clubs, trotting towards some unknown disturbance. And then came a remote disorder. But for the most part this remnant that worked, worked hopelessly. All the spirit that was left in fallen humanity was above in the streets that night, calling for the Master, and valiantly and noisily keeping its arms.

They emerged from these wanderings and stood blinking in the bright light of the middle passage of the platforms again. They became aware of the remote hooting and yelping of the machines of one of the General Intelligence Offices, and suddenly came men running, and along the platforms and about the ways everywhere was a shouting and crying. Then a woman with a face of mute white terror, and another who gasped and shrieked as she ran.

'What has happened now?' said Graham, puzzled, for he could not understand their thick speech. Then he heard it in English and perceived that the thing that everyone was shouting, that men yelled to one another, that women took up screaming, that was passing like the first breeze of a thunderstorm, chill and sudden through the city, was this: 'Ostrog has ordered the Black Police to London. The Black Police are coming from South Africa. . . . The Black Police. The Black Police.'

Asano's face was white and astonished; he hesitated, looked

at Graham's face, and told him the thing he already knew. 'But how can they know?' asked Asano.

Graham heard someone shouting. 'Stop all work. Stop all work,' and a swarthy hunchback, ridiculously gay in green and gold, came leaping down the platforms towards him, bawling again and again in good English, 'This is Ostrog's doing, Ostrog the Knave! The Master is betrayed.' His voice was hoarse and a thin foam dropped from his ugly shouting mouth. He yelled an unspeakable horror that the Black Police had done in Paris, and so passed shrieking, 'Ostrog the Knave!'

For a moment Graham stood still, for it had come upon him again that these things were a dream. He looked up at the great cliff of buildings on either side, vanishing into blue haze at last above the lights, and down to the roaring tiers of platforms, and the shouting, running people who were gesticulating past. 'The Master is betrayed!' they cried. 'The Master is betrayed!'

Suddenly the situation shaped itself in his mind real and urgent. His heart began to beat fast and strong.

'It has come,' he said. 'I might have known. The hour has come.'

He thought swiftly. 'What am I to do?'

'Go back to the Council House,' said Asano.

'Why should I not appeal –? The people are here.'

'You will lose time. They will doubt if it is you. But they will mass about the Council House. There you will find their leaders. Your strength is there – with them.'

'Suppose this is only a rumour?'

'It sounds true,' said Asano.

'Let us have the facts,' said Graham.

Asano shrugged his shoulders. 'We had better get towards the Council House,' he cried. 'That is where they will swarm. Even now the ruins may be impassable.'

Graham regarded him doubtfully and followed him.

They went up the stepped platforms to the swiftest one, and there Asano accosted a labourer. The answers to his questions were in the thick, vulgar speech.

'What did he say?' asked Graham.

'He knows little, but he told me that the Black Police would have arrived here before the people knew – had not someone in the wind-vane offices learnt. He said a girl.'

'A girl? Not—?'

'He said a girl – he did not know who she was. Who came out from the Council House crying aloud, and told the men at work among the ruins.'

And then another thing was shouted, something that turned an aimless tumult into determinate movements, it came like a wind along the street. 'To your Wards, to your Wards. Every man get arms. Every man to his Ward!'

CHAPTER 22
THE STRUGGLE IN THE COUNCIL HOUSE

As Asano and Graham hurried along to the ruins about the Council House, they saw everywhere the excitement of the people rising. 'To your Wards! To your Wards!' Everywhere men and women in blue were hurrying from unknown subterranean employments, up the staircases of the middle path; at one place Graham saw an arsenal of the revolutionary committee besieged by a crowd of shouting men, at another a couple of men in the hated yellow uniform of the Labour Police, pursued by a gathering crowd, fled precipitately along the swift way that went in the opposite direction.

The cries of 'To your Wards!' became at last a continuous shouting as they drew near the government quarter. Many of the shouts were unintelligible. 'Ostrog has betrayed us,' one man bawled in a hoarse voice, again and again, dinning that refrain into Graham's ear until it haunted him. This person stayed close beside Graham and Asano on the swift way, shouting to the people who swarmed on the lower platforms as he rushed past them. His cry about Ostrog alternated with some incomprehensible orders. Presently he went leaping down and disappeared.

Graham's mind was filled with the din. His plans were vague and unformed. He had one picture of some commanding position from which he could address the multitudes, another of meeting Ostrog face to face. He was full of rage, of tense muscular excitement, his hands gripped, his lips were pressed together.

The way to the Council House across the ruins was impassable, but Asano met that difficulty and took Graham into the premises of the central post-office. The post-office was nominally at work, but the blue-clothed porters moved sluggishly or had stopped to stare through the arches of their galleries at the shouting men who were going by outside. 'Every man to his Ward! Every man to his Ward!' Here, by Asano's advice, Graham revealed his identity.

They crossed to the Council House by a cable cradle. Already in the brief interval since the capitulation of the Councillors a great change had been wrought in the appearance of the ruins. The spurting cascades of the ruptured sea-water mains had been captured and tamed, and huge temporary pipes ran overhead along a flimsy-looking fabric of girders. The sky was laced with restored cables and wires that served the Council House, and a mass of new fabric with cranes and other building machines going to and fro upon it projected to the left of the white pile.

The moving ways that ran across this area had been restored, albeit for once running under the open sky. These were the ways that Graham had seen from the little balcony in the hour of his awakening, not nine days since, and the hall of his trance had been on the further side, where now shapeless piles of smashed and shattered masonry were heaped together.

It was already high day and the sun was shining brightly. Out of their tall caverns of blue electric light came the swift ways crowded with multitudes of people, who poured off them and gathered ever denser over the wreckage and confusion of the ruins. The air was full of their shouting, and they were pressing and swaying towards the central building. For the most part that shouting mass consisted of shapeless swarms, but here and there Graham could see that a rude discipline struggled to establish itself. And every voice clamoured for order in the chaos. 'To your Wards! Every man to his Ward!'

The cable carried them into a hall which Graham recognized as the antechamber to the Hall of the Atlas, about the gallery of which he had walked days ago with Howard to show himself to the vanished Council, an hour from his awakening. Now the place was empty except for two cable attendants. These men seemed hugely astonished to recognize the Sleeper in the man who swung down from the cross seat.

'Where is Ostrog?' he demanded. 'I must see Ostrog forth-with. He has disobeyed me. I have come back to take things out of his hands.' Without waiting for Asano, he went straight across the place, ascended the steps at the further end, and, pulling the curtain aside, found himself facing the perpetually labouring Titan.

The Hall was empty. Its appearance had changed very greatly since his first sight of it. It had suffered serious injury in the violent struggle of the first outbreak. On the right-hand side of the great figure the upper half of the wall had been torn away for nearly two hundred feet of its length, and a sheet of the same glassy film that had enclosed Graham at his awakening had been drawn across the gap. This deadened, but did not altogether exclude, the roar of the people outside. 'Wards! Wards! Wards!' they seemed to be saying. Through it there were visible the beams and supports of metal scaffoldings that rose and fell according to the requirements of a great crowd of workmen. An idle building machine, with lank arms of red painted metal, stretched gauntly across this green tinted picture. On it were still a number of workmen staring at the crowd below. For a moment he stood regarding these things, and Asano overtook him.

'Ostrog,' said Asano, 'will be in the small offices beyond there.' The little man looked livid now and his eyes searched Graham's face.

They had scarcely advanced ten paces from the curtain before a panel to the left of the Atlas rolled up, and Ostrog, accom-panied by Lincoln and followed by two black- and yellow-clad Negroes, appeared crossing the remote corner of the hall, towards a second panel that was raised and open. 'Ostrog,' shouted Graham, and at the sound in his voice the little party turned astonished.

Ostrog said something to Lincoln and advanced alone.

Graham was the first to speak. His voice was loud and dicta-torial. 'What is this I hear?' he asked. 'Are you bringing Negroes here – to keep the people down?'

'It is none too soon,' said Ostrog. 'They have been getting out of hand more and more, since the revolt. I under-estimated—'

'Do you mean that these infernal Negroes are on the way?'

'On the way. As it is, you have seen the people – outside?'

'No wonder! But – after what was said. You have taken too much on yourself, Ostrog.'

Ostrog said nothing, but drew nearer.

'These Negroes must not come to London,' said Graham. 'I am Master and they shall not come.'

Ostrog glanced at Lincoln, who at once came towards them with his two attendants close behind him. 'Why not?' asked Ostrog.

'White men must be mastered by white men. Besides—'

'The Negroes are only an instrument.'

'But that is not the question. I am the Master. I mean to be the Master. And I tell you these Negroes shall not come.'

'The people—'

'I believe in the people.'

'Because you are an anachronism. You are a man out of the Past – an accident. You are Owner perhaps of the world. Nominally – legally. But you are not Master. You do not know enough to be Master.'

He glanced at Lincoln again. 'I know now what you think – I can guess something of what you mean to do. Even now it is not too late to warn you. You dream of human equality – of some sort of socialistic order – you have all those worn-out dreams of the nineteenth century fresh and vivid in your mind, and you would rule this age that you do not understand.'

'Listen!' said Graham. 'You can hear it – a sound like the sea. Not voices – but a voice. Do *you* altogether understand?'

'We taught them that,' said Ostrog.

'Perhaps. Can you teach them to forget it? But enough of this! These Negroes must not come.'

There was a pause and Ostrog looked him in the eyes.

'They will,' he said.

'I forbid it,' said Graham.

'They have started.'

'I will not have it.'

'No,' said Ostrog. 'Sorry as I am to follow the method of the Council – For your own good – you must not side with –

Disorder. And now that you are here – It was kind of you to come here.'

Lincoln laid his hand on Graham's shoulder. Abruptly Graham realized the enormity of his blunder in coming to the Council House. He turned towards the curtains that separated the hall from the antechamber. The clutching hand of Asano intervened. In another moment Lincoln had grasped Graham's cloak.

He turned and struck at Lincoln's face, and incontinently a Negro had him by collar and arm. He wrenched himself away, his sleeve tore noisily, and he stumbled back, to be tripped by the other attendant. Then he struck the ground heavily and he was staring at the distant ceiling of the hall.

He shouted, rolled over, struggling fiercely, clutched an attendant's leg and threw him headlong, and struggled to his feet.

Lincoln appeared before him, went down again with a blow under the point of the jaw and lay still. Graham made two strides, stumbled. And then Ostrog's arm was round his neck, he was pulled over backward, fell, and his arms were pinned to the ground. After a few violent efforts he ceased to struggle and lay staring at Ostrog's heaving throat.

'You – are – a prisoner,' panted Ostrog, exulting. 'You – were rather a fool – to come back.'

Graham turned his head about and perceived through the irregular green window in the walls of the hall the men who had been working the building cranes gesticulating excitedly to the people below them. They had seen!

Ostrog followed his eyes and started. He shouted something to Lincoln, but Lincoln did not move. A bullet smashed among the mouldings above the Atlas. The two sheets of transparent matter that had been stretched across this gap were rent, the edges of the torn aperture darkened, curved, ran rapidly to-wards the framework, and in a moment the Council Chamber stood open to the air. A chilly gust blew in by the gap, bringing with it a war of voices from the ruinous spaces without, an elvish babblement, 'Save the Master!' 'What are they doing to the Master?' 'The Master is betrayed!'

And then he realized that Ostrog's attention was distracted, that Ostrog's grip had relaxed, and, wrenching his arms free, he struggled to his knees. In another moment he had thrust Ostrog back, and he was on one foot, his hand gripping Ostrog's throat, and Ostrog's hands clutching the silk about his neck.

But now men were coming towards them from the dais – men whose intentions he misunderstood. He had a glimpse of someone running in the distance towards the curtains of the antechamber, and then Ostrog had slipped from him and these newcomers were upon him. To his infinite astonishment, they seized him. They obeyed the shouts of Ostrog.

He was lugged a dozen yards before he realized that they were not friends – that they were dragging him towards the open panel. When he saw this he pulled back, he tried to fling himself down, he called for help with all his strength. And this time there were answering cries.

The grip upon his neck relaxed, and behold! in the lower corner of the rent upon the wall, first one and then a number of little black figures appeared hooting and waving arms. They came leaping down from the gap into the light gallery that had led to the Silent Rooms. They ran along it, so near were they that Graham could see the weapons in their hands. Then Ostrog was giving directions to the men who held him, and once more he was struggling with all his strength against their endeavours to thrust him towards the opening that yawned to receive him. 'They can't come down,' panted Ostrog. 'They daren't fire. It's all right. We'll save him from them yet.'

For long minutes as it seemed to Graham that inglorious struggle continued. His clothes were rent in a dozen places, he was covered in dust, one hand had been trodden upon. He could hear the shouts of his supporters, and once he heard shots. He could feel his strength giving way, feel his efforts wild and aimless. But no help came, and surely, irresistibly, that black, yawning opening came nearer.

The pressure upon him relaxed and he struggled up. He saw Ostrog's grey head receding and perceived that he was no longer held. He turned about and came full into a man in black. One of the green weapons cracked close to him, a drift of pungent smoke came into his face, and a steel blade flashed. The huge chamber span about him.

He saw a man in pale blue stabbing one of the black and yellow attendants not three yards from his face. Then hands were upon him again.

He was being pulled in two directions now. It seemed as though people were shouting to him. He wanted to understand and could not. Someone was clutching about his thighs, he was being hoisted in spite of his vigorous efforts. He understood suddenly, he ceased to struggle. He was lifted up on men's shoulders and carried away from that devouring panel. Ten thousand throats were cheering.

He saw men in blue and black hurrying after the retreating Ostrogites and firing. Lifted up, he saw now across the whole expanse of the hall beneath the Atlas image, saw that he was being carried towards the raised platform in the centre of the place. The far end of the hall was already full of people running towards him. They were looking at him and cheering.

He became aware that a bodyguard surrounded him. Active men about him gave vague orders. He saw close at hand the black-moustached man in yellow who had been among those who had greeted him in the public theatre, shouting directions. The hall was already densely packed with swaying people, the little metal gallery sagged with a howling load, the curtains at the end had been torn away, and the antechamber was revealed densely crowded. He could scarcely make the man near him hear for the tumult about them. 'Where has Ostrog gone?' he asked.

The man he questioned pointed over the heads towards the lower panels about the hall on the side opposite the gap. They stood open, and armed men, blue clad with black sashes, were running through them and vanishing into the chambers and passages beyond. It seemed to Graham that a sound of firing drifted through the riot. He was carried in a staggering curve across the great hall towards an opening beneath the gap.

He perceived men working with a sort of rude discipline to keep the crowd off him, to make a space clear about him. He

passed out of the hall, and saw a crude, new wall rising blankly
before him topped by blue sky. He was swung down to his feet;
someone gripped his arm and guided him. He found the man
in yellow close at hand. They were taking him up a narrow
stairway of brick, and above rose the great red-painted masses,
the cranes and levers and the still engines of the big building
machine.

He was at the top of the steps. He was hurried across a
narrow railed footway, and suddenly with a vast uproar the
amphitheatre of ruins opened again before him. 'The Master is
with us! The Master! The Master!' The cry swept athwart the
lake of faces like a wave, broke against the distant cliff of ruins,
and came back in a welter of sounds. 'The Master is on our side!'

Graham perceived that he was no longer encompassed by
people, that he was standing upon a little temporary platform
of white metal, part of a flimsy-seeming scaffolding that laced
about the great mass of the Council House. Over all the huge
expanse of the ruins swayed and eddied the people; and here
and there the black banners of the revolutionary societies
ducked and swayed and formed rare nuclei of organization in
the chaos. Up the steep stairs of wall and scaffolding by which
his rescuers had reached the opening in the Atlas Chamber
clung a solid crowd, and little energetic black figures clinging to
pillars and projections were strenuous to induce these congested
masses to stir. Behind him, at a higher point on the scaffolding,
a number of men struggled upwards with the flapping folds of
a huge black standard. Through the yawning gap in the walls
below him he could look down upon the packed attentive
multitudes in the Hall of the Atlas. The distant flying stages to
the south came out bright and vivid, brought nearer as it seemed
by an unusual translucency of the air. A solitary monoplane
beat up from the central stage as if to meet the coming aeroplanes.

'What has become of Ostrog?' asked Graham, and even as
he spoke he saw that all eyes were turned from him towards
the crest of the Council House building. He looked also in this
direction of universal attention. For a moment he saw nothing
but the jagged corner of a wall, hard and clear against the sky.

Then in the shadow he perceived the interior of a room and recognized with a start the green and white decorations of his former prison. And coming quickly across this opened room and up to the very verge of the cliff of the ruins came a little white-clad figure followed by two other smaller-seeming figures in black and yellow. He heard the man beside him exclaim 'Ostrog,' and turned to ask a question. But he never did, because of the startled exclamation of another of those who were with him and a lank finger suddenly pointing. And behold! the mono-plane that had been rising from the flying stage when last he had looked in that direction, was driving towards them. The swift steady flight was still novel enough to hold his attention.

Nearer it came, growing rapidly larger and larger, until it had swept over the further edge of the ruins and into view of the dense multitudes below. It drooped across the space and rose and passed overhead, rising to clear the mass of the Council House, a filmy translucent shape with the aeronaut peering down through its ribs. It vanished beyond the skyline of the ruins.

Graham transferred his attention to Ostrog. He was signal-ling with his hands, and his attendants were busy breaking down the wall beside him. In another moment the monoplane came into view again, a little thing far away, coming round in a wide curve and going slower.

Then suddenly the man in yellow shouted: 'What are they doing? What are the people doing? Why is Ostrog left there? Why is he not captured? They will lift him – the monoplane will lift him! Ah!'

The exclamation was echoed by a shout from the ruins. The rattling sound of the green weapons drifted across the intervening gulf to Graham, and, looking down, he saw a number of black and yellow uniforms running along one of the galleries that lay open to the air below the promontory upon which Ostrog stood. They fired as they ran at men unseen, and then emerged a number of pale-blue figures in pursuit. These minute fighting figures had the oddest effect; they seemed as they ran like little model soldiers in a toy. This queer appearance of a house cut open gave that struggle amidst furniture and passages a quality of unreality. It was perhaps two hundred yards away from him, and very nearly fifty above the heads in the ruins below. The black and yellow men ran into an open archway, and turned and fired a volley. One of the blue pursuers striding forward close to the edge, flung up his arms, staggered sideways, seemed to Graham's sense to hang over the edge for several seconds, and fell headlong down. Graham saw him strike a projecting corner, fly out, head over heels, head over heels, and vanish behind the red arm of the building machine.

And then a shadow came between Graham and the sun. He looked up and the sky was clear, but he knew the little monoplane had passed. Ostrog had vanished. The man in yellow thrust before him, zealous and perspiring, pointing and blatant.

'They are grounding!' cried the man in yellow. 'They are grounding. Tell the people to fire at him. Tell them to fire at him!'

Graham could not understand. He heard loud voices repeating these enigmatical orders.

Suddenly he saw the prow of the monoplane come gliding over the edge of the ruins and stop with a jerk. In a moment Graham understood that the thing had grounded in order that Ostrog might escape by it. He saw a blue haze climbing out of the gulf, perceived that the people below him were now firing up at the projecting stem.

A man beside him cheered hoarsely, and he saw that the blue rebels had gained the archway that had been contested by the men in black and yellow a moment before, and were running in a continual stream along the open passage.

And suddenly the monoplane slipped over the edge of the Council House and fell like a diving swallow. It dropped, tilting at an angle of forty-five degrees, so steeply that it seemed to Graham, it seemed perhaps to most of those below, that it could not possibly rise again.

It fell so closely past him that he could see Ostrog clutching the guides of the seat, with his grey hair streaming; see the white-faced aeronaut wrenching over the lever that turned the machine upward. He heard the apprehensive vague cry of innumerable men below.

Graham gripped the railing before him and gasped. The second seemed an age. The lower van of the monoplane passed within an ace of touching the people, who yelled and screamed and trampled one another below.

And then it rose.

For a moment it looked as if it could not possibly clear the opposite cliff, and then that it could not possibly clear the wind-wheel that rotated beyond.

And behold! it was clear and soaring, still heeling sideways, upward, upward into the wind-swept sky.

The suspense of the moment gave place to a fury of exasperation as the swarming people realized that Ostrog had escaped them. With belated activity they renewed their fire, until the rattling wove into a roar, until the whole area became dim and blue and the air pungent with the thin smoke of their weapons.

Too late! The flying machine dwindled smaller and smaller, and curved about and swept gracefully downward to the flying stage from which it had so lately risen. Ostrog had escaped.

For a while a confused babblement arose from the ruins, and then the universal attention came back to Graham, perched high among the scaffolding. He saw the faces of the people turned towards him, heard their shouts at his rescue. From the throat of the ways came the Song of the Revolt spreading like a breeze across that swaying sea of men.

The little group of men about him shouted congratulations on his escape. The man in yellow was close to him, with a set face and shining eyes. And the song was rising, louder and louder; tramp, tramp, tramp, tramp.

Slowly the realization came of the full meaning of these things to him, the perception of the swift change in his position. Ostrog, who had stood beside him whenever he had faced that shouting multitude before, was beyond there – the antagonist. There was no one to rule for him any longer. Even the people about him, the leaders and organizers of the multitude, looked to see what he would do, looked to him to act, awaited his orders. He was king indeed. His puppet reign was at an end.

He was very intent to do the thing that was expected of him. His nerves and muscles were quivering, his mind was perhaps a little confused, but he felt neither fear nor anger. His hand that had been trodden upon throbbed and was hot. He was a little nervous about his bearing. He knew he was not afraid, but he was anxious not to seem afraid. In his former life he had often been more excited in playing games of skill. He was desirous of immediate action, he knew he must not think too much in detail of the huge complexity of the struggle about him lest he should be paralysed by the sense of its intricacy.

Over there those square blue shapes, the flying stages, meant Ostrog; against Ostrog, who was so clear and definite and decisive, he who was so vague and undecided, was fighting for the whole future of the world.

CHAPTER 23
GRAHAM SPEAKS HIS WORD

For a time the Master of the Earth was not even master of his own mind. Even his will seemed a will not his own, his own acts surprised him and were but a part of the confusion of strange experiences that poured across his being. Three things were definite, the Negroes were coming, Helen Wotton had warned the people of their coming, and he was Master of the Earth. Each of these facts seemed struggling for complete possession of his thoughts. They protruded from a background of swarming halls, elevated passages, rooms jammed with ward leaders in council, kinematograph and telephone rooms, and windows looking out on a seething sea of marching men. The men in yellow, and men whom he fancied were called Ward Leaders, were either propelling him forward or following him obediently; it was hard to tell. Perhaps they were doing a little of both. Perhaps some power unseen and unsuspected propelled them all. He was aware that he was going to make a proclamation to the People of the Earth, aware of certain grandiose phrases floating in his mind as the thing he meant to say. He found himself with the man in yellow entering a little room where this proclamation of his was to be made.

This room was grotesquely latter-day in its appointments. In the centre was a bright oval lit by shaded electric lights from above. The rest was in shadow, and the double finely fitting doors through which he came from the swarming Hall of the Atlas made the place very still. The dead thud of these as they closed behind him, the sudden cessation of the tumult in which he had been living for hours, the quivering circle of light, the whispers and quick noiseless movements of vaguely visible attendants in the shadows, had a strange effect upon Graham. The huge ears of a phonographic mechanism gaped in a battery for his words, the black eyes of great photographic cameras awaited his beginning, beyond metal rods and coils glittered dimly, and something whirled about with a droning hum. He walked into the centre of the light, and his shadow drew together black and sharp to a little blot at his feet.

The vague shape of the words he meant to say was already in his mind. But this silence, this isolation, this withdrawal from that contagious crowd, this audience of gaping, glaring machines, had not been in his anticipation. All his supports seemed taken away; he seemed to have dropped into this suddenly, suddenly to have discovered himself. In a moment he was changed. He found that he now feared to be inadequate, he feared to be theatrical, he feared the quality of his voice, the quality of his wit; astonished, he turned to the man in yellow with a propitiatory gesture. 'Just for a little while,' he said, 'I must wait. I did not think it would be like this. I must think again of what I have to say.'

While he was still hesitating there came an agitated messenger with news that the foremost aeroplanes were passing over Madrid.

'What news of the flying stages?' he asked.

'The people of the south-west wards are ready.'

'Ready!'

He turned impatiently to the blank circles of the lenses again.

'I suppose it must be a sort of speech. Would to God I knew certainly the thing that should be said! Aeroplanes at Madrid! They must have started before the main fleet.

'Oh! what can it matter whether I speak well or ill?' he said, and felt the light grow brighter.

He had framed some vague sentence of democratic sentiment when suddenly doubts overwhelmed him. His belief in his heroic quality and calling he found had altogether lost its assured conviction. The picture of a little strutting futility in a windy waste of incomprehensible destinies replaced it. Abruptly it was perfectly clear to him that this revolt against Ostrog was premature, foredoomed to failure, the impulse of passionate inadequacy against inevitable things. He thought of that swift flight of aeroplanes like the swoop of Fate towards him. He was astonished that he could have seen things in any other light. In that final emergency he debated, thrust debate resolutely aside, determined at all costs to go through with the thing he had undertaken. And he could find no word to begin. Even as he stood, awkward, hesitating, with an indiscreet apology for his inability trembling on his lips, came the noise of many people crying out, the running to and fro of feet. 'Wait,' cried someone, and a door opened. Graham turned, and the watching lights waned.

Through the open doorway he saw a slight girlish figure approaching. His heart leapt. It was Helen Wotton. The man in yellow came out of the nearer shadows into the circle of light.

'This is the girl who told us what Ostrog had done,' he said.

She came in very quietly, and stood still, as if she did not want to interrupt Graham's eloquence. . . . But his doubts and questionings fled before her presence. He remembered the things that he had meant to say. He faced the cameras again and the light about him grew brighter. He turned back to her.

'You have helped me,' he said lamely – 'helped me very much. . . . This is very difficult.'

He paused. He addressed himself to the unseen multitudes who stared upon him through those grotesque black eyes. At first he spoke slowly.

'Men and women of the new age,' he said; 'you have arisen to do battle for the race! . . . There is no easy victory before us.'

He stopped to gather words. He wished passionately for the gift of moving speech.

'This night is a beginning,' he said. 'This battle that is coming, this battle that rushes upon us tonight, is only a beginning. All your lives, it may be, you must fight. Take no thought though I am beaten, though I am utterly overthrown. I think I may be overthrown.'

He found the thing in his mind too vague for words. He paused momentarily, and broke into vague exhortations, and then a rush of speech came upon him. Much that he said was but the humanitarian commonplace of a vanished age, but the conviction of his voice touched it to vitality. He stated the case of the old days to the people of the new age, to the girl at his side. 'I come out of the past to you', he said, 'with the memory of an age that hoped. My age was an age of dreams – of beginnings, an age of noble hopes; throughout the world we had made an end of slavery; throughout the world we had spread the desire and anticipation that wars might cease, that all men and women might live nobly, in freedom and peace. . . . So we hoped in the days that are past. And what of those hopes? How is it with man after two hundred years?

'Great cities, vast powers, a collective greatness beyond our dreams. For that we did not work, and that has come. But how is it with the little lives that make up this greater life? How is it with the common lives? As it has ever been – sorrow and labour, lives cramped and unfulfilled, lives tempted by power, tempted by wealth, and gone to waste and folly. The old faiths have faded and changed, the new faith – Is there a new faith?

'Charity and mercy,' he floundered; 'beauty and the love of beautiful things – effort and devotion! Give yourselves as I would give myself – as Christ gave Himself upon the Cross. It does not matter if you understand. It does not matter if you seem to fail. You *know* – in the core of your hearts you *know*. There is no promise, there is no security – nothing to go upon but Faith. There is no faith but faith – faith which is courage. . . .'

Things that he had long wished to believe, he found that he believed. He spoke gustily, in broken incomplete sentences, but with all his heart and strength, of this new faith within him. He spoke of the greatness of self-abnegation, of his belief in an immortal life of Humanity in which we live and move and have our being. His voice rose and fell, and the recording appliances hummed as he spoke, dim attendants watched him out of the shadow. . . .

His sense of that silent spectator beside him sustained his sincerity. For a few glorious moments he was carried away; he felt no doubt of his heroic quality, no doubt of his heroic words, he had it all straight and plain. His eloquence limped no longer.

And at last he made an end to speaking. 'Here and now,' he cried, 'I make my will. All that is mine in the world I give to the people of the world. All that is mine in the world I give to the people of the world. To all of you. I give it to you, and myself I give to you. And as God wills tonight, I will live for you, or I will die.'

He ended. He found the light of his present exaltation reflected in the face of the girl. Their eyes met; her eyes were swimming with tears of enthusiasm.

'I knew,' she whispered. 'Oh! Father of the World – *Sire*! I knew you would say these things. . . .'

'I have said what I could,' he answered lamely and for a moment held her outstretched hands.

CHAPTER 24
WHILE THE AEROPLANES WERE COMING*

The man in yellow was beside them. Neither had noted his coming. He was saying that the south-west wards were marching. 'I never expected it so soon,' he cried. 'They have done wonders. You must send them a word to help them on their way.'

Graham stared at him absent-mindedly. Then with a start he returned to his previous preoccupation about the flying stages.

'Yes,' he said. 'That is good, that is good.' He weighed a message. 'Tell them; – well done South West.'

He turned his eyes to Helen Wotton again. His face expressed his struggle between conflicting ideas. 'We must capture the flying stages,' he explained. 'Unless we can do that they will land Negroes. At all costs we must prevent that.'

He felt even as he spoke that this was not what had been in his mind before the interruption. He saw a touch of surprise in her eyes. She seemed about to speak and a shrill bell drowned her voice.

It occurred to Graham that she expected him to lead these marching people, that that was the thing he had to do. He made the offer abruptly. He addressed the man in yellow, but he spoke to her. He saw her face respond. 'Here I am doing nothing,' he said.

'It is impossible,' protested the man in yellow. 'It is a fight in a warren. Your place is here.'

He explained elaborately. He motioned towards the room where Graham must wait, he insisted no other course was possible. 'We must know where you are,' he said. 'At any

* These chapters were written fifteen years before there was any fighting in the air, and eleven before there was an aeroplane in the air.

moment a crisis may arise needing your presence and decision.'

A picture had drifted through his mind of such a vast dramatic struggle as the masses in the ruins had suggested. But here was no spectacular battlefield such as he imagined. Instead was seclusion – and suspense. It was only as the afternoon wore on that he pieced together a truer picture of the fight that was raging, inaudibly and invisibly, within four miles of him, beneath the Roehampton stage. A strange and unprecedented contest it was, a battle that was a hundred thousand little battles, a battle in a sponge of ways and channels, fought out of sight of sky or sun under the electric glare, fought out in a vast confusion by multitudes untrained in arms, led chiefly by acclamation, multitudes dulled by mindless labour and enervated by the tradition of two hundred years of servile security against multitudes demoralized by lives of venial privilege and sensual indulgence. They had no artillery, no differentiation into this force or that; the only weapon on either side was the little green metal carbine whose secret manufacture and sudden distribution in enormous quantities had been one of Ostrog's culminating moves against the Council. Few had had any experience with this weapon, many had never discharged one, many who carried it came unprovided with ammunition; never was wilder firing in the history of warfare. It was a battle of amateurs, a hideous experimental warfare, armed rioters fighting armed rioters, armed rioters swept forward by the words and fury of a song, by the tramping sympathy of their numbers, pouring in countless myriads towards the smaller ways, the disabled lifts, the galleries slippery with blood, the halls and passages choked with smoke beneath the flying stages, to learn there when retreat was hopeless the ancient mysteries of warfare. And overhead save for a few sharpshooters upon the roof spaces and for a few bands and threads of vapour that multiplied and darkened towards the evening, the day was a clear serenity. Ostrog it seems had no bombs at command and in all the earlier phases of the battle the flying machines played no part. Not the smallest cloud was there to break the empty brilliance of the sky. It was as though it held itself vacant until the aeroplanes should come.

Ever and again there was news of these, drawing nearer, from this Spanish town and then that, and presently from France. But of the new guns that Ostrog had made and which were known to be in the city came no news in spite of Graham's urgency, nor any report of successes from the dense felt of fighting strands about the flying stages. Section after section of the Labour Societies reported itself assembled, reported itself marching, and vanished from knowledge into the labyrinth of that warfare. What was happening there? Even the busy Ward Leaders did not know. In spite of the opening and closing of doors, the hasty messengers, the ringing of bells and the perpetual clitter-clack of recording implements, Graham felt isolated, strangely inactive, inoperative.

His isolation seemed at times the strangest, the most unexpected of all the things that had happened since his awakening. It had something of the quality of that inactivity that comes in dreams. A tumult, the stupendous realization of a world struggle between Ostrog and himself, and then this confined quiet little room with its mouthpieces and bells and broken mirror!

Now the door would be closed and Graham and Helen were alone together; they seemed sharply marked off then from all the unprecedented world storm that rushed together without, vividly aware of one another, only concerned with one another. Then the door would open again, messengers would enter, or a sharp bell would stab their privacy, and it was like a window in a brightly lit house flung open suddenly to a hurricane. The dark hurry and tumult, the stress and vehemence of the battle rushed in and overwhelmed them. They were no longer persons but mere spectators, mere impressions of a tremendous convulsion. They became unreal even to themselves, miniatures of personality, indescribably small, and the two antagonistic realities, the only realities in being were first the city, that throbbed and roared yonder in a belated frenzy of defence, and secondly the aeroplanes hurling inexorably towards them over the round shoulder of the world.

There came a sudden stir outside, a running to and fro, and cries. The girl stood up, speechless, incredulous.

Metallic voices were shouting 'Victory!' Yes it was 'Victory!'

Bursting through the curtains appeared the man in yellow, startled and dishevelled with excitement. 'Victory,' he cried, 'victory! The people are winning. Ostrog's people have collapsed.'

She rose. 'Victory?'

'What do you mean?' asked Graham. 'Tell me! *What*?'

'We have driven them out of the under galleries at Norwood, Streatham is afire and burning wildly, and Roehampton is ours. *Ours*! – and we have taken the monoplane that lay thereon.'

A shrill bell rang. An agitated grey-headed man appeared from the room of the Ward Leaders. 'It is all over,' he cried.

'What matters it now that we have Roehampton? The aeroplanes have been sighted at Boulogne!'[1]

'The Channel!' said the man in yellow. He calculated swiftly. 'Half an hour.'

'They still have three of the flying stages,' said the old man.

'Those guns?' cried Graham.

'We cannot mount them – in half an hour.'

'Do you mean they are found?'

'Too late,' said the old man.

'If we could stop them another hour!' cried the man in yellow.

'Nothing can stop them now,' said the old man. 'They have near a hundred aeroplanes in the first fleet.'

'Another hour?' asked Graham.

'To be so near!' said the Ward Leader. 'Now that we have found those guns. To be so near – If once we could get them out upon the roof spaces.'

'How long would that take?' asked Graham suddenly.

'An hour – certainly.'

'Too late,' cried the Ward Leader, 'too late.'

'*Is* it too late?' said Graham. 'Even now – An hour!'

He had suddenly perceived a possibility. He tried to speak calmly, but his face was white. 'There is one chance. You said there was a monoplane—?'

'On the Roehampton stage, Sire.'

'Smashed?'

'No. It is lying crossways to the carrier. It might be got upon the guides – easily. But there is no aeronaut—'

Graham glanced at the two men and then at Helen. He spoke after a long pause. '*We* have no aeronauts?'

'None.'

He turned suddenly to Helen. His decision was made. 'I must do it.'

'Do what?'

'Go to this flying stage – to this machine.'

'What do you mean?'

'I am an aeronaut. After all – Those days for which you reproached me were not altogether wasted.'

He turned to the old man in yellow. 'Tell them to put it upon the guides.'

The man in yellow hesitated.

'What do you mean to do?' cried Helen.

'This monoplane – it is a chance—'

'You don't mean—?'

'To fight – yes. To fight in the air. I have thought before – A big aeroplane is a clumsy thing. A resolute man—!'

'But – never since flying began –' cried the man in yellow.

'There has been no need. But now the time has come. Tell them now – send them my message – to put it upon the guides. I see now something to do. I see now why I am here!'

The old man dumbly interrogated the man in yellow, nodded, and hurried out.

Helen made a step towards Graham. Her face was white. 'But, Sire! – How can one fight? You will be killed.'

'Perhaps. Yet, not to do it – or to let someone else attempt it—'

'You will be killed,' she repeated.

'I've said my Word. Do you not see? It may save – London!'

He stopped, he could speak no more, he swept the alternative aside by a gesture, and they stood staring at one another.

There was no act of tenderness between them, no embrace, no parting word. The bare thought of personal love was swept aside by the tremendous necessities of his position. Her face expressed amazement and acceptance. A little movement of her hands gave him to his fate.

He turned towards the man in yellow. 'I am ready,' he said.

CHAPTER 25

THE COMING OF THE AEROPLANES

Two men in pale blue were lying in the irregular line that stretched along the edge of the captured Roehampton stage from end to end, grasping their carbines and peering into the shadows of the stage called Wimbledon Park. Now and then they spoke to one another. They spoke the mutilated English of their class and period. The fire of the Ostrogites had dwindled and ceased, and few of the enemy had been seen for some time. But the echoes of the fight that was going on now far below in the lower galleries of that stage, came every now and then between the staccato of shots from the popular side. One of these men was describing to the other how he had seen a man down below there dodge behind a girder, and had aimed at a guess and hit him cleanly as he dodged too far. 'He's down there still,' said the marksman. 'See that little patch. Yes. Between those bars.'

A few yards behind them lay a dead stranger, face upward to the sky, with the blue canvas of his jacket smouldering in a circle about the neat bullet hole on his chest. Close beside him a wounded man, with a leg swathed about, sat with an expressionless face and watched the progress of that burning. Behind them, athwart the carrier lay the captured monoplane.

'I can't see him *now*,' said the second man in a tone of provocation.

The marksman became foul-mouthed and high-voiced in his earnest endeavour to make things plain. And suddenly, interrupting him, came a noisy shouting from the substage.

'What's going on now?' he said, and raised himself on one arm to survey the stairheads in the central groove of the stage.

A number of blue figures were coming up these, and swarming across the stage.

'We don't want all these fools,' said his friend. 'They only crowd up and spoil shots. What are they after?'

'Ssh! – they're shouting something.'

The two men listened. The newcomers had crowded densely about the machine. Three Ward Leaders, conspicuous by their black mantles and badges, clambered into the body and appeared above it. The rank and file flung themselves upon the vans, gripping hold of the edges, until the entire outline of the thing was manned, in some places three deep. One of the marksmen knelt up. 'They're putting it on the carrier – that's what they're after.'

He rose to his feet, his friend rose also. 'What's the good?' said his friend. 'We've got no aeronauts.'

'That's what they're doing anyhow.' He looked at his rifle, looked at the struggling crowd, and suddenly turned to the wounded man. 'Mind these, mate,' he said, handing his carbine and cartridge belt; and in a moment he was running towards the monoplane. For a quarter of an hour he was lugging, thrusting, shouting and heeding shouts, and then the thing was done, and he stood with a multitude of others cheering their own achievement. By this time he knew, what indeed everyone in the city knew, that the Master, raw learner though he was, intended to fly this machine himself, was coming even now to take control of it, would let no other man attempt it.

'He who takes the greatest danger, he who bears the heaviest burthen, that man is King,' so the Master was reported to have spoken. And even as this man cheered, and while the beads of sweat still chased one another from the disorder of his hair, he heard the thunder of a greater tumult, and in fitful snatches the beat and impulse of the revolutionary song. He saw through a gap in the people that a thick stream of heads still poured up the stairway. 'The Master is coming,' shouted voices, 'the Master is coming,' and the crowd about him grew denser and denser. He began to thrust himself towards the central groove. 'The Master is coming!' 'The Sleeper, the Master!' 'God and the Master!' roared the voices.

And suddenly quite close to him were the black uniforms of the revolutionary guard, and for the first and last time in his life he saw Graham, saw him quite nearly. A tall, dark man in a flowing black robe he was, with a white, resolute face and eyes fixed steadfastly before him; a man who for all the little things about him had neither ears nor eyes nor thoughts. . . .

For all his days that man remembered the passing of Graham's bloodless face. In a moment it had gone and he was fighting in the swaying crowd. A lad weeping with terror thrust against him, pressing towards the stairways, yelling 'Clear for the start, you fools!' The bell that cleared the flying stage became a loud unmelodious clanging.

With that clanging in his ears Graham drew near the monoplane, marched into the shadow of its tilting wing. He became aware that a number of people about him were offering to accompany him, and waved their offers aside. He wanted to think how one started the engine. The bell clanged faster and faster, and the feet of the retreating people roared faster and louder. The man in yellow was assisting him to mount through the ribs of the body. He clambered into the aeronaut's place, fixing himself very carefully and deliberately. What was it? The man in yellow was pointing to two small flying machines driving upward in the southern sky. No doubt they were looking for the coming aeroplanes. That – presently – the thing to do now was to start. Things were being shouted at him, questions, warnings. They bothered him. He wanted to think about the machine, to recall every item of his previous experience. He waved the people from him, saw the man in yellow dropping off through the ribs, saw the crowd cleft down the line of the girders by his gesture.

For a moment he was motionless, staring at the levers, the wheel by which the engine shifted, and all the delicate appliances of which he knew so little. His eye caught a spirit level with the bubble towards him, and he remembered something, spent a dozen seconds in swinging the engine forward until the bubble floated in the centre of the tube. He noted that the people were not shouting, knew they watched his deliberation. A bullet smashed on the bar above his head. Who fired? Was the line clear of people? He stood up to see and sat down again.

In another second the propeller was spinning and he was gliding down the guides. He gripped the wheel and swung the engine back to lift the stem. Then it was the people shouted. He was throbbing with the quiver of the engine, and the shouts dwindled swiftly behind, rushed down to silence. The wind whistled over the edges of the screen, and the world sank away from him very swiftly.

Throb, throb, throb – throb, throb, throb; up he drove. He fancied himself free of all excitement, felt cool and deliberate. He lifted the stem still more, opened one valve on his left wing and swept round and up. He looked down with a steady head, and up. One of the Ostrogite monoplanes was driving across his course, so that he drove obliquely towards it and would pass below it at a steep angle. Its little aeronauts were peering down at him. What did they mean to do? His mind became active. One, he saw, held a weapon pointing, seemed prepared to fire. What did they think he meant to do? Instantly he understood their tactics and his resolution was taken. His momentary lethargy was past. He opened two more valves to his left, swung round, end on to this hostile machine, closed his valves, and shot straight at it, stem and windscreen shielding him from the shot. They tilted a little as if to clear him. He flung up his stem.

Throb, throb, throb – pause – throb, throb – he set his teeth, his face into an involuntary grimace, and crash! He struck it! He struck upward beneath the nearer wing.

Very slowly the wing of his antagonist seemed to broaden as the impetus of his blow turned it up. He saw the full breadth of it and then it slid downward out of his sight.

He felt his stem going down, his hands tightened on the levers, whirled and rammed the engine back. He felt the jerk of a clearance, the nose of the machine jerked upward steeply, and for a moment he seemed to be lying on his back. The machine was reeling and staggering, it seemed to be dancing on its screw. He made a huge effort, hung with all his weight on the levers, and slowly the engine came forward again. He was driving upward but no longer so steeply. He gasped for a moment and flung himself at the levers again. The wind whistled about him. One further effort and he was almost level. He could breathe. He turned his head for the first time to see what had become of his antagonists. Turned back to the levers and looked again. For a moment he could have believed they were annihilated. And then he saw between the two stages to the east was a chasm, and down this something, a slender edge, fell swiftly and vanished as a sixpence falls down a crack.

At first he did not understand, and then a wild joy possessed him. He shouted at the top of his voice, an inarticulate shout, and drove higher and higher up the sky. Throb, throb, throb, pause, throb, throb, throb. 'Where was the other?' he thought. 'They too –' As he looked round the empty heavens he had a momentary fear that this second machine had risen above him, and then he saw it alighting on the Norwood stage. They had meant shooting. To risk being rammed headlong two thousand feet in the air was beyond their latter-day courage. . . .

For a little while he circled, then swooped in a steep descent towards the westward stage. Throb throb throb, throb throb throb. The twilight was creeping on apace, the smoke from the Streatham stage that had been so dense and dark, was now a pillar of fire, and all the laced curves of the moving ways and the translucent roofs and domes and the chasms between the buildings were glowing softly now, lit by the tempered radiance of the electric light that the glare of the day overpowered. The three efficient stages that the Ostrogites held – for Wimbledon Park was useless because of the fire from Roehampton, and Streatham was a furnace – were glowing with guide lights for the coming aeroplanes. As he swept over the Roehampton stage he saw the dark masses of the people thereon. He heard a clap of frantic cheering, heard a bullet from the Wimbledon Park stage tweet through the air, and went beating up above the Surrey wastes. He felt a breath of wind from the south-west, and lifted his westward wing as he had learnt to do, and so drove upward heeling into the rare swift upper air. Whirr, whirr, whirr.

Up he drove and up, to that pulsating rhythm, until the country beneath was blue and indistinct, and London spread like a little map traced in light, like the mere model of a city near the brim of the horizon. The south-west was a sky of sapphire over the shadowy rim of the world, and ever as he drove upward the multitude of stars increased.

And behold! In the southward, low down and glittering swiftly nearer, were two little patches of nebulous light. And then two more, and then a glow of swiftly driving shapes. Presently he could count them. There were four and twenty. The first fleet of aeroplanes had come! Beyond appeared a yet greater glow.

He swept round in a half circle, staring at this advancing fleet. It flew in a wedge-like shape, a triangular flight of gigantic phosphorescent shapes sweeping nearer through the lower air. He made a swift calculation of their pace, and spun the little wheel that brought the engine forward. He touched a lever and the throbbing effort of the engine ceased. He began to fall, fell swifter and swifter. He aimed at the apex of the wedge. He dropped like a stone through the whistling air. It seemed scarce a second from that soaring moment before he struck the foremost aeroplane.

No man of all that black multitude saw the coming of his fate, no man among them dreamt of the hawk that struck downward upon him out of the sky. Those who were not limp in the agonies of air sickness, were craning their black necks and staring to see the filmy city that was rising out of the haze, the rich and splendid city to which 'Massa Boss' had brought their obedient muscles. Bright teeth gleamed and the glossy faces shone. They had heard of Paris. They knew they were to have lordly times among the poor white trash.[1]

Suddenly Graham hit them.

He had aimed at the body of the aeroplane, but at the very last instant a better idea had flashed into his mind. He twisted about and struck near the edge of the starboard wing with all his accumulated weight. He was jerked back as he struck. His prow went gliding across its smooth expanse towards the rim. He felt the forward rush of the huge fabric sweeping him and his monoplane along with it, and for a moment that seemed an age he could not tell what was happening. He heard a thousand throats yelling, and perceived that his machine was balanced on the edge of the gigantic float, and driving down, down; glanced over his shoulder and saw the backbone of the aeroplane and the opposite float swaying up. He had a vision through the ribs of sliding chairs, staring faces, and hands clutching at the tilting guide bars. The fenestrations in the further float flashed open as the aeronaut tried to right her. Beyond, he saw a second aeroplane leaping steeply to escape the whirl of its heeling[2] fellow. The broad area of swaying wings seemed to jerk upward. He felt he had dropped clear, that the monstrous fabric, clean overturned, hung like a sloping wall above him.

He did not clearly understand that he had struck the side float of the aeroplane and slipped off, but he perceived that he was flying free on the down glide and rapidly nearing earth. What had he done? His heart throbbed like a noisy engine in his throat and for a perilous instant he could not move his levers because of the paralysis of his hands. He wrenched the levers to throw his engine back, fought for two seconds against the weight of it, felt himself righting, driving horizontally, set the engine beating again.

He looked upward and saw two aeroplanes glide shouting far overhead, looked back, and saw the main body of the fleet opening out and rushing upward and outward; saw the one he had struck fall edgewise on and strike like a gigantic knife-blade along the wind-wheels below it.

He put down his stern and looked again. He drove up heedless of his direction as he watched. He saw the wind-vanes give, saw the huge fabric strike the earth, saw its downward vanes crumple with the weight of its descent, and then the whole mass turned over and smashed, upside down, upon the sloping wheels. Then from the heaving wreckage a thin tongue of white fire licked up towards the zenith. He was aware of a huge mass flying through the air towards him, and turned upwards just in time to escape the charge – if it was a charge – of a second aeroplane. It whirled by below, sucked him down a fathom, and nearly turned him over in the gust of its close passage.

He became aware of three others rushing towards him, aware

of the urgent necessity of beating above them. Aeroplanes were all about him, circling wildly to avoid him, as it seemed. They drove past him, above, below, eastward and westward. Far away to the westward was the sound of a collision, and two falling flares. Far away to the southward a second squadron was coming. Steadily he beat upward. Presently all the aeroplanes were below him, but he doubted the height he had of them, and did not swoop again immediately. And then he came down upon a second victim and all its load of soldiers saw him coming. The big machine heeled and swayed as the fear-maddened men scrambled to the stern for their weapons. A score of bullets sang through the air, and there flashed a star in the thick glass windscreen that protected him. The aeroplane slowed and dropped to foil his stroke, and dropped too low. Just in time he saw the wind-wheels of Bromley hill rushing up towards him, and spun about and up as the aeroplane he had chased crashed among them. All its voices wove into a felt of yelling. The great fabric seemed to be standing on end for a second among the heeling and splintering vanes, and then it flew to pieces. Huge splinters came flying through the air, its engines burst like shells. A hot rush of flame shot overhead into the darkling sky.

'*Two*!' he cried, with a bomb from overhead bursting as it fell, and forthwith he was beating up again. A glorious exhilaration possessed him now, a giant activity. His troubles about humanity, about his inadequacy, were gone for ever. He was a man in battle rejoicing in his power. Aeroplanes seemed radiating from him in every direction, intent only upon avoiding him, the yelling of their packed passengers came in short gusts as they swept by. He chose his third quarry, struck hastily and did but turn it on edge. It escaped him, to smash against the tall cliff of London Wall. Flying from that impact he skimmed the darkling ground so nearly he could see a frightened rabbit bolting up a slope. He jerked up steeply, and found himself driving over south London with the air about him vacant. To the right of him a wild riot of signal rockets from the Ostrogites banged tumultuously in the sky. To the south the wreckage of half a dozen air ships flamed, and east and west and north they fled before him. They drove away to the east and north, and went about in the south, for they could not pause in the air. In their present confusion any attempt at evolution would have meant disastrous collisions.

He passed two hundred feet or so above the Roehampton stage. It was black with people and noisy with their frantic shouting. But why was the Wimbledon Park stage black and cheering, too? The smoke and flame of Streatham now hid the three further stages. He curved about and rose to see them and the northern quarters. First came the square masses of Shooter's Hill into sight, from behind the smoke, lit and orderly with the aeroplane that had landed and its disembarking Negroes. Then came Blackheath, and then under the corner of the reek the Norwood stage. On Blackheath no aeroplane had landed. Norwood was covered by a swarm of little figures running to and fro in a passionate confusion. Why? Abruptly he understood. The stubborn defence of the flying stages was over, the people were pouring into the under-ways of these last strongholds of Ostrog's usurpation. And then, from far away on the northern border of the city, full of glorious import to him, came a sound, a signal, a note of triumph, the leaden thud of a gun. His lips fell apart, his face was disturbed with emotion.

He drew an immense breath. 'They win,' he shouted to the empty air; 'the people win!' The sound of a second gun came like an answer. And then he saw the monoplane on Blackheath was running down its guides to launch. It lifted clean and rose. It shot up into the air, driving straight southward and away from him.

In an instant it came to him what this meant. It must needs be Ostrog in flight. He shouted and dropped towards it. He had the momentum of his elevation and fell slanting down the air and very swiftly. The other machine rose steeply at his approach. He allowed for its velocity and drove straight upon it.

It suddenly became a mere flat edge, and behold! he was past it, and driving headlong down with all the force of his futile blow.

He was furiously angry. He reeled the engine back along its

shaft and went circling up. He saw Ostrog's machine beating up a spiral before him. He rose straight towards it, won above it by virtue of the impetus of his swoop and by the advantage and weight of a man. He dropped headlong – dropped and missed again! As he rushed past he saw the face of Ostrog's aeronaut confident and cool and in Ostrog's attitude a wincing resolution. Ostrog was looking steadfastly away from him – to the south. He realized with a gleam of wrath how bungling his flight must be. Below he saw the Croydon hills. He jerked upwards and once more he gained on his enemy.

He glanced over his shoulder and his attention was arrested. The eastward stage, the one on Shooter's Hill, appeared to lift; a flash changing to a tall grey shape, a cowled figure of smoke and dust, jerked into the air. For a moment this cowled figure stood motionless, dropping huge masses of metal from its shoulders, and then it began to uncoil a dense head of smoke. The people had blown it up, aeroplane and all! As suddenly a second flash and grey shape sprang up from the Norwood stage. And even as he stared at this came a dead report; and the air wave of the first explosion struck him. He was flung up and sideways.

For a moment his monoplane fell nearly edgewise with her nose down, and seemed to hesitate whether to overset altogether. He stood on his windshield, wrenching the wheel that swayed up over his head. And then the shock of the second explosion took his machine sideways.

He found himself clinging to one of the ribs of his machine, and the air was blowing past him and *upwards*. He seemed to be hanging quite still in the air, with the wind blowing up past him. But the world below was rotating – more and more rapidly. It occurred to him that he was falling. Then he was sure that he was falling. He could not look down.

He found himself recapitulating with incredible swiftness all that had happened since his awakening, the days of doubt, the days of Empire, and at last the tumultuous discovery of Ostrog's calculated treachery.

The vision had a quality of utter unreality. Who was he? Why was he holding so tightly with his hands? Why could he not let go? In such a fall as this countless dreams have ended. But in a moment he would wake. . . .

His thoughts ran swifter and swifter. He wondered if he should see Helen again. It seemed so unreasonable that he should not see her again.

Although he could not look at it, he was suddenly aware that the whirling earth below him was very near.

Came a shock and a great crackling and popping of bars and stays.

Note on Places in the Text

Places of significance mentioned in the text are noted individually except for two to which Wells gives dramatic weighting as well as the general sense of difference in the 'domed' London of his future. The first cluster is the Cornish coast, where Isbister first meets Graham, and the second is south-east England, especially viewed from the air. Wells set other novels, such as *The War of the Worlds* and *The Invisible Man*, in Surrey, including some of the territory he observes here (see below).

The Cornish Coast

Boscastle is on the north coast of Cornwall, 25 miles north-east of Newquay and 3 miles north-east of Tintagel, famous for its connections with the legend of King Arthur (chapter 18, note 2). Arthur is himself a 'sleeper', as Wells will make clear. According to many versions of the legend he was, after his final defeat by his nephew Mordred at Camelot, ferried to the Isle of Avalon, from where he will return when his country needs him. Five miles south-west of Tintagel is Camelford (chapter 2) which Douglas B. W. Sladen (1856–1947) suggested was the historical Camelot in his poem 'Camelford' (1885). Western and Eastern Blackapit (Penally Point overlooks Eastern Blackapit) are inlets near Boscastle, separated by a headland, but there is also a hint of a view into the 'black pit' of Hell. The Lizard is the eastern peninsula of Mount's Bay in Cornwall (opposite to Land's End), which marks England's most southerly point. Lulworth Cove, mentioned in this context, is in Dorset on the south coast of England about 10 miles east of

Weymouth. It is famous for its attractive coastline, and acts as a kind of thematic link between the west of England, where the story begins, and the south and south-east, where it continues into the future. Although Wells is vague about the location of the 'strange, voluptuous' Pleasure Cities, which may not even be in Britain, he puts them in the 'dim south-west' (chapter 14).

The Downs and South-east England

In chapter 16, Graham observes from the air the English countryside, seeing the familiar from an unfamiliar viewpoint. He is displaced in time, but also in space: as Wells points out in his preface, the description of an aerial dogfight was written some years before heavier-than-air aircraft actually flew, and his imagination is working from descriptions of balloon flights and his own vivid sense of a future. Wells is describing viewpoints he, and the vast majority of people alive at the time, had yet to see.

The North Downs are a chalk ridge that runs south of London through Surrey and Kent to meet the sea at the 'White Cliffs' of Dover in south-east Kent. Where the ridge narrows between the towns of Farnham and Guildford is the 'Hog's Back'. The 'Surrey Hills' mentioned in chapter 14 are the slopes of the North Downs extending from Farnham southwards to Haslemere and east to Oxted. They include many of the landmarks mentioned in chapter 16. Leith Hill, south of Dorking, is the highest place in south-east England. The Wealden Heights is a line of ridges and hills running through Surrey. Hindhead overlooks a large depression called the Devil's Punch Bowl and is a viewpoint from which Pitch Hill and Leith Hill, 16 miles to the north-east, can be seen. All these heights, as Wells imagines, make possible sites for 'wind farms', harvesting energy through wind power.

The River Wey is part of a network of canals and waterways that run north from Godalming through the gap where the town of Guildford stands, to Weybridge on the River Thames south-west of London. To the south, it is connected with the River Arun. The canal traffic ceased in the late 1860s because of competition from the railways, which have in this future been superseded by Eadhamite roads.

Aldershot, noted specifically in chapter 16, is a town in Hampshire 8 miles west of Guildford. It became an important base for the British Army in 1853 because of the surrounding 'sandy wastes', which were used for training troops, and is still a garrison town.

The South Downs are a line of chalk ridges running from Hampshire through Sussex, ending at the sea at Beachy Head (chapter 16), a chalk cliff south-west of Eastbourne on the Sussex coast.

Between 8 and 20 miles east of Lulworth Cove on the Dorset coast, famous for its attractive coastline (referred to in chapter 1), are the neighbouring towns of Bournemouth, Wareham and Swanage, envisaged by Wells as giant tower-blocks. Portsdown Hill is a ridge forming the northern edge of Portsmouth harbour in Hampshire. These ridges and cliffs produce spectacular rock formations: the Needles jut out of the sea off the western point of the Isle of Wight, which is separated from the mainland (the county of Hampshire) by the strait called the Solent.

Andy Sawyer

Notes

PREFACE TO THE ATLANTIC EDITION

1. *In 1911 I took the opportunity ... excisions and alterations:* Wells revised *When the Sleeper Wakes* in 1910 and retitled it *The Sleeper Awakes.*
2. *Anticipations:* Published as Volume 4 of the Atlantic Edition.

PREFACE [1921]

Mr Belloc's nightmare of the Servile State: Hilaire Belloc (1870–1953) was a novelist and political/religious journalist who argued, in *The Servile State* (1912: originally given as a lecture 1911), that the welfare socialism proposed by the Labour Party would only serve to confirm the grip of the ruling class upon the means of production.

CHAPTER I
INSOMNIA

1. *body fag:* Bodily tiredness or fatigue, as opposed to mental weariness.
2. *chloral:* Chloral hydrate: a compound of chlorine and oxygen used as an anaesthetic.
3. *monkshood:* Monkshood is an ornamental plant (*Aconitum napellus*) with violet-blue flowers, native to south-west England.
4. *darkling:* Having grown dark.
5. *delphinium:* Delphinium is the name given to numerous varieties of the *Ranunculaceae* family, including the larkspur. The colour is indigo-blue.

CHAPTER 2

THE TRANCE

1. *drill*: A coarse linen or cotton fabric used for hot-weather clothing.
2. *trap*: A small, usually two-wheeled carriage, drawn by a pony.
3. *Victoria's Jubilee*: Queen Victoria's Golden Jubilee, commemorating fifty years of her reign, was celebrated in 1887. The second jubilee, the 'Diamond Jubilee', was celebrated ten years later in June 1897.
4. *GP*: General Practitioner, or family doctor.
5. *the War*: Readers of the 1924 Atlantic edition may have taken this to refer to the Great War, or First World War (1914–18). However, the earlier editions of *When the Sleeper Wakes* include after the following sentence, 'From beginning to end,' Isbister's reply: 'And these Martians.' (See the Note on the Text.) Readers of these editions would have seen an echo of *The War of the Worlds* (1899) with *When the Sleeper Wakes* as in some way a sequel to that novel, although the 'War' and the 'Martians' seem to be mentioned as separate events. The lack of clarity may have been why Wells deleted reference to the Martians.
6. *Rip Van Winkle*: In the story of that name by Washington Irving (1783–1859) in *The Sketch-Book* (1820) he fell asleep in the Catskill Mountains and awoke twenty years later.
7. *Compound interest*: Interest paid on capital and the accumulated interest, rather than on the sum itself.

CHAPTER 3

THE AWAKENING

1. *maximum and minimum thermometer*: A thermometer which can be set to record the maximum and minimum temperatures.
2. *a steady, sweeping shadow*: Probably a flying machine (see chapter 7 note 7 below), but its regularity suggests that it could be one of the giant 'wind-vanes'.

CHAPTER 4

THE SOUND OF A TUMULT

1. *a gross of years*: 144 years (see note 9 below).
2. *Duchy of Cornwall*: Not to be confused with the county of

Cornwall (although the speaker may not know the difference). The Duchy of Cornwall was created by Edward III as an estate for the eldest sons of the monarch: thus the present Duke of Cornwall is Charles Windsor the Prince of Wales. Over half of the land owned by the Duchy is in Devon or elsewhere in southern England.

3. *A long strip of this apparently solid wall rolled up with a snap*: In this future, as in many science-fiction futures, everyday technology is made to look like magic from the viewpoint of a visitor from the past.

4. *kinetoscope*: A device invented by Thomas Alva Edison (1847–1931) in which a strip of film is passed behind a peephole through which the viewer can see the images. This was developed into the kinematograph (chapter 14 note 9), which projected images on to a screen.

5. *anaemic*: Pale-looking through lack of, or unhealthy, blood.

6. *some sort of force*: London's first large electric power station opened in Deptford in 1882. In 1895, a hydroelectric power station using electricity generated at Niagara Falls between the USA and Canada provided power to the city of Buffalo, 25 miles away, and opened up the possibility for the mass use of electrical power. See also chapter 10 note 1.

7. *mesmerist*: Franz Anton Mesmer (1734–1815) developed a form of healing based upon 'animal magnetism' which often involved placing people in hypnotic trances.

8. *capillotomist*: An invented word from the Latin '*capillus*' (hair) and 'anatomist', someone skilled in the dissection of the (human) body: hence, an expert in the cutting and treatment of the hair.

9. *sixdoz lions*: As explained in this conversation, 'lions' are the monetary units and the duodecimal (units of twelve), rather than the decimal (units of ten), system is used for counting. The former system of reckoning has not wholly been replaced: 'dozen' for twelve is commonly used, 'gross' for twelve twelves (144) is rarer. Before 1971, in British currency there were twelve pence to one shilling (but twenty shillings to one pound). The system and currency described here appear also in *A Modern Utopia* (1905).

CHAPTER 5
THE MOVING WAYS

1. *The Moving Ways*: Another feature of later science fiction, as in 'The Roads Must Roll' (1940) by Robert A. Heinlein (1907–88),

which mentions Wells, or *The Caves of Steel* (1954) by Isaac Asimov (1920–92).

2. *Titanic*: Vast and overwhelming. The word is capitalized as a reference to the giant Titans of ancient Greek mythology, children of the god Uranus and the goddess Gaea. They were said to have built the huge buildings of older cultures.

3. *tracery of translucent material*: London has been roofed over in a manner reminiscent of the Crystal Palace, constructed in Hyde Park for the Great Exhibition of 1851 and re-erected at Sydenham Hill in south London in 1854.

4. *Ostrog*: Possibly an echo of 'Ostrogoth', one of the tribes which ravaged the Roman Empire. There is a town in the Ukraine of that name, and the *Oxford English Dictionary* defines the word as 'a house or village in Siberia, surrounded by a palisade or wall, and serving as a fort or prison'. There are therefore sinister implications, and the name is not attached to a person until later in the novel. There may also be a reference to the Russian political theorist Moisei Ostrogorsky (1854–1919) (see the Introduction).

CHAPTER 6

THE HALL OF THE ATLAS

1. *white figure of Atlas*: In Greek mythology, Atlas, one of the Titans, was condemned to bear the weight of Heaven on his shoulders. The whiteness of the figure is that of a marble statue, but there may also be an allusion to the Imperial responsibility of the 'White Man's Burden', although the poem of that name by Rudyard Kipling (1865–1936) was not published until 1899.

2. *caryatidae*: Supporting columns in the shape of female figures.

CHAPTER 7

IN THE SILENT ROOMS

1. '*The Man who would be King*': Story published in 1888 by Rudyard Kipling.

2. '*The Heart of Darkness*' . . . '*The Madonna of the Future*': 'The Heart of Darkness' by Joseph Conrad (1857–1924) was published in Blackwood's Magazine (February–April 1899) and, as *Heart of Darkness*, in book form in 1902. 'The Madonna of the Future' by Henry James (1843–1916) was first published in the *Atlantic Monthly* in 1873. Well was on good terms with both

writers in the late 1890s, and the joke is on Graham, not Conrad and James.

3. *Tannhauser*: The subject of an opera by Richard Wagner (1813–83), set in medieval Germany. It begins with the minstrel-knight Tannhauser under the spell of the goddess Venus, who holds court in a mountain, Venusberg, which is identified with the Hörselberg, near the town of Eisenach.

4. *photographed realities*: Graham is watching what would in his (and Wells's) time be seen as pornographic representations of sexual activity. Whether in our time such images would be so regarded is unclear, but sexuality is much more open in this future than in Graham's time. Later in the chapter (and also in chapter 17) Graham is offered the services of a class of licensed prostitutes.

5. *Bellamy*: Edward Bellamy (1850–98), whose *Looking Backward: 2000–1887* (1888) also features a 'Sleeper' who awakens in a state-socialist utopia, in Boston. Bellamy's novel, which also featured many technological forecasts, was immensely popular as both a vision of the future and propaganda for social reform.

6. *Bulgarian atrocities*: The rebellion of the Bulgarians against the ruling Turkish Empire in 1876 was put down with great brutality, and famously denounced by the former British Prime Minister William Ewart Gladstone (1809–98).

7. *I suppose they can fly*: Although numerous experiments with balloons and airships were made during the late nineteenth century, the German inventor Ferdinand von Zeppelin (1838–1917) was the first to create a propeller-driven airship, which made its first flight on 2 July 1900. The first successful powered flight (120 feet) in a heavier-than-air machine was made by Orville Wright on 17 December 1903. Powered flight, for Wells, was *the* symbol of technological progress. In *The War in the Air* (1908) he describes the use of air power in warfare, and in *The Shape of Things to Come* (1933) it is the airmen who develop the World State.

8. *This also a Council had said*: The Sanhedrin, the Council of High Priests to whom Judas betrayed Jesus. This is a loose interpretation rather than a direct quotation.

CHAPTER 8

THE ROOF SPACES

1. *wind-vane police*: This future world has, as Graham is told in chapter 6, 'about fourteen' separate police forces. The 'wind-vane police' would be responsible for the giant windmills (see note 3 below) which generate electrical power.

2. *way-gearers*: The technicians responsible for the maintenance of the moving ways.

3. *the roof of the vast city structure*: As noted above (chapter 5, note 3), London is covered by a huge dome, reminiscent of the Crystal Palace, partly for protection from the elements, partly to enable giant wind-driven power generators to function more easily. In the 1936 film *Things to Come*, based upon *The Shape of Things to Come* (1933), Wells envisages an underground 'Everytown' following his technological revolution. Domed or underground cities of the future are features of much mid-twentieth century science fiction.

4. *the flying machine*: Earlier (chapters 3 and 7), there had been hints that the secret of powered flight had been achieved.

5. *proscenium*: The part of the stage in front of the curtain.

CHAPTER 9

THE PEOPLE MARCH

1. *Lincoln*: A reference, possibly, to Abraham Lincoln (1809–65) who became President of the United States of America in 1861, the year the Civil War broke out.

2. *the dominant blue*: Blue canvas is the uniform of the working class. In the world of *The Sleeper Awakes* people's clothing encodes their social function: red, for example, is the colour of the police.

CHAPTER 10

THE BATTLE OF THE DARKNESS

1. *globes of electric light*: The first large-scale use of street lighting in London was 1878, and the Edison Electric Lighting Company began operating the first power station for electric lighting in the world in London 1882.

2. *fenestrations*: Arrangements of windows.

3. *pneumatic*: Inflated with air.

4. *Eadhamite*: This substance is described later, and is Wells's extra-polation of tarmacadam or 'tarmac', the addition of tar to the mixture of graded stones used for paving roads by the engineer J. L. McAdam (1756–1836) that had been introduced by the 1880s. It is also described in Wells's (1899) novella 'A Story of the Days to Come'. This and the blue-clad work force are some of the factors which suggest that 'Days to Come' and *The Sleeper Awakes* are set in the same future.

5. *Labour Bureau – Little-Side*: 'Big-side' and 'Little-side' derive from public school divisions into senior and junior groups, especially in sport. The sense here could be that this is the Labour office for young workers.

6. *such a leap in time*: A reference to the tradition of fictions that feature 'sleepers' waking up in the future: not just 'Rip Van Winkle' and Bellamy's *Looking Backward*, but William Morris's *News from Nowhere* (1890), which, like his 'A Dream of John Ball', looks towards medieval dream-romances. Following Wells's *The Time Machine*, such fictions tended to transport people through time by means of 'machines' rather than mysteri-ously suspended sleep, although some authors have used sleep in the form of suspended animation or induced hibernation ('cold-sleep') as a way of bringing people into the future.

CHAPTER II

THE OLD MAN WHO KNEW EVERYTHING

1. *Boss*: The word here carries strong overtones of a meaning origin-ally American, 'a manager or dictator of a party organization' (*Oxford English Dictionary*).

2. *when the Paris people broke out*: The short-lived Paris Commune of 1871 was a left-wing protest against the surrender of France in the Franco-Prussian war.

3. *Babble Machine*: Loudspeakers broadcasting news and prop-aganda.

4. *Verneys*: An unexplained faction. Possibly there is an allusion to Jules Verne (1828–1905), to whose work Wells's *The War of the Worlds* had been compared. Another possibility might be Lionel Verney, the narrator of Mary Shelley's *The Lost Man* (1826).

5. *Julius Caesar*: Roman general (*c.*101–44 BC) who became dic-

tator and was murdered to prevent him from re-establishing the monarchy.

6. *Sanitary Company*: In this future services are provided by state-owned companies. The destruction of books by the 'Sanitary Company' is reminiscent of the later use by Ray Bradbury (1920–), in his novel *Fahrenheit 451* (1953), of 'firemen' to burn books.

7. *ashlarite*: Ashlar is 'A square hewn stone for building purposes or for pavement' (*Oxford English Dictionary*). 'Ashlarite' is thus an artificial building material one component of which is the ashes of books.

8. *silver photographs*: The action of light on silver nitrate was fundamental to the development of photography. Louis Daguerre (1787–1851) gave his name to the *daguerreotype*, which involved creating an image on a silver-plated sheet of copper.

9. *Wind Vanes Control*: The branch of the State cartel that controls the production of energy.

10. *I've worn the blue*: This means more than 'I have been a worker', as Graham is to discover, in chapter 18, that the blue-uniformed workers are virtual serfs of the Labour Department.

11. *Pleasure City*: One of the privileges in this world is being able to go to a resort given over to luxury.

12. *Capri*: Island off Naples, in Italy, which was a favourite luxury resort of the Roman Emperors, especially Tiberius (42 BC–AD 37).

13. *greener*: Someone who is 'green' or inexperienced; Wells may have been thinking of the American slang term 'greenhorn'.

CHAPTER 12

OSTROG

1. *pigeon English*: A simplified form of English, a kind of patois used as a 'common tongue' to aid communication between users of different languages. More normally spelled 'pidgin', but frequently spelled thus because of the similarity of sound. Wells uses 'pidgin' in chapter 14.

2. *large oval disc*: A television screen. The theory of television was being developed during the late nineteenth century. Paul Nipkow (1860–1940) had patented a means of sending images over wire in 1884.

3. *pull of the aeroplanes*: That is, the power of the pilots and engineers.

4. *kinetotelephotographs*: Literally 'moving-at-a-distance-images', what we simply call 'television': the word was coined in 1900.

CHAPTER 13
THE END OF THE OLD ORDER

1. *circumadjacent*: Surrounding.

CHAPTER 14
FROM THE CROW'S NEST

1. *Crow's Nest*: A platform on top of a mast where a ship's lookout was stationed.
2. *a telephone bell*: The telephone was patented by Alexander Graham Bell (1847–1922) in 1876. By 1880 there were 30,000 telephones operating around the world including a telephone exchange in London.
3. *specula*: Literally 'mirrors' or 'reflectors' but in this case a kind of television camera.
4. *Highgate and Muswell Hill*: Hills in north London, now part of London's suburbia.
5. *British Food Trust*: The state cartel concerned with agriculture and food production.
6. *the Pool*: The 'Pool of London', or the dockland area of the River Thames reaching upstream to London Bridge: the heart of London's maritime trading.
7. *great single wheels*: Among early speculations of powered transport were gyroscopically stabilized vehicles on two wheels, or even one. Wells speculated about 'gyroscopic motor-cars' in *The War in the Air*.
8. *monoplane*: The *Oxford English Dictionary* cites 1907 as the earliest use of 'monoplane' to mean a single-winged aeroplane. (Most early aeroplanes were biplanes with two wings on each side.) The 1899 first edition of *When the Sleeper Wakes* has 'aeropile'.
9. *kinematograph and phonograph*: The kinematograph was the name given to a device for projecting a series of photographs rapidly on to a screen to give the illusion of movement. It was patented by the Lumière brothers, Auguste (1862–1954) and Louis (1864–1948) in 1895, and became the foundation of the modern cinema. The phonograph, a means of recording and

replaying sound, was invented in 1877 by Thomas Alva Edison but not commercially developed until ten years later.

10. *Hindoo*: Now usually spelled 'Hindu'.

11. *reached to Antioch and Genoa . . . Cadiz*: Antioch (now Antakya) is in Syria on the Mediterranean coast. Genoa is a port city in north-eastern Italy. Cadiz is on the southern coast of Spain, west of the Straits of Gibraltar.

12. *Persia and Kurdistan*: Modern Iran and the areas of northern Iraq and eastern Turkey inhabited by the Kurdish people.

13. *Pekin*: Or Peking, now spelled Beijing, the capital of China, in the north of the country.

14. *Congo*: Region of central Africa surrounding the Congo River. In 1885 it was taken under the personal control of King Leopold II of Belgium (1835–1909). In 1908 it became the Belgian Congo. Formerly Zaire, it is now the Democratic Republic of Congo.

15. *Sybaris*: A city in south Italy which flourished in the sixth century BC and whose inhabitants were famous for their luxurious living.

CHAPTER 15

PROMINENT PEOPLE

1. *filigree*: Ornamental work of gold or silver wire.

2. *Rossetti*: Dante Gabriel Rossetti (1828–82), the English painter who was one of the founders of the Pre-Raphaelite Brotherhood, which looked for inspiration and subject-matter to the pre-Renaissance period.

3. *à la Marguerite*: A French style fashionable around 1875, with long hair in two plaits hanging at the back. It derived from a character in the 1846 work *La Damnation de Faust* by Hector Berlioz (1803–69).

4. *pigtail*: It was the custom of Chinese people to wear their hair in a long plait hanging from the back. This was introduced by the Manchu dynasty in the seventeenth century, at first to signify the inferiority of the Han majority to their Manchu rulers, but it became a symbol of identity and pride. Wells uses 'Manchurian' to signify 'Chinese' as a whole, although the Manchurians were a separate group who became assimilated to some extent by the majority population, as a warrior and ruling class.

5. *Leo the Tenth*: (1475–1521); born Giovanni de' Medici, he became Pope in 1513, at the time when the Italian Renaissance was at its height.

6. *embonpoint*: Stoutness or plumpness.

7. *First French Empire*: Napoleon Bonaparte (1769–1821) was declared Emperor in 1804. He was forced to abdicate in 1814, escaped from exile and was finally defeated in 1815 following the battle of Waterloo. During the Empire, fashions and clothing affected a neo-Classical style.

8. *Raphael's cartoons*: Raffaello Sanzio (1483–1520) was one of the greatest artists of the Italian Renaissance. His 'cartoons' are preliminary sketches for works such as the tapestries for the Sistine Chapel in Rome.

9. *Chaucer*: The poet Geoffrey Chaucer (*c.*1340–1400), author of *The Canterbury Tales*.

10. *Red Rose*: The Red Rose was the symbol of the Lancastrian dynasty during the Wars of the Roses in the fifteenth century. Henry Tudor (1457–1509) became king in 1485 and brought the wars to an end. The Tudor dynasty ruled until the death of Queen Elizabeth I (1533–1603).

11. *Asano*: Described in a passage deleted from the previous chapter as Graham's Japanese attendant.

12. *Stuart blood*: The Stuarts were the dynasty of British monarchs following the Tudors. Queen Elizabeth I was succeeded by James VI of Scotland (1566–1625), who became James I of England. Apart from the Civil War and the Republic between 1649 and 1658, the Stuarts ruled until James II (1633–1701) was expelled in the 'Glorious Revolution' of 1688.

13. *bluff 'aerial dog'*: 'Sea dog' is a term used for an experienced sailor. Like Admirals of old, the Master Aeronaut is presenting himself as a rough-and-ready, frank and hearty sort of fellow.

14. *Public Schools*: Not, it seems, 'public schools' in the modern British sense, which means private schools for the elite. Here, state-supported schooling for the entire population is meant, although Wells is, as throughout this scene, having fun with his stereotype of an educational bureaucrat.

15. *pince-nez*: Glasses fixed to the nose by a clip, rather than attached to the ears. From the French 'pinch-nose'.

16. *Cram*: Literally to pack or to stuff, here to prepare for examinations through a programme of concentrated study. In Wells's England 'Crammers' prepared students for University examinations.

17. *University Extension*: The University Extension movement was started during the late nineteenth century as a means of providing

a university-level education for disadvantaged groups, especially women.

18. *Plato and Swift ... Shelley, Hazlitt and Burns*: Plato (*c.* 427–347 BC) was a Greek philosopher whose *Republic* is one of the fundamental works of political philosophy, influencing Wells's own utopian writing. Jonathan Swift (1667–1745) was the author of the satire *Gulliver's Travels* (1726). Percy Bysshe Shelley (1792–1822) was a Romantic poet who in verses such as 'The Masque of Anarchy' (1819) urged English workers to 'Rise, like lions after slumber/In unvanquishable number!' William Hazlitt (1778–1830) was an English essayist and critic. The Scottish poet Robert Burns (1759–96) was celebrated for his love poetry and a robust sense of democracy. Wells is therefore associating figures noted for political and personal opposition with the second-hand and rigid ideas that pass for education in his future.

19. *Antibilious Pill*: 'Beecham's Pills' for indigestion were patented by Thomas Beecham (1820–1907) in 1847 and became one of Victorian Britain's best-known remedies. Wells was to satirize the patent medicine craze in *Tono-Bungay* (1909).

20. *Uncle Toby and the Widow*: An anecdote involving a flirtation scene from *Tristram Shandy* (1759–67) by Lawrence Sterne (1713–58).

21. *Caligula*: (AD 12–41). He became Emperor of Rome in AD 30 and was known for his debauchery and cruelty.

22. *Black Labour Master*: The administrator in charge of the African Companies.

23. *a rule of clerical monogamy*: The Church of England allows priests to marry but obviously has stood out against the new, more liberal sexual customs. Other branches of the Christian Church, such as the Roman Catholic, insist that priests remain celibate. The young woman's argument in favour of 'subsidiary wives' for the clergy is exactly the argument presented in favour of marriage for priests.

24. *œil de boeuf*: A circular or oval window in French seventeenth- and eighteenth-century architecture. Literally 'ox's eye'.

CHAPTER 16

THE MONOPLANE

1. *aluminium body skeleton*: The extraction of aluminium from bauxite was not economical until 1894. Zeppelin's first airship (see chapter 7 note 7) used aluminium for its lightness and strength.

2. *funicular railway*: A railway used in steep or mountainous regions, in which the carriage is pulled up by a cable.

3. *skerries*: The ruins appear like reefs or rocky islands.

4. *Bath Road*: The present A4 running westward from Hounslow.

5. *peewit*: Lapwing or green plover, named thus because of its distinctive call.

6. *Eiffel Tower*: Built by Gustave Eiffel (1832–1923) for the International Exhibition in Paris in 1889, the Eiffel Tower is one of Paris's most distinctive buildings and an icon of the city.

7. *wind-screw*: Propeller.

8. *Aeronautics is the secret – the privilege*: Wells is again stressing the potential power of mastery of the air, a 'mystery' like that of the medieval guilds. The association of 'aeronauts' is a cross between an elite professional organization and a trade union.

CHAPTER 17

THREE DAYS

1. *I'm not a Latin*: Graham is showing the English prejudice that the 'Latins' – French, Italians and Spanish – are sexual athletes. He has better things on his mind.

2. *bayadère*: French: Indian dancing girls.

3. *Milne Bramwell, Fechner, Liebault, William James, Myers and Gurney*: J. Milne Bramwell (1852–1905) was a researcher into hypnotism. Gustav Theodor Fechner (1801–87) was one of the pioneers of experimental psychology. August Ambroise Liebault (1823–1904) was one of the first investigators of hypnosis to consider it a science rather than a paranormal phenomenon. William James (1842–1910) was a psychologist and philosopher, and a member of the Society for Psychical Research. His brother Henry, the novelist, was a friend of Wells. Frederic William Henry Myers (1843–1901) was one of the founders of the Society for Psychical Research in 1882. Edmund Gurney (1847–88) was

a psychologist who, with Myers, helped to found the Society for Psychical Research.

4.   *hypnotists ready to imprint permanent memories*: More techno-logical means of this were forecast by Hugo Gernsback (1884–1967) in *Ralph 124C41+* (serialized 1911–12) and Aldous Huxley (1894–1963) in *Brave New World* (1932). A more recent version of this story is the film *Eternal Sunshine of the Spotless Mind* (2004), in which memories are technologically erased.

5.   *my London University days*: University College London was founded in 1836 building upon the University of London, founded ten years earlier. It offered education to wider social groups than did Oxford or Cambridge. Wells himself studied from 1884 to 1887 at the Normal School of Science (which later became part of the Imperial College of Science and Technology) in South Kensington.

6.   *Waterloo*: London railway station on the south bank of the River Thames, originally established in 1848 as a terminus for trains bringing passengers into the City of London on the north bank.

CHAPTER 18

GRAHAM REMEMBERS

1.   *Principalities, powers, dominions*: An echo of various biblical references, which are sometimes considered to be orders of Angels: 'For by him were all things created, that are in heaven, and that are in earth, visible and invisible, whether they be thrones, or dominions, or principalities, or powers.' (*Authorized Version*, Colossians 1:16)

2.   *King Arthur, Barbarossa*: According to Thomas Malory (*c.*1410–*c.*1471), whose *Morte d'Arthur* was published in 1485, the legend of King Arthur is that he will come again to his people: 'the once and future king'. The same story is told about many other hero-kings, including the German Frederick I ('Barbarossa') (*c.*1125–90), who became Holy Roman Emperor in 1152. A number of places mentioned in *The Sleeper Awakes* have Arthurian connections: see the Note on Places in the Text.

3.   *Mammon*: Literally 'riches' in Syriac, and partly because of the biblical warning 'Ye cannot serve God and mammon' (Matthew 6:24), taken to be a personification or god of money.

4.   *workhouse*: Workhouses were established from the seventeenth

century onwards to offer low-grade work to the poor to relieve poverty and unemployment. By the later nineteenth century, being forced to enter the workhouse was a social stigma made worse by the fact that for many there was no alternative.

5. *Salvation Army*: Formed in 1865 by William Booth (1829–1912) as a Christian campaign against urban poverty and homelessness.

6. *Euthanasy*: State-backed euthanasia, or assisted death for those who wish to die.

CHAPTER 19
OSTROG'S POINT OF VIEW

1. *Senegalese*: Senegal is a country in West Africa. During the nineteenth century it was a French colony.

2. *bowmen of Creçy*: In the Battle of Creçy (1346) volleys of arrows from the English archers defeated the heavily armoured French mounted knights.

3. *the Over-man*: The doctrine of the 'over-man' (sometimes translated 'super-man') who will replace normal humanity was proposed by the German philosopher Friedrich Wilhelm Nietzsche (1844–1900).

CHAPTER 20
IN THE CITY WAYS

1. *a procession parading the city seated*: They are of course on the 'moving ways'.

2. *the merchants of Phoenecia*: From Syria on the eastern Mediterranean coast, the Phoenecians were a trading nation who flourished between 1200 and 800 BC and who established many colonies throughout the Mediterranean, including Carthage.

3. *facsimile*: An exact copy.

4. *Theosophist*: Theosophy was a popular mixture of Eastern and Western religions synthesized by Helena Blavatsky (1831–91), who in various books published in the 1880s claimed to have been in touch with 'Secret Masters' in Tibet.

5. *Northumberland Avenue*: A street in London running from the Victoria Embankment to Charing Cross.

6. *scullery*: The room attached to a kitchen where the work of cleaning dishes and utensils takes place.

7. *wattle hut*: A hut made out of interwoven stakes.

8.   *Aërated Bread Shop*: By introducing carbon dioxide into dough, bread was made to rise faster. The Aerated Bread Company began, in 1864, to serve food and drink in its shops, thus opening up a mass market of small restaurants or 'tea shops' which provided a cheap and (for women) unthreatening alternative to eating and socializing in the home.

9.   *viand and condiment*: Food and seasoning or sauces.

10. *chemical wine*: A suggestion that either the wine is artificial or that it has been treated with chemicals.

11. *banderlog*: The monkeys in Kipling's *Jungle Book* (1894).

12. *Fuzzy Wuzzy*: The name given by British soldiers to the Sudanese during the 1880s. Kipling's poem 'Fuzzy Wuzzy', published in 1890 and incorporated in his *Barrack-Room Ballads* (1892), commemorates their bravery and fighting spirit and may be one of the 'songs' mentioned above by the Babble Machine.

13. *Niger and Timbuctoo*: Niger is a North African country south of Algeria and Libya. It came under French influence in the late nineteenth century, but did not become a formal colony until 1922. Timbuctoo, an important trading city on the river Niger, is now in the state of Mali.

14. *crèches*: French for 'cradles'. Nurseries for working mothers.

15. *wet nurses*: Originally women employed to breast-feed the babies of others, here they are mechanical nurses.

16. *Froebel*: Friedrich Froebel (1782–1852), the German educational reformer who devised the 'kindergarten' system for educating young children.

17. *cant*: Insincere expressions of pious or worthy sentiments.

18. *Grant Allen, Le Gallienne*: Charles Grant Allen (1848–99), a prolific writer whose output included early science fiction. He was a strong influence on Wells. His *The Woman Who Did* (1895) was a novel of female emancipation. Richard Le Gallienne (1866–1947), poet, essayist and novelist. Wells refers to his *The Quest of the Golden Girl* (1896) in *The History of Mr Polly* (1910).

19. *Godwin*: The philosopher and political writer William Godwin (1756–1836), the husband of the feminist writer Mary Wollstonecraft (1759–97) and father of the novelist Mary Shelley (1797–1851).

20. *Capella . . . Vega . . . Great Bear*: Capella is a bright star in the constellation Auriga (the Charioteer). *Vega*, the fifth brightest star in the night sky, is in the constellation Lyra (the Lyre). The

Great Bear is the constellation also known as the Plough or the Big Dipper.

21. *Orion*: The constellation representing Orion the Hunter of Greek mythology.

22. *PROPRAIET'R*: As noted in chapter 7, spelling has been reformed to reflect more closely the pronunciation of a word.

23. *Chaldea*: A civilization in the Middle East, on the river Euphrates in modern Iraq, which came into being around 625 BC with Babylon as its capital.

CHAPTER 21

THE UNDERSIDE

1. *The Underside*: As in *The Time Machine* and 'A Story of the Days to Come' Wells is making the common identification of the 'lower' (working) classes with a *physically* lower location.

2. *biscuit-making*: 'Biscuit' is pottery which is fired but not yet glazed.

3. *felspar*: Or feldspar. A crystalline mineral containing aluminium silicates together with sodium or calcium, important in the manufacture of porcelain.

4. *dray horse*: Horses pulling drays, or low carts for heavy goods.

5. *distinctly plain and flat-chested*: One of the anxieties about women's greater involvement in the workplace was that it would deprive them of their sexual roles and appearances. Wallace G. West's story 'The Last Man' (1929) sets the last man in a world of such 'unsexed' women.

6. *cloisonné tiles*: Enamel tiles divided by metal partitions.

7. *lips and nostrils a livid white*: In 1888 Wells had lived for a short time in the Potteries, where he would have observed some of the health hazards associated with the use of, for example, lead in the glaze. A letter to his father dated 29 April 1888, printed in the *Correspondence of H. G. Wells*, edited by David C. Smith (1998) refers to a factory with 'grinding mills', 'dim . . . with the dust of powdered feldspar and chert, and these are served by men who are whiter by far than any other millers that I have seen'. In the same year the 'Match Girls' Strike' brought to attention the facial disfigurement ('phossy jaw') caused by the use of white phosphorus in manufacture of matches.

CHAPTER 24

WHILE THE AEROPLANES WERE COMING

1. *Boulogne*: City on the north coast of France about 28 miles across the English Channel from Folkestone.

CHAPTER 25

THE COMING OF THE AEROPLANES

1. *poor white trash*: An American term to describe the white Southerners at the bottom of the social heap, who shared the poverty of their black neighbours and most of their disadvantages except the colour of their skin.
2. *heeling*: Leaning steeply to one side. Wells is adapting a nautical term to the air.

A. S.